Honor

Honor

A Novel By

Peter G. Andresen

TIMEWALKER
PRESS

Honor
A novel by Peter G. Andresen

Timewalker Press
P.O. Box 1434
Salinas, California, 93902
Facebook page: https://www.facebook.com/TimewalkerPress/
For special discounts, please contact Timewalker Press.

Printed in the United States of America

Publisher's Cataloging-in-Publication Data
Andresen, Peter Garth

     ISBN 978-0-98542852-5 (paperback book)
     ISBN 978-0-9854285-3-2 (e-book Kindle)
     ISBN 978-0-9854285-4-9 (e-book iBook)

Library of Congress Control Number: 2018902093

This is a novel. It's all made up.

There are no relationships, and there have been no relationships, which correlate to what you read here. All characters are entirely fictional.

There really *was* a 194th Tank Battalion, they *did* fight heroically in the Philippines, and most of them died there, or else they died from the effects of their POW years. Largely everything in the book about the 194th Tank Battalion is true. They are real-life heroes and their passing has left a gap in our town.

The Marine Corps is of course quite real, as are the bombings they endured in Lebanon. Most people have forgotten that the War on Terror, which most believe began on 9/11, began for the American military with the embassy kidnappings in Tehran in 1979, and entered its killing phase on October 23rd, 1983, with the unavenged bombing of BLT 1-8 at the Beirut airport.

Although I am proud to have served in the peacetime Marine Corps, I participated in none of the adventures described in this book. Everything you read in this book about the Marine Corps should be considered completely fictional.

The Bible quotes are also true, so much as my Bible is accurate.

Everything else . . . the whole novel . . .is fiction. Any religious experiences in the book are quite fictional, and I have no agenda spiritually. The religious experiences of the fictional characters in this work of fiction are themselves fictional.

It's all made up.

Though the righteous fall seven times, they rise again.

--Proverbs 24:16

For the revelation awaits an appointed time;

it speaks of the end

and will not prove false.

Though it linger, wait for it;

it will certainly come

and will not delay.

--Habakkuk 2:3 *New International V*

Chapter One

February 25, 2012

The view out the window was spectacular: a golf course surrounded by mansions in central California. The author John Steinbeck once wrote that these hills, right here, were "the pastures of heaven." Not for me. I'd rather be skiing. I'd rather be anywhere but here.

"Another of my angels," whispered Tommy, looking up at me from his hospital-style bed set up in his home. Friend and client. His bed overlooked the golf course. Beautiful. Peaceful. He himself was melted, disfigured, bloated with liver and kidney failure. I was shocked by how quickly his appearance had changed from our last visit, two weeks before. I could barely speak. Why I was shocked, I cannot know: I had seen others die like this before, too many, cancer-riddled, destroyed.

Long, slow, painful, ugly.

Tommy Narcisco. One of the most vital men I have ever known in my life. So physically destroyed. I felt the fear-sweat beading on my bald, shaven head. Calm down.

"Happy to be here, amigo," I whispered. *A lie.*

Tommy croaked incoherently, struggling to speak, writhing with effort. "I'm so grateful. Surrounded by people who help me. Some of them I don't even know. Like a circus in here sometimes.

"But you, I know," he continued with difficulty. "You've been a wonderful friend and an excellent investment advisor over the years. You've made me rich."

Yep, that was me. The money man. And, I hoped, the true friend I aspired to be.

Tommy's young Filipina wife, Angelica, hovered over him, her hopes of an American renaissance after life in Pampanga undoubtedly turned into a horror, while his two young children attempted to toss a small foam football around the room as if nothing was wrong. Indeed, for them, nothing really *was* wrong, since their father had been ill since they were babies.

Tommy looked up at me from his raised metal bed. He could barely lift his head. At that point, he had an infection in his esophagus, the nurse said, so it hurt to move, hurt to breathe, hurt to live. Pain with every pulse.

Five years of this, I thought. I sat there in a chair pulled up to the bedside, looking at his wasted form, his bloated abdomen like a caterpillar's, spindly limbs, hairless, his toothless head. Beyond the sliding glass doors, outside, down the hill, the beautiful golf course gleamed in the sun. There were people on the fairways, laughing, playing. Golf carts creeping about in the sunlight, like insects far away. Everything depends on the beige golf cart, I thought. Take me there.

Tommy played golf. I didn't. Of course, he'd been fighting leukemia for five years. All the devout family praying and praying and praying, and then nothing, no answer from God but the wasting, the repeated medical failures, the stern faces. There were small pictures of Jesus all over the room. Crosses. Crucifixes. Most of Angelica's Filipino family was Catholic. Tommy was possessed with a more activist Protestant faith: if we just pray hard enough, good things will certainly happen.

He looked at me. He smiled, or more precisely he grimaced.

"I'm not gonna die," he said.

I looked at him.

"I'm not gonna die," he repeated, "One more transfusion, I'll get it, I'll get through this. One day at a time. God is good."

I just looked at him. He smiled, or tried in vain. I attempted to force a smile back at him. Angelica's face was near tears. She quickly herded the chattering children from the bedroom, and

— Honor —

2

shut the door. Tommy and I were alone.

As the door shut, Tommy looked at my paltry attempt at a grin, and his face fell. No more fake smile. It was as though the bones in his face crumbled and his pallid potato head deflated.

I sat there and looked at him. I remembered him, in the past, bouncing up the steps to my office, into my home. Now he could not even raise his head from the pillow. His yellowed eyes stared at me. He said nothing.

I wanted to flee. Just four steps and I would be out that door and away, into the clean sunlight. Out there, out the front door, there was a warm, green, moist front lawn, and a sycamore tree stump which was sprouting coffee-colored mushrooms. I thought of them. Beautiful. Possibly poisonous.

"Take care of my wife," he whispered. "Take care of Cesar. Take care of Rose."

I sat and tried to savor the comfort of the chair: soft, almost a recliner. There was too much finality in any answer I could give. He looked at me, head turned towards me on the pillow, pain in his eyes. I could hear footsteps in the hallway, coming towards us.

I said, quietly, before anyone could enter, "Yes."

If I said that, and someone entered, I could leave honorably.

"Promise me, right? Everybody's gonna walk away a few months after. Not you, right?"

I waited. Nobody entered from the hallway. The sound of footsteps on the hardwood floor receded. I could escape out the back, out the sliding glass doors, go running on that golf course. Just run.

"Not me," I said.

Tommy's eyes widened. He seemed a little afraid, repulsed. He didn't understand. Perhaps he hadn't heard, or he thought I was telling him no. He raised his head off the pillow. Angry? In pain? I had to say more. He was struggling to speak.

"Tommy, I promise, I'll be there for them. I will take care of your wife and children. I will. I will." I spoke clearly. Loudly.

Tommy lowered his head back to the pillow, and closed his

eyes. "Bullshit. I know what will happen," he said.

I said nothing. I thought of cross country skiing. It was February. There was still snow in the Sierra Mountains, far away from this death bed. There would be the scent of pines there.

"It's what always happens," he whispered, "I'm a doctor, remember?"

I said nothing. His eyes stayed shut, his mouth moving slightly. He seemed to be rehearsing words. Perhaps he was not fully conscious. Time passed silently. I could hear people down the hallway, beyond the closed door, apparently waiting for us to finish. Tommy spoke again without moving, quietly.

"The people come, the people say nice things, the people promise. Then most of them will walk away. I can't really blame them." A pause. A deep breath. Several hiccoughs. Spasms, really. It looked painful.

"There are a few. Sometimes you don't even know their names. The ones who help. Perhaps they don't even know they're doing it. Accidental." He was whispering now, eyes closed, as though talking to himself.

"My situation is complicated, Garth. Perhaps I should have done better. I know what is happening. They think I don't know I'm dying, but I do."

His eyes were shut. Was he talking about his imminent death? I wasn't sure. Silence seemed the best choice, faced with such opacity. Perhaps Tommy was disoriented from the pain killers. In my own body I could feel the stiffness of uncertainty, a rising panic. *Oh, somebody, do something.* I focused on keeping my breathing slow and routine, counting to ten on the inhale, then to ten on the exhale.

Then I moved my thoughts beyond the room, beyond this home, beyond this street. I'll run for sixty minutes today, I thought, until I'm soaked with sweat and it's all burned away. Today I will run, one foot in front of the other, down Main Street in Old Town Salinas, past Patria and all the other restaurants, where they serve you the Caesar salads with grilled salmon, still crispy from the oak wood fire, or perhaps I will run at Toro Park, up the brush-covered hills, to look down into the Salinas Valley at the gray clouds creeping up the valley from the blue Pacific Ocean. Beautiful.

He opened his eyes and gazed at me and seemed to become angry, and he croaked at me.

"Promise me! You won't abandon me, right? I know your soul, Garth. I know what you are. I remember . . . I remember that you were in the Marines once. Remember that? I need that commitment." Louder now.

He gasped painfully, as though the words had hurt him, closing his eyes again.

"A warrior soul. That's what they will need. You *will* fight for my family. Promise me, I need to hear it."

He paused, lying rigid, eyes shut, apparently struggling to control a disorienting wave of pain. I sat there, wishing I was anywhere else. I certainly wasn't a warrior.

"Take care of Angelica," he whispered. "Take care of Angelica. Take care of Cesar. Take care of Rose. I want them to grow up in this home, live life, smile. Life is good, you know?"

I silently nodded my assent.

"Promise me," he repeated. "She's a good woman. They are good kids. It's going to be hard for you, for them. Promise me."

There was silence for a time. He lay there with his eyes shut, and I thought, has he died? Then I saw his chest moving, and he turned his head and looked me in the eye. He looked all the way through me. I looked back. I wanted to give him peace, reassure him. Whatever it took.

Finally I spoke, more loudly again. "Tommy, I promise."

I paused.

"I promise you that I will take care of Angelica, and take care of Cesar, and take care of Rose. I promise that I will fight for them. I will always be there for them. Always. I promise."

"I know you will," he whispered. "That's who you are. That's why we're here." Then he shut his eyes, and was silent. I watched him for a while, and realized that he wasn't going to say anything more.

— Chapter 1 —

"Goodbye, my friend," I said quietly. "Sushi next month, when you are better, right?"

His eyes were shut. He didn't respond. His breathing was irregular. Perhaps he was asleep. I remembered that when my own father died, after the car crash, the nurse had told us that the irregular breathing was the sign of the end of the fight. My father. I had not thought of him yet today.

I put my hand to the door and began to open it, dreaming of the sunlight beyond the front door. I heard a slight rustling and turned on my leather-soled shoes, the shoes I had bought for dancing, and I saw that Tommy seemed to rouse. "Garth, wait," he whispered.

He struggled for words. "It's complicated," he forced out.

"I can handle this, Tommy," I said. "It's money. It's what I do."

His eyes stayed shut, his face relaxed now.

"The angels know the truth," he whispered, smiling faintly. "The money is just there for love. Giving. We give, we give, and when we least expect, giving is all there is. It's all there is."

He seemed to fall asleep then. I watched him. His breath was sometimes deep, sometimes shallow, and sometimes even absent.

Walking out of there that day, away from the smells of decay, fermentation, feces, and medicinal alcohol, away from the fixed toothy smiles of the brown-skinned, black-haired Filipina women who were Tommy's caregivers, the pictures of smiling Jesus on the walls, into the brilliant sunlight of the front yard, beautiful warm green lawn, sycamore tree stump with mushrooms, I thought to myself, if anyone can live through this, Tommy can do it. Tommy was one of the toughest men I knew. Tommy was the very epitome of resilient.

I always take refuge in words.

Two days later: a sunny February day, chill with the promise of early spring in coastal California, and I was shooting a rifle, lying flat on a blue canvas shooting mat. On both sides of me, there were other shooters, absorbed as I was.

I was finishing a twenty-shot Swiss international rifle match, trying to fire a hole in a ten ring the size of a teacup on the paper international rifle target, 300 meters distant. Clear, cool air. Slight heat mirage off the 1954-made Swiss Schmidt Rubin rifle. Blued steel and brown birch wood. There was a ritual to it: slide the rifle into the shoulder so that the sling is tight, all weight to both elbows. Rattle the action shut on a fresh Swiss military GP-11 cartridge, align the sights, focus on the front sight, gentle trigger squeeze, let the recoil from the shot ripple through your body, score the shot. Repeat.

The Monterey County Swiss Rifle Club range was tucked into the spring-green mountains, which form the eastern boundaries of the Salinas Valley, near the coast at Monterey Bay in Central California. The first match of the spring season was always a challenge, and this, in February 2012, was no different. During the competition it often looked as though the front sight was wavering on the tiny black bullseye so far away. The hills beyond the row of targets were greening, sprouts amongst last year's brown grass. My final shot was a ten. Perfect.

I stood up, inserted a yellow plastic chamber flag into the open maw of the receiver as match regulations required, placed the rifle in the worn gray wooden gun rack behind the firing line, muzzle upright, and peeled off the sweat-soaked, stiff, thick camouflage shooting jacket. I pulled on a yellow cotton hooded sweatshirt. My cellphone was in a sweatshirt pocket. I lifted, looked, and there was a text message, from Lanie, a co-worker. She was also one of my closest friends.

"Tommy just died."

Somewhere the match was continuing; the repeated sound of rifle shots, scores being shouted from score keepers to shooters, the tinkle of empty brass cartridge cases ejected from rifles hitting the concrete firing platform. I looked at the text on my phone as my mind swam. Then I stared at my shooting jacket lying on a raw, unpainted plywood shooting table. The quilted white of the interior canvas lining of the coat steamed slightly in the cold sunlit air.

— Chapter 1 —

7

Chapter Two

March 2012

Tommy's funeral was a loud immensity, replete with vast tables of pan-Asian food including an entire roast pig, "lechon," and Hawaiian music. Five hundred people. A vaguely military, middle-aged paunchy color guard, wearing berets, graying facial hair, and motorcycle vests. As Tommy used to say, it had everything but dancing monkeys.

Tommy's family held the memorial service at the Steinbeck Cultural Center, the central venue for all our big events in Salinas. Our Salinas City fathers, back in the Age of Elvis, tore down most of the interesting Victorian architecture and replaced it with what was then regarded as chic, the "Space Age Cinder Block Gas Station" look, preferably painted white or beige. So in Salinas we made do with what we had, and our concert hall, appropriately located next to our dirt-track arena where we hold rodeos, monster truck rallies, and Hispanic rock concerts, was the ultimate place in town for volunteer talent shows and ballet recitals.

But this was a first in my memory, a multi-cultural event seating a mere five hundred. There was a ceremony in the midst of all this, a "celebration of life" sort of thing with people doing their best to ignore the reality that the cancer dragon had just eaten one of our own, skin, bone, and sinew.

Even at the edges of this celebration, I could hear people discussing, pledging, and promising: Tommy had been one of us, one of our family, our ohana, brown, yellow, and white, and across the peoples of different races and beliefs, I heard the murmur of commitment. Angelica and her two beautiful young children would be cherished, supported, and loved. This family would never be in want.

It was a honey-sound, a soothing rhythm of love and support and closeness, and I had never felt it so deeply before in my life.

Towards the end, there was a hula, performed by thirty of Tommy's distant pan-Asian cousins who had driven down from San Jose, now up on the stage moving in perfect step to Keali'i Reichel's "Wanting Memories" It was a plaintive, sad, beautiful Hawaiian song.

I sat in the audience in the dark, watching those thirty women of all ages, dancing slowly in the stage-light, all in unison, all in the trance of shared performance, beautiful black hair, gray hair on some, brown skin in a spectrum of tones, and I wondered at the life of someone such as Tommy who could produce such magic simply with his smile.

Finally there was the Navy ROTC color guard from North Salinas High School, where slightly overweight military retirees taught the kids to drill and march prettily and pretend that the killing isn't real. Teenagers, beardless boys and smooth-faced girls. The middle-aged men in faux military berets and motor-cycle vests folded a flag . . . no casket here to mar the party . . . and they gave the triangular, folded flag of a veteran to the ROTC teenagers, and they passed it to his widow, stood straight, and saluted.

Angelica sat alone on stage in the spotlight as she accepted the triangular flag: tiny in a calf-length black dress, the beams of light shadowing her exercise-defined arms and slender profile, beautiful, and yet so obviously full of sorrows. I asked myself as I sat in the dark behind five hundred other guests how a man could earn the love of such a woman as that. I was seated near a door, and as I watched her I realized that it was pouring rain outside. It was really coming down out there on the sidewalk. In here, in this dark cavernous auditorium, there was only quiet, peace, and a spotlight on a tiny beautiful woman in a black dress with a folded flag.

I was a veteran myself.

— Honor —
10

Chapter Three

March 22, 2003

"Is it true you used to be a major, sir? You took a demotion just to be with us?" said the teenaged lance corporal who was driving this massive six-by-six truck. A cargo of what appeared to be MREs were piled squarely in the back.

It was day three of the Iraqi invasion, midmorning. We had been driving our trucks for twenty-hour days since we'd launched, still sweltering in our camouflage, sun-absorbing MOPP suits, which we wore in the event of chemical attack. Wearing a MOPP suit was like wearing a thick, plastic garbage bag: wet, stifling, chafing, smelly, hot. Looking back at all my achievements, wearing a MOPP suit for three straight days ranks high.

I was exhausted. I didn't want to talk. But some response was necessary.

"Yes, Lance Corporal, you heard right. I took a demotion just to be with you." I had to smile. Actually, there was so much more to the story, and I did not believe in chronic bullshit. So I continued.

"I was in for most of two decades, infantry, Arabic foreign area officer, the whole bit. I got out sixteen years ago. I'm back in because of 9/11. Too much broken time. So I'm a warrant officer now." So much unsaid.

I had been infantry. After I came back in, I assailed the G-1 personnel department of 1 Marine Expeditionary Force on at least a weekly basis, reminding them of my Arabic language background and my reconnaissance special operations training.

Somehow, I found a weekly excuse to get into Camp Pendleton mainside, visit 1 MEF headquarters, and confront the G-1, the administrators and paper-pushers, about my mis-assignment.

Finally the administrator-captain behind the desk, young enough to be my son, and never once in the field since basic school, white-faced, wide-eyed, apoplectic from stress, shrieked at me, "I DON'T HAVE TIME FOR THIS! IT DOESN'T . . . MATTER! YOUR ARABIC . . . DOESN'T THE FUCK MAT-TER! GO BACK TO YOUR FUCKING TRUCKS . . . AND DO WHAT YOU ARE FUCKING . . . TOLD!"

So here I was.

I studied the pallid driver, a nineteen-year-old named Gus from Paradise, Tennessee, an eager reservist called to eager ac-tive duty, who had been attempting to discuss his relationship with his pregnant wife back home. I wasn't saying much. As his potential platoon commander I didn't want to get into give-and-take about relationships, and I had never seen this lance corporal before that morning, when he arrived as a replacement with a shipment of fan belts and tires. We were under orders to keep moving, keep rolling, and at this point, I didn't even know if he was actually part of my platoon, or just a temporary add-on for the day. We were all mixed up and moving too fast. But I needed to say something.

"Tell me more about home," I forced out. Not much, but enough.

Gus droned on. His wife was apparently "way horny" in her pregnancy, and Gus was here, not there. I recoiled emotionally. Too much information. But I said nothing. He kept talking and my mind wandered.

9/11. 9/11. We've all got our stories.

I learned about it when my mother called. I think she must be-gin watching the news at 3 a.m., still, so there was a call on the house phone . . . while I sat on the living couch typing a client newsletter about the dangers of excessively long bond maturi-ties, waiting to wake the children for school.

"Turn on the TV."

— Honor —

12

So I did. There was the first tower of the World Trade Center, wrapped in flame and smoke. Tragic. Undoubtedly some nut-ball airline pilot, pissed at his wife's lover. Probably an accident. After all, hadn't someone accidentally flown a B-25 into the Empire State Building in 1945?

Then I saw the live images of that second jetliner slamming into the second tower, and the whole world changed. Watching my wife, Margaret, as the second tower collapsed, seeing the color drain from her face, witnessing thousands of people die horribly, watching our dreams burn up in jet fuel.

When I came home a few days later and told her that I had re-enlisted, she had simply affirmed my statement with a cold nod of her head. No, "WHAT THE FUCK ARE YOU THINKING?" not even an, "I'll miss you." She had always been a homemaker, and we had enough saved so that she could remain a homemaker. She said nothing. Just a nod of her head. She helped me pack.

What happened after that was still a bit of a mystery.

I had concluded my prior service as a major in the Marine Corps Reserve. Given my giant absence between 1991 and 2001, I was permitted to re-enlist in the Marine Reserves as a warrant officer one, at age forty-seven, when most others are a few years from retirement.

The lieutenant doing the induction, perhaps twenty-one years old, told me that as far as he was concerned, my rejoining was an insult to warrant officers everywhere. He could say that because, of course, warrant officers of any age rank below lieutenants and thus he was safe from my hoary, bald-headed vengeance.

I was incompetent as a truck platoon commander, since I had never been one in my life, except as a passenger.

I was personally a bit puzzled about why we needed to invade Iraq, since we had known about the weapons of mass destruction back in the First Gulf War and decided to ignore them then. My guess was that the dictator of Iraq, Saddam Hussein, had fed one too many dissidents to a wood chipper, had played kissy-face with one terrorist too many. So here we were. Ours not to reason.

— Chapter 3 —

The truck hit a large pothole in the dirt road. I turned my attention back to reality. Gus rambled on. He was worried, clearly. Perhaps, he perseverated, there was a good 'ol boy back there in the Tennessee holler, with eyes on Gus's ever-swelling, pie-eating teenage bride. He said, "Staff Sergeant Smith says I'm a gonna go home and find my wife the same way I left her: freshly fucked!"

He said that as bright as a chipmunk, his southern accent rich in his words. I looked at him wordlessly. His sallow twelve-year-old, wide-eyed rodent face looked back at me, full of horror at what the good ol' boy and his expectant wife might be doing, since it was about 3 a.m. yesterday back in Coon Holler.

Lance Corporal Gus turned his face back to the road ahead, his wide eyes bulging. The boy had a scattering of whiteheads and pimples covering his unbearded face. For all that is holy, he was way too young to be here. *Damn.* I would have to counsel the staff sergeant about talk like that.

"That's a fear we all have. It's part of the experience," I said. Platitudes. Say something.

His breath was grotesquely bad from powdered coffee and lack of a toothbrush.

It was an astonishing reality that left unsupervised, some people don't brush their teeth.

I guessed I was probably his new platoon commander, so I would need to address dental hygiene for the entire platoon at the next break. In addition, the plastic bag MOPP suits were making us all ferment in our own sweat. A mandatory wipe-down of all personnel was definitely in order. Meanwhile, the sour stench from both sources filled the cabin.

Sitting in the bouncing passenger seat of the dust-filled truck as we jostled across the rutted sand, I was trying not to talk. My mind wandered again. I had my M-16A2 without optics stowed on the dash rack, magazine in place, chamber empty. I watched it gradually accumulate dust. I had started out in the 1970s with the M-16A1, that Matty-Mattel ever-jamming piece of garbage. But this M-16A2 was a whole different beast, heavier bullets, much better barrel and sights, an entire class above the tired 7.62 AKM's of the Iraqis, and I expected good things from it. I had always qualified Expert. I had competed in the West Coast USMC shooting team earlier in my life. But that was shooting without the target shooting back. This might be different. I supposed we were all wondering how we would perform in combat.

As we bounced along the rutted road and Gus continued to talk, I thought of the inscription which he had tattooed in large florid script on his flaccid right arm. I had seen the image that morning after his arrival, as he pulled on the rainsuit-like gear. Now the tattoo was covered by the coffee stain cammies and the MOPP suit: "USMC Death before Dishonor Don't bother to run, you'll only die tired." That was a lot to put on one small arm. As he chattered on, Gus revealed that during his last physical fitness test he had managed five pull-ups.

I was contemplating the likelihood of an engine breakdown in my truck platoon on this sand road as we passed disabled vehicles from other units at regular intervals. My thought was that the task force and the supply convoy were huge, beyond envisioning, and we seemed to be entering Iraq in a relatively slender column. Some breakdowns out of thousands of vehicles were probably normal.

Gus talked on. Apparently, his wife, who was but seventeen, was a superb cook. His words barely penetrated my mind, as the column began to accordion, to slow up to a near stop and speed back up to 15 miles per hour. That made the tan dust rise ahead. I reached for my map. Yes, we had GPS but I wanted to see if I could fix our position the old way.

On the road side we passed an unarmored Humvee communications vehicle, with radio antennas bristling about 5 meters high, clearly crammed with comm gear. Marines in combat gear and MOPP suits, no masks, just desert camo Kevlar helmets, were talking into handsets and peering through binoculars to our right. All of them looked tired and overheated: sweaty red faces, blank stares. A FAC (forward air control) team, perhaps ANGLICO (air-naval gunfire liaison company), they might be calling a fire mission for aircraft or artillery. Something might be brewing over there, beyond the gentle, tan sand dunes. I noticed several foreign uniforms, slight changes in camouflage patterns. It was probably ANGLICO, then. Air Naval Gunfire Liaison Team. Working with our allies.

Envy. These guys were getting to pound the snot out of the bad guys while I was merely riding a truck. I felt a small little kick of adrenaline. Something might be happening. But probably not. No cause to get all excited. No need to unlatch that M-16A2 rifle from its rack. I turned my mind back to the convoy. No need to check the map. Just follow the truck in front of us.

Then something crushed me, blotted everything black. I felt the air smashed out of my chest with a loud crunch, and I remembered nothing more.

I woke up unable to move my head or anything else, aching over every inch of my body.   I was in the sand, I thought. I moved my eyes. There was a roaring in my ears, and I shifted my hand. So there was movement there. I panicked; I was crippled, paralyzed. No. I could move my jaw, although something was crunching and salty in my mouth. I could feel my toes. I could hardly hear anything but the ringing in my head. It was as though people were talking through a blanket. There was a corpsman—a very young female corpsman—looking down at me, trying to speak to me, but I couldn't really hear her, and what I could hear, I couldn't understand.

What is she doing with that flashlight in my mouth? Someone was suctioning my mouth, like a dentist, and there were little loose rocks in there . . . no, teeth. They gently removed my helmet and latched my head down on the backboard. I could feel the straps. My head was now immobile, and I didn't know why. I moved my toes. I moved my fingers. There was salt and a metallic taste in my mouth: blood. I tried to spit it out, forced the blood and the bits out with my tongue, which seemed cut, and I felt the mess drool down the side of my cheek.

I became more aware of the young woman corpsman looking

down at me. She looked frightened, almost terrified. Very young. Teenaged. I felt a wave of parental concern. Whatever happens, whatever has happened to me, I must not frighten these youngsters. I must bolster their sense of competence, build their confidence. But I couldn't move effectively, couldn't really speak.

Then somebody unbuckled my pistol and pulled the web belt out from under me. My .45 1911 pistol. Don't take my pistol. I was feebly thrashing, trying to get their attention, when it occurred to me that I didn't want to embarrass myself in front of that girl. Let the pistol go. Let the pistol go. I'll get it back later when all this is over.

I did a quick mental check through my sensory fog. Was I moaning? Crying? Afraid? Had I pissed myself? No. Apparently, I was just lying there now. Good. Then I wondered: who was in charge now? Did we have security? Was everyone focused on the casualties? We needed to set out some sentries. Now. I tried to speak, but I couldn't talk.

"Let's do another assessment. Overall body. Saline, morphine, then roll him, roll him," someone said.

I felt with my hands: I was now in a basket litter: I could feel the rail. The IV slid into my hand: a little ant bite, and an intense coolness as something began to flow through my arm. I forced my eyes to the sides. There was the truck, flat on its back, held square by the undisturbed cargo. A giant beetle.

Then they rolled the entire litter on its side, with me strapped immobile, and irrigated my mouth to wash out my shattered molars. My mouth suddenly began to ache and burn when that saline solution sprayed into my mouth. I suppose I made a face, because I remember someone saying, "Xylocaine" and they sprayed something into my mouth, and some of the pain went away.

I could see the truck beyond the corpsmen. I was looking at the front axle. Not even broken. They'll be able to roll the truck back onto its wheels and just drive on. In a few minutes I'm going to jump right up, get my pistol back, and drive away with it.

Then they carried me away, rocking flat on the basket litter along with their strides, with the sun boring its way into my eyes. A mild jolt of excitement echoed through the painkillers: I had been wounded in action, and yet I was intact. A Purple Heart medal was in my future. I had finally been in combat . . . commanding a 6 by 6 truck platoon. Whatever, it was still action.

That was followed by another wave of concern. Had anyone else been hurt? Had my Marines been somehow involved in combat which I had missed entirely while I was unconscious?

Later at the hospital in Germany I learned that it was not combat, and there would be no Purple Heart. The forward observers of an allied artillery battery had made a mistake, and they had fired on the observer's grid coordinates with a 175 MM cannon. One shot, one shell, one truck, all an accident, all friendly fire. And even then, not too bad by the official standards.

I had crushed sinuses, a few broken molars, and a mild traumatic brain injury. Lance Corporal Gus had sustained greater head trauma, had suffered a profoundly greater head injury, and was quickly moved to Bethesda Naval Hospital, to an intensive brain care facility. He was expected to make a full recovery. Lance Corporal Gus had never been officially transferred into my platoon: he "experienced a non-combat injury" before his paperwork could catch up. I was advised that he was the concern of others. Let it go.

Let it go. Easier said than done. Nothing was ever the same, after that.

My mind returned to Tommy's funeral. I realized that everyone, everything, was now silent, except for the pounding rain on the pavement beyond the open door. The sun had orbited the earth nine more times since Iraq, I thought. Such noise so long ago, so much passion. Here was only quiet, peace, and a spotlight on a tiny beautiful woman in a black dress with a folded flag. A small part of me wished that folded flag was for me.

— Honor —

Chapter Four

March-April 2012

Lanie, my investment advisor partner, and I sat across the table from Angelica, the new widow. We were at the same hexagonal table that Tommy had sat at when he told me he was sick. Angelica was sitting in the same chair. I didn't tell her that.

There was a large brown paper grocery bag of bills on that little table. A full grocery bag. All these bills, all compressed and jumbled, layered paper leaves, where the family of a dying man had stored them, financial silage stored away against the inevitable reality that someday they would come due. Doubtlessly fermenting.

"I detest bills," I said, mostly to fill the emptiness.

"I know," answered Lanie. "But why?"

Nice of her to ask. Like me, she was undoubtedly trying to keep up a prattle to keep Angelica distracted from her awesome loss.

"As I see it, I am always one envelope from ruin. Have you noticed that bills seem to spawn like cockroaches, the same way coots migrate underground?" I added.

"What are coots?" asked Angelica, drawn out of her somber thoughts. Good.

"Kind of like a cross between a duck and a chicken. Wild water birds," I said, "They eat grass."

"I've never seen one," said Lanie to Angelica, smiling. "Don't let him fool you."

"You see? Underground," I added as I sorted papers out of the bag. I placed them in piles, attempting to cull out the junk.

"Bills are an unavoidable part of life," added Lanie.

"So are hemorrhoids, rattlesnakes, mountain oysters, and ticks. The less one sees of them, the better," I countered.

Finally Angelica smiled, albeit slightly.

Lanie began to open the envelopes, one after another, and to unfold them, rattling, to organize them into new piles to be paid, or possibly to be negotiated. She was in her well-dusted efficient element. Soon the table was full and we were lining the bills up on the nearby chocolate brown leather couch, covering the plush, overstuffed cushions with rows of papers and envelopes. Angelica sat there silently, looking somber, eyes wet.

"How did you know my husband?" asked Angelica, "He talked of you often."

"We grew up around each other, mostly. We knew each other as kids, in passing. He lived in Alisal, and I lived on a cattle ranch in the mountains down by Chualar," I replied.

"He said you were a soldier?" said Angelica.

"Marine infantry. And he joined the navy. Enlisted medical. Then worked his way up to medical school on the GI bill. Amazing." I added, "Really we got to know each other after we came back from all that. My father was a very established doctor and rancher, and Tommy was just getting started. They became friends, and I became an investment advisor as well as a friend. I managed your family money. That's where we spent the most time."

While we talked, I created a spreadsheet account on my laptop computer, and added up the assets. As I entered the account balances, it quickly became obvious that the estate was simply not big enough. I rechecked the numbers.

This couldn't be happening: Tommy had been frugal, and I had watched his wealth grow. Now I could see that except for the investments in the discount brokerage accounts, which I managed, the rest was gone. The family home was now deeply mortgaged. I tried to keep my face neutral.

"Is there something I'm not seeing?" I asked. Angelica became more silent and pale. Surely there were other accounts. Secret money somewhere. Lanie rummaged through the piles: nothing there but bills. There was no rescuing bank account statement, no hidden respite from the relentless tallies now stacked across my laptop's screen.

"And you went away to the soldiers again?" said Angelica. She sounded accusatory.

What? I thought.

"9/11. I thought I could make a difference. I'd been there before," I responded. "I really got to know your husband after I came back that second time and tried to restart my life. Tommy was very welcoming. Most people didn't know what to do. You helped."

"How did I help?" asked Angelica.

"You made him happy," I said, distracted by the pile of bills.

While we talked, the numbers I was seeing on the laptop silently astounded me. Tommy was a doctor. Tommy was well established, a high earner, a man of understated but emphatic prosperity. By all that was holy, he lived next to the golf course. I did not want to tell Angelica. This would terrify her.

"Did I make him happy?" asked Angelica. She looked down, face gently contorting. "Did I?" her voice cracked.

"Tommy had never been married before and he had no children. He had given up on love," I responded. "And there you were."

Tears fell from Angelica's eyes as she looked at me, smiling.

"You know Tommy was fifty-nine and I was thirty. We met because a cousin introduced us. It wasn't supposed to happen, but it did. I didn't expect it either. So what did you think?" asked Angelica.

I laughed. "Well, of course, we all thought that you were very young and very beautiful. The truth is that most of us thought that your marriage would blow up like a zeppelin, like the Hindenburg, you know, a great big ball of fire." I pantomimed a fireball.

"But it didn't. Two beautiful healthy kids. So wonderful."

— Chapter 4 —

I didn't mention that my own personal life had gone in exactly the opposite direction since I'd returned from the Marines. Headaches and fainting. Nightmares. Muscle pain. I exercised frantically but my weight was still gradually declining. Headaches. Doctors. Dentists.

My own romantic entanglements were the stuff of B-grade melodrama and church cautionary tales: a broken marriage, a thin, stern-lipped Anglo-Saxon professional ex-wife who was always dressed for success, and four wonderful children enwrapped in sparse shared custody and lush child support. Thus I knew an approaching train wreck simply by hearing the whistle.

"What's a zeppelin?" asked Angelica.

"A giant gas bag," I responded, diverted. While we were talking, Lanie had silently pointed out the deficits on my computer spreadsheets. I was agog.

Lanie showed us the shards of paper set in three well-organized piles on the walnut octagonal table and on the couch. Tommy had been generous. Here was a printout of a money transfer showing that before his death he had contributed to the education of a teeming multitude of Filipino in-laws, some of whom he had never met. Lanie brandished another paper showing that Tommy had bought several of the Filipino clan "jeepneys" to begin taxi services. One bank account transfer document, crumpled and used at some point in the past as a coaster for some sort of tea or coffee, revealed that Tommy had contributed an $80,000 check for the construction of a home for his in-laws.

Even worse, Tommy had been prompt and honest. When bills had arrived when he had been too sick to work, he had paid them to the full. There was a clear record: a surprisingly limited health insurance policy, monstrous hospital charges, doctors' bills as big as a Montana sunrise. While he was alive, Tommy had paid any bill he could find, while his savings and financial reserves had trickled away.

There was no recourse but to share this stark reality with Angelica. Lanie took the lead. She was good that way. Gentle, kind, yet truthful. As she spoke quietly, I saw tears welling up in Angelica's eyes. Beyond tolerance to watch her cry. To divert myself, I reviewed the stacks of bills.

I realized that the lifestyle Tommy had maintained for his family and himself had continued with unabated opulence until he'd breathed his final ragged breath. There, for example, were several bills for his golf club membership, unpaid since his final days, with garish red "Overdue" stamps diagonally across them. There as well was his last credit card bill, with a charge for a wide-screen plasma TV and two bicycles for the children-- for Christmas, Angelica said. There were a whopping $400,000 in unexplained withdrawals from his bank account. Angelica explained that these were for a final budget-wrecking trip to Massachusetts to attempt a last-ditch cure with peach-pit extract. Apparently not covered by health insurance.

Looking now at Tommy's beautiful young wife, pale-faced, wide-eyed, silent, tears coursing down her flawless, flan-colored cheeks, wearing jeans and a conservative white shirt, I could understand his thoughts, his choice to grasp for all the tangible joy a terminally ill man could apprehend. Had I been in his place, perhaps I would have done the same. I sat there unable to speak, attempting to formulate a plan within my mind, until I finally had it organized in my head.

So began our afternoons to rebuild the finances of the Narcisco family. We met daily after the stock market closed and I ended my trading. We sat there at that table, while the rain fell and the sun shone on the front yard outside. Lanie managed the bookkeeping. I talked with the creditors. My son Ernst, who was 19, working in the office and attending community college, handled the copying, organizing, and mailing. We were a team.

The days grew longer as spring passed into summer. Day after day, after the stock market closed, Angelica would bring her children and her pancit and her bills. She, Lanie, and I would comb through the accounts, and apportion what we could. There were the hidden small nuggets of insurance, which hide all over the American financial landscape, all offered as enticements by this credit card company or an unannounced benefit from that past employer, and we dug them all up, pulled them unwillingly from the earth, and so we grew the Narcisco family accounts.

As soon as we found money, we paid it out. Creditors grudgingly settled. I spent hours on the phone, negotiating. It was, however, almost impossible to dun a young widow with young children, especially when the numbers were laid via email before the creditors. At first, they were impassive, unresponsive, unmoved. One at a time, I faxed them or emailed them the vital spreadsheet, and they began to realize: it was either a partial payment, or no payment. The money simply wasn't there. And so, one by one, they settled.

One by one, the promises of the pig-eating attendees at Tommy's funeral proved empty. There was no resultant college fund for the children. There was no genuine support. Many of the single men who had been Tommy's friends dropped by the family home to gaze with longing as Angelica lost weight, to change a light bulb, to mow the lawn. But there was no money. We swam in an economy awash in cash, but there was so little for this family.

Chapter Five

May 2012

The fog had crept across the mountains all the way from the Pacific Ocean, thirty miles distant, to the deep river canyon of the Arroyo Seco River. The cool wouldn't last: the fog almost always burned off by 10 a.m. at the latest, especially this far inland. Then it would be hot.

It was Saturday. My plan was to run about 10 miles uphill on the Indians Road with my Uncle Otto's Marlin rifle and a pig tag. The Indians Road was a trail, really, a former four-wheel drive dirt road along the steep canyon slopes. It had been closed several decades earlier when too many off-the-grid illegal drug manufacturers, mostly emaciated, toothless meth tweakers with rusting old sedans, took to driving the uncertain, twisted dirt road at night with their lights off, to bring product to Soledad.

A few years ago, an especially blessed mud slump from uphill onto the road had stopped all traffic, and provided the National Forest Service with the opportunity to shut the track down to motor vehicles.

Now, in 2012, the road was a trail for runners, hikers, mountain bikers, and a few fortunate horse packers. Other rock slides and gullies had reduced the potential for vehicular traffic even more, and the deerweed, sage, and hop tree had been allowed to over grow the road. The path transected the steep green brush, dark green oak trees, and brown grasses of the ridges high above the clear waters of the Arroyo Seco River. Usually the sound of rushing water was ever present.

There I was, at dawn as always, and I had brought my

ninety-two-year-old mother, AKA date repellent, and my five-year-old daughter. My mother insisted she could watch Francesca, or at least call for help, and while I had deep misgivings about that, the lure of the trail was just too great. We were on good terms with Bill, the lumbering campground host. I had asked him to keep an eye out for my family, and he had agreed.

I parked the yellow XTerra in the day use area, near the river. At her age, Mom needed help out of the car and onto her walker, and then to a nearby picnic table under a sycamore tree. Francesca wandered down towards the flowing clear water, gathered up a few river rocks and began throwing them, attempting to skip them across. My mother beckoned to her: she wanted to see the pebbles.

I pondered that she certainly knew her rocks. After all, she was a geology graduate from Stanford in 1940, and she had worked through World War II as an invasion-planning geologist and later as a petroleum hunter in Central America. Then she'd moved back to Salinas with my father, and his medical practice, and his inherited ranch, and became an expert of Angus cattle and a school board doyenne.

A flooding of many, many memories of our early life along that river: babies toddling and falling in the sand, weaving tules with our Native American relatives, fishing, laughter, powdery dust, hot days, cold clean water, and the pungency of sycamore trees in the sun.

While she was pointing out a family of acorn woodpeckers in a nearby oak to Francesca, I began my stiff and painful run, turtle-speed up the hill, past the campground host Bill in his softly whirring beige electric golf cart. Undoubtedly, he was driving down to check on my family. Cowboy hat. Aviator sunglasses. Hawaiian shirt. Three hundred pounds. He waved.

Feeling my muscles unbinding. All the memories of life, life on the ranch before we lost it, friends living and dead, hunting deer, the many other runs on that road, relationships.

There was a tarantula hawk wasp clinging to a monkey flower. And there, in a rare sandy spot on the road: a circular animal track; a mountain lion had stepped there. The river far below: glittering as the fog lifted, a flowing path of translucent greens and transparent blues.

At 5 miles out, I found an almost-hidden trail head on the downhill side of the road, and stopped running. Down through the purple-blooming ceonothus brush, feet carefully on the trail to keep from sliding on dry brown prickly oak leaves, rifle held for balance, about 50 yards downhill, and there was my secret clearing.

It was May: all the wild oats were golden and not yet broken by dehydration, and the squirrels had rooted up some of the ground, leaving piles of dry moved dirt. Dark dirt. The Esselen Indians . . . our distant relations . . . had been here in this clearing hundreds of years before me. The clearing was about 10 yards across, a hidden place, with a light tan limestone rock in the center raised above the grass. Little white clam fossils speckled the rock, and as I slid down to it I could see them more clearly, small bumps and divots becoming clearer.

The arrowhead and the feather I had created and left the last time I had been here, several weeks ago, when the grass was seeded but still green, were both gone. That was fine; it was a sharing of sorts. Someone else had been here, had seen the magic.

I sat on the rock. My breath began to quiet. The hum of insects: bees. The lupine and the monkeyflower were blooming. I could smell them. There was a tiny jumping spider hunting on the rock, jerking and swiveling like a miniscule armored vehicle. Somewhere an acorn woodpecker was chattering to its clan. I was soaking wet from sweat, and beads were running down my face. A tick was crawling up my pant leg. I brushed it off.

I took a new arrowhead out of my running pack. I had made it in my backyard the week before, sitting under an olive tree. Green wine bottle glass, so no archaeologist could possibly think that the Eastern woodland Cahokia culture made it out this far west. I had carried it out here in a yellow plastic camping soap dish lined with a rag. Then I removed the small feather

— Chapter 5 —

27

from my pack: wild turkey, red felt. Plastic pastel beads.

I put the arrowhead on the rock. Then I sat. Quietly, counting my breath cycle, trying to slow it down. Talk to me, God, I thought. A wave of guilt washed over me. So much not done.

I began with the Lord's Prayer.

Then I asked, aloud, "Please forgive me for my past mistakes, God. Let me follow your path to bring goodness to the world. Give me courage. Help me to be strong."

A horned toad lizard jumped up on the rock next to me. Horned lizards are usually found in sand. This guy had waded through wild oats and brome to get here. He looked pissed. Horned lizards always look pissed. I looked back, unmoving, hoping I wouldn't drip sweat on the creature. The lizard looked back, tiny spikes and camouflaged skin, flat as a pancake. I thought. God, what do you mean to tell me?

The lizard wasn't saying. It suddenly jumped back down into the grass and shimmied away, and vanished quickly. Off to eat ants, I supposed.

There was blue in the sky now. The fog was melting away, and soon the heat would begin. I needed to move. A quick sip from the water bottle, a handful of Costco mixed nuts, and I began to run very slowly up to the trail, up to the road, back to the campground and engines and my mother and Francesca, and hopefully, mergansers.

I finished the run as the heat was rising in the blue sky. It was noon: time for the peanut butter sandwiches I had wrapped in the cooler in the back of the car. I walked down the road for my cool down and I could see my mother, sitting there at a picnic table in the shade of a sycamore tree, smiling, laughing at a woman. A beautiful, small woman . . . and I recognized her.

Angelica. She had come to see us. I struggled to remember: yes, I had mentioned I was going to be here. I *did* mention my mother, I *did* invite her to come out and see the river and bring the children. But I didn't expect her to act on that.

"Hi!" She flashed her brilliant smile. "I brought lunch." Her velvet voice. Her smile was bright as a mirror.

— Honor —

"She also brought the kids," said my mother. "They're playing with Francesca."

I could hear the laughter and see flashes of color down by the river. *We really should be closer to the water to watch them.* Distant children's laughter. Amazing. Wonderful.

The entire picnic table was covered with closed plastic containers of food.

"I thought you would enjoy this, and I could meet your mom." Angelica smiled shyly. Her voice was smooth and feminine.

"She's impressing me!" said my mom. "I was in the Philippines after the war and I *loved* it! I've been hungering for pancit ever since. Angelica, you are wonderful for bringing all this. Sit down and show me what I'm eating!"

Somehow, I had forgotten that my mother had been in the Philippines before.

I could see the children playing by the water now. Skipping rocks. Shouting, squealing with joy. Francesca was attempting to dam a rivulet with rocks. Wonderful. I looked at Angelica. A blessing. I felt Tommy's loss: to live so long, to find this treasure, and then to die.

I sat down to eat.

Later, the children played in the clear river water. Mom showed Angelica how to weave tules, and how the merganser ducks paddling down the stream nested in trees and carried their babies on their backs. The sun was hot, and the water was clear and cool.

I showed the children how to lift the underwater rocks in the crystal cold flow to expose crawfish, how to quickly grab them behind the claws with the fingers, to avoid getting pinched. I introduced them to ant lion insect larvae, tiny, comically hideous grubs with giant jaws. I sprayed sunblock on everyone, and swam away the sweat of my run.

As the sun went down, Cesar and I built a fire in the fire pit and I lit it with flint and steel. The dinner meal was more Filipino food from Angelica's ice chest, especially a frozen mango float. There was so much food that Bill the campground host and a game warden named Gene happily joined us as the evening gently cooled.

The darkness of night swept over us, and a giant moon rose up over the Salinas Valley to the east. It was time to go home. Angelica chivvied the reluctant Cesar and Rose into her car while I belted Francesca into her backseat booster. I hugged Angelica goodnight. Her small body simply melted into mine. I couldn't let go, and I thought what a lucky man Tommy had been . . . and how very, very unlucky.

We began to drive out of the valley on the winding canyon road, in the dark, asphalt ahead lit by our headlights. Francesca quickly fell asleep in the back seat. The full moon filled the sky. Mom was silent. I thought she might be asleep.

"We had a wonderful day," I said quietly, wondering if she might respond. "We thought we'd leave at noon and here we are, 10 p.m."

"You planned that?" said my mom. There was no sleep in her voice.

"If I had planned the day, I would have served MREs and jerky," I responded. Smiling in the dark.

Quiet. Lit by our headlights, a kangaroo rat hopped across the road ahead of us as we drove on.

"She just found us by magic?" Mom's voice was mildly joking.

"It was one of those someday invitations. Yes, I invited her. No, I did not expect her. But still, I'm glad she came. Look at the day she made."

"Yes, she did," Mom replied.

We drove on.

"Maybe she put a low jack on our car," I added.

Mom chuckled to herself. "She reminds me of me. Come to a place you don't know, with people you do not know, and make things happen. It's a skill."

Then we were silent, watching the far side of the Salinas Valley, the Gabilan Mountains tan in the brilliant moonlight. Soon we were on Highway 101, driving north to home.

— Honor —

30

Mom spoke again, as though to herself. "It's way too soon. It's too soon. Angelica is a joy. But she's a young woman, and she's just lost her husband and it's been horrible. So she's changeable as a rattlesnake, and sooner or later she's going to bite. And you know what it's like to get snake-bit. After the venom takes you, ya ain't worth shooting."

Chapter Six

June 2012

It was a somewhat overcast Thursday afternoon. The stock market had been diffident. Not unusual for the stock market.

Since my home and office began as my great grandfather's house in 1894 it has been in the center of Salinas's activity. The center of town. Margaret and I lived here when we were starting out. Then we grew so many children that we bought another house nearer to her parents and closer to my mother. These homes are all within walking distance. All within the original town, now subsumed in subdivisions sprawling to the north. My bed moved into the new home. My office, and occasional bed, remained in the place of our ancestors.

Now, beyond the old street trees, which my grandfather and my father had once climbed as a boy, we looked out into a Monterey County government parking lot. Beyond that, there was a new Monterey County office building, which blocked the mountains and Toro Peak from our sight. I used to enjoy those mountains, especially on winter days when they were frosted with snow. Now the square, ordered windows seem like dentures in a giant, black-toothed grimace.

But at least there was plenty to see. Family court is on Fridays and we can plan on at least one tattoo-marked couple yelling it out on our front lawn. Some discussions are more interesting than others.

I walked onto the front porch with my five-year-old daughter, Francesca. She wanted to be picked up. I lifted her in my arms, her blonde hair gusting in the wind, her matching baby-blue pinafore still clean, and she began to pretend that the porch was a ship, and the front lawn below us was the sea, and she was fishing.

Today, the Euro was under pressure. Greece was threatening to default on its debts. China was angry: they had forced down an American reconnaissance aircraft. Well, China is always angry.

I was pondering about two clients who were talking divorce, which means they were going to take half their wealth out into the backyard and burn it. Divorce to an investment advisor is worse than the Great Depression.

I was concerned about the relative performance of one of my mutual fund selections. The managers needed to step it up, or explain why.

My 19-year-old son Ernst, very talented in math and studying finance, was preparing for a career as an investment advisor. Today he was working in the office, analyzing mutual funds to determine potential risks. His selections, strongly edited by me, were likely to appear in client portfolios. A conference between my son and me was scheduled for that afternoon.

And here was my youngest daughter in my arms, on a balmy June day, pretending to catch trout.

Then Angelica pulled her gold Honda CRV into our driveway. She stepped lightly out of the car as we watched. Angelica's long, dark hair was gently waving, and she was dressed in a gold sleeveless shirt, tight jeans, and brown, tight, calf-high boots. She unbuckled the two children in the back seat. Seven-year-old Cesar and five-year-old Rose boiled out of the open car door and came running, screaming, and laughing, up the steps. My daughter squirmed to be let down and the three children went racing through the front door, shouting. The blast of sound undoubtedly captured the full attention of the staff in various rooms.

I had a surprise set up for the kids. I had erected a 1960's camouflage Austrian Army surplus tent in the backyard, and one of the staff had volunteered to watch them. When the children saw that tent through the open back door they shouted once again, raced into the backyard, and the noise in the building dropped at once. I thought of Rosemary, our administrative assistant, out in the open with the three children . . . she was going to have an active late afternoon.

Angelica walked into the kitchen and put down the sheet foil tray loaded with pancit, as always, big enough to feed ten people, undoubtedly dinner for everyone, undoubtedly to be shared with my mother. Lanie and I were waiting in the front alcove, at the hexagonal table, paperwork spread before us.

Angelica slowly walked towards us from the kitchen, graceful, lithe, small, smiling broadly, golden, and as she passed the living room couch, her small, delicate hand reached out and smoothed a wrinkle in a blanket, which was draped over the brown leather upholstered back.

That simple motion. I felt a hunger, a longing, an envy. I didn't know what to do. I didn't know what to say.

That night, after sunset. The dishes done. Francesca sleeping in her room. My ex-wife Margaret in the arms of another. I was alone in my bed in the dark, and the hunger came back and filled me.

I'm used to hunger. In fact, I think hunger makes us strong. But this was different: there was an unseen desperation, a disembodied recklessness. What was I to do with that? Unbidden. Unexpected. So sudden. This was the first time I had felt deeply since Margaret had left me.

I slid out of bed and began to pray desperately. I was kneeling, using my dirty laundry of the day as a cushion. I found myself praying to God and to Tommy and my father, Uncle Kurt, Uncle Otto, and Uncle Sid, all my deceased ancestors. All the saints.

That was a new thing for me, since I'm nominally a Presbyterian. I asked God what to do. I asked how to do it. God, please show me what I am to do. Please make it holy, please make it sacred, and God, it is way too soon since Tommy's death. If I can endure, it will pass, and we will all move on, and my love will be

— Chapter 6 —

a silent blessing, unrealized by anyone but me. How do I do that?

I have learned that to most people, God is a cosmic vending machine: people ask for what they want, throw scripture around like grass seed, and expect God to grow a car, or money, or health. Memories of wailing mullahs beseeching the Great Vendor in minarets during my Marine years. Lebanon. Kazakhstan, Saudi, Kuwait, Iraq, and more. I had learned Arabic at the Defense Language Institute. I could understand the broadcast prayers of our allies. Death to America. Death to the Great Satan. May God the Merciful, the Compassionate, Smite Them As We Smile To Their Faces.

Yet if God is truly God, Inshallah, then God is in charge. Not us.

So I didn't ask for God to give me Angelica. I asked Him, "What's the right thing?"

It was very hard getting to sleep that night.

The next day I was sitting at my desk trying to stay focused, fighting past the fatigue. I was down another three pounds. The headaches had gotten worse in the past weeks. All this was apparently due to my diagnosed PTSD. Ten-percent disability. The medication was not working. Guilt: I wasn't really worthy of PTSD. No combat. Press on.

The phone rang. Lanie answered in the adjoining office. I could hear her always-pleasant voice as she wished the caller a good morning. Shortly thereafter she appeared in the doorway. Always dressed in chic Italian designers, mostly black and white, intelligently bought at discount, honey-colored hair perfectly done. Astonishingly beautiful. Her husband was still crazy in love with her. Wise man.

"For you," she said. "It's Globalbank."

I stared blankly at her.

"Globalbank," she repeated. "They're the mortgage lenders for Tommy and Angelica. We're applying for a restructuring."

Ah, yes. That. I adjusted my headset and keyed the connection. "Good morning!" I said.

"Good morning," said a woman's voice. It sounded far away.

"You are Garth Ericson?"

The voice had an accent.

"Yes," I responded. "I'm the trustee for the Narcisco Family Trust. Have you received the restructuring package we sent?"

"Ah, yes, that's why I'm calling. We need a signed appointment of trustee from Thomas P. Narcisco stating that you are trustee," said the voice.

"It's all there," I responded. "Thomas P. Narcisco is deceased. You have his death certificate and an affidavit of trustee issued by the court. As you can see . . ."

I paged through the Narcisco file until I came to the appropriate page.

"I am named as trustee on page 32," I continued.

"We still require Thomas P. Narcisco's signature," the woman's voice responded.

"For what? He's dead," I answered.

"He needs to sign the affidavit of trustee. And then he needs to sign the restructuring documents," the voice continued.

"He's dead," I responded. "He's not alive. He's a former person. His soul has flown to heaven. His remains have been cremated."

"Can you obtain his signature from him?" asked the voice.

I didn't know what to say. I was silent.

"May I please speak with your supervisor?" I eventually asked.

"No, he is not here," responded the voice.

"Try again," I said. I was beginning to become angry.

"He is using the restroom," said the voice.

"I'll wait," I answered.

"Perhaps he will be gone a long time," the voice said.

"Where are you?" I asked.

"I am at Globalbank," the womanish voice said.

"No, I mean, where are you geographically?" I asked.

"We are not permitted to say," said the voice.

"Try me," I pressed.

"Vietnam," answered the voice.

— Chapter 6 —
37

"Ah," I responded. "Is your supervisor back now?"

"Let me find out," said the voice. There was a *click* as the phone line was placed on hold, then a dial tone as the connection was terminated.

Chapter Seven

June 2012

"Tell me again why you're choosing this fight," said Robert with a sigh, smoothing his red silk tie. Robert was Tommy's lawyer, like me, a lifetime resident of Salinas. Today, he was wearing a dark blue pinstripe suit and crisp white shirt to match the tie. His office was in the old part of the Main Street area, an antique, dense, brick building reeking of old paper. Many bookshelves of case law. Few windows.

Robert's partner had been my father's attorney as well. When I visited the office, I could still feel the emotions of the days after my father's death, when I had discovered the secret debts, the trading losses, the hidden life.

I remembered feeling the sure awareness that the ranch and all our centuries of traditions there were lost. I still felt the shame. Here I always felt like a child.

"Tommy was a good man, and there's no money," I responded. "Besides, it's wrong when corporations like Globalbank push people around."

"I agree, and it pains me. Big fish eat little fish. It happens every minute of every day, and nobody gives a damn," said Robert. "So why you, why now? Did you know Tommy well?

"Not as well as I should have," I replied. "Shared community. Social functions. We weren't close always. He was wonderful to me when I came back, though."

"Came back?" asked Robert. Then he remembered. "Oh yes, as I recall you had a military adventure after 9/11."

"What did you hear about that?" I asked. My vanity was

getting the better of me. "Forgive me, I'm just curious."

Robert smiled. Full head of dark hair, although he was a good ten years older than me. He seemed to radiate benign good will. Behind him, his worn wooden tennis racket hung on the wall. Local athlete.

"Some people thought that your adventure in the Marine Corps was more self-indulgent than patriotic," he said. "After all, you have a Master's degree in finance. For most people, you know, the military is for people who can't do anything else."

I pondered that.

"So 9/11 didn't matter?" I asked. "It mattered a hell of a lot to me."

Robert seemed thoughtful. "Oh, I think 9/11 scared everyone. But for most people? The fear passed quickly. Life went on. The war was about other people, other places," he said, leaning back. "Most people don't really have a connection to all that."

"Our ancestors would have fought like tigers," I said angrily. "Once upon a time, the core virtue for a man was to do more for the community than anyone else. First in line. Service."

"Think about it," responded Robert. "Most of the big families here got their sons farming deferments in World War II. The sons of working people went off to Bataan. Including my uncle. He never came back. You might ask for what."

"Perhaps you're right," I said.

"I remember that at least one farming family here made their fortune in confiscated Japanese-American farmland. They're still rich. Nobody remembers the Nisei families who lost their homes," said Robert.

"I remember," I said.

"You are unusual." Robert grinned. "Now it's my turn to be curious. What did people tell you when you got back?"

Inside I was trembling with anger, but I crammed it down. "Lots of comments. One client asked me if I intended to quit again soon to sail around the world or to walk the Appalachian Trail. He thought the whole thing was just a stunt. And at Christmas dinner, 2005, my wife asked me, 'Are you satisfied with your zig-zag course in life? Perhaps you should apologize to us.' That chilled the roast turkey damned quick."

Robert, so dapper, swiveled away in his chair, repelled. I had said too much.

"So why defend Tommy's family? Tommy is dead, nobody will notice," he asked.

"Perhaps I'm just fed up," I responded. "Or perhaps I'll notice."

"Be angry somewhere else, not at work. Go for a hike instead." he said. "What about your fee? There's no money in this. I'm already giving a 75-percent discount."

"I'm going to do it pro bono. For free," I said.

"For love of Tommy?" asked Robert. "You are some friend."

"It's not really about Tommy," I replied.

I was standing in the green expanse of the plaza at San Juan Bautista State Park, dressed in my classic 1850's rancher's outfit: straw boater, drop-front breeches, with pegged boots, vest, and suspenders. I was preparing to help teach a class on fire-starting with flint and steel. It's quite dramatic really: a few whacks with the flint, a few sparks into the char-cloth, blow, and then you have fire. The lead instructor was a gentleman known by the alias of Captain Jedidiah, the best of the twenty-first-century mountain men.

He was a school teacher in the modern world. Here, at San Juan Bautista once a month, with a few added weekends, and during the entire summers, he was a genuine, committed Rocky Mountain-rambling mountain man. He had carried his Lyman .54 caplock Great Plains rifle into more scrapes than most of the originals back in the nineteenth century. More unexpected summer blizzards, more rock slides, more upended canoes in chilling wilderness rapids. And here he was, pounding on flint, hunting for a spark.

Those entire summers spent up behind Grand Junction, Colorado probably accounted for his perennially troubled marital status. Captain Jedidiah confided in me that no matter how much he tried, he could not convince his wife to spend the entire summers in a brush-built wikiyup in the national forest, and after twenty years of marriage she still refused to help field dress the elk he shot each November. For some reason he wouldn't tell me about deer hunting with his wife at all.

Francesca was dressed in a purple 1850's prairie dress and bonnet, running across the grass in random arcs, later throwing the tomahawk against a sawn wood round, enjoying what I had known in my own childhood. Marbles and kites. The blessings of the non-electronic age. Perpetual motion, a purple whirligig bug. Then, unexpectedly, she began to make a beeline straight across the grass of the plaza.

There, perhaps a hundred paces away across the green lawn, were Angelica and the children, laughing, hugging Francesca, white teeth, black hair, and motion. Angelica led the three children towards us, slender, smiling, doe-walking tentatively, shy, long dark hair blown by the slight wind. Her voice, gentle and low, flutelike, reached out me as she approached.

"Hello, Garth."

I could feel my heart rabbiting in my chest. I smiled.

Angelica seemed mystified. "Why do you do this? It is like pretend play for grownups?" she asked.

"Yes, I guess," I responded. "Now that I don't have the ranch, this is as close as I can get to my own childhood. I lived on a cattle ranch near here in the 1960s, I mean. It's good for Francesca, and the others. A chance to experience the traditional ways."

Angelica nodded.

I thought of my life then and my life now. So different.

"Do you play cowboys?" she asked. "And Indians?"

She was smiling.

I laughed. "No, we don't. For one thing I'd be related to everyone so I couldn't pick a side."

Beyond us, on the open green lawn of the plaza, Francesca and other volunteer children were running with Cesar and Rose, a swirl of color and laughter.

"May we make fire?"

— Honor —

42

I motioned to the Ersatz mountain men who were watching. They came swarming, Burnside whiskers twitching. All elderly, out of shape. Angelica and the three children were carried off into a rotation of axe throwing, fur pelting, and yes, fire making. They blew their tinder into flames easily.

Later one of the living history women served a fire-cooked Dutch oven early dinner of beans, bacon, and cornbread. Angelica and the children seemed to take to it all so naturally. Francesca, normally so timid and diffident about food, quickly devoured her serving.

The sun began to set beyond the plaza. Behind us, the bells of the mission began to toll, as they have rung for two hundred years and more. The mission was beginning their Saturday evening service, locally known as "mattress mass" because attending it allows parishioners to sleep in on Sunday mornings.

Captain Jedidiah was folding up the white canvas of his tents, ready to leave, his Toyota pickup now parked nearby.

Angelica and I walked with the children into the mission church without saying a word, sat in the back pew, and listened quietly as the service began. I looked up at the painted high ceilings and all I could silently say to God was thank you, thank you, thank you. Help me turn this into something wonderful. Whatever that is.

We sat, but the children were restless. Rose, the liveliest of the three, was silently hopping, visibly suppressing a compulsive need to shout. Francesca had crept around to the back of the pew and was kneeling on the tiles, fingering a dog footprint, placed whenever the tile was wet. Perhaps two hundred years ago? Cesar stoically looked towards the altar as though he was about to receive an inoculation with a large needle.

Clearly, they needed a break. I had forgotten the rite of Catholic communion anyway.

As though reading my mind, Angelica whispered into my ear, "I will take the children outside. Meet you at the cross in the courtyard."

I nodded my assent. She whispered again into my ear, her

breath caressing my face, "I love you," and I felt the room move.

As she began to rise I pulled her back down, swept back her hair, and whispered into her ear, "I LOVE YOU." The people near us heard. One older woman, wrapped against the rising cold, smiled at us.

Angelica smiled softly. Her eyes were wet. She stood up, motioned the children into a swirling herd, and silently pushed the three little ones through the back door. I watched them until the door shut.

A cantor was leading singing and responses. He had a beautiful, soaring voice, but I didn't know the words and I was swept away by what Angelica had just said. I slipped out of the pews and walked over to the nearby candle rack, in an alcove, and lit a candle, got on my knees, and prayed.

God, God, God, Tommy, my dead father, my uncles, all my ancestors, thank you for this blessing, thank you, thank you, let me be worthy, let me be honorable, let me do God's will.

I never ever cry. I have attended the funerals of my family and have not shed a tear. My wife left me, and I did not shed a tear. When a helicopter crash in Mindoro wiped out most of my platoon, I did not cry. At the bombing in Lebanon, and afterwards through the unending aftermath and memorials, I did not cry. Yes, I've shed tears when a pugil stick or a horse's head or an angry drunk smashed me in the nose. But emotional tears? Never.

So I was amazed when tears began to run down my cheeks. Amazed. Confused. All I could do was stay on my knees and keep praying, keep focused on those blurry candles, keep saying to myself, "Your will be done."

I became aware that there was a priest kneeling alongside me, on his knees, in brown robes exactly like an original Spanish padre of 1812. I looked briefly as I tried to focus on my prayers. No glasses. No wristwatch, not even a tan line where a watch might be. No wedding ring. Tonsured head. Perhaps he was a living history person like me; after all, I was dressed in 1850's clothing. I looked at him again, briefly, my face wet. I was worried he might see. I didn't recognize him. Perhaps he was a genuine priest.

Then he said to me, in a low. even voice, *"Cuando el espíritu se abate, permitir éis entrar lo sagrado dentro de ti."*

Spanish. No kidding. I think he said, "When you are broken, it lets the sacred enter in." This guy took his reenacting seriously. And I wasn't broken I was just . . . crying. Crying. It was embarrassing. And it felt right.

I stared at the candles flickering through my wet eyes. *God, God, God, God, thank you for this blessing. Please help me.*

I looked at the monk. He was gone. Nowhere in sight.

Then I stood up, dried my eyes on the brown sleeve of my 1850's collarless shirt, and went out to the family waiting outside. The family.

Chapter Eight

July 2012

Tommy was one of the first to welcome me back from my truck-driving experience in the Iraqi sandbox. And now, here I was, six months after his agonizing death, and his widow was texting me "I love you," sometimes at 3 a.m. And I was texting her back every chance I got.

Previously our texting had gradually grown to about twenty times a day, all sorts of little tidbits such as, "What are you eating for lunch?" or "Cesar lost a tooth!" or "It's beautiful today."

Now the texting became constant, every little factoid about every little detail. Perhaps I should have resisted the complete collapse of my personal space, and certainly I should have waited. Somehow it felt so . . . right. The little smiley faces, the constant stream of praise. Now the text messages flew into my phone in a never-ending stream, digital lightning bolts, which jolted down to my toes as I read them: "I love you" and "I can't wait to be with you" and "You are my hero." I admit I puffed up a bit when I read these. Her words were a balm. I'd read and heard plenty of words telling me that I was less than perfect.

On Wednesday morning at 6 a.m., she texted me: "How ya doing?"

I considered how to respond.

I had arrived at the office at 5:30 a.m., in the pre-dawn, to discover a homeless person sleeping on the front porch engulfed in a dirty, square, old-fashioned sleeping bag. Black matted hair about a foot long protruded from the top of the bag. The hair looked filthy. There was a sleeping pad underneath the sleeping bag, and some sort of bottle in a brown paper bag alongside the sleeping form, and a worn red athletic tote, apparently of possessions. An iPhone 4 was plugged into the outdoor electrical socket on the other side of the sleeping form. I decided to simply leave well enough alone and went about my business.

I decided not to mention the homeless man to Angelica. There was a decided aura of filth. Of lice. Other than the itinerant sleeping on my front porch, I was struggling to keep my mind focused on my company, my business, my job: investment advising. Once upon a time, I had been an infantry company commander, sailing the seas in an amphibious assault ship with two hundred and eighty testosterone-crazed Marines under my direction. Two hundred and eighty crazed monkeys, no leashes, and guns. Now I commanded mutual funds and a desk.

My shirt-manufacturing client in Mozambique had requested a Skype call, so I was at work and at my desk at 6 a.m. That was normal, actually.

I texted her back: "Busy morning no breakfast. At least I'm not bored. ☺"

Margaret dropped off Francesca around 8 a.m. Francesca had been coming to the office since she was three months old. And now, school was out for summer break. As was her tradition, Margaret passed Francesca in through the front door. Margaret hadn't entered my office . . . my great grandfather's home . . . since the separation, six years ago. But still I offered.

"Come in," I said.

I glanced sideways, onto the porch. No homeless man. Not a trace. Hallelujah.

Margaret just shook her head. I looked at her: mid-length, full black hair, green eyes flecked with gold, and an expression of near-loathing on her face. What was I to do with that? As always, Margaret was superbly dressed, wearing a delightfully vibrant dress of white with splashes of red. She could always wear clothes well.

Francesca cavorted back into the home to say hello to the

staff, while Margaret stood there, a well-dressed wooden post. I could hear Francesca's laughter. Behind Margaret the paved sameness of the Monterey County parking lot with the small blue and white commuter buslet making the rounds, and beyond that, the new Monterey County office building which blocked our view of Mt. Toro. "Please come in." I said.

Margaret's answer was the same as always: a flat-faced blank look of a mind caught wandering far away. Margaret's gold-flecked eyes, staring at a wall, or into nothingness, anywhere but at me. In a moment she would blurt out a sarcastic, bitter rejoinder. Wait for it . . .

"No, thanks. I'll meet plenty of losers at work."

That was true. She now worked as a paralegal for one of the most prestigious real estate lawyers in Salinas. It was a job she did not necessarily choose, a path she had taken after I chose to reenter the corps, driven more by the gnawing perception of financial need than by love of the profession.

And now my former and forever wife was transmogrified by my own choice to be a patriot. Dour. A sucked lemon, picked green.

Meanwhile there was more laughter from the back room, this time from the staff as well as Francesca. Joy.

"See you this afternoon," said Margaret, flatly, as though she was reading the phonebook. She spun on her heels and walked down the stairs to the street, where her oh-so-practical gray Honda civic was waiting.

Around 9 a.m., my daughter and the financial markets were well into their play cycles. I was starving. The stock market . . . well what about the stock market? The Value Line Manager's Appreciation Index was indicating that the stock markets were overvalued. The bond markets were showing the symptoms of Federal Reserve stimulus: interest rates were declining to un-foreseeable lows. Yada, yada.

And just then, Angelica pulled her CRV into my drive-way, completely unannounced. She was just suddenly there:

— Chapter 8 —

beautiful, smiling, kids strapped into their child seats in back. Francesca heard the car, raced to the front porch, and greeted Cesar and Rose, hopping, squealing with joy.

The three children made a dash for the backyard. I had set the Austrian military surplus pup tent out there, in a box, rolled up and waiting to be assembled. Rosemary, tall, slender, girlish, and serene in her twenties, long blond hair and personality both unruffled by matrimony or mortgage, went out into the back yard to supervise the chaos.

Meanwhile Angelica and I sat in the front room at our table, where she had shed so many tears, and the sun streamed in through the front windows, and she revealed her surprise from a brown paper bag: hot oatmeal from Starbucks, complete with nuts.

Lanie walked into the room, expecting an unusual morning session of bills and crisis. She saw the oatmeal, stopped, and smiled beautifully.

"Hi," said Angelica, grinning. "I just brought Garth breakfast. Early morning."

"It's about time somebody got Garth to eat. Next, Angelica, get him to dress better, please," she said. "I'll let you eat in peace."

Behind her came our stolid computer technician and office manager, Tammy Fay. She stopped behind us, apparently drawn by curiosity and the smell of maple. She stopped at the door, and grinned toothily through her thick black-rimmed glasses.

In another room, the phone rang.

"I'll get that," said Lanie, still smiling. "Shall I say you are in conference?"

"Please," I answered.

Tammy Fay grinned out at us one last time, and shut the door to the other offices behind her. At last, we were alone. In the distance, in the backyard, I could hear the children shrieking happily.

"What do we do now?" Angelica said softly. "I need you so much."

— Honor —

50

I looked back at her. I needed her so much too.

"I guess we go slowly," I said. "If we can go slowly, honorably, so that your family, so everyone can respect us, then we can build something wonderful."

It hurt me to say that. I just wanted to jump at her and kiss her right there.

"I don't want to do that," Angelica replied. "I don't want to wait."

Her highlighted hair was pulled back from her impossibly high forehead. She had puffy eyes.

"I don't want to wait either," I responded. "But if we rush this, we dishonor ourselves. If we go slowly, we can build something to last."

Damn, I sounded like a broken record. I just wanted her. But I also wanted her forever, not for the next few months.

Or, if it was best, I wanted to be the loving friend she would remember and love forever as she went on with someone else.

"But you don't want to sit here eating oatmeal, do you?" She smiled widely.

"Nope," I answered.

We had both stopped eating.

I leaned across the little table and kissed her right there. Eyes shut, praying that nobody would walk in, that no client would pull into the driveway outside.

I couldn't pull away. Her lips were so soft, so welcoming, so giving, so lush. It was all there: nothing else mattered. No pain. No sorrow. No hunger. Just the sensation of her lips on mine, gently giving, gently opening . . . forever. Her lips were perfect. I allowed myself to peek: her eyes were closed. Beautiful, brown puffy eyes.

I slowly kissed her. I put my arms around her, finally, a lifetime of starvation in that hug. Pulling her from her seat, into me as I stood up. Her tight-fitting shirt was smooth under my hands, the curves of her sides so firm and small and perfect. I could feel the seams. I kept kissing. Her small breasts felt hard as rocks against my chest. Through my shirt. My lips drifted

— Chapter 8 —

51

down to her throat, impossibly smooth, and I could feel her bird-heart racing.

Then I heard the pounding of feet on the steps from the back-yard. We pulled apart just before the children raced in to share the news of the tent's successful erection. The noise of their shouts filled the room. The sun streamed in through the front window.

"Eat your oatmeal" I said to Angelica.

She smiled. "I'm going to call you Schatzi," she said.

"Why?"

"It's German. It means 'Lover.'".

"Why? Who is German?"

"I just like the sound of it," she said.

And as the children chased each other into the next room, she smiled, leaned up, and kissed me again.

I was sleepless that night. *What do I do now? It's way too soon. It's dishonorable.* And I gave my word to Tommy.

I wanted, I hungered, and I lay there in my bed in the dark. I was in our family home, and of course my bed was empty, save for me. My oldest daughter Sarah was away at college. Oldest son Wallace was in the Air Force in Germany, repairing B-58 bombers, apparently. My younger son Ernst was sound asleep in the room near mine, living frugally already, saving for a gradu-ate degree and a home of his own. Francesca was sleeping at her mother's home a few blocks away. The cell phone next to my bed buzzed. It was a text from Angelica.

"Schatzi," it read.

What did *that* mean?

"Yes? ☺" I texted back.

"Come here," she messaged.

"Now?" I texted back.

"Now," she responded.

I went to my Xterra in my driveway at one in the morning and I drove to her home, down the long straight path of Blanco Road to Highway 68, and out to Corral de Tierra, lit by a half-moon over Fremont's Peak and stars overhead. "Outside," I texted. Then I walked up the steps to her home.

The door was shut.

For a moment I wondered if somehow, I had made a mistake, if somehow, I had misunderstood, or perhaps the children were awake. I wrestled with my need. I needed to turn away from this, this is too soon, I thought. I stood there in the dark staring at the door. She's not coming, I thought. Besides, this is wrong, so wrong.

Then she opened the door. There was only one light on in her living room, but it was enough. She was barefoot, wearing a short white bathrobe with pastel polka dots. The house was quiet, utterly still.

Clearly Rose and Cesar were already asleep in their rooms.

She silently opened the door and I stepped across the threshold and pulled her into my arms, and her lips met mine instantly as though they simply belonged.

There was Tommy's picture on the wall. In fact, there was Tommy's picture on any wall that wasn't a window. The place was a shrine. I looked around the room as Angelica's lips moved to my neck. She reached up, grasped my hand from around her neck, and moved it inside her robe, to her bottom. Her perfect bottom. Perfect. She was wearing absolutely nothing under that robe.

I used that leverage to maneuver her to the couch, and fell lightly on top of her. Her robe began to open and she gripped me with her legs. My hand was trapped between her bottom and the couch. I wasn't sorry.

"Please stop. For just a moment," I whispered.

She looked up at me quizzically, cat's eyes shining in the very dim light.

"Why you want stop, Schatzi?" she whispered.

"This is Tommy's home. We are going too fast," I breathed. "I am falling in love. I want the best for you. I want this to last, to grow. It's too soon."

"You talk too much." She smiled. "I love you too. I want you now. Why not be happy with what God has given us? I love you."

"If we make love tonight, to me it will be like I am married to you. That's just how I am. The last woman I made love to was my wife. If we make love tonight, you will own me. There's no turning back for me. Are you ready for that?"

Her eyes flared. "You talk so much and you do so little. You ask that? For five years I watched my beloved Tommy die. I took care of him 24/7."

She rolled until she was on top of me, and continued, "Why you ask that? You know I marry you tonight too. I choose you."

Her words left me dizzy. I was speechless. This was wrong. I kissed her neck gently, playing for time as my lips played with her ears. She laughed softly as my lips roamed down her neck. There was a small scar there, just under her jaw on her right side. I kissed it. She gasped. "Tickles," she said.

"What about honoring Tommy?" I asked. "We can't disrespect him."

"We wait to be public," she whispered. "We enjoy what God has given us, and we are quiet for one year. Then we will be engaged in public and Tommy is respected."

My lips went lower. I thought, surely people have met and married with less time than I have had with Angelica. I lifted my head and bit her lightly on the neck. She gasped again.

"Then, after one year, we will become engaged?"

No response as I kissed her strongly on the neck and she groaned softly.

"Yes," she moaned, apparently frustrated.

"And then we marry when it is right for the children?" I asked.

Her arms were around me and she hit me lightly on the back with her closed fist. "Yes, YES! Now shut up. Keep it light." She laughed quietly.

"Hydrogen," I responded. "I can't keep this secret forever. And I can't make love unless you agree. If we do this tonight, you will own me. So choose," I whispered, as my lips moved lower again. Perfect joy was rising in me. I felt as though I was flying.

"What kind of ceremony we will have for our wedding?" she asked, as the robe seemed to fall away on its own.

I didn't answer.

It was a very good night.

Chapter Nine

July 2012

The following Monday afternoon I had child custody mediation with Margaret. We sat in the front room of my great-grandfather's home, at the hexagonal table which had been there for more than one hundred years. I looked at the cracks in the wood.

Tommy had sat here too. I thought about that. And now I was in love with his widow. *Damn. What a train wreck.*

The table needed refinishing.

Of course my older children with Margaret were in their early twenties. But mediation was still necessary for Francesca. I suppose it was an alternative to court.

Margaret was beautiful, slender, well-dressed as always, brunette hair pulled back. As always ,her mouth was a straight line as she stared at me with those gold-flecked eyes. I had seen those eyes many times before, of course, including curiously in a Weimaraner dog. Regardless, they were alluring, wide, clear, and deep. One always had the impression, looking into Margaret's eyes, that one was looking at a hidden galaxy inside her. I had met her when she was twenty-one, and I was thirty-five. After I had diverted into the reserves from the active duty Marine Corps, after Beirut, before the first Gulf War called me back.

I sat in that chair and pondered my first impressions of Margaret: beautiful then as now. Tall, curves like a 1950's pinup girl, brunette, hair almost black, eyes like constellations, flecked with gold, a serious Christian at First Presbyterian Church, who could waltz like love itself and run 10K races like an Olympian.

We had married quickly, probably to cope with the temptations of sex and dancing. We made three wonderful babies immediately. Long, all-night deliveries. First-name-basis with the obstetrician. Lots of secret prayer on my part. I had been praying hard ever since.

I thought back to 2003, in Germany, a military hospital, a week after my "industrial accident." They brought Margaret to see me, as I sat next to my hospital bed in my gray bathrobe and slippers after my first sinus re-inflation. It had been a full-anesthesia experience. My nose was packed full of gauze mini-tampons, which the staff called "rockets" and I was breathing only through my bad-tasting mouth. My face hurt, especially over my eyes. The tinnitus in my ears screeched. The anesthesia wasn't done yet, and staring at the wall seemed appropriate as I mustered the energy to think. Then Margaret walked into that sky-blue room with the rich German sunlight streaming in, and she looked as beautiful as a model, eyes brilliant, dark hair swept back. When she saw me her face lit up with a radiant smile, and I sat forward in my bathrobe and I remembered everything: our first kiss, our first time making love, our marriage, our life . . . but I couldn't remember her name.

Another memory: A crisp January morning in 2007, bright and blue, after the Marines, another surprising pregnancy, number four, who would become Francesca. After 9/11. After the sandbox. I drove from work to our routine prenatal meeting with the doctor. Margaret had not discussed it at all that morning. I had seen it written on the calendar stuck with souvenir magnets to the refrigerator door.

I had pulled my new-to-us yellow XTerra, which the kids had named "the school bus," into the parking lot of the doctor's office and I looked up into the cab of a very large, white, dual-tired pickup truck. White, with red trim, and it was turning out of the parking lot, leaving, and time seemed to freeze. I saw Margaret clearly in the passenger seat, looking fixedly straight ahead, frowning. After a moment of befuddlement I realized that the truck was driven by a longtime friend of mine, Jack, an agricultural produce broker. He sold broccoli, and best of all, he had a genuine stranglehold on the artichoke market. There's big money in that. Jack had been in my home more and more frequently, first as a fellow shooter on the rifle range, and then simply for friendship's sake. I realized, suddenly, like falling into an unexpected hole in the sidewalk, that perhaps Jack had a very good reason to be there after all.

Now, years later, meeting the mediator in my office, the world had finally changed. Power had shifted in the night, and nobody else at the table was aware. I was strong again, for the first time in years.

The professional mediator, Aaron Sanchez, was a brisk, efficient psychologist who wore a full professorial white beard, well-trimmed, to match his innately curly white hair. His bright blue eyes and pink pale face were, as always, smiling and intelligent. He watched us both as though appraising a particularly interesting aquarium populated by two fascinating and mutually combative gobies.

In the beginning, when she was pregnant, Margaret had spoken of naming the baby after Jack, of giving the baby Jack's last name. Her words had come close to destroying me: her words and the vision of my pregnant wife with Jack. Or, worse yet, my forever wife pregnant *by* Jack.

Jack had assembled the crib, Jack had painted the nursery, and Jack had gone shopping for baby clothes. All the small prenatal joys of growing a family had been Jack's honor. I had been excluded with the threat of a potential restraining order. I had desired beyond words to be part of all that, after all those years away.

When Francesca was three months old, when I was finally able to be away from Margaret's condominium with her, I had secretly done a quick paternity test swab in her tiny toothless cheek. I had mailed away the test, and I had received the answer. The anonymous geneticists somewhere out there were 99.5% sure that I was her father. For the sake of my older children, and for the sake of Francesca's perception of herself, I still kept that

— Chapter 9 —
59

paternity test for Francesca in my files.

I also had Margaret's engagement and wedding rings, kept in an envelope in the gun safe next to my great-grandfather's single action army pistol and my own new replacement 1911 Colt. Margaret had flung those rings across the living room at me during our final breakup scene. I remembered stooping down, picking them up, and walking out without another word, tearing apart inside. Since then I had despaired of giving our youngest daughter anything resembling an optimal life.

Now Angelica's love kept me at that table with a new sense of calm. I would be able to give Francesca an intact home of sorts after all.

"Garth has profound Post Traumatic Stress Disorder," said Margaret to the mediator. "He has a traumatic brain injury, confirmed by a doctor."

I sat there. She was wrong. But years of mediation had taught me the futility of raising my voice, of disagreeing, so I simply sat toad-like at the table.

Margaret went on. "He has profound insomnia. He has anorexia. He can't remember people's names. I feel very insecure with Francesca sleeping overnight at his home."

Our home, I thought. It HAD been our home. Now, Margaret, you are sharing a condo with Jack. That makes it a home?

I said nothing.

"Jack agrees with me," Margaret continued. The woman had ESP.

"Jack actually has nothing to do with this," replied Aaron evenly. "And it's not his place to make parenting decisions for Francesca. It's in your parenting agreement, between you and Garth."

"But Garth is barely functional. He can barely get through the day," said Margaret.

Before Angelica, perhaps she would have been right.

And then there was what neither Margaret nor Angelica knew about me. There was a broken part of me.

— Honor —

I simply couldn't discuss it, in the same way one does not discuss a hernia.

For a year or so in the early 1980s, out of US Marine Base 29 Palms, I had occasionally tracked illegal immigrants across the deserts of Arizona and California with the border patrol.

We flew in single-rotor Huey helicopters with doors pulled back and latched, racing low across the desert, seeking the tracks of walking people heading north. Trackways, we called them. I remembered the sound of rotors, the smell of the jet engine exhaust from the helicopter's rotary engines, the morning heat rising off the desert, the brilliance of the daylight against the white sand and the dark volcanic rocks flashing past below us as I wondered if my gunner's belt would hold me in the aircraft. In midday the invisible turbulent air would rise off the bajadas, making us lurch as we sped low, making me grip the door frame so hard my hands would become stiff.

Sometimes the smell of dead wetbacks lost in the scrub and rocks would reach all the way up into the Huey helicopter as we raced along. That's how we'd find them. We also found a lot of dead cattle that way. They all smell the same.

Sometimes we rode the front bumpers of border patrol trucks, sitting on the truck's hood as we cruised the four-wheel drive trails across the sand, searching for revealing footprints crossing the roads. Allegedly this was to hone our tracking skills. In reality we were man-hunting.

I remembered finding the illegal immigrants, mostly under rock overhangs, or under bushes, or under desert willow trees. Cowering, creeping, weeping dry tears, hiding. Dusty, all of them. Many Mexicans, many Central Americans, living and dead. War was raging in El Salvador, and too many were caught between the twin evils of both factions, and many tried for El Norte as their refuge.

I know that's what I would have done. I thought about it a lot: if I had been born in El Salvador or Nicaragua in that era, I would have packed up the discarded plastic soda bottle full of tepid water, the stale tortilla, the blanket, and headed north, just

— Chapter 9 —

like they did. When we found them, many had that thousand-yard stare, like the Vietnam veterans in my platoon.

The dead: desiccated, coyote-eaten, empty eye sockets, ants, dried husks of cloth and skin and bone. Or fresher, maggots making the corpse pulse, undulate, and swell. I remember the smell of sunbaked rotten death rising from the baking desert, the stench . . .

Most of all I remember the dead children we found, how I would look at the small empty shells, the remnants, and I would wonder why we didn't get there sooner. Why the hell I had gone back to base last night, why I had slept, why I had been taking a crap or a shower in the BOQ while that four-year-old kid was slowly baking to death under an ocotillo? While I was kicking back drinking a Budweiser.

The El Salvadorans hid from the helicopters. To them, helicopters meant machine guns, and machine guns meant death, and so they hid, and so they died. In their delirium they would take their clothes off before they died. I don't know why.

I came to a place psychologically where I dreamed of them. I dreamed I could track them, I dreamed I could follow their trackways as though they were glowing, magically, as though God and the Ancestors would lead me right to them.

We learned about the biology of death. First the scavengers, the coyotes, the vultures, the rats. Then the maggots and blow-flies for the soft and the wet. Finally, the dermestid beetles for the dry, the hair, the hard to reach places. Those dermestid beetles were really something. They would even eat wool sweaters, if a little body fluid got into the fibers. We could tell how old a corpse was by what was eating it at the moment.

We Marines, many of us Hispanics ourselves, coped with humor first, alcohol second, depression third. We joked about it. "Juan is Juan with the cosmos." "Maria we're not going to be able to shout *that* out" referring to a popular detergent commercial of the day. Greeting a skeleton: "Aye, Pedro, you've dieted way, way too much." And upon sighting a particularly maggoty corpse, "Ramon, the deodorant isn't working" with the

— Honor —

accompanying, "Such pets! You've got way too many."

Some of us collected dermestid beetles, put them in a foot-locker out in the sand behind the barracks at 29 Palms, and fed them the carrion of animals that we found. In this way the crew was able to produce some animal skulls for trophies, such as bobcats, dogs, a ring-tailed cat, and once even a desert bighorn sheep skull, complete with horns, which we illegally removed from the Twenty-Nine Palms National Park after we smelled the carcass from the helicopter.

The smell of those beetles and their work was stunning, acrid, sharp, and clinging. Our experiment with skeletonizing ended when some of the beetles rode one of the skulls into the company barracks and began to eat the dress green wool uniforms. After that the beetles and their footlocker went to live off-post in the waterless, tin-roofed squatter's hut occupied by a lance corporal and his girlfriend.

I wondered now if I should ever share those memories with Margaret. I had never really told her. Nothing much to talk about, really, and why vomit such unpleasantness? But . . . there were the many children we found in the desert, living, dead, damaged. And there were the many we'd failed to find. If she knew, she would know the secret about me, maybe.

Now, looking across that table, I didn't think it mattered. She had Jack, who hadn't served a day in green in his entire life, but who drove his chrome-adorned monster truck through town with a "F*** Bin Laden" bumper sticker on its backside. Jack was her reality, not El Salvadorans dead more than thirty years past. Jack, who wore a surplus army camo shirt when he went camping. Jack, who had his AR-15 tricked out with flashlights and optics for maximum coolness while plinking at the 50-yard range.

So far during this meeting I hadn't said a word.

"My parents can see how Garth is so incredibly damaged. They agree with me. Sometimes he gets this wild, crazy look in his eyes; it's indescribable. When that happens I honestly fear for me, fear for my daughter. I mean our safety, our physical safety."

— Chapter 9 —

63

Here, Margaret looked away, out the window at the people walking on the sidewalk outside, beyond the moist green lawn. I had learned that unconscious act: it was her tell. She was lying. Aaron the mediator couldn't see it.

"Garth is simply incapable of being a competent father for our daughter. I have a good home. Jack is like a father to her. Garth is alone in his own place. Garth has nobody, will never have anybody except his mother and she can't get around without a walker. It's only sensible. I want full custody."

"If I had a woman in my life, would that make a difference?" I asked.

"Of course," said Margaret. "If you had a good woman, a committed woman who could make sure that Francesca is properly loved, then that would make all the difference. I would know she was cared for, I would know she had consistency in her life with Garth."

She looked at the mediator. She looked at me. She looked at the table. "If you had a woman who loved you, it would change everything."

I didn't know why a woman would make a difference, but it didn't matter. What she was suggesting was wonderful news.

I smiled.

Chapter Ten

July 2012

The next Saturday was Angelica's son's birthday. Cesar was eight years old, all black thick hair and skinny motion, a bit like a spider monkey in a shirt. He was a beautiful young man, small for his age, usually with a giant smile, trying so hard to be strong, six months after his father's death.

I arrived early at Angelica's sprawling, ranch-style home overlooking the golf course to help set up for the party. Angelica had been vague about the details. I had the rope for the piñata. I myself was planning for what was normal for my family: about ten young children, hot dogs, cake, shared play, a piñata, and a quick finish.

I noticed as I pulled up in my XTerra that there was a large, white, commercial rented awning rising beyond the carved, pine-board driveway gate. There was a humming of people, unseen.

I walked up the lawn. The front door was open. Puzzled, I walked into a home swarming with Filipina women and a swirling hoard of small children. There were Tommy's photos covering the walls. Pictures of Angelica in her wedding dress. I had seen all this before. What was different was the swarm of Asian women, all moving rapidly and talking. In the midst of the entropy, each woman seemed to be performing a prear- ranged task.

There were many quick introductions, just as quickly for- gotten. My mind could see only Angelica, embarrassingly so. Then Angelica said, "Quick, come see documents." Everybody smiled and nodded. Business, of course.

With a small hand on my back, Angelica guided me down the central hallway of the home. Then, out of sight, she pulled me by the hand, down the hall, into Rose's bedroom towards the back of the home. She shut the door, and blocked it with her body. She pulled my face down to hers and her mouth eagerly found mine.

"Schatzi," she whispered. "Schatzi." A few fevered kisses. I ran my hands over her tight blouse, felt the solid curves of her waist and her belt line, down to her buttocks, and felt a spectacular burst of testosterone and adrenaline. By all that was holy, this woman was Tommy's widow. That sudden thought chilled me to my core.

Just as quickly, she was spinning away, grinning whitely in the dark, opening the door, guiding me stupefied back down the hall to the front of the home, letting go of my hand, my heart still racing from our kisses. More people had arrived in the few minutes we had been in that room. Angelica's sister Marta was watching me across the crowd, thoughtfully, tracking me. Not smiling.

I was still in the living room attempting to rediscover my feet when Francesca appeared at the front door of the crowded home, escorted by Margaret's mother, Victoria. That had been the deal at mediation: Margaret's mother would bring Francesca, and observe, and see if Angelica in fact had two heads or perhaps breathed fire, or practiced animal sacrifice when emotionally stressed.

There in the doorway with my daughter stood my ex-mother in law. Angelica, God bless her, had agreed to all this, and she met them both at the door, swelling with hospitality. Angelica gracefully escorted Victoria through the throng, introducing her, leading her through the people to the tables and the food in the driveway under the translucent white awning.

Francesca simply squealed with delight and chased into the back of the home to find the children, of which there were approximately thirty in some sort of conjoined, howling orbit.

— Honor —

Lodged in the living room, I was in a sea of people, from centenarians to toddling babies, and I dodged my way out to the driveway, since the piñata must be there. Over the fence I could see the golf course, bright green in the sun, with distant tiny multicolored figures of golfers playing.

My former mother-in-law Victoria was sitting at a white plastic rented table under a white plastic rented awning on a white plastic rented folding chair, surrounded by laughing people chattering in kapampangan dialect, in English, and even occasionally in what I assumed was Hawaiian. She was smiling happily and talking with the much smaller Filipina women who surrounded her.

A large white plastic plate of Asian food sat before her, steaming a bit, including, I noticed, a large portion of roasted lechon pig. It made me hungry to look at it. Victoria was fully caught up in the discussion around her, apparently enjoying herself. Francesca was somewhere else in the torrent of children.

Behind us, near the garage, there were three ten-foot rented tables laden with Asian food. There was the entire roast pig, a "lechon" in Filipino language. Marta, Angelica's sister from Pampanga, was in charge of all that food, which appeared to be arriving in the hands of dozens of Filipina women. There was Vietnamese pho, there was pancit, there was cabbage, an entire baked salmon filet, and some sort of lumpia. Enough for a battalion.

Towards the front of the driveway, I looped the piñata rope over a high limb of an oak tree in the front drive. That oak tree had been there hundreds of years, overlooking the pastures of heaven, out there on what would have been a wilderness ridge before the oak woodland turned into houses.

I pulled the rope so that the end hung down near the candy-swollen florescent green piñata, as big as a Labrador dog. I wondered if the wire bale, which would connect the piñata to the rope, was strong enough, or if it would come off in mid-yank and smash a blindfolded bat-wielding five-year-old. The piñata weighed about as much as a full ammo can of 7.62 ammo:

— Chapter 10 —

in other words, a lot. There was a plethora of candy in there, enough to keep these children wired for a week. The parents were smiling blissfully at me, unaware of the days of hyperactivity I was about to unleash upon them. Far down the ridgeline, the golf carts crept along the paths of the emerald golf course.

Meanwhile people kept pouring into the driveway. I watched as Angelica and her teenage niece, Rachaela, greeted the very elderly Filipinos by holding their hands to their own foreheads. I had no idea what was happening. Then my son, Ernst, escorted my mother down the stairs into the yard.

"I invited your family," Angelica whispered in my ear. "I want your family to be our family too."

At this point there were probably at least one hundred people crammed into the driveway and side yards and the house, sitting under the awning, milling about near the food, or simply standing and talking loudly. It was a sunny day, and the light illuminated the awnings.

The people seemed to be from all ethnic groups and all ages. People who had known Tommy as a doctor. Every child in Cesar's class. Apparently about half the congregation of First Presbyterian Church was there. Most of them knew me, and waved and smiled and spoke greetings. My tinnitus, the ringing in my ears, and the roar of conversation at nearby tables made it hard for me to hear. I smiled and waved back.

I knotted the rope onto the wire bale of the piñata with a bowline knot, and gave the rope a pull. That piñata weighed at least twenty pounds: I was going to score both tree and rope by pulling on it. I could go to the car and get a carabineer, but I didn't know if I had time. The XTerra was parked directly in front of the home. I looked over the driveway fence into the front yard. Two men in board shorts were assembling a rented bounce house, some sort of inflated red and yellow castle with a large slide on the front lawn.

Meanwhile the horde continued to go through the food line, and I saw Ernst and Marta helping my mother fill a plate. They gently coaxed people apart to get my mother through and they sat her directly across from Victoria. Drawn by decades of shared family life, Victoria and my mother began conversing cordially. Family indeed.

Later, I went through the food line myself. I took just a little, and most of that was for Francesca, who was hungry now and beginning to make sporadic visits to look wanly at me and ask for cheese puffs. I sat near my mother, and my son, and Victoria, but kept a few people between us, since I also wanted to mix with Angelica's family. Angelica saw us in the crowd and came over to where we were sitting.

"Why you not eat more?" she asked me. She put her hand lightly on my shoulder, and left it there, and bent down to look at me in the eye. Her smile was dazzling, and her tone was soft, personal. I looked at her long, slender fingernails. There were flowers painted on them.

I smiled. "Keeping my run times down. It's certainly delicious."

Actually it *was* quite delicious. As expected, that lechon was a greasy, salty delicacy. Had I permitted myself, I would have feasted.

I looked over at the tables nearby. Marta had her eyes glued onto Angelica's hand like lasers. She wasn't smiling. Around her, the Filipinos were laughing and chattering, lost in the moment. The children were swirling like paper in the wind, and little Francesca leapt up to join them, food forgotten. My mother looked across the people at Angelica's hand on my shoulder and smiled.

"I will get you more food. You must try more of the lechon," Angelica said softly in her musical voice. "Come, come with me and I will teach you about what we eat."

So I followed her from serving plate to serving plate on the three tables. The food was largely eaten. Still, there was enough for me to sample morsels. There was still a shred of pompano left, and a morsel of rice.

Then Angelica escorted me back to the chair next to my mother, and left me there as she walked back up the stairs into the kitchen. Tight designer blue jeans. I allowed myself to watch her walk away, a vision which Michelangelo would have immortalized. I gave myself up to it, allowed myself to simply watch, lumpia, pancit, and piñata forgotten.

The noise of the party returned. I looked around. People were staring at me. I glanced over at Marta. She was looking back at me. Her husband was regarding me stonily. Around them, the conversation had stilled. Angelica's immediate Filipino family was watching me as coyotes might watch an injured squirrel.

Chapter Eleven

July 2012

Before Tommy got sick, Angelica had worked part time as a caregiver at Heritage Bay Eldercare, a luxurious residential facility by the sea at Pebble Beach, between Pacific Grove and Carmel. It was quite swank, famous locally for the elderly retired San Francisco lawyer who, in the grip of Alzheimer's, attempted to smuggle himself out in a laundry hamper and was delivered to the cleaners curled at the bottom of the large wheeled bin, quite blue, quite stiff, and quite dead. Apparently, those sheets have a very high thread count.

Heritage Bay Eldercare was resplendently Christian, with a life-sized weeping stone Madonna gazing down on the front lawn, between trimmed pine trees, with a view of the beautiful beach. I'd weep too if that many neighborhood dogs peed on my feet. It was staffed mostly by a smiling staff of Filipino women who were known locally for their complete devotion to their patients and their complete indifference to bodily secretions.

This was where Angelica had decided to return to work. She had worked there before, before Tommy was ill, before the cancer had devoured all his days. She told me she needed to return to the world of the working, and of course, I had to agree with that. Since Heritage Bay Eldercare was familiar ground to her, Angelica wanted to give me a tour first. So there we went.

Angelica was looking beautiful as always: conservative, neat. Hair pulled back, black slacks, common-sense shoes. White blouse. No hiding those curves.

I parked my XTerra. There was a black Mercedes two-seater

coup in the director's parking space, the sort with the hard-top, which folds into the trunk. That set off my radar: I love that car, but an investment advisor driving a Mercedes is essentially telling the clients that he's going to fee the crap out of them. I wondered what a Mercedes meant in a director's parking space in an eldercare facility.

Through the large, church-like front doors, the spacious atrium was well-lit, with a hanging stained glass cross in the back. We walked in, and I unconsciously reached for Angelica's hand: I was more intimidated by this place than she was. She ignored my questing palm. Of course, I thought, we can't be public, and she works here. They know her as a widow, and it's right she should keep it that way.

The residential wing stretched off to the left. Clearly the common area and the dining area were to the left. Beyond was a resplendent patio with fire pits and a spectacular view of the bay.

In the front office, there was a gray-haired woman, clearly an employee, bent over a desk, with a tall, red-haired handsome man pointing out figures on a laptop. They stood.

"Angelica!" the woman smiled. She was tall, well-built, dressed professionally. She reached for Angelica's hand, then mine. "Great to see you again."

She turned to fully face me. "I'm Darla!" She handed me a business card. "And this is Jerome Totenkopf."

The man stood. Younger than me, by about ten years, taller, athletic, with a great thick crop of trimmed auburn hair. He was wearing expensive slacks, long-sleeved LL Bean shirt. Old fashioned gold watch. Yuppie. Very self-confident posture. Very expensive shoes. Solid handshake. No wedding ring.

"Jerome is the owner of Heritage Bay Eldercare, as well as some other facilities, and he's here to provide some management. We're between executive directors right now," said Darla.

Angelica smiled up at him. She stepped slightly away from me. "Hi," Angelica said shyly to Jerome.

"Hello, there!" Jerome responded, grinning, looking at Angelica.

So that was his Mercedes in the parking lot.

"Garth is my trustee and investment advisor," Angelica explained. No mention of anything else.

"Oh, so you're a financial guy. Good for you. That's my game too. I own eighteen facilities just like this. I'm the only stockholder. Maybe we should talk shop sometime," said Jerome.

"I'd enjoy that." I said politely. Maybe I could manage his pension plan.

Jerome looked at me. He smiled. He looked away at Angelica. Angelica looked back. They both laughed shyly. They seemed to know each other.

"Jerome was here before, when my husband was still alive," Angelica explained to me. Then she turned back to Darla and Jerome.

"Garth also should have a tour here," said Angelica. "His mother is ninety-two years old, and she still lives in her own home."

"Lives in her own home?" said Darla. "Why that's just an accident waiting to happen. We need to get her in here, get her in here as fast as you can, before something dreadful occurs."

I just looked at her. I tried to smile. The idea of my mother in an institution gave me chills.

"We see this all the time," said Darla. "They fall, they break something, and they die. It's so much better to get your mother in here *before* she falls, before she has that accident! Get her in here! Bring her in for a tour! I'll get my calendar!"

"No, not now," I said quietly. "We can plan that another time."

"Better do it quickly!" said Jerome. "Before she falls. That's why I created Heritage Bay Eldercare, to provide loving assisted living to people like your mom. We'll treat her right."

I was silent, looking at him. I was doing the math. Eighteen institutions. Let's say an average of fifty people in each. That's nine hundred elderly residents. Times say $7,000 a month. That's a cash flow of $6,300,000 a month. $75,600,000 a year. That would buy a lot of loving care, wouldn't it?

I made dinner that night. "Heritage Bay Eldercare is *such* a wonderful place to work," Angelica gushed. "Jerome took me out to lunch today at the Sardine Factory."

The Sardine Factory was a relatively expensive high-end restaurant in Monterey featuring quality Italian food. Capers. Chiante. Crustini.

"He flies his own Lear Jet, you know. He flies between his facilities and he supervises them all, and he has *thousands* of employees spread all over the United States."

"That's a lot of flying," I said.

I was scooping roast salmon for the three clamoring children. They all devoured it. Salmon was the go-to meal. "He's a *wonderful* man! He's a champion runner too!" said Angelica.

Ah. A runner.

"Who went to lunch with you and Jerome?" I asked. There was a centipede of jealousy crawling around somewhere inside me. I told myself it was nothing. After all, 50-percent of the world is men, and 50-percent is women. If we are going to work, we are going to have professional relationships with everyone.

"Oh we went by ourselves," Angelica said. "You know how it is, lunch snuck up on us, and we just went out. Jerome said he likes to meet all the new employees personally when they join the team."

The Sardine Factory was perhaps thirty minutes driving each way from Heritage Bay Eldercare. With many restaurants en route.

"I thought he already knew you," I said.

"Oh, yes, he was consultant before," Angelica corrected herself quickly.

"He's a consultant? I thought he was the boss," I asked. To me, a man and a woman alone at an expensive restaurant for lunch seemed a lot like a date. It occurred to me that my curiosity was getting out of control. "I thought he was the owner."

"Oh he is, he is," replied Angelica. "He's also the acting boss. There isn't an executive director now, so he's filling in. We're lucky to have him."

"But he already knew you," I said.

"He was just very happy to have me come back."

The children were chattering among themselves, laughing, animated. Making faces. They seemed so bonded, so natural together. I turned to my plate. The broccoli was just right; slightly al-dente. The pink teriyaki fish was perfect. I looked across the table at Angelica. She smiled back, radiantly, wonderful small teeth, clear brown eyes. Then she leaned deeply across the table, reaching far with those slender arms, and took both my hands in both of hers, right there at dinner with all three children watching, and looked deeply into my eyes. The kids didn't react at all. Angelica's gaze locked into mine, and I felt the doubt drain out as though a plug had been pulled in my heel. What a complete blessing this was. Angelica's new job was a blessing. The three children were a blessing. How could I be this lucky?

I'm full of irrational paranoia, I thought to myself, and laughed slightly.

Chapter Twelve

"Actually I like Angelica," announced Victoria. "I like her whole family."

Victoria was a woman of strong opinions, a woman which the French would term "formidable." Congenitally unable to keep an emotion, an opinion, or a secret to herself, she was an asset to any man seeking a transparent life. Assuming one didn't mind the verbal bronco ride, of course. Assuming that one wanted to live as transparently as a glass window.

Tonight, I was in the process of picking up Francesca from Victoria's home, a tidy, 1960's three-bedroom home near Hartnell Community College, only a few blocks from my own residence. I often met Francesca there, as Margaret's home across Blanco was infested with anger and a resident man.

This time, however, Margaret and Jack were visiting Victoria as well. Thus, in anticipation of a verbal conflict, Victoria's utterly inoffensive British husband Fred, my ex father-in-law, had wisely fled into the back of the home at my first knock on the clean red front door. He had been bombed as a child in London in World War II, his home utterly destroyed. Perhaps he could still hear falling explosives before they hit. That left Victoria, personality enough for two, a sulking Margaret, and a perennially glaring Jack.

Jack always wore a small sheath knife on his belt, one of the "camp and fish" variety favored in eastern Boy Scout camps, with a tasteful aluminum-capped handle of leather washers and with a blade about 4 inches long. I had often wondered what that meant. He was a produce broker, not a buffalo hunter. Still, there was no denying that for slicing strawberries or opening UPS boxes, a sheath knife was plenty handy.

I was allowed into the living room. Francesca was playing and chirping in the vicinity of her Barbie doll house on the other side of the room. I took my seat, buttocks poised for simian flight, on the edge of the brown leather couch opposite Margaret and Jack. We looked at each other, all apparently pondering Victoria's words with an enforced sagacity. None of us spoke. Margaret sat back on the couch and examined the brickwork of the fireplace, which had been converted into a black sheet metal pellet-burning stove. Jack sat close by Margaret, their legs touching. He had his arm around Margaret defensively, pulling her to contact. He glared directly at me. I tried not to glare back. Interesting stove, that.

"That was some party, wasn't it?" I offered to Victoria.

I was trying to understand how I was going to introduce Angelica and her family into our family dynamic. Because in my opinion, if you have children and both parents involved, you are still a family. Dysfunctional, unnecessarily complicated, gratuitously pain-filled, but still some sort of loose, disarticulated, shambling family. I didn't know what to do about this.

"She's just lost her husband, and she's trying to do the best she can," announced Victoria. "She has that wonderful large family, and they are surrounding her with love, as they should. Clearly, Garth, you are helping a lot too. She told me all about what you do for her and the children."

"It *is* wonderful, isn't it?" I offered. "She helps me more than I help her. It's great for Francesca. We are getting outside more because of her. It's a win-win."

"More like a lose-lose," said Margaret, her voice low and angry.

I looked to see if Francesca had heard. No, she was playing away at her doll house. For some reason Barbie and Ken appeared ready to jump off the roof. It was a two-story dollhouse.

My first aid training kicked in. A jump off two stories meant a fib-tib compound fracture at least, with probable serious spinal, neck, cranial . . . those dolls better stay safe. I had seen one of those compound tib-fibs when a Marine in 1st Force Recon's parachute team had an opening malfunction out of an OV-10 light aircraft. The man's leg bones had speared into the dirt like pickaxes. We had called him Toulouse Lautrec even after the casts came off.

"Please tell me more," I asked. Great therapy talk. My men's group at First Presbyterian Church, which I no longer attended, would be proud.

"Francesca is *not* a Filipina. Those aren't her people. She has no reason being with them," muttered Margaret.

"They can teach us a lot," I offered back. "What do you find difficult about that?"

Medium points from the phantom men's group for that comment. Challenging. I should have just asked for more.

"She already has a *mother!* She doesn't need another," she continued. "If you want to chase some LBFM then that's your business. But don't include Francesca. She already has a mother."

"LBFM?" I asked.

"Little Brown Fucking Machine," Margaret shot back. "That's what you're after, right? That's what *all* men want. Look, all you gave Francesca was your sperm. I did the rest. I'M HER MOTHER! Leave us alone!"

I sat there, stunned. I felt the anger rising up in me. She had no idea, no idea at all about my true feelings for her in the past, or my true feelings now for Angelica.

I looked at Victoria, looking large and younger than her seventy years. She was examining the large framed family photos on the wall opposite the pellet stove. I examined the photos as well. There were about six of them, of the family traveling, at Disneyland, in San Francisco; at Christmas around the tree. I saw Jack there, in the family photos. I noticed that I wasn't present in any of those portraits. All of my photos had been taken down. After more than two decades of marriage to Margaret, and there was Jack, smiling from those glass frames, with Francesca smiling in most of them as well. What the heck was I doing here at all, I wondered?

I looked at Francesca, across the room. She seemed oblivious, with a doll in each hand, talking happily to each in turn. Ken and Barbie apparently had given up on the roof jump and were walking down the stairs.

Victoria looked at us all, her mouth a straight line. I could sense an imminent detonation. If Victoria became angry, not even the paint was safe.

"It's been five years," I said softly. "Five years alone. Five years of watching you and Jack. Jack at the doctor visits. Jack assembling the crib. Jack holding Francesca just after she was born." I motioned to the wall.

"I had to paternity test my daughter because I had to be sure she wasn't Jack's. Apparently . . . . apparently, I wasn't the only one giving you—"

It immediately dawned on me that I should not have said that. The phantom men's group was definitely giving me a thumbs-down. But I had the bit between my teeth, and my adrenaline was overwhelming my common sense. I could feel it sweeping me into verbal hysteria.

Margaret hissed first. "YOU WERE NEVER HOME. YOU WERE ALWAYS GONE, RIDING IN THOSE TRUCKS OF YOURS. YOU DIDN'T CARE WHAT HAPPENED TO US, YOU JUST HAD TO GO DRIVE AROUND IN THE SAND, OR PIROUETTE AROUND IN THOSE GODDAMNED DRESS BLUES OF YOURS, AND YOU LEFT US!"

I stood there, silent. It seemed like hours, but it was probably ten seconds. "You sat on that couch and cried when you saw 9/11," I said. "I was there too. I saw you. And then I saw you, I heard you, you said over and over again that we had to fight back. I was a trained Marine infantry officer. What else was I to do?" I wrestled with myself not to yell.

"Well, you could'a actually fought someone. Like killed the bad guys. Sure as shit that's what I would'a done. Fucking coward. Embarrassing," muttered Jack.

"I went where I was sent," I replied. "I didn't see you there."

"I would'a gone but I was too old. And before that I had asthma." Jack chomped the words out. "At least I didn't fake it or take advantage of the system to hide in a truck."

"I was an infantry officer because I joined up at age twenty and rose through the ranks. I didn't have asthma. I went back in because I thought I could do some good for the nation. For all of us. I'll say it again, I didn't see you there, Jack." I responded.

Margaret's face was suffused with red, turning purple, and her eyes narrowed into slits as she responded, "Yes, you were an infantry officer, and I put up with your Tarzan chest pounding for years. But when you went back in, it was different. You were older, you had a business, and a master's degree. You had CHOICES! Only people WITHOUT CHOICES go into the military! Stupid people! People without any education! But no, you had to leave us to DRIVE TRUCKS! You never even heard a shot fired. You PIMPED OUT your family TO DANCE AROUND IN YOUR DRESS BLUES AND DRIVE TRUCKS! For that, you left us!"

I took a deep breath before I responded, "The best people, some of the most educated people, I ever met were in the Marines. I know you don't believe that, and you don't understand that. I won't try to change your mind. You are right about one thing: I went away thinking I was going to carry a rifle and instead I carried a clipboard. But I still went. I still went, and if that isn't good enough for you, then live with it. All I know is that the man who took my wife was a civilian."

I immediately realized that saying that was another mistake, and I visualized reaching out and plucking the words from the air right there.

Jack made an obscene gesture towards me with his fingers.

I turned to Jack. "And you . . . with your American flag and your Bin Laden bumper sticker. You were my friend. And a close friend you turned out to be. I came home to NOTHING thanks to your patriotism. Did you think of ME when you made love to Margaret? Pumping up the war effort? Injecting a little family support after I was wounded?"

"Meanwhile, while I was riding around in my trucks and eating MREs, you, Margaret . . ." I looked at her.

"You were doing your patriotic duty, I suppose."

"You, you can't speak to Margaret that way! That's abusive, that's abusive. I'm gonna kick your ass for that." That would be Jack.

"Oh, Jack." I laughed. "Bring it. Any time. Right here, in the driveway, whatever. You are the prince of adulterers as far as I'm concerned."

Jack glared at me, and I had a sudden picture of a mountain gorilla defending his forest nest. That's all we are, I thought. We are just chest-thumping primates. And I am out of control. Time to leave.

I rose. I looked at Francesca, across the room, still playing with her Barbie and Ken, and I ached when I realized what chaos we'd set loose in all our lives. I just ached.

"It's clear that I am not respected here. It's clear that Margaret . . ." I glared at her.

"And Jack . . ."

"And you too Victoria . . ."

"Have some kind of hidden contempt for me, or I would be in those pictures." I motioned at the framed portraits. "At least the older portraits, the ones we took when I was part of this family . . ."

That was true: the photos from all the years of my marriage to Margaret had been edited to specifically exclude me. Jack was on the wall. I wasn't. That said a lot about what Victoria and Fred thought about me, didn't it? I cringed inside.

"Francesca looks at those every day, Victoria, and look at what she sees. Jack. Her father, Jack."

"You don't deserve to have your photo on that wall," said Victoria, finally wading into the argument. This made it a *real* family feud, because Victoria was the heavyweight, the contender, the Muhammad Ali of verbal disagreements.

— Honor —

Victoria's face became a mask of contempt. She continued to speak, as though passing sentence. "You are abusive; just listen to what you've said today. Good riddance. You should have found an Iraqi bullet over there. That would have been more honorable. Then your photos would still be on these walls."

Silence. Everyone looked at Victoria.

"Do you really mean that?" I asked Victoria quietly. At last, honesty. Somehow, unexpectedly, a line had been crossed between us. Our relationship had changed in an instant.

Victoria moved across the room and sat next to Jack. "You were gone, pretending to go to war, and we know what was really happening. You were simply getting away from all this responsibility. But Jack was here. Your daughter deserves *squeals of joy*. When she shouts, "Catch me, Daddy," at the park, Jack catches her as much as you do."

"I guess in your opinion I'm out of Francesca's life," I said quietly.

"Oh bullshit, Garth. Fred worked for forty years in a grocery store and he saw his daughters about fifteen minutes a day, and that was enough for him. He is a very good man. Unlike you, he knows the meaning of hard work. He worked at that grocery store twelve hours a day, and when he came home, the girls were in bed. He made a happy life anyway. Man up, Garth. This is the twenty-first century and you're missing it!"

The loudness of Victoria's voice. Francesca looked up in alarm from her play. I went over to her, into an area where I was normally not allowed, bent down and hugged her, smiling. She was silent, and eventually refocused her attention on Barbie and Ken. She put the dolls into a plastic convertible car and began to push them out of the room. I stepped back towards Victoria, Margaret, and Jack. They seemed to shrink into the couch.

"Give my best wishes to Fred when he comes out from under the bed," I said. I walked to the front door, and I departed without slamming it, hoping as I left that a meteorite would smash me dead as I walked into the driveway.

The door opened behind me. "And you WEREN'T

— Chapter 12 —

83

WOUNDED! NOTHING HAPPENED, AND THEN YOU
WERE INJURED!" Jack shouted behind me, and I heard the
door slam shut.

Chapter Thirteen

August 2012

"Here's the question: since I'm in a romantic relationship with the beneficiary, am I too compromised, is there too much conflict of interest, to continue serving as trustee for the Narcisco Trust?" I asked.

It was the following afternoon. A board of directors' meeting for Ericson and Associates, fee-only investment advisors. In our front room, in the window, at the table, where it all had happened before.

I had told them everything.

"Good question," responded Sarah, my twenty-three year old daughter. "I'd say yes."

"Is Angelica fully informed?" asked Ernst, my twenty year old son. "It seems to me that she's a grown-up, and she's intelligent. She can make this choice."

"Either you provide exceptional service or you resign," said Lanie. "It seems to me that you are doing that. We've provided outstanding care. We're doing it for free, pro-bono. If we billed, it would cost Angelica tens of thousands of dollars, which she doesn't have."

"What do you think, Garth?" asked Robert, the lawyer. "Answer your own question." I had asked him to attend the meeting specifically to address this issue.

"I think we are doing superb work, and we're honoring my promises to Tommy," I responded. "Almost everyone else who promised to help has fallen away. We're it. And we're doing it for free. So I feel I should continue as trustee. But I need to make sure I stay on task."

"I have reservations," responded Sarah. "There's an obvious conflict of interest."

"Yes," I agreed.

"However," Ernst said to Sarah, "is there anyone else prepared to deal with all this, for free, when there is no money? How are we taking advantage if we aren't being rewarded?"

"Sexual coercion?" said Sarah. "And what about your faith?"

"She came to me," I said quickly. "And you are right. I'm struggling about the Christian aspect of this. There must be commitment."

"We know you're starving emotionally," said Lanie. "That's obvious."

"It's obvious to me too. I'm guessing Angelica is just as broken," I replied.

"With all that in mind," said Ernst, "we need some boundaries. I think it's okay to stay as trustee, and okay to pursue the relationship, but what are the guidelines?"

"I propose the following," said Robert. "I should monitor, and the board should monitor your actions to make sure you remain a good trustee for Tommy. We will watch you keep your promises. We will watch you do the right thing."

"Can you do this?" asked Sarah. "Do both?"

"I also feel that you should take the maximum opportunity to grow, heal, and be a better investment advisor and father and man. Can you do that?" asked Ernst.

Their questions took me aback. Could I really do this?

"Let's find out," I responded.

Chapter Fourteen

August 2012

The following Saturday we celebrated the Salinas California Rodeo, a tradition of more than a century.

A long time ago, a man named Sherwood liked to race horses. He donated the ground for a rodeo arena on the outskirts of town, with the proviso that cultured horseracing should take place every year alongside the lowbrow escapades of bronc riding, steer wrestling, and roping.

Back then, in the late nineteenth century, irrigation with deep wells hadn't been developed, so the town was surrounded by giant cattle ranches and dry farming.

The ranchers ran the town back then. They were the big money, and they set the social agenda. Their sons attended the newly-created Stanford University and were born to a life in the saddle. In my childhood, ranch owners and cowboys routinely read Robert Louis Stevenson and Sir Walter Scott.

Since then, irrigated row crops have replaced the cattle and the bean fields, and the rodeo grounds themselves have been surrounded by housing developments and strip malls. The worn red wooden horse barns, with their stalls stained and chewed by a century of bored equines, have now been quietly replaced by metal stock pens and aluminum sheds. Probably intentionally, not a trace remains of those barns in which the county's Japanese-Americans were sequestered in early World War II, prior to being shipped off to internment camps.

When my family owned our ancestral cattle ranch, the rodeo was a big deal, lasting a week. It was a bit like Christmas in summer, and we would ride our horses up Old Stage Road, past the ranches of our friends, to attend all five days of the rodeo fiesta.

Even now, decades later, in my memory I sometimes found myself riding to the rodeo, a child again, on horseback, cresting the fingers of the Gabilan Mountains on the overgrown dirt trail. The slopes, ridges, and ravines would stretch below us, brown in the desiccation of August. They would extend before us with their dry summer grass and dark green patches of oaks and brush. There, down the slope ahead would be a white blanket of coastal fog ,which hid our hometown and the Monterey coast. We would ride our steaming horses in the clear early morning light with the sun rising behind us, and ahead there was the white sea of cloud flowing beneath the mountains, endless and forever and timeless. All was in place in the universe and our place in the world was secure.

Of course, it wasn't timeless and it wasn't secure. Everything changed. And in recent decades the rodeo has become less relevant to me, since my father died, after the ranch was sold to satisfy the conflicts of the myriad debtors. I had walked away from the cowboy lifestyle to focus on family and life.

Meanwhile the local rodeo competitors have been replaced by the national bull riding stars, and it had become more about the circus than the livestock.

Before his death so many years ago, my father had loved it all.

By Salinas's standards, rodeo 2012 was a hot day, perhaps 80 degrees. I bought straw cowboy hats for Francesca and her two young guests, Cesar and Rose. Ernst, and Sarah, who had known the ranch and horses early in life, wore their well-used hats and plain, polished cowboy boots, looking relaxed and bemused. Cesar, Francesca, and Rose capered and bounced loudly through the new rattling sheet metal bleachers, laughing and calling, mindless of the history they had never known.

We arrived to our bleacher seats early, above the more expensive box seats and the vastly more expensive sponsor's paddock. Since losing the ranch, since the Marines, those costlier "see-and-be-seen" choices seemed extravagant, and the children certainly seemed content up in the cheap seats.

Gradually, Francesca, Cesar, and Rose quieted as the stands filled with spectators around us. Ernst, and Sarah were somewhere visiting their friends, their lengths of bleacher seats empty. In the bright arena, down in the plowed and harrowed dirt, the last of the slack roping—the out-of-the-money calf roping contestants—finished their runs, horses pounding after small steers, the rope snaking out, horse skidding to a stop, calf whiplashed off its feet to slam into the ground.

I was pondering that: on the ranch we would never have treated an animal that way. Too rough. We were in the shade from the giant metal half-roof, but I could see the sunlight creeping towards us as the sun moved overhead in the sky.

"Hey, look, it's Mom!!!" shouted Cesar, pointing down into the sponsor's enclosure. I felt a jolt of adrenaline. I peered down, cursing my lack of binoculars. Yes, there in the distance was a woman who looked very much like Angelica, colorful gold urban-western short sleeved shirt, black skin-tight jeans, brilliant smile. Her cowboy hat was a double-rolled open weave, the kind you see on Hollywood celebrities, a faux-hat really.

The woman was very animated, joyful, face turned up to a tall, trim, auburn-haired man with a blocked cowboy hat and aviator sunglasses, square-jawed, fit, plaid western shirt, and tight blue jeans. A spear of adrenaline coursed through my whole body. The couple disappeared from sight into the sponsor's tent, a place legendary for its chef-prepared barbecue and its ongoing party of the elites of Salinas. Before, in my life, that had been my place. Not now. I didn't want to be there. Too much wealth lost when my father had died. Too much dislocation after the Marines.

"Let's go down and see her!" shouted Cesar, rising and beginning to hop down the stairs. I reached out, grabbed him by the collar gently, and his small butt thumped back on the aluminum bench. "Text first," I said, as I plucked out my phone.

"Where are you?" I texted Angelica. "We are at the rodeo and we think we see you."

— Chapter 14 —

89

Long silence. No response. On the track, the grand entry began, a horse parade, well-groomed horses, riders shining in brilliantly colored western outfits. Many American flags. We stood. We sat. We stood again. Hats off. Hats on.

Then there was a pageant of historical flags, slender, beautiful young women in sequined outfits astride galloping horses, racing their horses at full speed down the track. They carried the flags of the history of California, the colorful cloth banners straight out in the wind, cracking, snapping, alive. A tall, slender black man in a cowboy hat stepped forward and sang, "I love you, California," the state anthem, and the volunteer band far below thumped and crashed through the music.

I sat down and there was a response from Angelica on my phone.

"Enjoy the rodeo! I am home. Enjoy. I love you all."

There was a photo of Angelica on my phone. A selfie portrait. She was smiling, beautiful, looking straight at the camera, hair swept to one side. I thought of her at home. Waiting for us. Lips waiting to kiss. I looked again down into the sponsor's area. The woman and man had disappeared, apparently seeking shelter in the luxurious open-sided dining tent. We couldn't see into it.

Then I looked at the photo again. In the background of her portrait, on the shelf in the bay window over the kitchen sink behind her, there was a tiny pumpkin, the kind that people buy to decorate around Halloween and Thanksgiving. Alongside it was a small plastic jack-o'-lantern.

It was August.

In the arena, the bull riding began.

Chapter Fifteen

August 2012

The following Sunday was the Salinas Buddhist Temple Obon celebration. For native Salinas residents, it was a genuine holiday. For me it was full of childhood memories, and so I awoke as if to Easter.

I ran early that morning as the first dawn light cut through the fog, past the houses of my neighborhood, into the old Main Street area. En route I ran to Peninsula Bakery, a tiny place, windows bright, opaque from steam in the pre-dawn, the rich delicious smells of sugar, vanilla, yeast, and chocolate filling the air a block away. They knew me: five chocolate-almond croissants, each dripping with the butter baked into the dough, each in its own brown paper bag.

On I ran, jostling the small bagged pastries as I loped over the sidewalks. One bag went to the homeless man awakening on my front porch on Gabilan Street. He seemed to have taken up semi-permanent residence, despite my referrals to a nearby city-run homeless shelter. This morning he was still asleep.

Then I ran to my mother's home in full morning light, another two miles, used my key, and left the bagged and somewhat battered chocolate almond croissant on the kitchen counter for her to discover when she awoke later.

I left the other croissants on the porches of other neighbors, including Victoria and Fred's, each croissant in its respective brown paper bag. Then I continued my run home to a shower and oatmeal.

I have been attending Obon since birth, thanks to growing up with a Japanese-American nanny who was left with three small hakujin children for weeks while my parents were elsewhere. She brought us to the Buddhist Temple for many family nights, when she could enjoy the company of her own family and share her culture with us. As a result, I grew up with Toshiro Mifune movies projected using a white bed sheet on the gym wall, with inari, unagi, teriyaki, and rice. To me, it was simply life as a child. Traditional Salinas.

I often wonder about how my nanny must have felt: to raise three children not your own, and mix them with yours, as part of your work. I sometimes wonder how intrusive we white Christian children must have been.

Now I think back and wonder what is genuinely my heritage, what is real, and what is "Disneyland with kimonos," which we experienced because my parents paid for it.

Whatever it was, it was my genuine childhood experience. And so, when I had children of my own, I shared the celebrations of the Salinas Buddhist Temple with my family.

In 2012, that meant dance rehearsals each Tuesday night for the entire months of June and July. Each Tuesday night I drove Cesar, Rose, and Francesca to the Salinas Buddhist Temple gymnasium, each in casual exercise clothes with a fan, a tea towel, and Japanese castanets. The veteran dancers such as Gordon Yoshida and Annie Tokugawa would teach them, circle after circle of dancing, the boombox-generated shrill Japanese music as timeless as the temple itself. Of course there were the relatively new Japanese hits as well, including the protest song from the 1960s, "Sukiyaki," which the gentle Buddhists had transformed into a playful children's fan dance.

In past years, before, when I was in Salinas and not in the Marines, I would dance with ever-reluctant Margaret and the children.

"We are *white* people and we look like halibuts in these clothes!" Margaret would say. "What are you going to do, give Sarah a Quincinera too? And Ernst a Bar Mitzvah?"

After our divorce, attending became more important to

Margaret because the children continued to dance each year. She and Jack would attend to watch sullenly from the sidelines with her parents, all chewing delicious, savory skewers of chicken yakitori.

In 2012, however, given our renewed state of conflict, Margaret and Jack decided to not attend, with a loudly expressed, profound sense of deprivation. I instantly filled the emptiness with Angelica, Cesar, and Rose.

Thus it was a boiling triad of childhood energy, which came rocketing from the XTerra for that 2012 Obon, followed at great distance by my mother with her walker, greeting the many friends she knew as she trundled on, and, given her macular degeneration, expressing her best wishes to an unusually statuesque boulder in the rock garden.

Angelica was right behind in her own Honda Pilot. She quickly caught up to my mother, and I shepherded Rose and Francesca into the dressing room, where the ladies of the temple could wrestle the girls into yukata, brilliantly colored cotton summer kimonos, which our friend Snow Tanaka had most thoughtfully given us. Men are easy to dress for Obon: a simple purple cotton jacket, and a headband, and any man is ready to dance.

The music began, the circle of costumed dancers began to move and I saw my son Ernst join us from the side, wearing his purple, fan in hand. I looked out to where Cesar, Rose, and Francesca were already dancing. I looked across the circle of people and there was Angelica, standing alongside my mother who was sitting on her walker. Angelica had put her navy blue wool pea coat around my mother's shoulders as the fog moved in. The day was ending, the darkness of evening was increasing, and the gray overcast was floating in from the sea.

Overhead, the multicolored Japanese paper lanterns were glowing in a line across the dance floor, glowing, swaying gently in the soft cool moist wind.

Afterwards, we all wandered over to the Temple gymnasium for food. This year was unique: in addition to the udon noodles and the inari sushi, Ernst appeared at our table with an entire teriyaki chicken and a saba, a barbecued mackerel.

I sampled a piece of saba and savored the salty oiliness as it melted upon my tongue. Francesca was chewing it diffidently, Rose as always was eating heartily, and Angelica was, as ever, eating with enthusiasm.

Somehow, there was a bit of oyster shell or pebble in the saba. I imagine it was grit from the oysters they were barbecuing on the same red-hot grill, or perhaps it was a sand grain from the oak wood which fueled the fire. It was a tiny, tiny fragment of rock, but I unknowingly bit down on it with an excess of zeal and I felt an upper molar snap like glass, simply shatter into my mouth.

The pain surged up into my sinuses, and I was speechless for a few seconds. Then I spat the tooth bits and the old tooth cap from the molar into my hand. It was one of the teeth badly damaged by my accident in Iraq. Everybody seemed mildly interested, sympathetic, their minds more on the coming strawberry short-cake than the demolition taking place between my jaws.

But Angelica looked at me, apparently genuinely frightened, seemingly on the verge of tears. "That is what happened to Tommy," she said quietly.

I looked at her as expressionlessly as possible as the dazzling flood of pain ebbed from my face.

"That is what he did with all his teeth, one at a time, during the chemo," she whispered, visibly cringing. I could see her eyes widening.

She was deeply terrified, and as I watched, her expression changed to immense sorrow, resignation, a sense of something irretrievably lost.

"You are old, after all," she whispered.

I looked around the table at my family. Beyond our table, the hundreds of participants ate and talked happily and noisily and the auditorium was bright, filled with the hum of life.

I was the only one who had heard her.

Several days later, I visited the dentist and felt him drill down my tooth, smelled the burning dentin, and finally bit down on command to install a temporary crown.Angelica would not respond to my texts suggesting a lunch of soft udon at Kokoro's, nor did she ask how I was doing. Her text responses were monosyllabic, grudging, withdrawn, a smiley face when I texted a picture of the three children dancing at the Obon.

Her Facebook page was cluttered with Bible quotes and encouraging phrases from Payton Opp, the Christian motivator and televangelist, that something good was in store for us all, if we could only allow God to change us. Somehow, God was going to drop a miracle into our laps. Somehow, if we could only *believe,* God was going to bless us with incalculable joy. We were merely to wait, and to pray hard for that miracle.

I hungered for Angelica as though there was no other food in the world. I felt embarrassed as though I had somehow committed an unforgiveable faux pas at the Obon, perhaps defecated in the rock garden or vomited on the shining bald head of a sitting elderly Bonsai master.

Chapter Sixteen

September 2012

For the past months we had texted at least every half hour, so long as we were both awake. Now, nothing. I assumed that she was grieving for Tommy, appropriately. We had started this relationship much too soon. Surely some emotional confusion would be unavoidable. I remembered my plans and my prayers that I could love, let go, accept. Good luck with that.

Our weeks together had bonded us, at least in my own mind, and it felt like a large piece of my anatomy was missing, misplaced somehow, removed from somewhere near my lungs.

Two days later, that Tuesday, was the Jewish food festival at Temple Beth El. I am a Presbyterian, of course, but once a year I convert, to worship the pastrami on rye sold to me at Temple Beth El by my smiling neighbors. Apparently half of our town converts as well, because the lines are long and the tickets are usually sold out. I had been careful to buy meals for my entire office staff weeks in advance, and I had promised Angelica that I would bring her one of Salinas' culinary marvels.

Before receiving my seven sandwiches, an assortment of pastrami and corned beef, I visited the florist, Swenson and Silacci, in the same building where I had taken my pig-infected hand so long ago. I stood reverently before their glass-fronted refrigerated displays, and carefully selected a medium-priced bouquet of mixed blooms, white and red roses, a green glass vase, and a cardboard carrier to keep it all from tipping as I carried it in my car. Living beauty, all of it, a wonderful, memory-filled smell, and a smile of a small gift.

After a beautiful sunny drive to Pebble Beach, I parked the XTerra in the clear light of midday in the Heritage Bay Eldercare parking lot. I picked one sandwich out of many in the large brown paper shopping bag, and I pried the green vase of flowers out of the cardboard protector. There was Angelica's car, parked next to the director's parking space. In the director's parking space, there was the black, two-seat Mercedes convertible.

I walked into the well-lit foyer, and off to the side, at her desk, there was Angelica. Dressed perfectly, conservatively, beautifully, hair pulled back, small, white pearl earrings, white shirt, and brown skin. She was typing away at a computer when she looked up and saw me, and I felt a jolt of delight. But that quickly changed: as I watched in the sunlight through the large windows behind, her mouth fell open, shocked. She was alarmed. I felt a small boot of adrenaline, an unexpected tiny bat-squeak of fear.

She was not happy at all. She seemed afraid. She stood up, small, slender, tottered on her high heels, and she walked towards me, angry, making a bulldog face, eyes glaring, and she clutched me on the bicep, and pulled me rapidly towards the door. Around the corner I could see Darla, who saw me, saw Angelica, stared at the flowers, and quickly ducked back into the hallway beyond with a neutral expression.

Angelica continued to push me angrily back out through the front doors, almost causing me to stumble.

Once outside, she spoke quietly, sharply, sternly. "Why you here? This my work! Why you come here?"

I held up the sandwich, wrapped in white paper. "Corned beef. The Jewish food festival. We discussed it last week."

"You bring me sandwich?"

"I brought you lunch."

"You should not be here. Take it, take the flowers, and go." Her face was stern.

"IS IT THE JEWISH FOOD FESTIVAL OVER IN SALINAS?" said a loud quavering older woman's voice behind me.

Angelica wheeled, horrified. "Selma!" she almost shouted. "What you doing out?"

I turned to look.

The woman was ancient, curled like a dried pear, clutching her walker, too old to ever have been young, brown-dyed hair fading to red and grown out, so that a skunk-stripe of white crossed the top of her head where her hair was parted. Her loudly pastel floral print shirt, pink, yellow, red, and purple flowers on black, hung over pink polyester pants, and her slipper shoes were white. She had 1960's style sunglasses with upturns and rhinestones along the top. She was of European origin, pale skin, bulbous Walter Matthau nose. She looked utterly unfazed by Angelica's comments, determined to stay right where she was.

"I am escaping from my cell. I am stickin' it to da MAN!" Selma declared, looking steadily at Angelica, voice quavering as she smiled widely. Her teeth were cream colored, a little crooked, real.

"That's a synagogue special, isn't it sweetie?" she continued, looking at me, and then at the white paper bag. One hand left the walker and gestured.

"Most assuredly." I smiled back. Selma's confidence was bringing forth my own.

"Well, ASSUREDLY then, is it corned beef or pastrami? What did you bring our little Angelica? And flowers too! Angelica . . ." Selma shifted her walker.

Angelica stifled a response. She clenched her jaw. "You should not have come here without permission," she muttered.

"Permission? Him or me, dearie?" replied Selma, looking at Angelica.

Angelica seemed flustered.

Selma grinned, her basset face crinkling.

"Hell, if he's got pastrami I give him permission," said Selma.

Then she turned to me. "Everyone wants to visit Angelica. The UPS man, the EMT, the orderlies, and now you, kind sir," said Selma brightly, ignoring Angelica's obvious anger and impatience.

"When I want to bring joy to my own day I just go into Angelica's office and see what new flowers she's got. But nobody else has brought her a synagogue sandwich. I'm officially envious. The food here is only slightly better than the food I had on a troop ship in the North Atlantic in 1944."

A spasm of jealousy squeezed my stomach. Flowers from other men. Yet it would normal. After all, Angelica was beautiful.

Selma smiled brightly, all wrinkles. Her eyes almost vanished in her face, and she looked at Angelica. "Lighten up, kid, in twenty years you'll remember this and smile. And when you are my age, you'll give all you have to remember it. You should be taking pictures. Tempis fugit."

Angelica stared at her puzzled, still angry.

"That means time's gonna kick your ass. Actually it's gonna sag your ass, then kick it," said Selma. "But first, the breasts. I gotta tell you, someday you are gonna look in the mirror and scare yourself. It happens to all of us. You too, Mister Sunshine."

I felt a surge of affection mix with my anxiety.

Angelica turned away from Selma, and looked at me steadily, unsmiling. She seemed afraid and angry. "Garth, please take sandwich, and flowers, and go. You aren't invite here, and you should go."

I was deeply hurt. I wanted to reach out and hold her, as we had held each other a week ago. What had changed?

Selma interjected, "Tell you what, Angelica, you can disinvite him. Then I'll invite him, right now. I'll walk him to his wheels."

Selma looked at me. "That yellow box on wheels yours, Mister Sunshine?" Selma nodded towards my XTerra. "Let's saddle up." She shifted her walker.

Angelica shook her head, anger barely suppressed. And something else, impatience . . . fear. Why was she afraid? Apparently, she needed to get me out of here as fast as possible.

"He should not be here," she said to Selma, "He need leave now."

"Angelica, I got him. I promise I won't get lost," said Selma to Angelica. With that, Selma began steering her walker towards my car.

"Okay," said Angelica emphatically. "Garth, I will text after work. Have a good day. I'm sorry." She turned abruptly and walked back into the office.

Selma walked me to the XTerra and parked her walker near the driver's side door.

"You gonna eat that?" she asked, looking at the sandwich.

"Actually I brought it for you," I responded. "I hear that it's better than troop ship food." I tucked the white paper wrapped sandwich into the carry basket of the walker. "It was nice to meet you."

I looked up at the clear blue sky. The fall day was heating up, and under my blue sports coat I was sweating. In the distance, I could hear the ocean.

"Why thank you, kind sir!" said Selma. "You are the money guy, right? You're the guy who saved Angelica's butt with the budget and the bills, right?"

"Is that what she said?" I smiled. "I saved her butt?" I felt a warmth, a gratitude when I heard those words.

"Well, Angelica and I, we talk." said Selma. "You were Marine, right?"

"Yes, I am proud to say that I was a jarhead," I said. This was nice.

"Well," said Selma, "I was a BAM."

"A BAM?" I asked. "What's a BAM?"

"A broad-ass Marine." Selma laughed. "I was a woman Marine. They sent me to England instead of the Pacific! I got to type in the combined headquarters in London. SHEAF. That's how I met my husband, Isaac."

There followed twenty minutes of discussion of England in 1944, of the values of being fluent in German as she was, being a Yiddish immigrant from Poland before the war, the virtues of the M-1 carbine, and the attractiveness of a certain combat-injured army combat engineer staff sergeant, himself fluent in German and a prewar Yiddish refugee, and their later adventures translating captured Nazi documents across liberated Europe after D Day. Fascinating.

— Chapter 16 —

She revealed that she owned a Walther PPK/S pistol, complete with Nazi markings. We agreed that it was a superb gun, light, handy, reliable.

At length I could feel the sun burning my bald head. And the sandwiches for my office staff were getting warm.

"I have to go," I said.

"Can you come back?" said Selma. "You are the only person I've met who seems interested in my life. And this place . . . it's like the slammer."

I looked beyond the glass of the atrium at the ocean. Behind us, across the parking lot, was a pine forest. There were surfers out there on the beach now. The sun was shining. This place was possibly the most luxurious residential eldercare complex I had ever visited.

"You ever been in the slammer before?" I asked.

"No, silly!" replied Selma. "Unless of course you count my forty years as an English teacher at Washington Middle School, over in Salinas. I could tell you . . ." She laughed and looked away into the pine forest. I wondered what she was thinking.

I had to fill the silence. "Oh, yes, of course. I forgot, I brought flowers for you too." I propped the green water-filled vase with the white and red roses into the cargo hamper of Selma's walker. "Tell someone to get those out for you, okay?"

"You're a sweetheart, sunshine," said Selma. "I know it hurts now. Angelica told me you broke up. She and I . . . we talk. She's not interested in much except shoes, and my purses. But she's very nice. The rest of the staff thinks I'm furniture."

I stepped back, working hard to hide the shock I was feeling. We broke up? Our relationship wasn't even public yet.

"Chin up," Selma continued quietly. "Don't let 'em see it on your face."

She reached out and touched my arm. "You are a wonderful man. But Jerome, well, he's a millionaire and then some. He's handsome, he's young, he's a *pilot,* and he shows her a good time. He owns this place. He takes her flying. How you gonna compete, when that's what the woman wants?"

— Honor —

I nodded politely and wheeled to leave, trying with all my strength to control myself. Brilliant sunlight. Bright blue sky. I could feel small bits of gravel under my leather dress shoe sole as I spun around on the pavement. Walk to the car. Walk to the car.

Selma yelled at me, "HEY!"

I turned to look back. I stopped where I was.

She learned over her walker, and she seemed to radiate a gentle affection, some kind of love, and she spoke quietly, slowly, as though she was imparting the combination to a steel safe containing a fortune.

"The understanding is that there's no understanding," she said.

I just looked at her. Her tortoise eyes drilled into mine.

"You didn't know that?" she said.

Chapter Seventeen

September 2012

I am not entirely sure how I drove the forty minutes back to the office. The sandwiches did not rot in my car, so somehow, they were distributed, although I drove with a scent of pastrami for days later. I remember the financial markets were mixed. I remember meeting with clients, smiling, listening as though I was underwater, making some sorts of comments which must have made sense, since the clients did not fire me on the spot. Several of our long maturity bond mutual funds were doing exceptionally well due to falling interest rates created by the Federal Reserve. Perhaps, I thought, these mutual funds have longer maturity bonds than they are revealing. Stay focused: this could backfire badly.

I remember fixing an Asian stir-fry for dinner, the meal I create when I have no creativity, and that my five-year-old daughter gave the almonds in the stir-fry to my mother, on the grounds that nuts shouldn't belong in a cooked dish.

But aside from that, I don't remember much.

At 9 p.m., after Francesca had gone to spend the sleeping hours with her mother, there was a text. It read, "Cesar has more panic attack. He wants you now. Please come here please."

Service, I thought. Let go. Expect nothing. Follow the path.

Angelica opened the front door for me before I could knock. Clearly, she had seen my car through the front window. She was dressed in her white bathrobe with large pastel polka dots. Many memories. Bare brown legs. Bare brown tiny feet. Memories. I focused on being kind, loving Cesar, and leaving her alone.

Cesar was curled up on the living room couch, encased in a ball of beige blankets, thick black hair sticking straight out the top. His scowling, small, long face was framed by wraps of blanket, his eyes shut, face pressed against the brown leather couch. He looked ill. I went over to him, sat down next to him, reached out, and his small slender arms reached up through the blankets, and he hugged me as tightly as he could, eyes screwed shut, face pressed against my shoulder.

"Hey," I said.

"Uncle Garth," he said quietly with his face still pressed against my yellow hoodie sweatshirt. "Uncle Garth, everything was so big again, and I couldn't touch it. And you were there, and Mommy, and Daddy. And I couldn't touch Daddy. I couldn't touch Daddy."

He sobbed a few times. He hugged tighter, and I hugged back.

"I want Daddy," he said quietly.

I looked at Angelica. She was seated across the room, legs folded up under her like a cat, the polka dot bathrobe, looking grave, concerned, focused on us. Small slender hands. No wedding ring. That was new.

Between us, over the fireplace, the many pictures of Tommy looked down. Tommy golfing. Tommy piloting a plane. Tommy in his wedding tuxedo. Family with Tommy. Children with Tommy. Framed quotes from the Bible. In the middle of it all, the polished walnut box of ashes, about the size of a square box where one might keep a softball.

Silence. I held Cesar, and Cesar held me, and finally, I said, "I know you do."

But by then he was asleep. I continued to hold him. I looked down at his black hair, thick, shiny from washing. I lowered my face and smelled the scent of conditioner. I felt his breathing now, more regular, slower. I looked across the room at Angelica, still with legs folded under her. She simply gazed back, serious, wordless. Enclosed. I thought of today, of Jerome, of what Selma had said.

"Is Rose asleep already?" I asked.

— Honor —

"In my bed," she answered. She did not move.

"I call you only for Cesar," she said.

A punch of grief and adrenaline went through my chest. I tried to say nothing, do nothing, stay focused on the sleeping boy who still had his arms wrapped around me. I looked down. Cesar's face had slid. He was drooling slightly on my sweatshirt. I felt a surge of affection. I had run today. The sweatshirt was already destined for a wash.

"What happened?" I asked.

"What happened what?" said Angelica.

"What happened between us?" I asked.

"You reject me. You don't give me what I need. You say you want to wait. But I need now. You starve me. You are cheap with me, with love," she said.

"Tommy's been dead seven months," I replied. "I am trying to do the right thing."

"You don't do the right thing," she replied quietly.

I was silent. I savored holding Cesar.

"I starve," she added. "You are cheap with everything."

I sat silently. I didn't know what to say.

"I love you," I said finally.

"You are . . . old," she replied. "I am sorry I hurt you. It is like Tommy."

Who can understand the brutal calculus of the human heart? My chest hurt. Badly.

I replied after a few minutes. "A few days ago you said you loved me. We made love . . . in there." My head gestured towards the bedroom. "I spent the night. We are both Christian, right? For us if we make love, it is a commitment, right?"

She looked at me. Just looked, unsmiling. "I sorry," she said again. "I don't fill it. I love you but I'm not in love with you."

I felt as though I had been hit.

We sat for minutes. Cesar continued to sleep, his breathing regular, continued to drool on my sweatshirt. I let him drool. The glistening drool was quickly absorbed into the yellow cotton fabric. Let it happen, I thought. A man has only a finite

— Chapter 17 —

number of opportunities to be drooled upon by a sleeping child.

Angelica unfolded her legs, and walked back into the bedroom. I heard her feet receding, slipping along the polished hardwood.

I sat in the quiet. I savored. I looked at the pictures on the wall. Tommy.

I heard Angelica's feet, returning down the hallway.

"Can you bring Cesar to bed?" she asked.

I simply stood, holding Cesar, and I carried him down the hall. Rose was sprawled widely across the bed in sleep, as always. While Angelica softly pulled her to one side of the bed, I gently lowered Cesar. He curled tighter and gripped me harder, and I realized I would have to unwrap the blanket or he would overheat. I gently shucked away his hands, and Angelica came to my side and peeled away the blanket, and pulled the sheets up around the sleeping boy.

I turned towards the door, and Angelica turned to me, and we gently collided. And there we were. And there were my lips on her smooth neck, kissing gently, and she pulled slightly away for a moment, and then her arms were around me. Her arms were around me. Her arms were around me, pulling me close.

I was breathless. My lips slid down, and Angelica tipped back, onto the foot of the giant bed. I looked up at the two sleeping children, both up at the headboard, both sleeping soundly. I looked down at Angelica, hair now spread across the comforter, and I lowered my lips to hers.

Chapter Eighteen

October 2012

Friday night in Salinas, and me without children around. Angelica was with her sister Marta, texting only monosyllabic responses from a Filipino comedy club in Burlingame, Cesar and Rose home with Mike and Rachaela. I was hungering to be with Angelica, a starving feeling, distracting.

It drove me out of my home, wandering solo, and tonight I was in the old Main Street section of Salinas, at 201 Main, the newly-opened restaurant in Salinas. I walked into the great high-ceilinged room, a converted 1920's bank, now dark and loud with evening revels. For eight decades some of the biggest financial deals in Monterey County were made, the stuff of legend, right here in this room. Now they made mixed drinks. This place boasted an incredible martini bar: underlit, translucent green marble, long as a tennis court, U-shaped with scurrying bartenders in the center and glasses hung upside down overhead. The dark room was crowded and loud, smiles white in the dimness, a buzz, busy. Many women.

Two months before, I had attended a Rotary meeting in the yet-unfinished restaurant. The owner had been absent, and the club president had loudly cajoled and convinced the fifty or so men and women, well-dressed strivers all, to use chairs as stepstools, climb up, and stand on the glowing marble bar. I was the designated photographer. I remembered the young professional women laughing and clustering atop the bar in their high heels and skirts, legs lit by the green glow of the florescent stone below, with the dapper professional men standing next to them, looking attentive. I remembered watching the young restaurant owner, family money in the pursuit of his dreams, walk into the room unexpectedly and freeze in shock. I remembered seeing the panic rising in his eyes as his mind attempted to encompass the prospect of several tons of well-groomed networking professionals standing on his precious rock slab, which had required several hundred thousand dollars to select, cut, polish, and install. There had been words between him and the club president. A hurried descent by the members before the loud "snap" of shattering fossil foraminifera filled the room. The meeting had concluded eyes averted, with a quick departure and hidden rueful smiles on the evening street. Wonderful photographs, shared away from Facebook.

Tonight, as my eyes searched the warmly-heated room, I could see that most of the Rotary members were here, including the club president, with his long seventies hair triumphant, tucked into a booth with several women members, laughing in the din, half-eaten plates of Italian food before them on the table. Beyond them the smiling young owner, thinning hair somehow peaked with hair gel into a nebulous Mohawk, stood looking down on them beatifically. Commerce had trumped embarrassment yet again.

There, in the corner booth, was the man I had come here to meet. Thanks to his Danish ancestry, his given name was Gunnar Iversen. In family lore, he was my distant cousin. Our family's ranches had been side by side. I had spent much of my childhood with him, tossing hay bales, cutting wood, camping, and hunting. On horses, until he became too huge for a horse to carry. That was in high school.

Those of us who grew up with him took to calling him "Bull" because he was a walking Minotaur, a behemoth on the Salinas High School football field. Most of us ranch kids did not play football. But we knew cattle. Now apparently, he had talked with my mother, and he was spreading the word. What word was he spreading, however?

He sat in his western finery, three hundred pounds at least, at least six and a half feet tall, a half-eaten order of French fries and a scattered dinner salad set before him. I reflected that somehow our Salinas High School class of 1972 offensive line was mostly quite heavy these days. For some reason they had all become obese. Enriching knee replacement doctors throughout the county, and beyond.

Bull was wearing a light-colored felt cowboy hat, incongruous indoors, tan western coat, aviator sunglasses. So many memories from childhood. Back then he had been small, quick, blond, and smiling. Now he was a storm cloud walking. His large round face glowered up at me as I approached. He motioned that I should sit.

"Greetings, cousin. So when you gonna come shoot a tusker with me?" he asked.

I said I didn't know.

He pulled an album up from the cushioned seat as I slid into the booth opposite him. He opened it. On the front page there was a full-page photo of him, dressed identically to how he was dressed now, crouched smiling broadly next to a gigantic dead gray elephant, surrounded by brightly dressed smiling black African people. Men, women, children. In the photo he was holding a large, blued rifle with a brown wooden stock, a Ruger #1 single shot by the looks of it. .375 H&H Magnum, I guessed. The elephant—eyes half-opened, mildly confused expression, gray, large tusks, a small black hole oozing a red stripe all the way down the elephant's forehead. Certainly quite dead.

"God damned crop killer, that's what he was," said Bull, looking down at the photo.

I was thinking that we had grown far apart since our shared childhood. I said nothing.

Bull started paging through the album: Bull in an open-topped Land Rover, smiling at the camera. Camp life. The elephant in the distance. The stalk, good by the look of it. Wind in the face. One shot. Then the pictures of triumph, the gutting, the dismembering.

In one photograph, the upright elephant rib cage, surrounded

— Chapter 18 —
111

by a posing, smiling Bull and his chainsaw-bearing African friends, looked like a fence of meat.

"You know I can't bring the ivory here, God damned tree huggers. I can't bring anything but the photos. Fuck, I paid $150,000 for it. You would think I could gold-plate a turd or something." He kept looking down at the photos, not spinning the book in my direction.

"Times have changed, Garth. And not for the better. Why look at these goat fuckers." He gestured with sausage fingers at a photo of a crowd of smiling black Africans in worn athletic t shirts and bright cotton dresses, surrounding and standing on the elephant carcass, while Bull sat in front on the elephant's legs, with his rifle skyward, grinning at the camera.

"They are so happy that *someone* has given them so much meat. Dang they should a' hung a medal on me."

$150,000? I wanted to shout. I was silent.

Bull kept looking at the book, flipping the pages slowly.

"Remember when we were on your ranch, and your dad told us to shoot all the cats, and we did? Then the wild pigs ate 'em. Ha! Those were the days. Not like now. Buncha pussies."

I thought for a bit. Bull had grown up an only child on his family's large Gabilan cattle ranch, the Tortuga Ranch. That ranch: beautiful as heaven, including some flat, dry farming land, which had a hidden treasure of petroleum underneath. Rising up and away from the farmed Salinas Valley floor were oak-covered wilderness mountains above. The Iversens had been reluctantly wealthy. Bull had inherited it, inherited the oil wells, the portfolio of stocks and bonds. The entire world had been his at birth. He was richer, and possibly larger, than God. And he had stayed right here in Salinas. No college, no marriage, no military service, no children, a bit of travel. I wondered if there was a horse on earth large enough to support him now. Perhaps a Percheron, a draft horse.

The waiter came over, dressed to emulate an employee at an Italian bistro. White shirt. Red skinny pants. Fauxhawked blonde hair.

"I'll take another mar-toony!" said Bull, leering. Surely, he wasn't going to drive like that.

The waiter nodded sagely. His sleeves were rolled up and there were black dragons wrapping around a coffin tattooed on his arm. I wondered what that meant. The waiter was in his mid-twenties. He was apparently mildly bored.

"Shaken not stirred!" Bull added.

"And you?" said the waiter, looking at me.

"I'll take food," I said. I looked at Bull. "You should eat something."

"Nope. I'm good with the soul food," Bull told the waiter. "Maybe a steak later."

I ordered the salmon risotto. No cheese. The waiter walked away. It was loud here, I thought.

"So what's new?" asked Bull.

"You know, for me it's always like being inside a barrel and rolling downhill," I responded, smiling.

"Oh, well." Bull smiled back. "I spoke with your mom."

I smiled.

"Got some brown action, huh?" said Bull.

I pondered that. It took a while to sink in.

"I've fallen in love, if that's what you mean." I smiled back. "It was not what I expected at all, but it's happened. It's good."

"Ah, well. I could understand why Maggie left. You were gone a long time hunting the sand niggers. Waste of time. Not worth shooting. And you didn't get any, did you? Can't blame her if another guy started hanging around. Women got needs, and Maggie's still beautiful." Bull laughed and slapped his hand on the table.

Well, gosh. Thanks for that. I said nothing. I just stared at him. Crude bastard. This was more like spying than a social meeting. I was already counting the minutes. I thought about target shooting. That's it. With an M-1 Garand, a real rifle, at 200 yards. Or my own family's ranch, now lost. Dos Cabesas. The clear bubbling creek there. Pacific pond turtles. Clemmys marmorata.

— Chapter 18 —

"How many kids you got?" he asked.

"Four. Three big, one little," I replied, smiling, shaking my head. Many.

"You sure that little one's yours?" asked Bull. "After all Jack was all over Margaret while you was driving trucks."

Anger churned somewhere deep in me. Was my family, my clan, so obnoxious? Had I grown up like this? Why yes, I had.

"Thank you for your service by the way," said Bull.

The waiter arrived. He brought my salmon risotto and the martini and a complimentary plate of fried calamari. This time the waiter was fast, all business, no eye contact. They must be getting busy.

"Thanks, I'll take a glass of house red," I said to the waiter as he spun around to leave. He nodded absently and paced away into the dark restaurant. Beyond, I could see a young city councilman, smiling, a woman on each side of him.

"You are welcome. It's not like I shot Bin Laden," I said to Bull.

"Hey, yeah, what the fuck was THAT?" said Bull. "I'd pay $150,000 to shoot Bin Laden. Hey, I wonder if they'd let me bring THAT head back?"

I forced a smile. My wine arrived. White wine. I considered calling the waiter back. White wine: simple-minded. The complexity of a doorknob. All the same. Oh, for a glass of red. I drank deeply. It was cold. It was carbonated. Actually it tasted surprisingly good.

"So anyway I talked with your mom," said Bull, looking at the calamari. He reached out and brought a piece to his mouth.

"And?" I asked.

He ate another piece, and then another. His fingers were hairy, huge, and thick.

"Hey, look, buddy, if you need to stick it to some brown, you do what you need to do. But you don't marry it," said Bull. "It isn't Christian, for Christ's sake."

Amazing that such words could come out of a lifelong friend's mouth. The world had changed. Or was it the God-like omnipotence created by so much wealth and so little family? Clearly the man wasn't house-broken.

"Did my mother say that?" I asked.

"Here's what your mom don't know," said Bull. "I had myself some of that action a while back. I kept her up in San Francisco. She liked . . . spanking. Anyway you don't shit in your own nest, capiche?"

I looked at him.

"Christ, women," continued Bull. "If they didn't have vaginas and make babies, there'd be a bounty on 'em."

The wine was beginning to seep into my awareness. One glass. Good choice. The key was to have no more.

Bull gestured with his fork. "But look, eventually we all gotta grow up. Even you. Even though I *can* understand a nice young piece of tail."

I smiled thinly as I pondered the part about growing up. I focused on my risotto.

"Do you miss the Dos Cabesas?" asked Bull.

"Every damned day," I responded. "Every hour. Try living in town. It's loud. And you can't shoot off the back porch."

We both smiled then. And I thought of how different the world was now.

"Well, you *can*," responded Bull. "But you'll probably have sirens in your front yard in ten minutes."

"Twenty," I answered.

I wondered why I was there.

After dinner we stood outside together at the restaurant door. I looked up. The lights of Main Street dimmed the stars above us. Bull was smoking, dragging deeply on his unfiltered cigarette, the smoke drifting around and above his cowboy hat. He had consumed three martinis during our time together and I wondered how they were affecting him. And how could he see with those aviator sunglasses at night? A giant gut slopped over his belt. Pointy little cowboy boots, embroidered with silver toes glinted in the light of the street lamps. He was looking down the street, smoking aggressively. He seemed nervous.

I stepped upwind from his smoke, and the stench of fertilizer, the acrid smell of dung, came with the wind from the west. Bull turned his face up into the night, closed his eyes and inhaled deeply.

"Is it true you never fired a shot in anger the whole time you were over there?" he asked. He was smelling the wind.

"Who says that?" I asked.

"Oh, your mom," answered Bull.

"She's right," I replied.

"What a fucked-up waste of time," said Bull. "How fucking embarrassing for you."

I looked at my watch.

"Time to go," I said. "Thanks for meeting with me."

I held out my hand to shake, and his giant baseball-glove sized palm enveloped it.

Bull wouldn't let go of my hand. He gave it a slight tug and held his pumpkin head up, cowboy hat tilted back. He looked at the sky, closed his eyes, and sniffed.

"Ya smell that? Ya smell that? Beautiful. Right here in Salinas. That's the smell of success, of fortunes being made, of the whole valley growing the green things that make us all rich. It's the smell of money itself. The fact that it smells exactly like cow shit is entirely coincidental." He paused.

The acrid smell of the fertilizer on the wind burned my nose. But he was right.

Bull gestured with his cigarette. "Oh thank God for my frugal Danish ancestors. They made it possible for me to just wake up in the morning, open my eyes, and be a wealthy man. Damn, what idiots." He laughed. "They lived their whole lives growing beans in the dust, when they could have been anywhere."

He finally let go of my hand.

Were they really idiots? I wondered. What would his ancestors think about paying $150,000 to shoot an elephant? They had been so frugal out on that ranch that they had re-used tea bags. We were both quiet for a time. Bull smoked, blowing

— Honor —

the smoke high into the air. Then he shifted and his movement broke our reverie.

"Anyway time to go. It's another big day tomorrow. Ya know, like waking up and cashing checks. Keep yer topknot," said Bull, and he turned dismissively and walked thickly away down Main Street with the lamplight shining on his cowboy hat and reflecting off his boot tips. The hat was tan, not white.

"Oh, one more thing! I almost forgot." His voice came thinly from a distance as I was walking away.

"Yes, sir?" I braced myself for something repulsive.

"I got this rifle. My father got it from his brother after the war. You know, my Uncle Gunnar. I was named after him. Went to fight the Russians with the Finns, in World War II, he was a Nazi, some kind a' shit. Anyway the rifle's a piece a shit too. A Russian Mosin. I'm gonna sell it. Before I do, though, I want you to look at it. You like that history shit, right?"

I stood there in the cold night with the reek of ammonia fertilizer in the air. It certainly did smell just like fermenting cow manure. I thought about that. Uncle Gunnar had done the unthinkable: he was in Denmark visiting relatives in 1939, when the Soviet Union brutally invaded Finland. Somehow, he had found himself fighting Russians with the Swedish volunteers, and almost certainly he was no Nazi at all. From my perspective Bull had the story wrong.

Uncle Gunnar had come home in 1948, with his silence and his rifle, sparking a frenzy of rumors. After a few months of stares and whispers he had returned to Scandinavia, and had never been heard from again. Now Bull had that rifle. I had only seen it once or twice but somehow it had exuded history and adventure. If only it could talk.

"I'd love to see it," I responded. I instantly realized that now he'd ask me to come out to the ranch. I found that stressful. Too many memories. Too close to my former home.

"Call me when you want me to visit," I said. That was an easy escape. Bull never called anyone. People always called him.

"Will do. And think about it: gotta big-tusk bull elephant just waitin' for ya out in Rhodesia. Let's go put 'em down," he said. He raised his hand, shaped it like a pistol, and mimicked shooting an invisible elephant.

"Giants, I tell ya," he said.

Then he turned and lumbered off into the darkness.

I stood under the light of the street lamp. I looked down at my phone.

Angelica had posted on Facebook for all her friends during my dinner with Bull. "God is good!" said the caption and there was a photo of her delicate hand, with her fingernails carefully tricolored, holding a glass of white wine. On her small brown wrist was a silver Pandora bracelet with a small Lear jet airplane charm on it, which I had never seen before. And the photo location was tagged automatically.

She was in Oakland, not Burlingame.

Chapter Nineteen

October 2012

Cesar and Rose came over for dinner the next day. Angelica dropped them off, blew me a kiss, and drove away. I fed the three children salmon, broccoli, and brown rice, and they ran in circles screeching and laughing in the back yard, climbing up on the hot tub cover and leaping down onto the unwatered lawn in some imaginary adventure. I took comfort in the motion and the noise.

The next day there were a few photos of the children, a starvation of texts, a famine of contact. On Wednesday, I sent badgering texts to Angelica until she met me at Kokoro's for our traditional lunch: jalapeño bombs for her, sushi, grilled salmon. She reached out and squeezed my hand, inflamed my desperation, and drove away.

On Thursday it rained in the morning. A small drizzle, hardly a real rain by Oklahoma standards, and only in showers. At least it was enough for puddles.

I walked Francesca to her kindergarten class at University Park, as she chirped like a beautiful overdressed tiny bird and speculated about the Rapunzel Halloween costume, which Victoria was sewing for her by hand. Wearing her rain boots, Francesca leapt happily into every pool of rainwater on the wet sidewalk. Victoria was a talented seamstress. Francesca was absorbed. I was barely listening, embarrassingly barely there at all.

I forced myself to rescue a few earthworms from the sidewalk. We placed them back on the adjoining lawns, free from the threat of crushing galoshes.

I took a phone photo of the great worm rescue effort and sent it to Angelica, and waited for her customary response. Usually there was a responding phone photo of Cesar and Rose, usually perfectly dressed, usually smiling happily en route to school.

Today there was nothing at all. No texted response. Nothing on Facebook. After an hour I phoned. It quickly went to message. Angelica was seeing my messages, but not responding. At all.

It continued to rain in showers that morning. I stepped out onto the chill front porch at the office, still dry, to retrieve the *Wall Street Journal.* I still like to read a real newspaper. The homeless man was gone: so far as I could tell, he hadn't been there for several weeks. But there, where his sleeping bag had been, was a human turd. Someone had shat on the front porch, wiped him or herself with an undershirt, smeared shit on the front wall of my home office, and then left the undershirt behind. There was surely great anger behind that. So revolting. The turd smelled of shit and booze. I wondered if there were parasites. After standing and staring, and pondering, I went back inside, told Lanie and Tammy Fay what had happened, went to the store, purchased the needed disinfecting supplies, and cleaned it up.

Afterwards I washed my hands with cleanser and sat at my desk feeling that the entire world was made of excrement. I pretended to work. Lanie and Tammy Fay could tell I was absent, could tell that I was missing while sitting there at my desk. That was rare: usually the diversions of the global market fascinated me.

Lanie placed a report on Greek debt on the desk before me, surely a living rat before a python. Yet my senses didn't ignite. It rained. Inside and out. I phoned, and it went to message. I texted with feigned casualness about the rain. I texted about lunch, asked her to lunch. And I texted about the afternoon. She viewed my texts, about hourly, but she didn't respond. She had never done this before.

At 3:00 we closed down the office as the rain trickled out.

I changed into my running gear, drove out to Fort Ord, and I pounded out a seven-mile run at Fort Ord. I ran up the hill from the parking lot to the vista overlooking Salinas, blind to the view, not feeling the heavy, rain-swollen wind, unsensing. I stopped, took a photo of the vista, as I so often did, and sent the photo to Angelica. No response. I kept the phone in my sweating hand minute by minute, waiting for a call, waiting for any response. None.

After the run, I looked at the message thread. During the entire day I had sent her a total of about thirty texts, with no response, and she had seen them. No response. Embarrassing. I was out of control, clearly.

Something was wrong in my relationship to Angelica, but what was it? Was the family okay? Perhaps I should go there now.

Clearly, I was losing my self-discipline in a way I had not ever known, not even when I was under much more stress. Something was wrong with me. Something was also wrong out there, unseen. Somehow, I had to regain my self-control, at least enough to get home, to get my family fed, to get to bedtime. I was shaking. Yet I didn't really know that anything was wrong, I reasoned. Perhaps she was simply contemplating. A lot had happened in her life.

I looked out over the Salinas Valley, at the brown and green patchwork of the farm fields, with a layer of low hanging gray clouds. Mid-October in the Salinas Valley. I felt the chill wind from the ocean penetrate my sweat-soaked long sleeve cotton t-shirt. How long had I been cold? A seven-mile run. I should be thirsty, hurting, hungry. There were the oak trees, immediately before me. Beyond, the Salinas Valley, the town, and the Memorial Hospital to the south. All still there. Overhead a gray cotton layer of solid clouds, as sharply defined as a layer of batting, pushing inland with the wind from the sea. Straight up, overhead, I could look into the gray swirling as it pushed by. A V of black geese scudded overhead, pushed by the steady breeze. Honking. What were they saying? I focused on my breathing.

— Chapter 19 —

Calm, calm, calm.

Dinner? I don't remember dinner. I know I fixed it. Ernst could see that I was largely disabled for some reason unknown to him. I'm sure he had some insight: when he asked me if Cesar and Rose were coming to dinner, I remember I simply looked at him, and perhaps my lips moved.

Francesca played and danced, now a paleontologist, digging fossils from the blankets on the couch. The fossils somehow emerged as perfectly formed plastic dinosaurs.

My mother gazed at me from the table, wordlessly. I sent several more texts through dinner, photos of the food, a photo of Francesca with her dinosaur discoveries. Two weeks ago my messages would have evoked rapid response, matching photos of Angelica's culinary creations, of Cesar and Rose with their own dinosaur toys. Today, nothing. She didn't even look at them.

The reheated teriyaki salmon was eaten for a second day, the mint ice cream was served in the mismatched bowls that my mother detested for their lack of uniformity. I could feel her reproachful eyes resting on those chipped, beaten bowls, and then on me.

Inwardly, I knew from experience, my mother was grieving my relative lack of wealth, of class, compared to what we had known. In my absence of aesthetics, she could see the family's decline after my father's death. I drove her back to her to her home, wordlessly.

Francesca had her bath and went to bed, singing, and fell asleep. Ernst went to his own bed. I sat alone on the living room couch, obsessively staring at the phone, waiting for a response. Any response, even an indication that Angelica had seen the messages. Nothing.

Finally, at midnight, I walked into Ernst's dark bedroom, and told him I was going over to Angelica's home. Something must be wrong. Watch over sleeping Francesca. He spoke from the darkness, "Of course, Dad. You do what you feel you need to do. Let me know if you need anything."

I had never gone over there unannounced before.

The driveway was empty. Her gold Honda was not there. She was not home.

I sat, pondering what that implied.

"Are you okay?" I texted. Concerned. Perhaps Cesar had had another panic attack. Perhaps Angelica's sister Marta was ill. I should be there. No response.

But then she read her messages, all six hours of messages. Too many messages. So she was receiving them. I could guess that she herself was not in the hospital, not in a car accident, at least not a serious wreck.

I called when I saw that. The call went straight to message.

I sat in the parked car, and I waited. While I waited I listened to an Audible book, *American Caesar* by William Manchester. About Douglas MacArthur. Amazing man.

Finally, at 2 a.m., the golden Honda drove down the street, pulled into the driveway, and parked. I stepped out of the XTerra, and Angelica saw me. It's not hard to see a bright yellow XTerra. She looked at me across the street. Her hair was disheveled, her eyes puffy, makeup vaguely uneven. Frown. She gave me an appraising, angry stare. She pulled her gaze away and hurried into the home, and left the front door open.

I entered. She was in the back, in her bathroom. I sat there, on that couch of so many memories, for minutes. Hours. Days. At some point I heard her small bare feet brushing back down the hall.

When she entered the room she was in her white polka dot bathrobe, makeup off, hair pulled back, her shapely small brown legs bare beneath the robe.

"What are you doing here?" she asked.

"Is everything okay?" I asked. "You just went dark."

She grunted. Frustration. Anger.

"Can you just tell me what is happening?" I asked.

She stared at me, unsmiling. "I am free woman, yes?"

I looked at her evenly. "You are free if you think you are. We have made love. For me, that's big. I don't regard myself as free."

— Chapter 19 —

123

She just stared at me, frowning, wordless. The silence was intolerable.

It seemed to last minutes. She stood more defiantly now, legs apart, hands on hips, scowling.

"I am free woman," she stated.

Perhaps she stared at me for a minute, perhaps even more. Her hair was pulled back, her little apricot ears exposed.

"You should go home now," she said. "Go home, Garth. Please."

"I need an answer," I responded. "Let's be clear about where we are. You decide. Tell me and I'll go."

I sat on that couch. I felt like death.

She turned away evasively, and grunted again. Finally she seemed to will herself to turn to me, to speak. Her eyes were flat, level, and she looked directly into mine. "I am with Jerome today, all day, and all tonight. We have made love. He is my boyfriend now."

Chapter Twenty

October 2012

"That went well," said Sarah. Marvelous hair. When she had been a child, she had been utterly blond. Now she was almost brunette.

I had called a meeting of the board of directors. I felt that they should be fully informed. The fall sunlight was streaming in the windows like crystal, illuminating the hexagonal table.

"I guess the question remains, can you do your job as trustee?" asked Robert, the attorney. He was looking a bit worn, tired.

"I'm guessing we'll know by Garth's actions," responded Lanie. "As soon as I don't see the best behavior, it's time to step aside."

"Agreed," I responded.

"How are you feeling?" asked Ernst. He seemed very concerned.

"I have to say, I'm not surprised," I answered. "It's only been a few months after Tommy died, so let's have some empathy for Angelica. She can't know her own mind yet."

"I mean, how are *you* feeling?" asked Ernst again. Serious. Smooth face lit by the brilliant sunlight.

"I guess my emotional starvation is showing," I said. "I'm stunned." I chuckled self-consciously. "I'm not sure what to do. I'm hurting."

"Dazed and confused," said Sarah.

"Yep."

"Here's that opportunity we discussed earlier," said Lanie. "Now is the time to make big, positive changes in your life."

"Harder to do than to talk about," I said.

"If you must fail in life, fail fast, fail completely, fail cheap. Then move on," said Ernst. "That's from my tech entrepreneurship class. Be done. Walk away. Make a decisive change. Start something different."

"Good advice," said Sarah.

"This is as good a time as any for an intervention," said Lanie.

"What?" I responded. "I called this meeting to discuss my situation with Angelica."

"It's gone beyond that," said Lanie. "Weight loss, insomnia, headaches, distracting thoughts, muscle pain, and you live in the damn bathroom. We all lived through years of this. Promise us that you will address your PTSD now. Take advantage of this situation."

"It's hard, but there it is. Like running," said Sarah. She was a runner herself. Cross country in high school. Steeplechase at University of California San Diego.

"I think Lanie has a good idea," said Ernst. "Stanford and the Palo Alto Veteran's Affairs has a new program for PTSD. You go to it, Dad, and get on with life. We'll help you in any way we can."

"Got vodka?" I quipped. Nobody laughed.

"You are a lucky man, to be surrounded by people who love you like this," said Robert. "Meanwhile you will remain as trustee for Tommy, and Lanie will let me know how it goes."

"Fail fast, fail completely, fail cheap, learn the lessons, move on," said Ernst. "Show us how it's done."

I felt the emotional load of that comment press down on me.

"As a dog returns to its own vomit," quoted Sarah.

"So a fool repeats his folly," I replied. "Got it."

Later that Friday morning, I went by Margaret's home to walk Francesca to school. Francesca was having a great kindergarten year, the very nexus of childish joy. I had not slept, but I had showered. Body aching with fatigue, hollow with insatiable hunger, I stood there in my business clothes and looked at her, pretending all was well. Margaret looked a bit haggard herself, in truth. I said nothing.

Margaret could smell the loss on me, the scent of a crushed ant, that formic acid aroma that comes from the descent of a massive weight. She looked at me sternly, speculatively. She then announced that she would visit friends in Camarillo with Jack, with Francesca, of course. Tomorrow.

Of course, to Lanie and Tammy Fay at the office, the hollowness should have been evident, should have been as obvious as an RPG wound, center chest, right on the sternum. Aside from my relative obliviousness, it seemed unnoticed.

I contemplated the prospect of an empty Friday night. My mother was in a wool spinning clinic, with her walker, her spinning wheel, her skeins, and a gaggle of smiling friends eager to drive her to the event and card fleece afterwards.

By now, Francesca was on the road with Margaret and Jack.

Angelica and her children were out of my life, allegedly forever, certainly for now. My adult children were off on their adventures.

If I remained at home, sitting, pondering, I felt that I might go insane. It was time to just go, time to just move, somewhere, try to leave the pain somewhere in the exhaust. I packed my backpacking gear, hurriedly, throwing MREs into the Gregory backpack as though I was back in the corps. I grabbed my Pedersoli Jaeger flintlock rifle, the shoulder bag of plastic powder charges, prime, .54 caliber ball, and cleaning gear, and began to drive east. I didn't know where I would go. I just drove. I followed the road.

The road went on, and somehow, I found myself wandering in the Sierra Mountains in the dark on the two-lane rural Highway 88, past the ski resort at Kirkwood, the black road winding and turning in the headlights. I had driven across the entire Pacheco Pass and across the Central Valley without thinking. My gas tank was half full, so somewhere I had refueled. I had no memory.

— Chapter 20 —

On I drove. I was lost in my thoughts in the darkness. Jerome. . . Jerome . . . Jerome . . . and my Angelica. My Angelica. What would they do this weekend, while I was camping? I wanted to tear, rip, even burn the images out of my head. Images of them smiling hugging, snuggling, making love. Visiting the places I had experienced with Angelica: Big Sur. Monterey. Abalonetti's, San Francisco.

I drove on.

Should I sleep or keep driving east? I stopped at Sorensen's Resort to check the dry-erase weatherboard outside the office. Twenty-percent chance of showers, which in the Sierras usually means "dry". Forty-six degrees minimum tonight. Fall would definitely be in the air.

So camping it was. I returned to the XTerra as the sun finally disappeared behind the western mountains. I turned left onto a dirt road I remembered at the intersection of Highway 88 and 89. The two-track was a sparse little unpaved 4X4 trail, ten miles to Burnside Lake. One of my favorite places.

I drove, bumping over the ruts, until the road ran out and there was the small, ingrown lake to the right, and a rock with a campfire pit in the headlights, and I was there. Not that I particularly wanted to be there. God, I thought, I don't know what else to do.

Out of the car, I realized that the wind from the north was rising. It was a cold, chilling, gusting wind, a cutting wind, and I shrugged into a Gore-Tex shell and the backpack, picked up the flintlock rifle, and started walking into the Mokelemne Wilderness.

There was a spectacular full moon almost directly overhead. Venus was radiant. The broad band of the Milky Way reached across the sky and I reflected that it was invisible in Salinas, washed away by light pollution. Here, the sky was ablaze. My legs were cold in the wind. Small puffs of black clouds, windblown, seemed to tumble east across the brilliant stars.

My headlamp provided a small disk of illumination of the trail ahead as I walked into a dark grove of lodge pole pines. They were roaring in the wind, branches clattering. Granite slabs on the path, the visible remnants of the old gold rush era dam which had created the lake. I realized dimly that if I continued hiking like this, I would eventually walk down into Grover Hot Springs State Park, and I didn't want to face the treacherous descent in the dark. So I would camp on the far side of the meadow, before the trail started down. Here I was at about 9,000-foot elevation. Relatively high up. I could feel the altitude in my lungs.

I walked out of the trees, and onto the spongy footing of the alpine meadow. The trail was grooved into the field, clear in the moon and starlight. Suddenly I saw a dark form out of the corner of my eye, racing out of the trees, a dog? A very large dog? Running straight for me. A bear.

I don't like to carry flintlock rifles loaded. Loading a flintlock is a laborious process. The black powder attracts moisture, like salt. That promotes a wet, unusable charge, and it creates rust. Flintlocks are a bitch to clean: you have to scrub them with soap and hot water. At the moment, my rifle was utterly unloaded. And the bear was 200 yards away, now 150 yards away, closing at a flat-out run.

Encumbered by the backpack, I snatched a plastic charger tube full of black powder from the shoulder bag, ripped off the rubber lid with my teeth, and poured the powder down the barrel. Some of the powder went down. The frigid wind blew the rest away. I let the plastic cylinder drop into the darkness, fumbled for a cloth patch, a lead ball, a short starter to push the ball into the barrel, quickly, quickly, adrenaline surging. Ramrod: pound the lead ball down hard, hard and hard again. Replace ramrod, rifle up, charge the pan with the small brass loader, frizzen down, cock the hammer. Fast. Fast.

I let myself look up finally, in time to see the bear race past me, perhaps ten feet away, rushing past then curving away at a full run, a frolicking giant dog. I began to wonder whether I was truly in danger or witnessing something else.

Now here it came again. I shouldered the rifle. In the moonlight, I could barely center the front sight into the rear notch. The chill wind was making me unsteady, gusting into my back, pushing my aim away from the rushing animal. I could hear the bear panting like a bellows, running with all the heart it possessed.

It ran past me again as I tracked it with my shouldered rifle, and arched away yet again. An animal possessed. Perhaps an animal with rabies. Or, perhaps, a giant Labrador dog romping euphorically on Carmel beach.

As it curved around yet again and began to return I could see its white teeth and its gleaming eyes. Seen dimly, it appeared to be smiling. A large, happy, 400-pound pet.

I began to continue down the trail, rifle at high carry, as the bear circled around me again, and again, and again. All the way across the moonlit meadow, stepping over the tiny creek, with the bear circling the entire time. When I set up my small dome backpacking tent, the bear stood and watched, occasionally spinning on its own paws, frantic from sheer energy.

Should I get inside the tent or continue to watch the bear? To the north and east, looking into the wind, I could see a black wall of cloud approaching, blotting out the stars. I was beginning to chill. I should get warm. So I took the bear canister of food—MREs—from my backpack, slung my Jaeger rifle, and carried the plastic bear-resistant can about 50 yards from the tent and set it down. I wasn't hungry.

At some point during the night the storm hit, and the rain came down in sheets. My four-season tent bent with the force. I realized that perhaps camping in the high Sierra in late October alone wasn't the wisest plan. Weather reports in these mountains were fickle, after all. Snow would be easier, but wet like this could kill. I needed to stay dry.

I checked my watch. 2 a.m. I pictured Jerome and Angelica, warm in bed, warm in each other's arms, making love, perhaps for the second time tonight, in a hotel room in San Francisco or Carmel, the luxurious hotel room that only a very rich man could afford. Spanish Bay, La Playa in Carmel. A second time. I was aware that perhaps I was perceiving a torrid sexual need, which did not exist. That made me smile.

The rain poured down. Deafening. Somewhere in the distance there was thunder. Unbidden, my thoughts returned to Jerome and Angelica. They might take a shower together, the soap making their bodies slippery, hands gliding across each other as they embraced and the warm water cascaded down their nakedness. All I wanted in life. Warmth, love, peace.

It was very dark in the tent. But I could make out the shape pushing the fabric in, in, in, almost to breaking. Wind? A loud snort and a fetid smell of carrion filled the tent. It was the bear. The bear was pushing into my tent.

I shouted, I smashed it in the nose. The bulge disappeared. Then it returned. Bigger than before, snorts and stench from outside, the bear leaned down on me. The carbon fiber tent poles bowing and bending unbelievably. This bear was going to eat me like an egg. Crunchy on the outside, soft on the inside. I smashed it again through the nylon, and I could feel the teeth and fur through the fabric, and through my gloves.

To hell with this. I would take this discussion outside. Headlamp on. I crammed my Randall Bowie knife into the elastic waist band of my long underwear, where it promptly began to slide down my leg between my skin and the fabric. I picked up the flintlock rifle and stepped into the storm.

The full freezing wind hit me full in the face, and the rain covered my glasses. I put my hand over the flintlock action. There was the bear: only 10 feet away. Wet. Breath steaming, great clouds of steam, eyes reflecting the headlamp.

It clicked its jaws.

I raised the rifle up to aim between the bear's eyes.

The bear stepped forward, jaws snapping. It huffed. It arched its back.

The rain was going to get into the charge, and make the rifle misfire. If I was going to shoot, I needed to shoot now. It was now, or never.

I aimed the rifle ten feet over the bear, into the dark, wind-battered trees. I pulled the trigger. I heard the hammer drop. The frizzen snapped forward. Nothing happened.

— Chapter 20 —

The prime was already wet. The wind blew whatever was dry into my face.

I stood there immobile.

The bear looked at me through the steam of its own breath. It seemed mildly disgusted. It snapped once more, halfheartedly, as though this was a required part of the performance.

I thought to myself, I can't even shoot over a bear. I groped for the Bowie knife and discovered it had slid inside my long underwear down past my knee, unreachable. So I grabbed the muzzle end of the still-loaded Jaeger rifle, and raised it up like a club, Daniel Boone at the Alamo, last stand.

Nothing happened. The bear stood on its four legs and looked at me. It seemed bored. It looked around as though something out there in the dark might be more interesting.

The rain was freezing me, soaking through, and reaching down into my groin and armpits, chilling me through. I thought, suddenly, there is too much loss in this world. Overwhelming confusion. So much rejection. Frustration. If I must die, what a great place to die. Right here, right now, I cannot bear this anymore. I cannot bear another second of this.

I shouted, I screamed, "GOD! TAKE ME NOW! TAKE ME NOW! TAKE ME NOW!"

The roaring wind carried the words away. I could barely hear myself. The rain poured down. I was shivering now, teeth chattering, body shaking. The bear looked at me as though I was puzzling, as though it was a pampered basset hound and I, its owner, had just said something in baby talk, mildly embarrassing, profoundly incomprehensible. Then it sat down, like a dog.

Chapter Twenty-one

October 2012

The sunlight pouring yellow and blue through the fabric of the tent woke me up. I came awake immediately, with a shock, somehow grasping, reaching for Angelica, wondering where she was. Of course she was not with me. The adrenaline surged: she was with Jerome in Cancun, La Playa, San Francisco, or perhaps Oakland.

I lay there in my sleeping bag. The memories of the past night came back. The cold. The shivering. The creeping hypothermia, the soaking icy wetness, retreating into the tent, shivering, cold, and then unconsciousness. The sunlight was full now. I looked over at the flintlock rifle, laying on the tent floor propped on my muddy boots. The black snot of the wet black powder prime drooled down the side of the gun barrel with a tracery of orange rust. I was too tired to react to that. I just looked at it.

The sleeping bag was warm. Angelica was with Jerome. The pain of that, the weakness of that, the embarrassment of that . . . that I should be so old, so lost, so alone, here in this tent, wet, with the sunlight streaming in through the fabric onto such emptiness.

And yet. And yet the light was beautiful. The day outside must be marvelous.

I fumbled into my backpack, found a plastic garbage bag full of dry clothes and changed into dry polypropylene fleece long underwear. My sleeping bag itself was wet, and my abdominal muscles cramped as I pulled the fresh clothes onto my chilled body. Finally, I pulled myself into a sitting position, laced up my boots and stepped into the brilliant morning light.

The alpine meadow lay steaming, glowing around me, crisp cool, wet from last night's rain.

The sun behind me in the cloudless deep blue sky created a sharp shadow of my image on the ground before the tent. I raised an arm. The shadow raised an arm. The shadow on the rain-flattened meadow grass was sharp as a cutout silhouette. I watched it. I wiggled my fingers, and watched the shadow fingers move. I let my arm fall. The shadow arm dropped abruptly.

My breath was steaming. I watched the cloud as I exhaled dissipate into nothing. Just like that. I had to smile, just a little. And then...then I had to laugh. The absurdity of my situation was too bizarre for my sense of humor to ignore.

There was nobody else camping here. I was at the edge of the meadow, by the trees, where the ground rose into rocky outcrops then into the tops of mountains, here, so high, so green, so blue. There were sparse lodge pole pines up the slopes, thin brown trunks, patchy limbs with short needles, midget inadequate cones littering the ground around them.

On the closest tree, a tiny stubby gray nuthatch bird, a grey egg-shaped ball of feathers, hopped straight down the trunk, distaining gravity, probing the bark for insects. I could hear it scratching when I listened.

Silence. I listened more carefully. Pine branches rattling in the slight wind in the trees higher up. Somewhere a jay was squabbling over something. Crisp air. Clear as glass forever. A blue, blue cloudless sky.

Across the meadow, around 50 yards away, a brown rock stirred. The bear. I felt a sudden pulse of adrenaline, then realized that I didn't care. I had let go of fear, somehow. The hunger for Angelica was so great that it filled me, coated me inside into my fingertips, my toes. I thought of her with Jerome. But what could I do about any of that?

I could be here. I could be here in my mud and wetness and sunshine and pine trees, and I could simply love, in my own way, and let Jerome love in his, and accept whatever God wanted.

— Honor —

Oh, that hurt. It felt like the ground opened up.

But then I could guess that regardless of his wealth Jerome had never had a pet bear, a pet ordesh in my mother's language. Ordesh. That made me smile. I had to grin: old, tired, alone, cold, wet, and feeling quite sorry for myself, I had nevertheless had an astounding adventure. I had been here. Joy. I am here.

The bear got to its feet. It was muddy, wet, steaming, bedraggled. It seemed tired and resigned, like me. It began to walk towards me. Bring it, I thought. I can heat some tea. We can both sit down for a cup of Tetley's and discuss the night.

Then the bear circled around, far from me, apparently a bit jaded by the teasing nature of our relationship, and began to walk the trail back to Burnside Lake. I watched its muddy rear end waddle down the trail for minutes before it disappeared in the pines on the far side of the meadow.

I leaned into the tent and packed my wet gear into my backpack. It would take hours of drying at home to keep all this from mildewing. With everything damply packed, I put the bear canister of food on top within the pack, pulled the drawstrings closed, set the pack upright against a nearby pine tree and leaned the flintlock rifle against it. I paused, walked to a nearby low shelf of rock.

From a bellows pocket in my pants, I removed a blue plastic soap dish lined with hand-cut squares of sponge sleeping pad. I opened it. Nestled in the foam were three hand-knapped glass spear points, each about two inches long. Nowadays I knapped them in my backyard flower bed, up against the fence where the deboutage and spall couldn't cut playing children, while I sat on a plastic lawn chair in the shade of a walnut tree.

One arrow point was made from the glass of a blue Welsh water bottle, from a trip full of loving memories which Margaret and I had made to Stinson Beach during our married time. I sat down on a rock, and forced Angelica from my mind. I picked out the blue arrow point and raised it to the sky in the palm of my hand. I forced myself to pray the way I had been taught as a child. Thank you, God for everything. Thank you, God for my

— Chapter 21 —

life. Thank you, God, for Margaret, for my children, including Cesar and Rose, for Angelica, and for Jerome. That last part came hard.

And thank you for the bear. Ordesh. The teaching bear. Nitaatik pesache. I accept stewardship of what you bring into my life. Make my life worthy. Open me to the Holy Spirit so I might change, might become better, might serve You better.

Then I placed a glass arrow point on a small rock nearby. It would remain here until someone found it. As it should be.

Before beginning the hike, I pulled the ramrod from the flintlock rifle, and screwed a threaded unloading tool onto the brass-tipped end. The loaded patched ball, packed deeply and firmly over the powder, came out with difficulty, but finally I was able to pull it free and pour most of the clumped, sodden black powder from the barrel onto the ground. Somewhere I had read that it was fertilizer. I began to throw the used, screw-damaged lead ball into the trees but then changed my mind-it was a souvenir of something unbelievable-so I slipped it into a bellows pocket of my BDU pants.

Then I pulled on the wet backpack, slung the unloaded flintlock Jaeger rifle, wet black powder smearing down the stock from the lock pan. Then I followed the bear back to the XTerra, and drove towards home.

As I drove past Kirkwood, heading downhill and west towards the coast and home, cell phone coverage returned. Ping after ping came from my phone as a cluster of text and phone messages downloaded all at once. I pulled over the XTerra, into the parking lot of the old Kirkwood log cabin. There were at least twenty text messages from Marta, Angelica's conservative Filipina sister.

"Where have you taken my Angelica? I have Cesar and Rose and they miss their mother."

Another: "She said she was going to work overnight at Heritage Bay Eldercare to take care of a patient but she is NOT ANSWERING her cell phone. I KNOW SHE IS WITH YOU!"

More: "Sinful man to debauch my sister in the eyes of God! Lying, deceitful, corrupting man!"

"My brother in law is not dead one full year and already you DESTROY his memory!"

And more.

And more.

There was also a text from my son Ernst: "Hi, Dad, I hope your camping trip is going well. Just letting you know that I'm feeding all the chocolate low fat ice cream in the freezer to visiting friends. You might want to pick up more on the way back. ☺"

I texted back to that: "Hope you ate it all. Great trip, coming home wet. I met a nice bear. I love you."

There were five recorded phone messages too, barely intelligible. Heavily accented English, shouts, raised voice, even a "GOD CURSE YOU!" surrounded by the unintelligible Pampangan rant.

I waited to call her back, until I drove through Stockton. Then I parked and dialed. Marta answered instantly. "Where are you?" she shouted.

"I'm not with Angelica," I responded. "I haven't seen her all weekend."

"Liar," she said. "Angelica came and got the children just now and she said that she was at Heritage Bay Eldercare, but I went there last night, at midnight, while Rachaela watched the children, and she was not there. So I KNOW YOU LIE! DEBAUCHER! BLASPHEMER!"

Her voice began to swell over the phone.

"MARTA!" I shouted back. "STOP! I am in the mountains, driving home from a camping trip. I WAS NOT WITH ANGELICA THIS WEEKEND. We should talk. I will be there in two hours."

I hung up the phone, and I did not answer when she called back. I drove two hours to her home, refueling in Los Banos, feeling resigned. I arrived at Marta's home in North Salinas as the sun was setting into the distant unseen ocean to the west.

Marta met me at the door to her large, well-kept family home in North Salinas. I stood there on the doorstep, disheveled in my camping clothing, unshaven, unwashed, sleep-deprived, and slightly damp. She looked me up and down, skeptically. "You smell like mushrooms," she muttered. Clearly, she was angry. Actually, I *did* smell a bit like fungus, since my very wet clothing inside the XTerra had begun to mildew slightly.

Marta made no offer to invite me inside. She simply looked at me, glaring. Actually, I realized, Marta was beautiful when she glared. Her hair was natural black, much longer and fuller than Angelica's. Angelica's hair was tinted. Marta was as small as Angelica, perhaps five feet tall, slightly heavier, but whereas Angelica's clothing was always tightly fitted, Marta was dressed much more conservatively. Right now that felt reassuring.

Marta had arrived in the United States from Pampanga only after Angelica and Tommy were married. When Tommy and Angelica had visited the Philippines with their first child, Cesar, Tommy's close friend Mike had come along to rediscover his partial Filipino roots. Mike had found Marta, and a marriage had resulted. Marta had been in the United States only about five years. So far as I knew, she was utterly devoted to her husband in every way.

At this point, I was shaking. Cold, lack of food, another unnamed hunger. I didn't even try to hide it. Finally, Marta relented. "Take your boots off," she said. "I don't want mud."

I unlaced my boots, slipped them off, and left them on the front step. Yes, they *were* muddy and damp. My thick brown boot socks were wet as well. I left them on anyway. I walked into the home, in my damp socks. As I looked back down at the tiles in the entryway, I saw clear wet footprints behind me on the pristine, cream-colored floor.

Marta led the way into the very neat living room, and motioned for me to sit down on the brown leather couch. There was Mike, her husband, sitting there in the low light, looking slender, Chinese, and dour. But then I had never seen him look any other way. As I turned to sit down I realized that Angelica's cousin Irene was also sitting across the room, in the partial darkness. She was a nurse at Salinas Valley Memorial Hospital, and she was wearing some sort of cotton white coat.

I remembered that these people had always been present when Tommy was ill. Especially Irene and Marta had always been there, always at Tommy's bedside, always quietly serving. They had been through their own fire, hadn't they?

My love for Angelica, while valid, intense, and genuine, was to them an alien presence, a dissonance, an unknown quantity. Indeed, largely unknown. I had no idea what Angelica had told them. I was twenty-one years older than Angelica. From their perspective, I was intrusive, morally suspect, and old. An aged roué.

Marta clicked on a torchiere, and sat down next to Mike. "Tell us where you took Angelica this weekend," she uttered quietly, clipping her words.

"I wasn't with her," I replied.

Quiet. Marta looked at me. She looked at Mike, who stared stoically back at her. Then she looked wordlessly at Irene.

"Where were you?" she asked again.

I explained.

"God will punish you if you lie, Garth. God will DESTROY YOU! If you are debauching my sister during her time of grief, God will PUNISH you!"

Mike moved a slender hand onto his wife's thigh, and seemed to squeeze. Hard, perhaps. Marta looked at him. Then she glared at me. Black eyes. Voluptuous black hair. It was admirable how close she sat to her husband.

"What has Angelica told you about my relationship with her?" I asked quietly.

"Very little. Yet we have eyes. We see your Facebook pictures together. We know you spend nights. This DISRESPECT TOMMY SO MUCH! You are WHITE AMERICAN MAN, AND YOU HAVE NO MORAL! Therefore, we know you lie now. You lie now, and God will punish you."

I looked at Irene and Irene looked steadily back at me. I looked at Marta. She continued to glare. I looked at Mike. He looked

— Chapter 21 —
139

slender and serene. Why would I keep secrets here? These were good people. They were devoted to Tommy and the children, as I aspired to be. If I was guilty of any sin, then let us name it. The home was warm. I realized that a mild smell of composting was emanating from my sock-covered feet.

I opened the photos on my IPhone and handed it to Marta. She sat next to Mike and fingered through the photos, and I could see her eyes widen, illuminated by the light of the phone. There was a sharp intake of breath, and Irene moved around behind Marta, looking over the back of the couch, studying the photos. Her eyes widened as well.

There was nothing risqué in those images. But there were hundreds, literally hundreds, of family photos, Angelica holding my hand, Angelica and I together, Angelica and I at dinner. I realized as I watched them: Angelica had told them nothing at all about me.

"You didn't know we were going out, did you?" I asked.

"She said she was with friends on those nights," Marta responded.

So I told them everything. Everything. How it began, how I was crazy in love with the children, with Angelica, and how Jerome had come into our lives. I burst open like a dropped melon.

"You are SINNER!" shouted Marta.

"Yes," I agreed. "I am a sinner."

Marta looked at me and I could see awareness spread across her face. "Angelica lie to me," she said to the room. "She lie to us, she USE US! We go to her now. I go now to CONFRONT HER SIN! God's will be done."

I shook my head. "No."

"What you mean no? Who are you to say?"

"Angelica is simply hurting. Tommy has been dead nine months. It's been hard. Let's be kind," I responded.

"Oh. MY GOD, SHE SEDUCE YOU! You have sex with my sister? YOU HAVE SEX WITH MY SISTER?" she shouted at me.

I said nothing. I saw her eyes widen in shock, again. "You and your whole family are wonderful people, Marta. I'm not going to lie to you. My relationship with your sister appears to be over, by her own choice. I need to respect that."

Marta exploded. "You white American pig, to debauch my sister. But now, this Jerome, he has her like . . . like a common whore. You will marry her. You admit your sin. But he . . . he is twice a pig. Three times a babuee. Now, I go!"

And she stormed from the room, into the garage, into her car, with Irene chasing after her. Mike remained on the sofa, scowling silently at me. Disappointment. He shook his head at me. Negative. I saw myself out, struggled into my boots on the doorstep, and ran to my own SUV. I could feel the cold damp in my feet.

Chapter Twenty-two

October 2012

I drove behind Marta. She swerved through traffic across the town of Salinas, out onto Highway 68 to the plush subdivisions around the golf course at Corral de Tierra. She was driving an orange Chevrolet Suburban: easy to spot. She pulled up in front of Angelica's home, stormed up to the door, rang the doorbell. I pulled up as I saw her rush inside, Irene close behind, as I parked my own car. The door was left open. I walked in. Loud voices in Kapampangan, raised in the bedroom. Shouting. Screaming. Crying. This was not going well at all. I shucked off my own damp hiking boots in the hallway, still crusted in trail mud. I hurried, slipping and sliding, down the hardwood corridor.

Marta, Irene, and Angelica were in the master bathroom, loud, arms waving, rooster-like, angry, the foreign words running together into one shrieking sound. The lights were bright, and I could see tears coursing down Angelica's cheeks. Cesar and Rose were huddled on the large bed in the adjoining bedroom, holding each other, faces registering shock, looking at the lit bathroom drama. I rushed over to them.

"Hey, kids," I said.

They looked at me, light from the bathroom illuminating the sorrow and fear transforming their faces. This was big.

I tried to comfort them. "Sometimes when people love each other, they disagree. They get loud. Everything will be okay. It's gonna be loud, but we'll all get over it. Okay?"

The children looked at me, immobilized by shock. I thought

to myself that I should shut the door, keep the sight from them.

Irene walked into the bedroom. Behind her, the squabble was getting louder and faster, if that was possible. "Watch the kids," I said as I moved past her towards the light.

She nodded her assent. Suddenly, slapping sounds and screams erupted. I hurried into the bathroom, shutting the door behind me.

Marta and Angelica had each other by the hair. Marta had a few floating strands in her hand. She had pulled them from Angelica's head. Both now had a hand firmly gripping each other's black locks, had twisted each other's heads around and were deliberately aiming slaps at each other's faces. As I watched, Angelica balled her free hand into a fist and brought it down onto Marta. It glanced feebly off Marta's head.

My first impression was to laugh. This was anything but Marine Corps combatives: it seemed almost a parody of physical fighting. It was the Two Stooges. But these two small women were very serious, both with tears running from their eyes, both shouting nonstop in Kapampangan. I moved quickly between them, trying to hug Angelica.

As I enfolded her in my arms, Angelica writhed and swung her fists wildly against me and the empty air. The pace of the shouting continued, and Marta reached over my shoulders to attempt a few halfhearted slaps. Then she stepped back, and Angelica collapsed into my arms sobbing, wailing, and shrieking.

She began gagging, then turned to the toilet and began vomiting. She heaved. I held her hair. The acrid smell of vomit filled the room as Angelica heaved, and heaved again. It was a handicapped toilet, from Tommy's final days. Angelica didn't have to bend down much.

She continued to sob and wail between heaves.

Marta reached around me to touch Angelica. I raised an arm and fended her off, and Marta stood back. Angelica kept her face over the toilet. The heaving gave way to nonstop sobs, then crying, and finally silence. I continued to hold Angelica's head. Her hair.

— Honor —
144

Finally, she slumped back into my arms. I reached around her and flushed the toilet, while avoiding at looking at what was in it. The contents splashed loudly down. As I held Angelica's small body, her breath came in spasms, the mild reek of vomit from Angelica and the vegetal smell of my socks blending. I was aware that I was unwashed, unshaven. Angelica leaned back against me, eyes shut, as Marta watched us eyes wide, disbelieving.

Angelica spoke quietly, almost whispering. "Marta, I will break with Jerome." Her face screwed up and I thought she would cry again. "I will sacrifice for Tommy's memory."

Marta looked at me questioningly. "You will stay?" she asked. I nodded, yes.

Angelica was limp now, her back against my chest, and her head back on my shoulder. "I'm going to move you to the couch in the front room, okay? The kids need the bathroom," I said quietly in her ear. Then I picked her up from the floor, light as air. She kept her eyes shut, and I rolled her in my arms so that her face pressed against my shoulder.

I was melting with affection for her. It had changed somehow. It wasn't romantic so much anymore, and the lust was evaporated. It was more simply love, and let go. This was all too different from my own life experience. There was the insanity of loss, and something else, beyond the light of understanding. A part of me wanted to simply get up and walk away. But there was my promise to Tommy, and my own commitment, which I had made, body and soul.

"Marta, please bathe the children, please make sure they are fed, and I will take Angelica to the living room. Please," I whispered.

Marta nodded. I carried Angelica to the couch and held her, cradling her in my arms, and she cried silently, face pressed into the hollow of my shoulder, and her tears soaked my already moist stale camping shirt.

It was about 10 p.m., two hours later at least, when Marta and

Irene crept quietly from the back bedroom. They looked at me, still sitting there, still holding Angelica. I laid her down, went to use the bathroom while they watched over Angelica's huddled form, returned. I settled back into the couch and held Angelica in my arms again. She snuggled in.

"Marta, Irene, I am so sorry. I am so sorry for bringing all this drama into your lives," I whispered. Angelica stayed huddled, face burrowed into my wet shoulder, snuffling slightly. I shifted to become more comfortable. I was aware that I was still damp from camping, and I still smelled vaguely of mildew. Angelica smelled mildly of vomit.

"I think this must happen," said Irene. "Too much sorrow."

Marta reached into a footstool, and pulled out a blanket. She put it over both Angelica and me, and as my eyes welled up, she said, "The children are asleep. Stay here as long as you need."

She and Irene walked to the door.

"Please wait," I whispered loudly. "It's time for me to leave too." I stood up, gently untangling myself, lowering the sleeping Angelica onto the couch, she stirred slightly. I turned and there was Irene with the blanket, which she spread over Angelica.

Marta stood in the doorway, turned to look back in. "Garth," she said, "You are a good man. You are crazy, and you smell like dirt, but you are good."

She paused.

"If you can't control your lusts I expect you to marry Angelica at once."

Lust. Lust was the last thing on my mind. Quiet. A silent awareness of sanctity, of the sacred. A sense that I had horribly trespassed, before. A sense that I was committed to this family in several ways. A sense that here was a path I had chosen to walk, and I should walk it, and try to harm no more. Harming no more meant leaving, letting Angelica sort out her grief and her need for Jerome.

I didn't respond to the comment. I simply walked to my XTerra, and drove away. Smelling deeply of mildew, and thinking of bears.

— Honor —

Chapter Twenty-three

October 2012

Halloween. Francesca was with Margaret, at her parent's home, dressing as "Silverlight," apparently one of the fairies in a children's movie. That night I made a special effort to focus, pull myself past my own hunger, to be present for Francesca. Margaret and I stolidly walked the streets in the dark, beneath stars and moon, as Francesca and her neighborhood friends ran laughing from home to home in our neighborhood begging for sweets. Jack was manning the door at the condo, handing out candy, and we visited him there. Margaret was a cat in a room full of dogs, moving slowing around me, never looking at me, always studying something at the edge of darkness.

We visited my mother, Margaret's parents, and our shared friends. Halloween lights of orange and yellow. Chill darkness, so cold our breath was steaming. Walking with Margaret on sidewalks, Margaret smiling for Francesca's sake, all attention turned toward the laughing girls who orbited around us. Francesca was a fairy, and she was five years old, when it was real for her. Real, and good.

Afterwards, when Margaret had taken Francesca skipping to her gray Honda sedan, then to her bed at the condominium, I walked home alone in the night. Only the teenagers were out roaming now, the younger children were all home with their piles of loot. I left the front door shut, I sat down on my front steps next to a lit Jack o' lantern, Francesca's artwork. I sat on the cold, smooth cement step of my small, run-down home and felt the chill rise into my butt through my jeans and I looked at the stars beyond the avocado tree.

I lifted the Jack o' lantern's lid. The invisible smell of roasted pumpkin swirled up out of the hollow squash and embraced me. For a short moment I shut my eyes and let the smell have its way, the childhood memories and the memories of my own older children's Halloweens. I missed them at their younger ages. Before the tall buildings collapsing, and the flames.

But those older children were mostly grown now, out somewhere in town and the world pursuing the joys of young people in their twenties. I was sitting here alone in the dark on this small cold front step, which had once echoed with their childish laughter. Still, they were happy. That was a serene thought.

Then I looked at the stars. Somewhere, Angelica was out there, probably with Jerome. All the brandy on earth wasn't going to wash that reality away.

Fail fast, fail cheap, fail quick. Easier said than done.

The next morning the stock market was up again. Valuations were high. A 1987-style event was unlikely unless some big news, such as rising interest rates, triggered a downturn. Meanwhile biotech and technology were on the rise.

According to the news, the war in Iraq was essentially over. The war in Afghanistan continued with two more unnamed American dead. Opinion columns in the *Wall Street Journal* and other magazines—I was reading old copy—were ranting about the death of the US ambassador in Libya at the hands of Islamic radicals the previous month. It all seemed so far away. It was so quiet here. More importantly, apparently, a starlet had coated her naked rear end with baby oil and posted a nude selfie. I saw the picture. It was indeed a capacious backside. Apparently, this was the new defining moment of fame for rising young women.

Iraq was another place, somebody else's war, fought by someone else's husbands and wives, someone else's sons and daughters. On the walls of my office were my children's art works, framed. A Cossack sashka sword with a Nazi swastika on the hilt, probably fake, leaned in the corner with a giant pair of wooden skis from the nineteenth century. No military pictures of me were visible at all in my office. No evidence. That was better. It was soothing somehow.

The phone rang and Lanie answered. "It's for you!" she said loudly from the adjoining office. "Globalbank! Angelica's mortgage!"

What was I to do? Angelica was with Jerome now, but I had promised to protect her. I felt the ice in my chest. I put on the headset and pushed on the line.

"Good morning," I said.

"Good morning, Mr. Ericson?" said the young man's voice on the other end of the phone.

"Are you the trustee of the Narcisco Trust?" asked the voice.

"I am," I responded. "How may I help you?"

"I'm calling to let you know that we've rejected your petition for a HAMP mortgage modification," said the voice. "We need an application signed by Thomas P. Narcisco."

"Hmmmm. May I ask to whom I am speaking?" I asked, my adrenaline surging.

"I am Samir," said the voice. "It doesn't really matter. What matters is that we can't accept the application without the signature of the trustor, who signed the mortgage, Thomas P. Narcisco."

"Samir, Thomas P. Narcisco is deceased. He's dead. He's been dead for months," I replied.

"Yes, Mr. Ericson, I understand. Nevertheless, we require his signature. Is there any possible way you might obtain it?"

I sat there. Perhaps I hadn't heard correctly.

"Samir, Thomas P. Narcisco is deceased, and his remains have been cremated. He is dead. He's been dead for nine months. That's why the widow is applying for a restructuring. She now exists on a small pension and social security, and she needs a HAMP mortgage modification to continue to live in the home. How do we do that?"

"Yes, Mr. Ericson, I understand. However, we cannot accept your signature, or that of Angelica C. Narcisco. We need

Thomas P. Narcisco to sign the documents. Perhaps you could ask him to sign the documents?"

"I can't see how that's possible," I responded quietly.

"Then perhaps you could call me in his presence and he can give me his verbal authorization? Yes, that would be acceptable. Please call me back and let me speak with Thomas P. Narcisco. When should I expect your call?"

"Samir . . . ," I paused. I was dumbfounded. "Where are you calling from?"

"I am calling from Globalbank," the voice responded flatly.

"Where, geographically?" I asked.

"I'm calling from India," said Samir.

"Samir, here's the deal: here in America, the dead can't sign documents, and they can't talk. At least as far as I've heard. I've never heard a dead person talk. Have you?"

There was a pause.

"Well, Mr. Ericson," said the voice. "In that case we have no alternative but to foreclose on the property immediately. Our foreclosure division will contact you at once."

"It's not going to happen," I responded, and terminated the call.

I phoned Angelica. She wouldn't answer the phone. I had Lanie call her on her cell phone. Angelica answered.

"She said she doesn't want to hear from you ever again," said Lanie.

Ouch.

"You are to leave her alone," emphasized Lanie.

"I understand," I said. "But let her know that if Globalbank calls, they should talk with me first."

Chapter Twenty-four

February 2013

Our oldest daughter Sarah was twenty-three and a college graduate, and she was marrying Osten, a Norwegian exchange student whom she had met at the University of California at San Diego. She had studied finance. He had studied theoretical economics, AKA, the stuff that doesn't work. I pondered that. Marxism versus capitalism. They seemed to hit it off rather well.

Osten seemed affable, large, extremely blond. There was a presence in him, a silent combed-hair looming Nordic superiority. He tolerated Salinas, California, and the United States in a bemused, European sort of way. Now he stood by the altar in a white tuxedo, his full, reddish-blonde hair shining, looking down the aisle at us as my first-born daughter and I paced towards him as rehearsed, in time to the soaring organ music: Pachelbel's Canon in D, with variations. The same music Margaret and I had chosen for our own wedding so long ago. I wondered if perhaps Sarah had discussed that with Margaret.

We were at our own ancestral church, our own First Presbyterian Church, the original building on Padre Drive, off Acacia, built in 1954, the year I was born. It was a beautiful old red brick, dark oak, stained-glass window church, capacity about three hundred, as close to an archaic cathedral as Salinas possesses. This was where Sarah had attended preschool, and the elementary school night program, JYC, Junior Youth for Christ, and later the high school group. The builder had been my grandfather. He once told me, shortly before his death at age ninety-five, that if there was ever a nuclear war, head for that church. Poured concrete and rebar and brick: it was not only a church, it was a bomb shelter.

He had also told me that when he had finished building that great pile, he had climbed up on the roof one last time, seventy feet in the air. He had stood gazing down at our then-small town and wondered what his grandson's life would be like, and asked God that I should see his love in this building, this monument.

Now here I was, his grandson, now so many years past birth, at the marriage of his great-granddaughter who remembered my grandfather only dimly from her infancy. As he had hoped, I was thinking of him. I wondered if somehow, he could see us all. So much of our life had been right there, in that red brick church. Most of us now attended weekly service at the new warehouse, on Main Street, and the old church, the masterpiece of stained glass and polished wood, had been largely forgotten.

There was a hot branding iron in the center of my solar plexus, that burn of missing Angelica, wondering where she was, with her millionaire. Then I silently rebuked my thoughts. Thanksgiving, Christmas, so many empty days and nights, all had come and gone. I had pretended so well. I had taken the family skiing in January. I had shared their joy. All the time there had been part of me somewhere else, unknown to everyone around me. Oh, God, by all that is holy, let me be present at least for my daughter's wedding.

Nobody could see the loss in me, so far as I could tell. I worked so hard to appear as though life was perfect. But still, I wondered, it was almost a year since Tommy's death. I thought of him every day. It was time enough for Angelica and Jerome to marry.

I walked the very beautiful bride, Sarah, with her kick-ass attitude to life, her own Euro-contempt merely embryonic at this young age, down the aisle to her waiting groom. She was beautiful in a fitted ivory, lace-covered dress, full gauze veil, and a very moderate satin train. Dr. Latham had been our pastor throughout Sarah's entire life, and before. Now he gazed serenely at me from the altar, possibly wondering how we had both gotten so old, or perhaps wondering what had happened to my intact Christian family. He was still slender, handsome, and authoritative in his clerical collar. He didn't ask me who gave this woman to be married. He didn't have to ask. He simply smiled and nodded at me. Okay, Garth. Your time is up.

I kissed Sarah on the cheek, stepped back, and expected her to simply turn to Osten. Instead she turned to me, smiled, and reached up and straightened my black bow tie. She kissed me on the cheek, and hugged me, and whispered in my ear, "Thank you, I love you."

I stood there for a few seconds awkwardly, my black tuxedo amidst the white of my sons and Osten and Sarah, with Francesca as the flower child, somehow unwilling to let her step forward into her new life with my throat tight and a smile glued on my face. Then she turned on her own and took her place besides Osten, and faced Dr. Latham. Dr. Latham smiled and nodded at me, as if to say, okay, Garth, your time is really up now.

I turned to walk back to my seat. I noticed the people. So many. There were about three hundred people in that church, about as much as the church could legally hold. Of course my mother was there, right behind us, walker folded, smiling benignly as I turned away from the altar. I could see my daughter's boss, a prominent candidate for sheriff. Sarah was working as a political consultant now, as well as serving on my corporate board of directors. There were my childhood friends, and newscasters with whom I had done television financial reports, and so many, many people who had known me such a long, long time. All the faces looking at me, or past me, to the radiance of Osten and Sarah. Where they should be looking.

I went back into the oaken pews in the first row, and I sat down next to Margaret. She was crying at the sight of her oldest daughter marrying.

Jack was not there. I had heard childish rumors from Francesca during her time with me, comments about Mommy crying,

Mommy alone, and Jack's clothes gone. He was gone from my own family, thank you very much. Why he was gone remained a mystery.

Margaret looked shocked, devastated, pale. She was carefully groomed, every hair in place, very formal in a deep, almost black, purple which contrasted perfectly with her brunette hair.

I looked at her. She looked at the ceremony with her lips and chin slightly quivering. I looked up at the altar. There was Dr. Latham, working his magic again, somehow drawing light into the room. The whole tableaux seemed illuminated. Our two sons lined up in their white tuxedos—white, for all that is holy, they looked like milkmen. I thought our oldest, Wallace, now a sergeant in the air force, should have worn his blues. However, that would have spoiled the Euro-symmetry of the presentation, so there was twenty-three year-old Wallace wearing white with the rest of them. And there was Osten, thick, billowing gold-red hair, pink skin, white smile, all in white, as he placed a golden ring on our beloved daughter's hand.

Sarah insisted that the reception be in the First Presbyterian Church gymnasium, where we had played, danced, and attended Bible study since she could toddle across the laminated wooden floor. We had the best food for such a situation, catered by a local Italian restaurant, Gino's. Industrial white-aproned food servers sliding foil trays of heated cannelloni and blackened chicken Alfredo onto tables against the wooden walls, onto hot, stainless-steel steam trays waiting to receive them. Good food. A place full of memories and love.

The food was served by high school students who were raising money for their mission trip to Mexicali. That was a nice touch by Sarah and Osten, I thought. Pointing my money in the right direction.

There were toasts. Long, rambling, youthful toasts. I heard from several Norwegian groomsmen of Osten's drinking exploits, when he had apparently confessed his undying love for Sarah, and then passed out. I heard again from a white-dressed dreadlocked bridesmaid of how Sarah flipped a raft during her time as a guide on the American River when she was talking about her distant Norwegian love, Osten.

I thought of Angelica: her visor, or perhaps her straw hat, her white smile, how she would look as a bride. My bride? No, that was impossible now. She was with Jerome. I had a stab of adrenaline. No, I would not think of that. At all.

I looked across the gymnasium. Hundreds of shining, smiling faces, genuine love, genuine connection with this event, this love, this joining. I was in a sea of agape, an ocean of love, and I was dying of thirst. What insanity. My insanity.

The ceremony of new life and new love continued. Eventually we came to the dancing, and there was the first dance shared between the bride and the groom. Some sort of slow music. I can't remember. Osten danced like a well-rehearsed bear. Sarah was her own aggressive self, chafing at the lead, and I thought that this was going to be an interesting relationship. As their faltering two-step progressed, Osten churned the turns like he was stirring cake mix, and Sarah spun out ahead of him, leading him in all but name. Interesting indeed.

Then there was my dance with Sarah, and I thought to myself, how am I here? How did life go by like this? I am bald, wrinkled, and single, although still fit, and once I danced with my own bride Margaret in this same place, when I had a full head of brown hair, and Margaret . . . well she pretty much looked then as she looks now, only she was in white then, and as young as Sarah is today. Time is an implacable, unrelenting bitch.

Then it was my turn to perform. I led Sarah, once a baby in this very room, across the polished basketball court into a swirling foxtrot. She was so beautiful. She was athletic from her years of competitive running, her years of ballet, and her work as a rafting guide. Our family enthusiasm for dance had somehow taken root in her and she danced with me with the perfect blend of following my lead and creating her own style. After her slow first dance with Osten, our foxtrot was lively and fast, as she herself had been when a child. We finished and Osten was waiting there patiently, standing straight, and looking slightly bored, all blond and white, with his arm out, ready to escort his bride to their table.

Instead, Sarah pulled him out onto the dance floor as the guests surged out of their chairs to join them. In that pause in the music, the bee-buzz of guests milling and talking, I found myself facing Margaret, who in all truth I had hoped to avoid. But it was as though other hands and the press of bodies pushed us together, two floating wood chips in the current of a stream.

There was another urge to push through the people around me and escape. She was the last person I wished to dance with: pale, wan, opaque, clearly distraught and distracted. I looked at her from a vantage point of emotional distance, viewing her as another man's woman, still beautiful. Still Margaret. She was the mother of my four children. I let myself step forward to her hand, and ask, quietly, formally, may I have this dance? As though we had never met. I managed a slight classic bow. She nodded her head in agreement. Forced smile.

Unexpectedly, the next song was a waltz. Playing a waltz for Margaret was like showing a rabbit to a greyhound. As the second stanza echoed across the room, I felt my own arms come up involuntarily, into a classic form, my left hand joining with hers, and I felt Margaret lean back against my hand, her steps matching my own, inviting my lead, my command. Oh my.

That waltz was in me, too, from our years together. I could not resist. I stepped into her as she stepped back, and we were away, turning, moving together into the music and we were alone in a world of our own, and she was turning into a full six-beat classic ball-room turn, arm outstretched as though she would fly away from me. I stepped into her, I brought her back, and we flew across that unseen dance floor as though we had never been apart. The waltz carried us, as it always had, and we were one. Just one. No time. No space. No pain. No hurt. No war. No kids. All one. Just one. All the time she was daring me with her movements, teasing me with her almost precognitive ability to predict my next step. I put us into a promenade and she matched every move I made, daring me for more. Another six-count wide sweeping turn and the music ended with one last coming together. She was in my arms again.

I bowed instinctively to her, smiling, and she curtsied to me, smiling back. We both woke up, startled into reality by the silence, the absence of the music. We were in a gymnasium, the same gymnasium in which we had waltzed at our own wedding.

Somehow, two decades and more had slipped away. We looked at each other, shocked. I had to glance around the room to make sure that I was here. Friends we had known for years were watching us, and smiling.

The next song, the next few bars of music, shocked Margaret and me together. I saw her eyes widen as the first few saccharine strings of "When I Fall in Love" by Nat King Cole began to play. Margaret stepped back, attempted to pull away. For some reason I would not let that happen. I drew her into me, almost harshly, and she made a few mild attempts to pull away before she surrendered into my arms for a slow enfolding two step, barely a dance at all. She began to cry, to sob, and I didn't know what to do.

Margaret pressed her cheek up against my ear. "You don't understand," she whispered.

A few months ago, I would have insisted that yes, I *did* understand. This time I just whispered into her ear. "Perhaps. Tell me."

Her tears were making my cheek wet, and my face was beginning to stick to hers. That was uncomfortable. However, I didn't want to move away. It was *our* song, after all, our song; we had danced to it at our wedding, and at my departure for the Marines.

She was quiet then, cheek pressed against mine. I wanted to pull my head back to break the bond, but somehow, I didn't. The music, the words, we were barely moving, and I remembered all those nights when the children were babies, so many babies, and they would somehow finally all sleep, and we would dance to the unseen song of our marriage, "When I Fall In Love." So we stood there, barely moving.

I looked up, feeling the suction of tears against my cheek. There were Osten and Sarah, wrapped together. There were Wallace and his wife, Alexis, dancing wrapped together. There was Francesca baltering around the room. She did that when she was happy.

Margaret and I stepped apart awkwardly. "Please tell me what I don't understand," I said softly to her.

Margaret's eyes filled with tears and she looked away.

"Jack . . . Jack has commitment problems."

I instantly controlled my face, kept it still, fighting back a blasting guffaw, which would instantly destroy our emotional connection. Jack, my home-wrecking friend, apparently had commitment problems. I wrestled my face into submission. Ten-count breathing, just like in sniper school. Keep it light, dimmer switch to medium, no expression.

"He has commitment problems?" I wanted to roar that at her. We were still holding each other instinctively. Not cheek to cheek, but our arms still around each other.

"Yes," she responded without a hint of awareness of the irony. "He says he's fallen out of love with me. He says he's in love with Terry." She wiped her eyes. "He says he loves me, but he's not *in* love with me. He's *in* love with Terry now. He wants me . . . he wants me to be cool about it."

"Who is Terry?" I asked. Straight face. Oh, please God. Please, ancestors, please keep my mouth shut.

"Terry is a receptionist at Jack's office. He met her . . . he says he met her when she came there seeking a clerical job. Something." She waved her hand dismissively.

"How could he fall out of love with you? I don't understand. Sorry, but you're a catch," I said, just to be nice.

Margaret was a person of substance, of depth. I really *couldn't* understand it. Her eyes widened and anger spread across her face.

"Terry is just taking him because she can. I know that kind of woman. If you can drive a man crazy and if you can own a man, why not?"

— Honor —

I wanted to ask what Terry had done to drive Jack crazy. The thought made me uncomfortable. That a woman could drive a man crazy with just sex.

Margaret went on, "I've met her, she goes to In Shape Fitness when I'm there sometimes. She treats men like walking, talking toys. She goes through them like batteries. She turns them on until they run out of juice."

I considered that. I wanted to ask: why denigrate the man who worships your body, who regards your physical form as a flesh-made temple, who considers your advice as a subject of serious regard? Why do you want a man who is a breathing recreational vehicle? Why not a man who literally cannot live without you, instead of a man who will think of you only whenever he's bored? Why would Terry live like that?

I said nothing. I looked up. Somehow, I had stopped hearing the music. But it was still playing: when I refocused my mind, I heard Bruce Springsteen, "Dancing In The Dark."

I watched everyone dancing. A good song. A good beat. Not about love at all though. Margaret was talking, continuing to vent, and I turned my attention back to her.

"I don't understand how I didn't see the signs, didn't see it happening. My friend Jane, remember her? At our wedding? She once told me that men are like horses, you ride them hard, and then change them when they falter, and pick another from the herd. Then you repeat."

"That doesn't sound like a successful lifestyle to me," I said quietly.

She was silent for a moment as we danced.

"Why did Jack pick Terry? Why not me?" She began to cry.

I held her and we shuffled. Not really dancing, not even in time to the music. Just holding each other. This felt much too intimate to me. I wondered what Angelica was thinking, where she was right now. She was probably with Jerome.

We are all insane, I thought.

I just held Margaret. Not cheek-to-cheek but just looking in her eyes, like we once did so frequently. It wasn't that we intentionally did that, it was just habit, while dancing and while doing everything else. While washing dishes. While making love. We just looked at each other. She had very unusual eyes, hazel with genuine gold flecks. So many memories raced through my mind. We had been partners, not just a couple. Everything. Babies. Business. Dancing. Running. Shooting, everything.

I wanted to say something comforting. Why? I don't know. Margaret had broken my soul. Jack had destroyed me. His involvement in the birth of my daughter had torn me in half, left my spirit dismembered. I should bray in her face like a donkey. I should recite how she had cheated and lied. But I was just so tired of all that.

"Are you sure you have this right?" I asked her. I instantly regretted that, but I had to backstop it, I had to support it. "Jack has really run off with Terry?"

"Garth, you magnificent fool...you believe the best in everyone," she said.

She continued, choking, "He told me himself, just as I have told you."

We were now simply holding each other and swaying slightly, barely a pretense at dancing.

"People make mistakes in the passion of the moment," I said. "Jack will probably be back."

"Garth . . . there's something about Jack you should know," said Margaret, leaning against me. I prepared myself emotionally. She was going to say he was magnificent, he was wonderful at making love, he was a superb father to Francesca.

"He doesn't *do* anything. He just watches," she said.

That was unexpected. I fought my urge to question aggressively. "Tell me more," I said.

"He just watches. You know how you and I camped? Our shooting competitions? Our hikes? Our Maui? Our horse riding with the kids? All that? Well, Jack *said* he was going to do that. He did shoot with me a few times, but you know, just blasting. He just watches football, baseball. He's good with the boys, he cheers them on. He can fix *anything.*"

— Honor —
160

"I can scarcely change the oil on a car." I laughed.

"I mean, when I was expecting Francesca," she said.

Now I could feel my pulse rising, my breath shortening. Anger. Loss. I had wanted to be there for all those moments, to feel the baby growing, to feel our love. I said nothing.

"Garth, he didn't *do* anything." She was crying again now.

"What do you mean?" I asked quietly. I wanted to scream, "TELL ME! TELL ME!" Inform her how I had died wanting to be with her, had shriveled like dried fruit waiting to participate in that pregnancy.

She went on, a few tears flowing down her cheeks. "He went to one doctor visit, then it grossed him out, and he left, and during every other visit he stayed outside and waited."

"The heartbeat? The ultrasound?" I asked.

I had hungered so deeply for those.

"Oh, he came in for those. The technician went and got him. Then he went right back out. He doesn't have any kids of his own, you know. My belly . . . it sort of grossed him out."

Unexpectedly I felt a jolt of her sorrow pass through me. To have moved her allegiance to this man, and then felt his awareness that the baby inside her was not his.

"He did a great job on the crib, and the bedroom, and he painted everything in the home," she said.

"Men show their love in different ways," I said. "People show their love in different ways."

"Now, now he's really distant. He's always watching TV. He's always preoccupied. He won't show me his phone."

"Well, now he's with Terry," I commented. I regretted the words instantly.

We were still on the dance floor, still barely moving, arms around each other, and she moved into me and put her head on my shoulder and I could feel her sobbing silently.

"I'm sorry, Garth, I'm sorry, I'm sorry," she said. "I'm sorry I didn't really understand why you left. I didn't really understand why you felt you had to go. I just felt that you left us. I just felt abandoned, and Jack was there, and he really cared about us."

— Chapter 24 —

She was speaking into my padded tuxedo shoulder. I could feel the dampness through the jacket.

"You *are* a hero to me," she added. "You always keep your word, and you always care for the people in your life. I just don't feel in love with you anymore. If I had stayed with you, it would have been a lie."

She raised her head up and looked at me. Hazel eyes, gold flecks. I felt the vast gulf between us again.

"I'm sorry I left you to go to the war. I was doing what I thought was right," I said quietly. "It was a promise I made when I signed up. Against all enemies."

"You never asked me for my opinion about what we should do as a family," she said quietly. Her jaw tensed. When she did that I could see the muscles in her neck stand out. Beautiful.

I realized that Angelica only played at exercising, stayed slim, but not fit. This sleek woman in my arms as we pretended to dance was a proven 10K runner, the real deal. Jack could not run across the parking lot for a six-pack of beer.

"I'm sorry," I said. "What do we do now?"

"Garth, I'm sorry but I love Jack. I don't know why. You and I will never be together, not after all the hardship between us." She put her face back down on my shoulder. "Perhaps God has a new man for me," she added.

"I love you," she said "But I'm not in love with you. God knows I tried for years."

I held her, we moved like amateurs to the music, and Margaret cried silently into the shoulder of my tuxedo. I looked down. The small red rose pinned to my lapel was crushed.

Chapter Twenty-five

March 2013

A few days later, Bull called me at the office. Bull never calls anyone. He certainly hadn't called me for months.

He had been a client, but had abruptly fired me, years before. I had shown him a graph and a spreadsheet detailing his annual spending. I had thought that he should know what he was doing to himself. His spending was consuming his liquid assets. Too many $150,000 elephant hunts. Too many spank-loving girlfriends up in San Francisco. Of course, I hadn't mentioned any of that. I had only placed the color, multiyear line graph on the hexagonal oak table before him. Then I had placed an Excel spreadsheet, an amortization, of his remaining liquid assets quantifying his burn rate. Out of money within fifteen years, and he had been only forty at the time. Of course he had never worked. Oil wells did his work for him.

I had suggested a bit of savings. I had suggested selling his development rights to the back half of the ranch to preserve its wilderness to a land conservation agency. Play up the tiger salamander and the burrowing owls. That would preserve his ranch for him. Then invest the proceeds in plain ol' can't bust 'em diversified mutual funds, away from the risks of fraud and speculation, and live on a 5-percent or even 10-percent annual payout, whatever that was, for the rest of his life. That was more, much more, than any normal person could expect to make as a working professional. And he wouldn't be working.

He had looked at both reports silently, stood up from the table in all his immenseness, and walked out the front door. He had fired me via letter days later. The rest of the story soon emerged at family gatherings; a prestigious New York investment manager, himself a billionaire, flew to Bull's ranch in a helicopter. Annual jetaways to New York for investment meetings. Annual meetings in Hawaii. Bull gently informed me at the time that I wasn't playing in the big leagues at all.

That was before 9/11.

Now he was calling me at work. This was a first. Lanie took the call.

"Gunnar Iversen on line 1," said Lanie from the other room. My tinnitus was screaming as always.

"We should talk," said Bull abruptly, cutting through my greetings.

"Of course," I responded. "Where?"

"Come out here. To Tortuga," he said.

"Business or pleasure?" I asked.

"Family."

"When?" I asked.

"Now."

I looked through the hall at Lanie at her desk. She was working away, beautiful and serene as always. Her husband was a lucky man. But then, unusually for men, he knew that. They had a good relationship. And then there were Bull and me: him single, multimillionaire, no kids. Me, not so wealthy, four kids, scraping the bottom of the barrel for the dregs of relationship skills. Bull, that racist trophy hunting obese misogynist, was my first cousin. Apparently, he needed me. So I would go.

"On the way," I replied.

In March, the hills of the Salinas Valley usually reach the fullness of emerald green before the water from April's rains is finally consumed and the grass—mostly annual grass now— dries up and goes to seed. March is perhaps a good month here. The air is crisp, yet warming, the skies are most often blue, and the cattle are fat. Delayed by the cold and wet of recent winter, the flies and hornets haven't followed their annual Malthusian cycle to maximum Biblical-plague capacity. That usually happens around August or September on a Salinas Valley cattle ranch. So March is splendid. Today the sky was a brilliant blue with a few tiny white clouds, far off and high. The grass in the pastures was still green, still sprouting from the rains of winter.

The gate to the homestead of the Tortuga Ranch was at the very corner of the property. As I stepped out of my XTerra and faced the gate, the low rolling hills of Tortuga Ranch stretched away to my right, dotted by the occasional oil extracting machinery. They looked for all the world like giant bobbing cartoon steel birds. Someone with a sense of humor had painted eyes and beaks on them.

Behind me, to my right, were the strawberry fields, owned by Tortuga but leased out. A strong, steady reliable source of income, I thought. Sure as hell, we weren't ancestral strawberry farmers. Strawberry production was high tech: chemicals and plastic and high fences. In strawberry farming, the land was really just a factory and nothing, absolutely nothing, lived on or in it without the farmer putting it there. I had grown up on a cattle ranch in which man adapted to what nature provided, had always provided, and our footprint had been as minimal as our waistlines.

To my left, over the fence, the pastures were green and completely ungrazed. That was Dos Cabesas Ranch. My childhood home, the home of generations of my ancestors. Still beautiful.

I had gone years avoiding seeing it again. The main gate was a few miles back, a dirt road leading up a valley with a clear creek. Were there still Pacific pond turtles living their whole lives in that creek?

Imagine a childhood lived in and around a creek like that: the smell of sycamores in the heat of summer, the clear water for daily diving and soaking and exploring, horse and boy together.

More childhood memories: on crisp, clear winter mornings, steaming breath, steaming horses, the early green grass frosted with white. We broke up the few inches of surface ice in the creek. As the ice bits floated down stream they were moving

— Chapter 25 —
165

targets and we shot at them with our pistols—mine my grandfather's USMC-marked .45 Colt New Service revolver. Blessed beyond words. I was still adapting to the life change. I was a city man now. Deaf, from all that shooting pre-ear protection.

Across the fence, on the Tortuga Ranch, I saw a lifted red custom pickup, worth literally $100,000, on the dirt access speeding towards me. That would be Bull. Big man, big truck. Round head, I noticed. He hadn't inherited the hair gene either. I looked up the slope at Dos Cabesas. It was a beautiful day. All my special childhood places were out there, across that fence. The creek. Mammary Springs. The Hunter's Cabin. All there, in the bright sunlight.

Bull lumbered out of his giant pickup. He seemed preoccupied. He waved. He opened the gate for me and I drove my XTerra through. I waited in my car. He walked up, leaned down, and spoke into the window,

"Thanks for coming. Let's go to the house."

He continued to walk to his lifted behemoth of a truck, u-turned it in the road, and began driving. I drove after him.

As we rounded the final bend to the house I was stunned. The old home was gone, replaced by a modern, soaring edifice with many windows and solar panels on the roof, and a walled garden. There were several people walking around apparently doing chores. One was a very small Hispanic man who looked vaguely familiar. He was riding a quad, all-terrain vehicle with several large potted evergreen trees in the cargo bed. Incongruous, as we were surrounded by beautiful natural oaks that were hundreds of years old. They seemed to be the tallest coastal live oaks I had ever seen.

The old barn was still there, still white. And the "white house," an old bunk house/party room was still standing as I drove past. But the main home was gone. In my boyish memories there had been a large, square, prim, two-story Victorian, properly maintained. Now there was this monument. So modern.

Bull parked his truck in the covered parking area alongside the house—complete with concrete floor and electric lights. Ah yes, the solar panels had brought electricity. I parked my yellow XTerra alongside. I stepped out. I looked across to the barn and I was stunned: no horses. Not one in sight. There were several all-terrain vehicles parked farther down the garage, and there were several out on the grounds. But no horses. Now that I noticed: no cattle. No cows.

Bull had opened a black, wrought iron gate into a court-yard and was motioning to me. As I approached, he turned and walked ahead of me. There was a large, carefully-tended swimming pool. Astonishing. Undoubtedly, I gaped, literally standing there with my jaw open, staring around the pool area. There was a young blonde woman in a flesh-colored bikini, reading under an umbrella, and she looked up and flashed a brilliant white smile. She stood up, looking quite nude, and walked to us, smile widening, hand outstretched. She had a perfect body. Her abdominal muscles were defined, stomach unravaged by stretch marks, skin unblotched by sun damage beneath her tan.

"Kathleen!" she said warmly. "Pleased to meet you."

I suppose at that point I shut my mouth.

I gaped my way through the rest of the house. Modern, high ceilings, many windows. Neo-Western art. Remington Bronze sculpture copies: "Coming Through The Rye" with four cowboys galloping and "The Mountain Man." As we walked past I looked at the brass bases of the statues: no foundry marks, no numbers. Recent recastings. There was a metal sculpture of John Wayne as a cowboy. Navajo rugs on the walls. A few kachinas. Some local Native American grinding rocks by the giant fireplace, which appeared unused. One grinding rock I recognized: pink granite, large, deep. If only it could talk, I thought. Finally, we arrived in Bull's study. High ceilings. Clean. Large oak desk. Guns in a Plexiglas room along one wall, with a Plexiglas combination lock door to access the firearms. Bull stopped at the desk and sat down, and motioned for me to sit as well.

"Nice," I said.

Bull reached down in a side drawer and pulled out a stack of legal papers, and a large rolled up cardboard tube. He said nothing.

"Kathleen is nice," I added.

In the following silence, I thought how far we had come from each other. I was living in my small, overcrowded house in Salinas. Bull was living here. I had traveled all over the world, and had little to show for it. Bull had remained here, except for tourism, and had much to show for it. We had both started out in life about three miles apart, on different dirt roads, in ancestral homes, the sons of brothers.

"Don't worry I'm clipped," said Bull.

I said nothing.

Bull added, "Kathleen doesn't want kids, I don't either. We just want to enjoy. That's what life is about, isn't it?"

I nodded affirmation.Bull shook his head as he gazed down at the papers. "I mean, women are like horses, right? They like lots of hay and they want regular breeding. They wear out or they run away, you buy another."

I sat there. No use responding to that. I wondered why he had asked me to come out to his ranch. Perhaps just to show off?

I watched as he pulled a bottle of aquavit, Danish vodka, out of a deep side drawer in the oak desk. He unscrewed the bottle's cap, pulled out two small glasses, and filled them with an amber liquid. Bull leaned forward and gently pushed the small, round glass across the table. I lifted it. Smelled. Rich alcohol-and-cardamom. Savoring. I contemplated that the thick glass of the bottle would also knap into superb arrowheads. I took a sip.

Bull looked out the large window onto the garden, which was enclosed from the ranch by an adobe wall. Green lawn. Sunlight. Roses. Beautiful. So different from what I remembered.

"I'm gonna sell Tortuga," he said.

Impossible.

"How many generations has your family been here?" I asked.

"I'm number eight," he replied. "Just like you're number eight. And before that? No ranch. We got by just fine. You lost your ranch. You seem fine. Poor. Fucked up. But otherwise fine."

"Yet you are here," I replied. "Why do you want to sell?"

He looked at the floor. "I'm in debt up to my fucking eyeballs," he said quietly. He drank the aquavit in his glass and poured more.

I looked around the room. So much here that was newly bought, surely within the past decade. Starting with the entire house. There weren't many memories here, at least for me. Across the room, there was that Plexiglas wall, and beyond it at least fifty rifles. So many antiques such as a Brown Bess musket and an antique Spanish escopeta but also some very modern guns. Weatherbys. Double guns of some sort. Apparently, a Barrett .50. A man could only shoot so many firearms. Then there was that custom truck parked outside. Bull hadn't been saving his pennies.

"How much?" I asked.

"With the oil rights, twenty million," he answered, looking at his aquavit.

That was a lot of dead elephants.

"I meant, how much do you owe?"

"About eight million," he answered.

"And the debt service is outrunning your oil royalties," I responded.

"Yep. This drop in energy prices has really kicked me in the nuts," he said.

We were both silent after that. Eight million dollars? He owed eight million dollars? How did that happen?

"How did eight million happen?" I asked.

"I should have stayed invested with you." Now Bull looked downright embarrassed.

The realization smacked me with a blow of adrenaline. That famous New York hedge fund manager, with his helicopter and his estate in Hawaii, had recently been indicted for running a Ponzi scheme, for fraud. All that sophisticated investment strategy had simply been an old-fashioned con. I hadn't remembered Bull's involvement.

"What did he do to you?" I asked quietly. *Damn.*

"I wanted more. Ya know I always want more. More of everything. It's just my nature," said Bull, slumping massively in his

— Chapter 25 —

giant, high-backed desk chair.

That was true.

I stayed silent.

"He told me he could make a killing in shorting the market, all the signs were there, and he was going to make me twice as rich as I had ever been. Then he asked me to borrow six million from the ranch to invest. Said he'd make much more than cattle could."

There it was again, I thought. Demon debt.

"And the other two million?" I asked.

"His fraud was revealed right when oil prices tanked. So six million went up in smoke right there. Then I had to finish the house. I had to keep living, ya know? A man's got to live."

He turned and looked out the full-length windows. I followed his gaze. Kathleen was lying in her bikini, reading, looking utterly flawless. Kathleen and Bull seemed to be living quite well. I bit back a comment.

"How can I help?" I asked.

Bull stood up and removed a rolled map from the cardboard tube, and unrolled it. It was a map of Tortuga. Developed into homesites, ranchettes, drives, and cul-de-sacs snaking across all five thousand acres of the Gabilan Mountain eastern half of the ranch. It would be suburbanized. All of it. I looked at it and thought of my memories and I wanted to gag, vomit, or flee. I did nothing. I just stood there.

"Where would you live?" I asked Bull.

"I dunno. I like Pebble Beach. I'm not sure Kathleen would like it. Too cold," said Bull.

"Do you want to keep living here?" I asked him.

"Damn straight. You know tradition doesn't mean much to me. I don't ride a horse anymore. Too damn fat. No cattle. The hill pastures are all leased out to Barsotti, over the fence, and he grazes the fuck out of it. But yeah, this place is still my home. Got the 'lil family graveyard up the hill. You know. Memories. So yep, I'd rather stay, all things considered. But not if I'm surrounded by this."

— Honor —

He gestured at the map.

I spoke my thoughts suddenly. "It'll be like a freeway up here. About five hundred houses, that's what they plan. Even a convenience store."

The thought made me ill, literally. Was I going to have a panic attack right here? I had a Xanax in my backpack. Oh the hell with that.

"Is there enough water for this?" I added. "Last I remember, there are only enough springs to water cattle."

"Oh, you know, a little money here, a little money there, and the county politicians will vote for a subdivision in the desert. Then the state water system will come in and bail their asses out," said Bull quietly. "They're already famous for paving paradise."

"What about the burrowing owls? The red-legged frogs? All the endangered species?" I asked.

"Ah well, see this little green dot?" Bull pointed to the map.

"It's infinitesimally small," I said.

"That's their reservation," said Bull. "I think it's about fifty yards in diameter. With a solar-powered water pumping system."

"All those animals living in that small space?" I said.

"Worked for the Indians," said Bull. "The planning commission has already said they'll support it, informally. Campaign contributions were mentioned."

Silence. Enormous. Somehow, when we lose our childhood homes we dream that they remain unchanged.

"When do you have to decide?" I asked.

"I think I have six months before the bank starts to foreclose," said Bull.

"Can you give me five months? I'll see what I can do," I asked him.

"You got it," said Bull.

"I'm sorry you're going through this," I added.

"Ah, well, life happens," Bull said, looking down at the map. "Oh, one more thing please."

"Sure, what is it?"

"Don't tell your mother. She'll kick my ass. For that matter, don't tell anyone."

I was all the way to the highway, driving the Xterra on 101, when I realized that I had forgotten to look at Bull's Mosin Nagant rifle. For an instant I contemplated calling him and turning back. Then I nixed that idea. It was going to be a busy day back at the office. Lanie was probably already overwhelmed, although of course she would camouflage the chaos as serenity.

As I drove I glanced down at my feet in their black polished dress shoes. Imagine. I had been to my uncle's ranch, in city dress shoes, and they hadn't even gotten dusty. My feet hadn't touched honest dirt once. What would my uncle or my father have said to that? What would my twenty-year-old self say, to see me as I was today? What would my twenty-year-old self say about selling the Tortuga?

Considering that concept, I realized that I would try to keep the eastern half of Bull's ranch undeveloped. Keep it as close to wilderness as possible. Let the wind whistle over the graves of my ancestors and the graves of my memories for as long as the world permits. And I realized who I would have to call: the Billionaire, the tech billionaire who now owned Dos Cabesas, my family's former home.

Chapter Twenty-six

April 2013

I woke up early. I always woke up early now. My body was trained to wake up early for holding, for loving, for caresses, for soft whispers, and then to go back to sleep.

When Angelica and I were together, it was a ritual. I would wake up at 3:30 and drive my XTerra through the darkness to her home, and then text her when I parked: "Outside."

She would always let me in.

So now, I woke up at 3:30 every morning, ready to go to Angelica. Except Angelica didn't want me there. She wanted Jerome there now.

This morning, as I lay in the dark in my bed, utterly wide awake, fighting the need, my phone buzzed. A surge of adrenaline. I picked it up, fumbled until it lit up, found the message.

It was Angelica. Texting me. "Do you love me?"

I should have waited, at least stalled to provide the illusion that I was asleep at 3:30 a.m. A small white lie to preserve my dignity.

"What's happening?" I texted back as rapidly as my fingers could move.

She was crying silently when she opened her door in her polka dot bathrobe. As I sat across the room from the couch where I had held her so many times, where we had made love, where I had sheltered her after her fight with Marta, she quietly sobbed out her story.

Jerome was too busy for her. He insisted that for the time

being, they should have only their bi-weekly meetings at the La Playa, and nothing more. He must protect his reputation, he said. He must not damage her reputation, he said. Perhaps, he told her, she wanted more than he could provide. He would not take her to his home. He would not fly her to his own home in his Lear jet. All he could provide right now were the daily phone calls and the visits.

Later, he might consider buying a home in Carmel or Pebble Beach, quitting the business, retiring to rest on his wealth, and marrying Angelica. Then she and the children could join him in his daily life. That was years in the future.

For now, there were a thousand employees who needed him, who required his daily vigilance. A thousand employees. Angelica said that several times.

So, Angelica said, Jerome would only see her about once every two weeks. He continued to call at least once a day, sometimes more, and he constantly reminded her of how much he loved her. He loved her, he said, and he loved the children, and he asked her to be patient. Angelica leaned towards me, as she sat on that couch, her robe slipped open slightly, and I pushed myself back and away into the padded chair until my legs ached. Temptation be damned.

"Let me get this straight," I responded.

"You drive to him, to the La Playa, meet him there, right?" My anger was beginning to rise. "He doesn't pick you up?"

"No," Angelica whispered back. "Please, be quiet for the children. No, I mean, yes, I drive to him."

"Why?" I asked. I knew that whatever was happening, this was a sauropod-sized deception, and I wanted no part of it.

"Because for the first time in my life I am queen. For the first time in my life I have no cares, no responsibility, no worry. Jerome cares for all."

That made sense, actually. Tommy had been a long time dying.

"Tell me more," I said. *Masochist.*

"It is always the same," she said. Her voice brightened happily in the dark. "Always we meet in room number 407, up high.

From there you can see Point Lobos, beautiful, far away across the bay, and the sunset over the beach, to the west. There is the beautiful garden below, and the flag on its pole, and the elegant pool. With elegant stylish people. He is always waiting in the room for me. So romantic. So perfect. I am a queen. People park my car for me."

I didn't want to know more.

"Has he met Cesar and Rose at all?" I asked.

"He was going to meet them but then Cesar got sick," she replied.

"Oh," I whispered back.

"And you seriously think that Jerome wants to marry you?" I asked.

"Yes, but he is modern. He is willing to share with other men and to let me make up my mind," she whispered back breathlessly.

I sat there stunned.

"Would you want a husband who can share you with another man?" I asked.

"No, no, of course not," she responded, her voice breaking above a whisper.

"Then why do you want a man who can share you now?" I asked, trying to be quiet. The adrenaline was filling me with the need to move. I looked up at the walnut box of ashes on the mantel. Tommy's ashes.

"Why do you want a man who can share you now?" I asked again.

She was silent for a time. Then she responded in a whisper. "Love is sacrifice."

I whispered back to her, "Forgive me, but that is the biggest barrel of bullshit I have heard in my life. Love is when *two* people give. Right now you are his concubine."

She twisted her face away from me angrily when I said that. I could see the anguish ripple briefly across her face as she comprehended the full meaning of my words. She growled quietly in frustration, and then was calm.

We sat there silently. My legs ached from wanting to run, and from pushing myself away. I felt the children's beloved presence in the bedroom, felt the walls pulsing with the power of Ohana, the family.

I must stay, I must do what is right.

"Do you love him?" I asked her.

"Yes, yes, yes," she said.

"Does he love you?" I asked. I felt my own body begin to shake as I asked that question. I was surprised I cared so much.

"He says he loves me every day," she whispered back.

Oh, I prayed so hard. I prayed to God, Tommy, my father, the ancestors, God. Please free me. Let me set any romantic needs aside, and be a good steward. What should I do, how should I do it? What is the right thing?

If God had an answer, God wasn't telling.

I could not eat. I lost five pounds in a week. I could not sleep at all. Perhaps three hours a night. I tried Ambien, I tried Lunesta. I was of one mind. My body, however, clearly had other thoughts.

I relearned another reality that week: there are few things in life which one glass of red wine does not make better. There are few things in life which four glasses of red wine does not make worse.

I quickly confided my situation to Lanie at work. She came into my office each day and guided me through the daily routine, through the trades, through the research. I stayed focused and got through. Day by day, my mind became more liberated. And while we worked together, she hand-walked me through that vital phone call with the VA, up at Stanford. Take advantage of the opportunity, Lanie said. Get started. Make a reservation. Easier said than done.

Then, on Friday, Globalbank called. They needed more documents. They needed a new signature on line 36 of the HAMP document.

I texted Angelica. I called her on her cell, and at her home. No answers. After two hours, no answers. I called Heritage Bay Eldercare. They said she was in, but not taking calls.

I was trustee, and I needed a signature. I suppose I should have had a staff member get the signature. But I wanted to keep them out of it. Also at that point, I was deeply sleep-deprived. It was as though I was on week number five of Reconnaissance School. I was a walking zombie. All I could do was what seemed right, what I was trained to do. I called Heritage Bay Eldercare. I told them that I was on my way over there.

"You probably won't like what you find," was all Lanie said as I walked out the door.

The sunlight was brilliant, eye-piercing. There was the ocean, shining gem-like, flat. A few seabirds perching on the kelp.

There was Angelica's Honda CRV in the parking lot. And there was a black Mercedes two seat convertible in the director's parking space. Jerome was here. I felt a punch, a blow. After I parked the XTerra, I sat behind the steering wheel as I felt my pulse race, and thought about what I would do: go in, get the signature from Angelica, and leave. Go in, get the signature, and leave.

I got out of the car, walked past the statue of Virgin Mary, and through the broad front doors. One step at a time.

Angelica was behind her desk in the alcove to the right. I walked straight there, looking neither left nor right.

Angelica looked up from her computer. By all that is holy, she was so beautiful. She scowled. Less beautiful. "Just get the signature and leave," she said, sharply.

She looked at the paperwork hastily, signed it, and thrust it back at me. "I don't need your help. I will replace you at this. Now go."

Her rejection burned. I spun around. There was Jerome, looking concerned, coming across the foyer to me from his office. He was tall, handsome, in khakis, a blue shirt. A full head of perfectly layered auburn hair. I had immediate hair envy.

"Who are you?" he asked. Then he recognized me.

"Oh, the trustee, the money guy. Right." He turned away, waved his hand. He seemed dismissive, bored. That bothered me.

"Got a second?" I asked, impulsively.

"Not really," he said.

"Let's share a moment," I directed. He fled to his office, intending to shut the door, but I walked in behind him as the door closed behind us.

Jerome looked angry. Then a look of fear flashed across his perfect face, for a second or two, and then a look of defiance, scorn. "You are beneath me," said his face.

Jerome sat down in his office chair, putting his desk between us. It was a clean desk, I noted. Almost devoid of papers, very organized. So utterly unlike mine. Now Jerome looked replete with ennui.

"I hear that you are having a relationship with Angelica. I just want to know that you're doing the right thing. She's been hurt enough," I said.

Jerome stared at me blankly. A buck in the headlights. A few moments passed. They seemed interminable. Finally, Jerome shrugged. He spoke slowly. "Angelica and I are good friends," he said quietly.

He was trying to act bored, or imposed upon, but his face softened as he said it.

"Good to hear it," I responded. "Angelica needs you. The children need you. Get in there. Be a father, a husband, a man. She loves you. Love her back."

He looked at me sideways. "Who are you to talk? What business is it of yours? It's my life, right? My life, Angelica's life. What do you know?"

I had to answer. "Actually I'm just a friend of the family. Angelica and I talk. The biweekly romps are not enough for her. As I said, she's been hurt enough."

"She said you were just the money guy," said Jerome. "Guess she was right."

I looked around for a chair. I needed to sit down. But there

— Honor —

178

was no chair. This was clearly the office of someone else most of the time, a Hispanic woman whose pictures coated the walls. Pictures of her, husband, children. All smiles. I had a sinking sensation, like the floor was tilting. My impulsive move was backfiring badly.

"You some kind of shakedown artist? Do you want blackmail?" He seemed in pain. I knew the feeling.

"Not even close. I don't want a penny. But she deserves honor and commitment. So do the kids." I spoke more loudly. "What happens next?"

I waited for his response. I expected him to say, "I love her" or, "Of course I'll be a gentleman." Bull elk syndrome. We all want to be masters of our own anthills.

Instead, Jerome stood up, and his face reddened. "Get out, get out now. I will sue you if you make this public. You can have Angelica for all I care. Go away. If you come back here again I'll get a restraining order. I'm a lawyer. Don't fuck with me."

He turned and faced the bookshelf on the wall. He wasn't looking at me now.

I hadn't expected this. I had expected him to do what I would have done: step up, emotionally and financially. That wasn't what was happening. I felt terrible.

I went on, "She tells me that you call her every day and you tell her that you love her. Surely, she doesn't lie. And I'm sure you wouldn't lie to her either."

Jerome just kept staring at the wall. I studied the books. They were books about eldercare and financing eldercare facilities. Not that interesting.

"Why would she talk with you about us?" he asked. Apparently to himself.

Chipmunk-helpful, I answered him, "She's still deeply, deeply hurt by her husband's death, and he took *five miserable years* to breathe his last. His ashes are sitting on her living room mantle. So if she's not 100-percent consistent, she's got a great excuse in my book. All she wants is true, deep, dependable love."

Jerome studied his shoes, eyes wet. His eyes were wet. *Damn.*

Damn. Damn. I realized I needed to shut up fast. I cinched up my backpack, opened the door, and walked across the foyer to the exit. The sunlight was streaming through the glass. Far off, beyond the windows, the ocean was as beautiful as ever. As I left, I saw Angelica's face, as she looked at me from her alcove, pale with shock. Her eyes were also wet, and red.

Chapter Twenty-seven

April 2013

Young, cheerful, attractive Miranda, complete with smile, a wheat grass smoothie, and a garnet nose stud processed me through the reception area for my first traumatic brain injury MRI at Stanford. She gave me the standard checklist to fill out concerning my mental state. She sat patiently while I completed the multiple-choice questionnaire, smiling as though she had won the lottery. Then she took the questionnaire and graciously ushered me down the stairs into the basement, where the machine was waiting.

I was changing into the metal-free pajamas, when my office called. They knew that they should phone only when it was important. I took the call. There was static on the line. Basements don't give you too many reception bars.

"You're in big trouble," said Tammy Fay at the other end of the line. Those were her first words. Not even hello. That meant I really *was* in big trouble.

"You are being sued," Tammy Fay continued. I felt a surge of adrenaline.

"I'm about to go into an MRI so you have two minutes." I was scared to death, actually. How could this be happening? I knew Jerome wasn't happy when I left him but I didn't think he'd do this.

"Jerome didn't enjoy you barging into his office and threatening him," said Tammy Fay sharply. "Now Angelica has called five times, she says you've ruined her life, and she says that Jerome is going to sue you."

Her voice seemed resigned to my imminent financial ruin. There it is, Buster. Somehow, I thought all men would act like me. A text appeared on the phone, superimposed on the phone data. From Angelica: "YOU RUIN MY LIFE." Yep, that much was true. Angelica was in this now as well.

Tammy Fay went on, "It turns out that you freaked Jerome out so much that he thinks Angelica is just after his money. So he's dropped her cold, says he doesn't want anything to do with her."

That wasn't what I expected. I had expected Jerome to do what I would have done. I had expected that he would step up to the challenge, marry Angelica. Happily ever after. Even after the disaster of my confrontation, I had expected that he would come to his senses. But what if I was the person who needed to gain sanity? Was I mistaken about all this?

No.

"YOU RUIN MY LIFE! I HATE YOU!" appeared on the screen of my phone.

"What happened?" I texted back. I already knew, but it didn't hurt to ask.

"Jerome leave me. You told him lies and now he leave me. YOU RUIN MY LIFE!"

I thought over my discussion with him. I hadn't told any lies that I knew of. Somehow, that didn't take away the feeling that I had done something terrible.

"I am sorry," I texted back.

"YOU RUIN MY LIFE! GOODBYE! NEVER I SEE YOU AGAIN! I KNOW YOUR TECHNIQUE OF POISON MY LIFE! YOU MANIPULATE CHILDREN FOR CONTROL ME AND YOU HUNT JEROME DOWN!"

I gave a big sigh. My bare feet were cold on the tile floor. It was a white basement floor, spotlessly clean, gleaming in the florescent light. I studied it to get my self-control back.

From Jerome'e perspective, Angelica was manipulating him for blackmail.

Like most men, his brains were in his pants. Uniquely for Jerome, they appeared to be in his wallet.

— Honor —

I knew the feeling.

There was a knock, and the door opened. Miranda's head appeared, with her ear to ear smile. "We're ready for you now," she said.

"Your questionnaire indicates that you might be depressed. Would you agree that you are stuck in your recovery? That's how it seems to us. We've decided to try a new treatment, with your permission."

This from Häyhä Pekk, possibly the most attractive woman shrink ever to work for the Etkin Center for Psychiatric Research at Stanford. The woman was classic Finnish beautiful.

"Your MRIs look good. Your sinuses still have a lot of scar tissue. Your brain injury seems to be gradually resolving, and your brain is rewiring. It's the post-traumatic stress disorder that seems to be unresolved," said Dr. Pekk.

"Post traumatic spouse disorder," I joked. Dr. Pekk smiled thinly.

"We have a research study underway, using TMS to resolve post-traumatic stress disorder," responded Dr. Pekk. She was smiling, but she wasn't recognizing the joke at all. Her classic features remained professional, compassionate yet focused. Deep blue eyes locked on to mine. The woman could make a killing as a commodities trader.

"TMS. Too Much Salsa?" I joked. Nice try.

"Transcranial Magnetic Stimulation," said Dr. Pekk.

I pondered. What did that mean?

"It's a new mechanistic treatment for traumatic brain injury. It is electro-magnetic stimulation for the brain, much, much better than electroshock therapy, much less confusion and memory loss, and since you will participate in a pilot study, we'll pay you, not the other way around. It's worth tens of thousands of dollars, and since you are older, your data will be very helpful. We've got lots of combat injuries here."

Well, if you put it that way. My ever-present guilt floated up to the surface of my mind, cream in whole milk. The scum also rises.

"May I think about it?" I asked Dr. Pekk.

"Of course," she said. "Take your time."

My phone buzzed. "I HATE YOU!" it read. From Angelica.

"I'll do it," I said to Dr. Pekk.

Chapter Twenty-eight

May-July 2013

A month of no contact with Angelica. Then another month. No contact with Cesar and Rose either. It was summer. I felt as though I was running while holding my breath.

I lost more weight.

I could not sleep.

When I awoke every morning at 3:30 a.m., I would lie in my bed and stare up at the dark ceiling above. "Jerome is not sleeping," I would hear myself say. "Jerome and his Lear jet, and all the successful men in the world, they do not rest, they do not agonize, and they do not grieve. Fail fast, fail cheap, fail completely, embrace the suck, and get on with life. Do something, Lieutenant."

The only response I could imagine was to run. I would get out of bed, shaking, at 4 a.m., dress in my running gear with pants and sweatshirt, and pull an elastic banded headlamp over my hat. I would run through the dark streets of Salinas, run through the night, sometimes in the beautiful moonlight of a glimmering full moon, sometimes on overcast ,early mornings with only the headlamp to light the way down the asphalt streets. Old Salinas town in the early pre-dawn. Sleeping streets. A few early cars. Cats. Raccoons. A few early habitual walkers, the fellow emotionally wounded, who soon learned to wave, not flee. I ran. I ran. I ran. I ran.

Meanwhile the work went on. The stock market continued to rise fitfully, although the why of that mystified me. The lives of clients also continued; there were two deaths, two births, and one divorce, between a man who literally went insane and his tech-executive wife.

Since it was summer, Francesca was usually at the office all day with me, until we could escape to the swimming pool or the hills. That meant that there was always a happy hum of family life in our ancestral home when I worked, and it meant that we had wonderful staff lunches with our own garden-grown tomatoes, our own squash, and berries picked from vines planted by my great-grandparents, now feeding us as the days progressed in joy.

And as the weeks passed there were five more human turds on the front porch. The police said that there was nothing to be done about them. I cleaned them up. I could not ask another to do what I would not do myself. I bought an entire carton of rubber gloves and a canister of Lysol from Costco.

After several months, Angelica reappeared in my Facebook feed, and I was able to see whatever she made public. I checked daily. Through the summer she gradually posted about forty pictures of herself with Tommy, long-ago photos of her and Tommy getting married, one photo at a time. She posted pictures of the children with Tommy, of herself with Tommy during their marriage, the family together. All the smiles. I could watch the progress of the battle through those pictures: first, Tommy standing at the wedding, then kneeling with the children, then sitting because he could not stand, then finally Tommy lying hairless and chemo-poisoned on the couch pretending he was napping.

At church, I sat in the balcony and watched the back of Angelica's head throughout the sermons. I wondered what might happen if I simply launched myself off the railing, down into the aisle beneath, ended all this longing and all this hunger, just gave myself to God and the concrete slab thirty feet below.

Of course that wasn't giving myself to God at all, was it? That was just the hunger talking.

The next week, at Stanford, they slid me into the tube of an

MRI machine, completely immobilized, yellow nylon webbing straps with black plastic buckles holding me in place.

I was wearing their metal-free pajamas. Miranda and another technician adjusted the magnet over my head. Then I was entirely strapped down, alone in that room inside the torpedo tube of that giant MRI machine.

"All set?" came Miranda's metallic voice over the loudspeaker.

I pondered the implications of electroshocking my brain, if only with magnets.

"As ready as I'll ever be," I responded.

When they triggered the magnetic impulse, it sent an electric wave through my body, slapping the back of my head, creating a mild spasm through my arms and legs. It was like being hit on the head by a plastic baseball bat wielded by an energetic five-year-old child. It was not overtly painful, but by the hundredth pulse that smacked into my head and rippled down to my toes, I was ready to rip that magnet off its mounts and throw it into the next county.

I tried to pray and to maintain ten-count breathing the entire time. God, Father, my ancestors, Tommy, I surrender. This may heal me, this may destroy me, but God, I accept your will and your path. I accept your plan. Give me the courage.

Late June. Several more threatening letters from Globalbank. Several more threatening phone calls with Globalbank. I spoke on the phone with Globalbank representatives named Jackie Mason, Dick Tracy, and Joe Jitsu. They threatened. I baited them (a bit). They insisted on talking with Tommy. Tommy was unable to respond.

Chapter Twenty-nine

July 2013

With July came the rodeo. I had no intention of attending.

Then I pondered. What was I trying to accomplish in my life? Move on. Embrace what is good, which must surely include the rodeo with its memories.

Besides, Jerome wasn't resting, was he? The successful people were not cowering, like me. They were embracing life in all its richness. Therefore, I needed to get my ass off the couch and down to that rodeo.

I put on my best Angelica-provided jeans, and slipped into the cowboy boots and hat given to me by my deceased father many years before. I no longer managed a ranch, but I could play the part. It was an overcast morning, which was normal for July in Salinas. I wore a jean jacket as part of my cowboy clothing, and I was barely warm enough.

I dragooned Ernst into going with me, if only so I could have a decent bathroom interval without taking Francesca into the stall with me. Once there, like me, he soon found the sights interesting enough. Francesca was fascinated by it all, in constant motion, dressed by Margaret in child-sized Western pants, pink boots, and a bandana T-shirt. I bought her a straw hat.

I found myself wondering if Angelica was there, watching the events, perhaps sitting in a wealthy person's private box in the main grandstands, perhaps over the bucking chutes on the far side of the arena. She would be meticulously dressed; hair and nails perfect, and her boots would be designer-embossed snake-skin mockeries of anything that had ever seen a stirrup.

Jerome would be with her, with his perfect hair, perfect clothes, muscled physique, undoubtedly wearing a very expensive private brand of rotary dial watch to complement his matching Western wardrobe and smooth manicured hands.

These days, top-end people such as Angelica and Jerome were the very essence of the cash cow that was the new Salinas California Rodeo. Where, as a teenager, I had happily galloped horseback about the arena with a grease bucket for slopping the chutes, there was now a carefully choreographed Roman circus of performers and livestock.

At a vending stand, we bought two carne asada burritos, exquisitely done, the meat crunchy from the grill and the salsa just spicy enough to add a bit of snap, warm garlic aromas wafting up to us from the large, folded hot flour tortillas with a little scorch on them. Delicious. Then, eating as we walked, we wandered through the crowded tunnels of the stadium, and into the stands.

The team penning had already started on the track directly in front of us. It was what I had done on the ranch at every possible moment in my teen years: ride fast, pen the livestock, cut out the chosen beast. The horses and riders pounded after the cattle, forcing them around green panel fences into enclosures.

Beyond the track, the bull riding was underway, which to me seemed ever more like a circus stunt. Certainly, we had never done *that* on the ranch. The crowd loved it though, and each time a gate opened, a roar rose from the masses, until the loud buzzer signaled an end to an eight-second ride.

Ahead of us on the grass in front of the grandstands was a row of patients in wheelchairs, with a carefully printed cardboard sign, yellow letters on blue cardboard, from the Veteran's Administration hospital in San Francisco. They were lined up on the grass in front of the stands, all men, as far as I could see, no women, all facing the rodeo arena.

I immediately noticed a man with a missing leg at the hip,

then another. A man farther down the row was missing an arm at the shoulder. There were a few catheters snaking from under blankets, with brown or yellow liquid draining through the transparent tubes, and even one IV. There was an assortment of labels on the stainless steel and beige plastic wheelchairs, "Oak Knolls Naval Hospital" stenciled on several. I had thought that the Oak Knolls hospital had closed. Perhaps I was wrong.

There were attendants behind the patients, some older, some younger, standing near the wheelchair patients or sitting on folding chairs behind the men, wearing casual civilian clothes and blue and yellow vests with "American Legion Volunteer" on a round, blue embroidered logo on the back.

At the nearest end of the line of wheelchairs sat a young man, limbs contorted, face twisted. He was wearing a light blue plastic hockey helmet with a glittering USMC roundel on the side. His eyes were each roaming individually, like a chameleon, hands pulled up, crab claws, fingers twisted and bent. He saw me and began making loud squeaking noises, and his limbs twitched and flopped. Poor man, I thought to myself. Sweat sprang up under my shirt. Unconsciously I reached down and damply took Francesca's hand, and began to steer her around to the back of the row of wheelchair patients, to avoid passing between them and the performance unfolding on the other side of the chain link fence. Ernst followed behind us. I could feel my pulse rise.

A young woman walked around the patient's wheelchair and knelt down to look him in the eye. She appeared to be a teenager, blonde with her hair in an unkempt ponytail under her straw, coarsely woven cowboy hat; slightly plump, a small roll of fat squeezing out above her tight blue jeans, long red artificial nails, chipped and uneven. Under her blue and yellow volunteer vest, she was wearing a chocolate-colored, sleeveless t-shirt, with the gold words "I see F%^&ktards" across her ample bosom. She leaned down so that her face was directly in front of the eyes of the disabled man, only inches away, intimately present, and she spoke to him in a low, soothing voice.

"Jody went for a burrito. A carne asada beef burrito. She

been wantin' one all mornin'. Don't worry; she'll be right back, Daddy."

Southern accent. The woman smiled down at the patient. The young man, slender, hair cut in Marine fashion under his light blue hockey helmet, with flecks of gray in the black hair, continued to contort spastically and grunt. He contorted harder to turn to see me he wheezed. As I tried to pass behind him, as I tried to pretend he wasn't there, he was trying harder to twist around to keep me in his vision and to get my attention. There was no way to ignore him. I stopped and looked down at him, Francesca's hand in my own wet palm. I looked into his blue eyes. I recognized him.

He was Lance Corporal Gus, my truck driver from the accident.

I looked at his maladjusted light blue eyes wandering across my face. He couldn't control them. There were dimples in both sinuses, what looked like acne scars across his cheeks. He was trying to speak. He was trying to smile.

I was horrified. I felt the sudden urge to panic, to run, and felt a vast tsunami of guilt: they had told me that he had a worse brain injury than I did, but as his leader I should have checked, I should have inquired, I should not have simply focused on my own recovery. Why had I not inquired?

He was twisting, trying to move, the cords of emaciated tendons standing out in his neck, and I saw a smile tremble onto his face, revealing now-perfect white teeth, which could only be dentures, and then the young woman with the gold words "I see F%^&ktards" emblazoned across her ever-so-tight, chocolate-colored sleeveless shirt leaned into me and said, "Greetins! I'm Honey, I'm Gus's wife," and she shook my hand energetically. I responded limply, forcing a smile. This was the once-pregnant wife from the hollers of Paradise, Tennessee?

"Oh, y'all be Warrant Officer Ericson! Y'all from Iraq! I recognize ya from the photos!"

Oh.

I mouthed some greetings. She continued, "We're up at the

hospital at San Francisco. Gus is doin' better all the time. He's healin' a little every day, with God's grace."

Oh my God, he was injured nine years ago. And he is still in a hospital.

Lance Corporal Gus was clearly smiling now. I could see the line in his gums where the dentures ended wetly and pink living tissue began.

"We are so-o-o proud that Gus was able to serve, able to defend our nation. We've always wanted to thank ya for leading him, for being thare with him. He has always felt that y'all's leadership was such a gift."

I stood there, speechless. Then I reached out my hand, and took hers. I didn't know what else to say.

"Thank you for your service. Thank you for being there for our lance corporal.'

I ignored the reality that I had never, ever, inquired after his wellbeing after I was injured, after they had told me that he wasn't in my platoon. Not my problem.

"How are you both?" I asked. Inane. Insensitive. I wondered if perhaps I had already said that.

She smiled broadly, warmly. "Oh, we are doin' just fine. We got an apartment near the hospital, and Gus has perm'nent gov'ment diz'bility, and we have to save here and there, but we *do* get by."

"Good," I said quietly. Secretly, I wanted to run.

"And Gus, he's a stubborn cuss, but he get use to this a bit ev'ry day, and Jody, our daughter, she grows strong and good like a weed, and she minds her books. We have so much to be thankful for."

My mind was racing. Let me get this straight. This woman is the pie-eating illiterate from Paradise, Tennessee, and her husband has the brain of a frog, and she's standing by him, heart, soul, and everything.

I studied her tightly stretched t-shirt. Here she was, with Lance Corporal Gus, a terminal lance, and he was smiling a brainless smile, each eye spinning off individually, and twitching, with

— Chapter 29 —

his hands clutched and twisted up by his face. They seemed genuinely happy to see me.

She clearly thought I was looking at her chest: she twittered and covered her mouth with her hand, and she looked to the arena, where a rodeo performer was riding a massive gray Brahma hump-backed bull, twisting and turning, the bell on that bull clanging as it jumped. The bull twisted, rolling inside its own skin, muscles and tendons showing, and the cowboy clung to its back and then the buzzer sounded the end of the eight seconds and the man—a small slender man with a very curved white cowboy hat—

leapt off gracefully and landed on his feet, chaps flaring, while the kicking bull arched towards the exit from the arena, and applause and cheering made the stadium echo and roar.

I looked up. The summer fog was burning away. I could see a hole in the gray cloud ceiling, blue sky overhead. It would get warmer soon. It was going to be a beautiful day after all. Angelica was nowhere in sight.

Chapter Thirty

July 2013

The phone call from Selma, the walker-wielding BAM World War II veteran at Heritage Harbor, came a few weeks later, around noon. I was at work. The stock markets were continuing to climb, even though I thought they were overvalued.

"Angelica's not working here anymore," said Selma over the phone. "Jerome isn't here either. He flew off to his next adventure."

"I'm sorry," I said. "I'm sorry to involve you in this."

"I know they went to the rodeo a few weeks ago. I think Jerome flew in especially for that. That's how they met last year, I think. Angelica asked him to the rodeo last July, in 2012. I remember Jerome had never seen a bull ride before last year, so it was something they laughed a lot about later. This time they went from here in Jerome's Mercedes but they didn't come back smiling. In fact, Angelica was crying."

"I'm sorry this happened," I automatically responded through my headset, leaning back in my chair, my eyes shut. I was doing the math. If they went to the rodeo in 2012, that would mean that she had been at the rodeo with Jerome, during the very core of our romance, right when she had been saying, "I love you" to me, and making love with me. Even before she told me she had met Jerome. This also meant that they were still, even now, in contact with each other. Seeing each other. Bad news in terms of what I thought my relationship with Angelica had been. Good news in terms of the present, actually. Fail fast, fail cheap, move on.

"Before that, Jerome was pretty shook up when Angelica

didn't come to work one day," said Selma. "She came to see me before she gave Darla her resignation letter. She said goodbye. She was crying."

I was silent when she said that.

"It's been a couple of months. Long months?" she asked.

"As long as they can be," I said. "You know, I'm sure. When your husband died? That was so much greater than whatever I am experiencing. I don't know how you did it."

Now the line was silent on her end. I waited.

Finally, she responded, "You know, I'm hungry for Chinese food."

"Oh yeah?" I had to smile.

"Yes, that Eagle restaurant in Salinas makes such good chicken and green beans in black bean sauce. Can you spring me from the pen, here? Come pick me up. When?"

"I'm hungry now," I answered.

Selma was standing out in front with her walker when I pulled up to Heritage Bay Eldercare. There was a man with her, bent, impossibly old, with his own wheeled walker. There was a much younger Filipina woman with them.

"This is Leonard. And this is Fergie," said Selma, motioning towards the young Filipina woman.

"Fergie's a princess of England," quipped Leonard, straightening slightly. He grinned, head unnaturally canted. His shaving job was uneven. I noticed tuffs of ear hair protruding whitely, Yoda-like.

"Leonard's the court jester," replied Fergie, smiling whitely. She was genuinely pretty. Fergie looked a bit like an Asian Jennifer Lopez. Statuesque.

"Leonard covets the throne," said Selma, smiling, and everyone laughed for a moment.

I loaded them both into the XTerra. Selma asked to be folded into the back seat with Leonard. XTerras are not built for four adults. Ever-smiling Fergie sat in the front with me. As we drove on Highway 68, past oaks and mansions to the Eagle restaurant,

Selma fiddled with the toggles until the rear window went half-way down, then she put her face to the wind like a dog.

"I'll have that chicken and green beans I've been craving," said Selma, apparently talking to herself.

"When my wife had a craving for Chinese food it turned out she was pregnant with our second daughter, in 1957. Hm-mmm," said Leonard in the backseat. I parked the XTerra on Alisal Street, in front of the Eagle. I looked back at Leonard. He raised his eyebrows inquiringly and looked at Selma.

"In your dreams, handsome," said Fergie, laughing, slapping his shoulder playfully as she opened the rear door to help him out on the sidewalk.

"Oh I wasn't talking to you, beautiful," replied Leonard. "You aren't the pretty girl with the cravings."

Still seated in the backseat, Selma blushed. "Maybe I should go to the doctor, Leonard." She laughed.

"Do they still have the frog test?" asked Leonard. "Did it lay eggs?"

Fergie and I whisked Leonard and Selma into the restaurant as fast as their walkers would wheel.

Selma and Leonard sat on one side of the booth. I sat on the other side. Fergie insisted on the aisle seat, the better to care for Selma and Leonard.

This felt a lot like a double date. That perception was re-inforced after a slender young Asian man with great hair and black plastic-rimmed glasses delivered our food. Selma fed Leonard a sample of her chicken and green beans in black bean sauce. Leonard smiled and gently took the forked offering into his mouth. His eyes never left Selma's.

I turned and looked at Fergie. She was smiling radiantly at the two, as though their happiness was entirely due to her own ef-forts. She seemed rapt, caught up, full of enjoyment. Her food, salmon and broccoli, sat before her untouched. She was feeding upon the joy.

"Eat. It's warm now," I said to Fergie. I motioned to the food. She turned to me and said, "Good times we make. Bad times come by themselves," with a strong Filipina accent.

"Yep," said Leonard, "love is rare. Selma and I have found that out the hard way."

He reached out and took Selma's hand.

I sat there watching them, bemused.

"Oh, Garth," said Selma. "I thought I would die when my husband passed on. I just thought I would die. Was it like that for you too, Leonard?"

Leonard's face grew somber, "I was married for fifty-six years. I got married in World War II. I was a landing craft sailor, in all those Pacific landings, against the Japanese. So many died."

Then his hound dog face pulled itself into a wide smile again. "You know I used to pray that God would protect me, prayed that God would pull me through. I did twelve landings! Then I took a 6.5 Japanese round here." He pointed to his chest. "Nicked a lung. I was spitting blood. Best thing that ever happened to me."

"How was *that* the best thing that ever happened to you?" I asked.

"Well for starters I missed Okinawa. After I left, my LST ship got blown up by a kamikaze. Just blown to hell. Hardly anyone survived." His eyes grew wet.

"But more importantly, believe it or not, I came home to Plains, Iowa, for a few months recuperation. The *first girl* I met, I married in only six weeks. God, we were crazy in love. We both thought I would die when I went back out to the Pacific, especially after we heard about the ship." A tear trickled down his cheeks. Selma reached out and enfolded his hand tightly with both of hers.

"What did you do?" I asked. "That must have been hard."

"Why, hell, son, we made a baby!" said Leonard, and started to laugh. "Didn't you?"

I didn't want to tell him that I had been nowhere near combat.

Selma added, "Finding a person who adores you is rare, Garth. It's rarer than people think. It's not even *who* we expect, either. Love prevails. Somehow, we have angels looking out for us. It's best not to wonder too much."

— Honor —

Leonard added quietly, "I'd never guess my angel was a Japanese Rikusentai sniper, but there it is."

I thought about Angelica watching Tommy die for five years. Not a lot of purses and cars and prestige in that situation.

Selma looked deeply at Leonard, and they smiled at each other. "Hi, handsome," she said. Leonard grinned back.

"But you must follow your heart, yes?" asked Fergie.

"Hell, dearie, if I followed my heart I would have shot my husband thirty times, beat all three kids, slept with the postman, and run off with that magnificent milk man. God what an ass he had, back in 1954," said Selma.

I began to laugh. Trying not to choke on the kung pao chicken.

Selma smiled and continued, "No, honey, love isn't really a feeling. It is a decision, a choice, a commitment you make to yourself. I mean, the attraction has to be there, but . . . love is really a mirror of your own values."

"You know when my wife said she was loved the most?" asked Leonard.

"At your wedding?" asked Fergie.

"My wife used to tell me that she felt most loved when she was pregnant and she had *terrible* morning sickness, she would vomit just to look at food. And she had this hair, this beautiful, long, dark black hair and it flowed like a river, and when she'd vomit in the toilet that beautiful hair would all fall around her face."

"Not your wedding?" asked Fergie. "But the wedding is so romantic!"

Leonard smiled, and continued. "Anyway she used to say that after we were married, she was so afraid, so afraid that we'd made a mistake getting married, made a mistake getting pregnant. I mean, I had orders to go back out for the invasion of Japan, and I had only a few months left with her before I shipped out. They had me at Treasure Island, near San Francisco, for a few months."

"Was it like a honeymoon?" asked Fergie, smiling back.

"We had no money." He laughed once, and smiled, and poked

at his food. Silence. He was lost in his thoughts. "We lived in a Quonset hut."

I thought about the Quonset hut. I'd lived in one of those sheet metal half-tubes, at Camp Pendleton. I considered that those Quonset huts had been in constant use for more than sixty years. All the life, love, tears, loss, joy…

Leonard continued, quietly. "God, we had fun though. Yes, it was romantic. But not in the way you think." Silence again. I looked at Fergie. She smiled whitely back at me. Dark skin. A beautiful woman. I looked away. I seized a peanut with my chopsticks and looked down at it.

"She used to say—" His voice broke. Selma put her fork down and held his hand with both of hers. Their hands, joined, looked like gnarled chicken feet.

"She used to say that she knew I really loved her when she threw up into the toilet one morning in that cold dark little Quonset hut, and I kneeled down and pulled her hair back behind and held it there, while she barfed. *That's* when she said she realized that I was really there for her, really committed." He laughed. His eyes were wet.

"You know that's one of the best memories of my life? Isn't that strange? I came back from the war, and smack-doodle I went to college while I was married, I took over my father in law's lumber business, we had four children, all of them married well, and I'm still doing great financially. And what do I remember as the best moment of my life? My wife is twenty-three years old and she's pregnant . . ." He laughed while a tear ran down his wrinkled face. He let go of Selma's hands and made a shape of pregnancy in front of his own stomach.

"And she's kneeling on our little bed in our Quonset hut just before bedtime, one bare light bulb, and she's telling me she knows I love her because I hold her hair when she pukes!" He laughed again, and looked at his half-eaten food.

"True love!" said Fergie, smiling whitely, tilting her beautiful head.

Selma reached out again and enfolded Leonard's hand in her

own, smiling, a few tears in her own eyes.

"I would die this instant if I could go back to that moment, right there," he said quietly. "But life is for the living, and to make the most of life, you have to be willing to love."

We all looked at our plates for a minute after that. Silence. A nice silence.

"Fifty-six years of marriage," he continued. "And I treasure every second of it."

Chapter Thirty-one

August 2013

Stanford. Dr. Häyhä Pekk's office window looked into the courtyard over the delicatessen on the first floor of the Etkin Psychology Laboratory building. Out the window, I could see people eating spinach arugula protein wraps and quinoa free-range breakfast folds. Dr. Pekk sat opposite me in a comfortable chair, looking blonde, trim, fit, young, well dressed, and intelligent. That was a powerful combination. I sat in a chair with my back to the opposite wall.

I looked at the black and white pictures of Nordic skiing on the beige walls. That might be her in those pictures but there were no portraits of her, which indicated a lack of narcissism on her part. Good for her. I was praying silently. It was ten weeks since I had received that magnetic treatment, Transcranial Magnetic Stimulation. Too Much Salsa.

Since then I had endured non-stop tinnitus. The ringing in my ears was never truly loud, but it also was never truly gone, either. It was a constant high-pitched cicada hum, unceasing, just as it had been for months after the explosion. The misfortune. The industrial accident. I was wondering if the tinnitus was the memory coming back, hearing damage from the explosion, or hearing damage from the MRI. I didn't know.

This was my fourth visit. It didn't seem to me that we were making a great deal of progress. In fact, my insomnia was raging and my hunger for Angelica seemed enlarged. I wasn't crazy per se, as far as I could tell. I simply awoke at 3:30 a.m. every morning, physically aching for Angelica, gasping for her as though she were oxygen. She was an amputated limb through the entire day, until I fell fitfully asleep late in the evening.

I weighed 159 pounds. By necessity, to calm my racing mind, I ran at least six miles every day, and I lifted weights compulsively. Even those strategies were barely enough. Fortunately, my staff at work was an emotional plaster cast, keeping me in line and focused during the workday. Then the raging mind, after work, raging until medication blasted me into slumber.

"I'm fine," I said to Häyhä.

"Hmmm . . . really? Well you *do* look fit," replied Häyhä. "Today we're going back to the imaginal."

Ah yes, the imaginal. An imaginal meant that I sat with my eyes closed and relived the explosion, again and again. Again and again and again. It wasn't that long a recounting, actually. But then she kept asking how I felt afterwards, and that was more complicated. Lots more complicated.

I went through it again, eyes closed. The blast, the truck on its back, me on the stretcher, the tooth bits rinsed out of my mouth. I felt the responsibility again, to remain calm, lead those young medical people through it.

"How long do you think you were unconscious?" she asked.

I thought about that.

"I think the sun moved in the sky while I was unconscious. The shadows had moved. I'm guessing forty-five minutes," I replied.

"That correlates to the severity of the brain injury we're seeing," she replied.

"Bad?" I asked.

"No, I think you know your brain injury is rather mild. Rewiring is definitely a possibility with you," she replied evenly. Always evenly. Very controlled, always.

I thought about Lance Corporal Gus. That was more severe, wasn't it?

"So what now?" I asked. "I'm no longer feeling much from that imaginal."

She seemed to reflect on that.

— Honor —

"Go back a bit," she said. "You wake up in the sand. The medics . . ."

"Corpsmen," I automatically responded.

"Corpsmen," she replied. "The corpsmen are working on you. Feel that? What do you feel?"

"Hmmmm. Confused," I replied.

"Okay, follow that back," she said. "I'm curious. What else? Feel it . . ."

I sat there.

"Responsible?" I replied.

"Responsible for what?" she asked.

"Those corpsmen were really young. I felt responsible for their ability to do the work; I thought the situation might panic them," I said.

"Okay, what do you feel responsible for now?" she asked. Cool as glass.

Brilliant blue eyes. Light blonde hair. She was even more beautiful when she smiled.

"Go with it," she said. "Just say what you are feeling. Responsible for? When you think back, what are you responsible for?"

I looked at her. So beautiful.

"Focus," she said. "You are responsible for . . ."

"The men, the platoon, the woman corpsman, she was so young, she didn't know what was happening," I replied.

"Get back onto the theme here. Responsible for?" she asked.

"The men, the platoon, the woman corpsman, the blast, the sand." I was grasping now.

"The blast?" said Häyhä. "You mean the explosion? Stay with it."

I was confused now. "Yeah . . . the blast, the explosion, the corpsmen . . ."

"The explosion?" asked Häyhä.

"Yes, the blast. I am responsible for the blast," I said, and as I spoke, I realized how ridiculous that was.

"Responsible for the blast? Follow that. Track it," said Häyhä.

"Yes," I responded. The thought was unfolding in my mind now, the clarity of it. "Yes, I *do* feel responsible for the explosion, the artillery impact."

That was very strange. Then Häyhä took the thoughts out of my head.

"But wait a minute," she said. "Weren't you where you were supposed to be when the artillery shell exploded?"

"Yes," I said. "We were just following the truck in front, as ordered."

Häyhä looked at me steadily. "Okay, let's focus on this. Did you ask for that artillery shell to hit you in *any way?*"

"No," I replied. "It just hit us." I thought about that.

Silence.

"Wow," I said.

Häyhä said nothing. She just looked at me tranquilly.

"What are you thinking?" she asked. "I can guess but I want to hear it from you."

"If I didn't cause the artillery shell, then who made it happen? And you can't tell me that I went to Iraq, and Margaret left with Jack, and my whole world ended, because I did *nothing* wrong," I said.

Häyhä looked at me. "Think about what you just said," she responded, slowly.

Chapter Thirty-two

August 2013

It was sunset, late August. 8 p.m., and the sun was setting somewhere beyond the fog. The world beneath the grey sky was growing darker.

Because of my sleep difficulties after my breakup with Angelica, I was still taking Ambien. Ambien creates sleep walking, so our mediator Aaron Sanchez and Margaret had ended the tradition of Francesca spending overnights at my home. That was why, as the sun set, I prepared to drive Francesca to Margaret's home out in Unhappy Acres.

As I slipped Francesca into her pink cotton pea coat, complete with wide flat pink plastic buttons, my phone buzzed. A text, from Margaret.

"Please take Francesca to Victoria and Fred's home. They are waiting for her."

"What's up?" I texted back.

"Jack and I need some alone time."

I remembered seeing them drive out of the doctor's office parking lot, in Jack's monster truck, before Francesca had been born. I fought back the need to respond with something long, something inflammatory, something angry.

Of course Victoria lived only two blocks away. I told Francesca that she was spending the night with them. Francesca hopped for joy. Walking distance. I grabbed a headlamp from my bedroom headboard, set the house alarm, and headed down the walkway from my home to the sidewalk. After about ten paces, Francesca asked to be carried on my shoulders. I lofted her up, with her small legs on either side of my neck, as she whooped.

We walked down the dark sidewalk, under the avocado tree in my front yard, and turned right towards Victoria and Fred's home.

"Why am I spending the night at *their* house?" asked Francesca as she placed her hands on my bald scalp. She liked to do that. She said it kept her hands warm.

"Your mommy says that she and Jack need some alone time," I responded.

"Yes, I know," she said matter-of-factly, her small girl's voice coming down from the darkness above my head.

I was silent. I didn't know what to say.

"Mommy and Jack fight all the time," she said. "They try to hide it but I hear them. Mommy cries."

"You know," I responded, "I'm not so sure it's sad. You can make good things come from disagreements." I had to say something.

"Arguing? How?" she asked above me. I walked on, steadily.

"It's something I've learned," I responded. "You can figure out what's important to the other person, and you can listen, and you can admit your mistakes."

"Oh".

"But it makes me sad," the little voice above me said.

We walked the last few yards without speaking.

Victoria and Fred answered their front door in stony silence. Scowls. I lifted Francesca from my shoulders and set her down in the doorway. Francesca hugged me on the threshold. "I love you," she chirped at me, smiling.

"I love you too," I responded, and as I smiled at her, the front door was closed sharply in my face.

It was a quick walk home through the darkness. I was pondering Margaret's text message, about the door shut in my face. I walked faster, stewing with anger. The fog above was misting slightly. It was fully dark now.

My phone buzzed.

— Honor —
208

A text from Angelica: "You ruin my life."

Ahhh yes. After months, that was the message. Stale crackers.

The phone buzzed again. "I hate yoooooouuuuuuuu!"

I was preparing myself to deliver a detailed response, a solid, fact-based rebuttal. But my fingers moved by themselves. "Sorry," I typed back. Move on.

"I need help," read the text from Angelica.

"How can I help you?" I responded.

"I have bad problem."

"Bad problem?" I asked. Something big must be happening.

"Yes, from Rose's birthday party. I have crabs."

"What?' I wrote back. Damn. That must have been some party.

"I have crabs"

I reread the text. Against my better judgement, beset by wonder, I typed back.

"How can I help?" Not much, I was guessing. Curiosity came at me like a tiger, consuming.

Then I texted, "Need a can of lighter fluid? An electric razor? An ice pick? A comb?" I erased all that before I sent it.

"Can you take shells? To garbage. If I leave here, they stink," came the answer.

Ahhhh . . . now I understood. At this point, my curiosity was overwhelming. So I responded.

"Yes. When?"

"Now," came the text.

Ten minutes later, I drove up to her home in my 1989 Ranger pickup. I had kept that truck after I gave up managing the cattle ranch. My decision then had been easy: it was paid for, it was battered, it was four-wheel drive, and I thought that I needed a truck to carry dead pigs when I hunted. I had seldom hunted since giving up the ranch. Now, sitting in the foggy darkness outside of her home, I thought that keeping that little brown truck had been one of the wisest decisions of my life.

I texted, "Outside."

She came out onto the front steps. By the dim light of the

porch, I could see her small, slender form. She was wearing olive-colored exercise sweats, velour, white trim. Even the looseness of the clothing could not hide her solid curves. I looked at her long, thick, black hair, plaited and hanging down over her shoulder. I saw her round face, her full lips. I felt my heart jump, once, twice. That was unexpected. Be calm, I said to myself. I took a deep breath. I got out of the truck and walked towards her.

"Hi," she said softly.

I didn't stand too close.

"We go round the side yard, to the back," she said.

"How are Cesar and Rose?" I asked.

"It was a great party," she said. "Maybe two hundred people, a bounce house. It was good."

I felt a flare of resentment that Francesca had not been invited. I said nothing. She turned and walked to the tall wooden gate, unpainted, which led to the backyard. She opened it and walked before me into the darkness.

I could smell the garbage before I saw it. An oceanic reek burned my nostrils. The garbage was in a plastic bag, one of the biggest plastic bags ever, white in the darkness. Angelica stood next to it.

"You take, okay?" Angelica asked.

I responded by reaching out and grabbing the neck of the bag. I was wishing I had worn gloves. The lifting motion caused some warm air to belch from the bag, as paper plates and paper tablecloths settled, and the stench of decaying seafood enveloped me. I lifted the bag higher. Agape, I thought. Curiosity satisfied.

"No problem," I responded. "How are the kids?"

"They shouldn't see you, okay?" she responded.

I didn't answer. I began to walk back towards the front yard holding the white plastic bag in front of me, at arm's length, the Saint Nicolas of garbage, the Santa of . . .

I could hear liquid trickling inside the bag.

"This thing's sealed, right?" I asked.

— Honor —

"Of course," she responded quietly. "Thank you for doing this. Goodnight." She walked back through the front door and into the house.

The next morning I woke up at 3:30 a.m., up like a shot. Exhausted.

I contemplated that I was now the garbage man. I had to smile. That gargantuan white plastic garbage bag was in the dumpster at the office, replete with the remnants of Dungeness crab and pancit and fish bones, fermenting. Cats had probably already plundered it.

I lay back in bed. So tired. Then I realized, for the thousandth time, that Jerome wasn't resting. Somewhere out there, Jerome was probably already at work, at 4 a.m., combing his wealth, stepping into his elegant clothes in his resplendent bedroom, preparing for yet another solid, efficient, productive, wealth-building day.

I rolled myself out of bed, fumbled into my athletic clothes, and walked out to the driveway. Caught by surprise, three raccoons caromed around the truck bed, two small kits and a parent. They jumped out, claws scraping on metal, landed on the cement driveway with small plopping sounds, and dashed off into the predawn black. I was too tired to care. I drove the XTerra through the stygian darkness to the YMCA to lift weights. It was foggier and colder than it had been the night before.

Later that morning I was dressed, ready for the day, still at home, browsing the Internet about the stock markets of the world. My understanding—my continuing perception—was that stock markets were overvalued. We would reallocate assets soon, make the clients' portfolios less risky, and prepare for an October correction that must surely be out there.

Alongside me on the green leather couch, my cell phone buzzed. Lanie. I answered.

"Globalbank needs to talk with you. Angelica didn't pay her mortgage. They're going to foreclose."

"*That's* not good," I responded. "Why did they call me? I'm no longer trustee, am I?"

"Apparently they think you are. Apparently, Angelica didn't file the letter releasing you."

"I'm not telling them any different," I replied. "Be right there."

If I didn't keep my promise to Tommy, then nothing else mattered. It was a question of character to me. If I didn't respond to this, they would run Angelica in circles and foreclose for sure. It was about Tommy now, not his widow. When I defended Tommy, I defended myself. My entire life was on the line. Do this, get it done, and move on.

I put on my blue sports coat. I set the house alarm, walked out into the driveway, and . . . there was no XTerra. I remembered that Ernst had taken it to work. I walked to the little Ranger truck. In the battered bed of the truck I saw a large oil stain, which had dribbled out the back, under the tail gate and onto the driveway. It reeked of sesame oil and rotting crab. The garbage had leaked last night.

When I drove the truck into the driveway of my office, Lanie came out to greet me. "You better call them back right now," she said. "They're pretty angry. What smells?"

I stepped out of the truck. "I don't smell anything."

Lanie looked at me, feigning amazement. "No seriously, I smell something," she said as she circled the truck. "Oh, what is that? That is *foul!"*

She saw the oil stain. She pointed. "What did you do? Kill a skunk?"

I considered that. Given my current life habits, she might assume anything.

I told her what had happened. Then I parked the truck out on the street.

The voice of the man on the other end of the phone was calmly emphatic. "Look, Mr. Ericson, we *can't* refinance this loan because the residence is *not* owner-occupied. Now the resident is *not* making the monthly payment. It's just time to end this."

"The owner is dead," I responded. "His widow and his children are now living in the home, and they have inherited this property."

"That's not clear to us. Perhaps we can talk with the owner."

"He's a box of ashes on the mantle."

"I understand that, but the regulations say we have to speak with the owner."

"He's dead. We may expect that his soul is in heaven."

"He's at home, right?"

"In a sense, yes."

"Then may we speak with him?"

"Know any good mediums?"

"Mr. Ericson, I know that you mean well, but the fact is, the owner hasn't paid his mortgage for months. We've sent him warning letters. We sent him a certified letter. It says here that the certified letter was accepted by his wife, Angelica Narcisco."

"When did that happen?" I asked.

"A few weeks ago, she accepted it."

"Hmmm." I was working my mental calendar. That would be right before the crab feed.

"Yes, sir, she signed for him. That indicates that he's read it by now. And you are listed as trustee."

"Who is listed as trustee?" I shot back.

"You are," replied the tired voice.

"Why wouldn't Thomas be trustee of his own trust, if he was still alive?"

"I don't know, sir, that's not my business. All I know is that I need to speak to him now and we keep leaving messages on his home phone. That's why we're calling you."

"Well, he's not going to call you back. Can you guess why?"

"Tell me, sir."

"It's because he's dead, deceased, passed on to his final reward, defunct, expired, mort, muerto, cashed in his chips, expired, breathed his last, and he's a box of ashes on the mantle. It's a bit hard to talk when you don't have vocal cords or a jaw

— Chapter 32 —

213

or lips. Did your barbecue ever talk to you?"

"No, sir, I still have to speak with him, sir."

"You should have a death certificate. I have sent you three certified copies, three different times. I sent *those* via certified mail too. Clearly, you can see that Thomas Narcisco MD is deceased."

"I can see that, sir, we have receipts for them. But somehow, we lost them, so technically, to us, Mr. Narcisco is still alive."

"He'll be delighted to hear it. His family will probably be delighted and terrified at the same time. I mean, you know, that living dead thing. Where can we pick him up, to bring him home?"

"No, sir, I mean we only think he's alive technically, from a legal perspective."

"That's good, because all I know is a box of ashes on the mantle. I could open it up, look in, see if there's a little man or something running around in there. A little legal man of some kind."

"That won't be necessary, sir. We still have to foreclose on the house if he can't talk to us. It's regulations. This is a courtesy call to let you know that a law enforcement person and a representative of the bank will be by tomorrow afternoon to put up the notice."

"You have to inform the owner by mail of that."

Silence. Some garbled discussion on the other end, then the comment, "We already did that, sir, two weeks ago, and his wife signed for the letter. Technically, legally, I mean, she's not his widow, she's his wife, since we lost his death certificate. That means he's alive, and I need to talk with him, or foreclose."

I was silent for a few minutes while I let my mind expand to encompass that. Finally I spoke. I tried not to shriek with rage, to be reasonable, to be businesslike.

"Well, here's my plan. Either you can have your supervisor call me back, and we can discuss a mortgage restructuring, as is legal and proper, or I'll see you there at the residence tomorrow afternoon with a professional camera crew. I'll have your minions on camera on YouTube within thirty minutes of their arrival. Picture it: 'Globalbank forecloses on minority widow and orphans.'"

"That may bring a lawsuit, sir."

"AND WHAT KIND OF LAWSUIT WILL WE COUNTER-FILE? THINK ABOUT THAT."

"Shouting isn't necessary, sir. You are harassing me."

Harassing my ass. An axe between the eyes is harassment. Defense against unlawful seizure is rational. "My apologies, I'm just trying to create dialogue. Here's the bottom line: you show up, you are on film, and it becomes a racial issue. Keep negotiating or *60 Minutes.* Make your choice."

"Sir, given the circumstances I'm going to have my supervisor call you to see if we can't find a way to avoid any theatrics when we foreclose. By regulation, I must insist that you communicate to Mr. Narcisco that foreclosure is imminent."

I sighed. "Oh, I'll do that," I said.

"Have him call us if you are able to make contact," said the voice.

"I'll buy a Ouija board tonight," I said.

There was a click as the line went dead.

Chapter Thirty-three

October 2013

S tanford. Dr. Häyhä Pekk was as beautiful as ever. As always, she wasn't smiling. All business. I looked out the window to see who was at the cafeteria below us. Only a few were eating, looking at their phones, the brilliant beauty of the morning light on the trees unseen. I wanted to be down there.

"Beirut," said Dr. Pekk.

Shit. I felt nauseated at once.

"What?" I said.

"It says here that you were in Beirut for the bombing of the Marine barracks on October 23, 1983. Thirty years ago, exactly."

"Well, I wasn't really there until afterwards," I responded. I felt like a child confronted with shoplifting a toy.

Dr. Pekk leaned forward, her smooth, blonde hair cascading down the side of her face. "Tell me more."

"That is what I least want to do," I replied.

I looked at her stonily and contemplated leaping from the window, clutching the willow limbs waving just a few yards distance in the sunlight. Climbing down to freedom from there.

"Go to the pain," she commanded.

"I was an FAO. I was on the Iwo Jima. That's a helicopter aircraft carrier. I was supposed to be there at the BLT, but I wasn't. I had been delayed for a few weeks in Germany, in Berlin, a conference about the Red Army Faction. Bader Meinholf. Terrorists," I responded. I felt queasier. I pondered bolting from the office, bee lining to the bathroom.

"What's a BLT, and what's an FAO?"

"BLT. Battalion Landing Team. An infantry fighting unit of about one thousand people. Back then, all men. They were sent there by the American government to safeguard lives and property during the Israeli invasion the year before," I said evenly. "Instead they found themselves in a war, about four different factions kicking the crap out of each other, with the Marines in the middle."

"Okay. And what's an FAO?" she asked.

I focused on her light blue eyes. There was comfort there. She seemed all business, but sympathetic. The need to vomit had passed. I was sweating now, hands wet, and slightly dizzy. Chest pains.

Keep talking. Keep looking at those light blue eyes. Forgive me, doctor, if I cling to what is good in the world. Beauty, wherever it is. Right now, it is in you.

"An FAO is a specially-trained officer who studies and becomes an expert in a certain country. Mine was Lebanon," I responded.

"Had you been to Lebanon before then?" she asked.

"Yes, at the Embassy. I was a talking head for six weeks. My stay there happened before the first bombing, which blew off the front of the embassy. Killed many. You would think we would have considered that a warning."

"There was another bombing?" she asked.

"Oh, yes. Months before the Marines. Killed the whole CIA staff. Good people."

Then I was silent, contemplating that first explosion. The morning light in the light green willow leaves outside the window.

"Please go on. Tell me about your own experience," said Dr. Pekk.

"That day, thirty years ago, I was in a CH-46 helicopter, in the back by the bubble windows, flying off the Iwo Jima, and when I saw that big column of smoke rising in the sky, black as burning tires, and I thought, my God, it's happened again. We were dumb as a box of nails. Damn."

— Honor —
218

"Was anyone shooting at you?" she asked.

"Oh, yes," I responded. "A few shots from Hooterville hit the helicopter. They sounded like someone beating on the aircraft with hammers. But they didn't do any damage, and we landed right next to the place where the bomb had gone off."

"Hooterville?" she asked.

I continued, ignoring her question. "I came off the helicopter and the whole building had collapsed,"

I motioned with my arms. Sweat was running down my armpits beneath my undershirt.

"Nothing left of this great big building. Smoke rising. Smell like gasoline and gunpowder and burning and chalk and blood and shit. Marines, Lebanese civilians, just like little ants climbing on this big pancaked four-story building. Debris, twisted rebar, giant concrete blocks, all around, and some of it was body parts, torsos, heads, arms, legs, all covered in dust. And it sounded like the wind was blowing through the wreckage, but it wasn't the wind." I stopped and gulped down a hiccup.

I looked in her beautiful light blue eyes and I saw tears. Oh bless you, doctor.

"What was it?" she asked.

"It was the sound of hundreds of people, trapped inside the collapsed building, screaming, shouting, calling for help," I said. "I think there must have been a fire down there in the wreckage."

Silence. The psychiatrist looked at me and waited.

"Now I know I was listening to people die," I said quietly.

"Did you get them out?" she asked.

"Oh, no," I said. "They were able to save the chaplain. The rest died before they could move away the giant concrete blocks. The sounds just got quieter and quieter, and then it was still."

"What did you do?" she asked.

"Not much," I said. "I could speak Arabic, so I coordinated the Lebanese construction workers. Quite helpful. They brought the big cranes we needed. Also, later, a lot of celebrities showed up to gawk at the wreckage. I helped with them. Congressmen.

Vice-president Bush. That sort."

I felt calmer now.

"What happened then?" she asked.

"Well, I didn't do shit," I responded.

"What do you mean?" she asked.

"I ask myself damned near every day. What would have happened if I hadn't stopped for that two weeks in Berlin? What would have happened if I had just been there, just talked to one more Lebanese, picked up the warnings somehow, somehow kept all those men from dying? I mean, my God, the state department was telling them to keep the magazines out of their M-16s to avoid looking threatening. It shouldn't have happened."

My sweating hands gripped the armrests of the chair. It occurred to me that I might pull them off.

"Think that through," she offered.

"I didn't do anything," I responded.

"Think that through," she said again.

"If only I had done something," I said.

"Come on, now. Push that thought," she said.

"I really couldn't have done anything, could I?" I explored the thought in my mind.

"What do you think, really?" asked Dr. Pekk.

Vivian, the woman loan officer on the other end of the phone at Seaforth Bank was silent after I outlined my plan. Then she spoke. "Yes, Mr. Ericson, you can do that. We have a very successful relationship with you dating back several decades. Five very successful real estate purchases. We would need Mrs. Narcisco to cosign."

"No problem there," I replied.

"Will there be a down payment?" she asked.

"Yes, I'll get that from my own investments," I replied.

The woman was silent. "Mr. Ericson, are you aware that by doing this you will comingle that down payment with the Narcisco Trust? It's like giving it to the Narcisco trust."

I considered that. "I'll have a lawyer draw up a bifurcation agreement which stipulates that the investment will remain separate."

"Does Mrs. Narcisco have any income?" asked Vivian.

"Not really," I responded. "She's a widow."

"You will probably want to consider resigning as trustee of the Narcisco Trust to prevent conflict of interest questions," Vivian offered.

"Yes," I said.

"Well . . . ," said Vivian, "I've run the numbers, and as far as I can determine, to buy real estate of this magnitude outright, and to assume the payments, we can get your interest rate to the lowest possible level if you also list your family trust income and assets. Can you do that?"

The family trust. I was the manager, the talking head, the smiling dog, for our pooled family money. The owners were my mother, my sister, all our children, and ourselves. We had carefully nurtured it as separate property, investing patiently over the decades in the financial markets and in real estate, successfully keeping it safe from divorces or profligates. Now, collectively, we had millions.

"Not pledging as collateral? The trust has a spendthrift clause," I asked.

"Oh, no," said Vivian's voice on the phone. "Just list the assets and the income."

Well, actually that was honest, wasn't it? My percentage of ownership *was* mine. I paid taxes on the income, even though I never spent any of it.

"List the trust. Let's get that interest rate down as low as possible," I replied.

"3.5-percent," Vivian responded. "Does that work for you?"

"Perfectly," I replied.

After I hung up the phone, I sat at my office desk, awash in client files and mutual fund information. As always, my desk looked as though a windstorm had scattered papers randomly. No clearly-defined piles. Yet I knew where everything was.

Through the open doors of the bathroom that connected us,

I could see Lanie working away at her own desk, oblivious to the fact that I had just created the means to join, or at least list, my life savings with that of a woman who had only loved me in passing. Most probably, Angelica had never loved me, had simply reached out to me in her need. Was I doing the right thing? I didn't know. It seemed right. I knew that part of this was driven by emotional hunger and part by lust, but was it *right?*

To distract myself I read the news in the *Wall Street Journal.* I'm still a paper newspaper person: I want to hold it, page through it, smell it. Islamic radicals, styling themselves as Islamic State, were reconquering Iraq. They had blown up a turquoise mosque. Why would Moslems blow up their own mosque? Apparently, hundreds were dead. Were those radicals now where I had once been?

I couldn't sit still. I reached behind me and gathered up the four battered tomahawks on the floor beneath my desk, and walked past Lanie with axes in hand.

She looked up, noted the tomahawks, and nodded.

"Tough day?" she asked.

"I just need a break," I replied.

"I couldn't help but overhear," she responded. Lanie. Hearing like an Ozark big-eared bat.

"Thoughts?"

"Angelica is broken," she said. "I've seen that in our meetings."

Thanks, Buddha.

She continued. "Everybody's broken, and broken people are in pain. People in pain are selfish. And selfish people think mostly of themselves."

"So that makes Angelica selfish?" I asked. The tomahawks were heavy in my hands. I needed to throw them.

"Actually I was thinking of you. You've been through a lot," responded Lanie.

She was right.

"So I can't pin this on her?" I asked.

"Nope. So you need to ask yourself, does this financial deal make sense? Think rationally. Think like a warrior. Is it the right thing?" she asked.

"Not at the full value of the note," I replied. "That's way too overvalued. But buy the home out of a short sale or a foreclosure, and it's worth it."

"Hmmmm. She's not going to love you for this, you know," said Lanie. "She's just not that into you. If you do it, it should be because it's a good investment for you too."

"What else?" I asked.

"I've discussed the mortgage with Angelica," continued Lanie. "No, she has not made the monthly payments. One of her Filipino family had advised her that the best thing she could do was to force a restructuring by simply not sending the mortgage check each month."

"That's not going to work well," I replied.

"It's likely to cost her the home," said Lanie.

I told Lanie about the 3.5-percent refinance offer from Vivian. "Please have Robert review the papers, and please have Angelica sign them if Robert approves," I added.

"What? You don't want to be with Angelica?" Lanie laughed. "What's changing?"

I grinned. "All I know is that I'll help everyone more if I'm not actually there."

Chapter Thirty-four

November 2013

Three weeks later. The morning dawned bright and crisp. Fall is often spectacular in central California. I had gone out for a 5 a.m. run, headlamp and all, so now, at around 10 a.m., I was feeling accomplished. It was a few days before my fifty-ninth birthday.

Angelica sat across from me at the table at the Cherry Bean, a locally-owned coffee shop. The Dow Jones Industrial Average was down about two hundred points, far less than it needed to fall, in my opinion. I studied the chart surreptitiously on my iPhone. I was deeply glad that we had stayed in the stock markets, at least partially. The clients and I were making real money these days.

Angelica's eyes were covered by large, round Louis Vuitton sunglasses against the brilliant November sunshine that poured through the glass of the front window. Another drought year. It was too warm. The gold LV monograms on the temples of her glasses glittered in the sunlight, looking hot. Angelica was wearing a different hat, summerier, and a string-strapped summer dress. Beautiful shoulders. She had to be slightly chilled. Before her sat a small bowl of oatmeal and a tall paper cup of latte mocha expresso something. There had to be enough caffeine and sugar in that giant vessel to reanimate Frankenstein.

Angelica herself had been silent since Lanie had met with her to sign. She hadn't even asked about the house, or the status of our pooled loan. With that approved, I was waiting for a short sale, waiting for some sort of price break, before I moved to purchase Tommy's home. That new power in itself had brought me a new sense of calm, regardless of whatever man might be in Angelica's life.

Mostly I was deeply curious, about her, and about the future. Where was Jerome now?

"My friends turn me on for this singles site, and I'm on it, and you should see men who contact me! Doctors and lawyers love me, want to marry me," she said.

"It call Tinder," she added after a moment's silence.

Tinder. The prospect of venereal disease reared its tapeworm head, somewhere in the back of my mind. *Tinder. No Jerome then. Just chaos.*

The thought came to my mind that we were in two very separate emotional places, far apart.

"How can I help you?" I asked.

She looked squarely at me, not smiling. "I need you," she said. That was probably true, in a non-romantic way, I thought. Words like this were honest, but they were a bit like hearing the dentist's drill in the cubicle next to yours.

I thought about that. There, there is the brokenness, I thought. My brokenness, not hers.

"You need to help me; my family is coming to visit."

"How can I help?" I said quietly.

"I need you. I mean, I need a man," she replied.

I said nothing. That fact seemed already evident. I pondered how to say no.

"I need you to show my father and my mother and my brothers and sisters California," she replied. 'They are coming to visit."

I had always enjoyed her family, via Facebook and Skype.

"Why not another?" I asked.

"Oh, Garth!" She threw up her hands. "It is PRIVACY! I will dishonor if Jerome revealed now. It too soon since Tommy dies."

So was she seeing doctors and lawyers who loved her, or Jerome, or both? And who was dishonored?

"Do you understand that I don't wish to deceive?" I responded. "My whole life is built on truth. Or at least my best efforts

— Honor —

226

at truth."

"Grrrr! If you really love me then you will help!"

I contemplated how to say no and escape with minimum pain to everyone. Boundaries. Agape. Meanwhile, she glared at me. Silence.

Then she said, flatly: "Maybe I pregnant."

She was looking somewhere far away, behind those sunglasses. She didn't look happy.

Now it was my turn to stare at her.

"Jerome is the father, I think. I am not sure," she said, almost whispering.

"You think? You guess?" I asked. I kept my voice to almost a whisper.

A tear appeared behind her sunglasses. She had been sitting serenely, but the turmoil inside her, and behind those sunglasses, must be immense. Now . . . nothing but that single tear. Her expression was unchanged.

"You love me, don't you? You love Cesar and Rose," asked Angelica. "I want to feel that the baby will be loved by somebody. I need to know that. My family needs to know that. The child needs to know that. Now, I don't know. Unless someone decides to be a father."

So. Several possible fathers. I thought about the terrible effects of a completely fatherless pregnancy on her entire traditional family. Challenging. So much better if a father would be involved. So much better for Rose and Cesar. They would need a living, breathing father in their lives more than ever.

"Why not just share this with Jerome?" I asked.

"He already think I chase for money. If I am pregnant then he feel I trick him with baby," she responded. "Also it is too soon after Tommy."

We sat there while the world turned. I was way too old for this.

"Tell me what you need," I responded.

"I promise I will tell everything to Jerome before my family visits, but we must plan now. I don't want to seem a foreigner to Jerome, and I don't want to be needy. Besides, if my family meets you, then later perhaps you will help them accept the American way, to accept my child. Not now, but later. First, they just meet you. When they visit, where do I take them?" she asked. "Where does a native Californian take visitors?"

We had gone from family to a baby to Disneyland. That left me spinning.

"Well, certainly, San Francisco, Yosemite, and a Carmel Beach fire," I answered. "Everybody wants to visit Disneyland. You do that. I can take them shooting."

It occurred to me that I was suddenly all-in. Damn. For Tommy.

"Hmmm. Yes. Can you make reservations?" she replied.

"Yes, but they are expensive. For me, it's a big deal," I responded.

"The money always big deal to you, Garth. One reason Jerome so attractive is that nothing is a big deal to him. He is rich. Rich in money and rich in spirit. He have everything, so everything bore him. Not big deal to him. So it is not big deal to me."

"And yet you are sitting here with me," I said dryly.

She ignored the comment.

"Okay, here's the plan." I was suddenly decisive. "I have reservations at the Ahwahnee at Yosemite. I made them months ago. They were for just you and me. I'll change them to a family room at Curry or at the Yosemite Lodge, if there's an opening. Also I'll get reservations for another hotel, not the Marine's Memorial, in San Francisco for New Years for you all. And, if Jerome funds this—you *are* paying me back, right?"

"Oh, yes, thank you," Angelica said. "I pay you back. Thank you. Can we still have beach fire?"

"Of course," I answered. "I want to meet your family, after talking with them and Facebooking them all this time. It will be great to see Cesar and Rose. I look forward to seeing Jerome again. It might as well be now. January 2nd?"

I contemplated that I was now lying. See Jerome again? I'd rather get a discount colonoscopy. Ah well, anything to make nice. Hopefully God and my ancestors would forgive.

"Yes. Thank you again. See you then," she said. Apparently she couldn't read my mind. She stood up, picked up that colossal paper cup of coffee, and gracefully walked out the front door.

Chapter Thirty-five

December 2013

December 27, 2013, was another up day for the stock market. I arrived at the office in the cold predawn darkness, around 5:45 a.m. The sky was very overcast, very dark. I had hopes for rain.

As I pulled my yellow XTerra into the driveway of my family's ancestral home, I saw a small reflection on the front porch. There was the homeless man in his soiled sleeping bag. I walked onto the porch, which was lit by a dim overhead light. The man was moving within the bag. His long brown hair, even more matted than before, protruded from the top. Beside him the iPhone—with a broken screen, I noted—was plugged into the outlet, charging.

It was the holiday season. Most people still had their Christmas decorations in place. In fact most people weren't even working. Here was this man: had he vandalized my porch all those times, or was someone else guilty of stealth defecation? My immediate reaction was to call the police, to have him evicted. But it was cold, and this was the holiday season.

Instead I got back in my XTerra and drove to Peninsula Bakery as the sun began to rise, stood in line with other drowsy overcoated citizens in that blessed smell of yeast, and purchased one chocolate-almond croissant. Still hot in its bag. The smell of the pastry filled the car. Worth the price by itself. Then I walked onto the porch of my office, where my great grandfather and all his descendants had sat, and I placed the small, butter-greased paper bag next to the sleeping homeless man. I went inside and began to work.

I sat at my desk, headset on, and watched as holiday sales came in higher than expected. The stock markets opened up.

The weekend was planned: I was taking Francesca to the California Academy of Sciences in San Francisco on Saturday, and then all the adult children would gather with me for a four-days-late family Christmas on Sunday with my mother.

Angelica would be in Yosemite at Camp Curry tonight with her family, at the lodgings that I had arranged by transferring my Ahwahnee luxury hotel reservations, for one night, to three nights at a family room at Curry. We were very lucky that we had been able to do that.

So many plans.

From my seat, I looked out the front window. The homeless man was half out of his bag, huddling in his dirty military surplus field jacket, breath steaming, with the croissant held up close to his densely long-bearded face, eating, staring straight ahead. I stood, put on my own coat, and walked out the front door onto the porch, feeling the slap of the cold, and I stood before him. This was the first time I had ever actually met him.

"How's the croissant?" I asked.

"*I don't speak your stupid English,*" he said in Spanish. Matter of factly, as though he was discussing TV shows.

He didn't look at me. He stared emphatically, angrily, at the croissant. His breath steamed as he chewed.

I replied in Spanish, a remnant of my life before, the language of my ancestors the caballeros on the ranch. *"Merry Christmas. You are welcome to be here. But someone has been defecating here, and I don't like cleaning it up. Please keep this porch clean. The shelter is two blocks away. It will be warmer there. God bless you."*

I reached into my pocket and took out two twenty dollar bills. It was intended as lunch money for the office staff and me, a sort of thank you from me to them for working through the holiday. I handed the bills to him. He didn't look at me: he just reached out an arm elliptically and snatched them out of my grasp.

"Fuck you, rich bastard," he said in Spanish. He had finished the croissant, and now he looked at me. *"Fuck you to hell for your whiteness. Fuck you for your wealth. Fuck you for this house and fuck you for your car and fuck you for your whole life. I shit here whenever I can. It's what you deserve. I tear down your fucking gringo flag and I wipe my ass with it."*

He spoke quietly. Now he was staring at me. Hatred twisted his face. I realized he was probably quite mentally ill.

"So you defecate here?" I asked in Spanish. Never mind the flag.

"It is my joy to spray shit on your perfect world. If I ever get inside your home, I will strangle your children and shit on them, fuck your wife, then strangle her too," he said.

Well, then. I looked straight at him. So much anger all over the world. I wondered why he thought I had a wife. He might be thinking of Lanie. Was Lanie here yet? Whatever else happened, I had to keep Lanie and the staff safe.

I spoke in Spanish. *"It is time for you to leave, and not return."*

"Fuck you," he responded. *"I will leave when I choose. But first I might beat you to death, and then go in your home and fuck your wife. I haven't decided yet. It's still early."*

I replied, *"I will call the police now. They will be here in ten minutes. If you come inside this home and attack us, you will die. Go now."* I turned on my heels, walked back into the home, shut and locked the door. Then I called the police.

The dispatcher on the other end of the phone was equivocal. "I'm not sure you have a right to threaten him like that." She sounded concerned.

"He threatened my family and he's on my property. I need him gone," I said.

The voice on the phone sounded worried. "He has no place to go, and it's cold, and he's mentally ill. How can you treat a poor mentally ill person like that? You know he's not responsible for his behavior. Also you know that the police are busy with more important public safety matters. It might take them hours. Perhaps you and your family should simply go have a cup of coffee away from your home and let him alone. Perhaps he won't come in if he isn't triggered by your actions."

I responded. "I'm staying here. I'm armed with a Remington 870 Mariner 12-gauge shotgun. If he forces his way in here, and he attempts to carry out his threats, I will respond. If that's what you want, I can live with it."

Two officers arrived ten minutes later to find the homeless man sitting on the porch next to a large fresh steaming turd. Apparently, he had wiped himself on a t-shirt, which was laying stained with brown next to his deposit. The man's sleeping bag was rolled, and he sat hunched over drinking from his paper-wrapped bottle. The officers approached with their hands on their Glock pistols, speaking to the homeless man quietly in Spanish. He stood. He turned. They searched him. They found a large rusted kitchen knife in his waistband. It was simply a kitchen knife. It was very large. They took the knife, confiscated the paper-bag covered bottle, turned the man, walked him to the squad car, and inserted him into the back seat. He was docile.

As the police officers were gently placing the man into the back seat of the squad car, with his breath steaming, a civilian car pulled up and blocked the driveway. It was a small hybrid Ford Escape car, white, with a State of California emblem on the door. A slight red-haired man emerged, dapper, clean, red tie. Tan raincoat. He walked up to me as I stood on the porch watching.

"Sir, I'm here to represent the homeless man you just evicted," said the man. He seemed to be in his late twenties.

"You mean the man who just took a shit on my front porch?" I said, gesturing towards the still-steaming turd and the brown-stained t-shirt lying alongside it, next to the filthy sleeping bag. Also there was the iPhone, still plugged in.

"The dispatcher said you threatened my client with a gun," said the young red-haired man. He seemed offended. "She was very concerned for his safety."

"I have a gun safe with a pump action shotgun, an M-1

— Honor —
234

Garand from World War II, and a pistol, which is in my office if you wish to see it. Do you have a warrant?"

The young man's face flushed. "It's possible that you have committed a racist hate crime. We don't need a warrant. I could call those police officers here right now," he responded with rising anger, "So the state has probable cause."

"Probable cause of what?" I asked. "A person on my front porch illegally said that he was contemplating killing my family. I didn't brandish. I didn't threaten, except to warn him not to enter my home. Instead, I called the police. And it worked, didn't it?"

The young man gritted his teeth. "You probably violated his rights," he said. "You own guns. That makes you dangerous."

I pondered that. "He violated my home," I answered. "And there's that."

I gestured toward the mess.

"Are you going to clean that up?" I asked. "Many thanks if you do. I'm tired of cleaning them up."

"If you installed a public bathroom on your property as you were advised then the homeless people wouldn't need to do that," said the young red-haired man.

"No," I responded. "I'd rather pay for a fence, really. That way my children can enjoy their ancestral home without that."

Again I gestured towards the mess on the front porch.

The young man glared at me. He was so well dressed. Red tie. Red hair. Now, red face.

"I'll . . . I'll secure the client's personal possessions and I'll be gone," he said.

He pulled blue rubber gloves from the pockets of his rain coat and drew them over his hands. He then withdrew a giant green garbage bag and began to stuff the homeless man's possessions into it, carefully stepping around the feces. Then he stood, sealed the bag, glared at me, and marched to his car.

The turd and the t-shirt were still there. The turd was no longer steaming. The sun had risen. It was much lighter outside.

I stepped back into the living room and shut the door. I felt

— Chapter 35 —

exhausted. I went into the back of the home to get the Lysol, the rubber gloves, and the new scrub brush, and piece of cardboard for scraping. I saw Lanie, working at her desk.

"I was so preoccupied with all that that I didn't even know you had come in," I said quietly.

"I saw the police when I drove up," Lanie responded. "I didn't want to get involved in all that . . . stuff." She laughed quietly. "Well, at least you solved the problem, I hope."

I laughed. God, I hoped so. Then I went to the porch and began to clean.

Later I was back at my desk, with my brain back into the stock market as much as possible. Emerging markets might be a bargain, so long as we ignored China. The baton seemed to be passing from the U.S. to the rest of the world. The economic greatness of America was fading. Perhaps it might be time to reflect that in our portfolios.

In a few hours, the weekend would begin. Something to anticipate with joy.

A text from Margaret: "Sudden change! I'm taking Francesca to visit Jack's family with my parents."

My text response: "We were planning on our family Christmas on Sunday!!!"

A text from Margaret: "We are already loading the car. You know this is traditionally my weekend."

I was burning inside. I wanted to shout, to call Margaret and yell. I didn't.

I took refuge in Facebook. Angelica and I were still friends there. It did me good to see Cesar and Rose smiling. There they were at Lake Tahoe. Jerome' estate. So Jerome was still definitely in the picture. Did he know of Angelica's pregnancy? What had she told him? Whatever was happening was now between the two of them. I could only hope that he was genuinely the father of this new baby.

Lake Tahoe was five hours away from Yosemite. They should be in Yosemite now. And yes, Angelica was still married to

Tommy, at least on Facebook.

I texted Angelica. "Your reservations are for tonight. Are you there yet?"

Angelica texted back: "Oh, sorry, our plans changed. We will stay at Lake Tahoe. We aren't going to Yosemite after all."

I texted back. "That's six hundred dollars' worth of plans changing. Are you and Jerome going to pay for it?"

Angelica texted back: "Sorry. We won't be there so why should I pay?"

A quick call to Yosemite reservations. "No, sir, it's inside the cancellation deadline. We can't refund your reservation on such short notice."

So I was going to eat six hundred dollars. My mind was working. Francesca wasn't going to be with us this weekend. That was unavoidable. The three adult children and my mother would be happy whatever I decided.

"Can you move the reservation to someplace cheaper, for one person, then roll the money we save forward into next year for a new reservation?" I asked the man.

"Oh, yes, we can do that, as long as you have three nights, starting tonight, in Yosemite," said the man.

"What's the cheapest you have?" I asked.

"It's the *only* thing we have," replied the man. "Everything else is full. The only thing left is an unheated tent in Curry Village," responded the man.

"I'll take it," I said. "Three nights in an unheated tent, Curry Village. Roll the remaining balance into three nights at Yosemite Lodge in 2014. I'll pay the additional cost on that next year."

I had just kept hundreds of dollars from being squandered. Self-congratulations. I turned to Lanie in the other office, and I smiled. "Guess who's going to Yosemite tonight?" I said.

"Whoever it is, he's going to freeze his ass off," Lanie responded, smiling.

Chapter Thirty-six

December 2013

Long after dark, I arrived at Curry Village and checked into my unheated tent, a white canvas affair with black metal bunks, one of hundreds ranked closely in the dark and dusty lanes. Immediately a disadvantage became clear: unlike a genuine campsite, there was no campfire for warming, no alternative to an immediate retreat to the arctic sleeping bag. No cell reception, either.

I disrobed and climbed into my chill sleeping bag as quickly as possible, ducking my head deeply inside. Visions of a warming fire danced in my mind, together with the family tradition of a gin martini at the Ahwahnee, as sleep took me unawares.

A chattering awoke me in the night, a woman's voice, angry, scolding in some unknown language, apparently Asian. She continued on, with a man grunting his responses occasionally as the volume and pitch of her voice rose. I pushed the illumination button on my digital wrist watch. 4:30 a.m. *Oh my.*

When I extended my arm outside the bag to see my watch, my fingers chilled instantly in the biting cold. Those tents . . . so close together. Forced to listen to the discussion in an unknown language only a few feet away.

"How could you EVER talk me into this?" the woman's voice seemed to be saying. "What demon from the underworld convinced you to drag me into this frozen hell?"

Actually, she sounded like Dino the dinosaur dog from the Flintstones. The translation was all in my half-awake, Ambien-soaked mind.

The man's voice grunted like a samurai in an old Japanese black and white film. "I'm sorry," he seemed to say. "It looked so good on the Internet!" The voice seemed weary.

"Bakaaaah!" said the woman's voice. "You know all the Internet pictures are taken in spring don't you?" she seemed to say. "You owe me bigtime for this one, buster."

Perhaps they were on their honeymoon. Without a winter-capable sleeping bag, they must be freezing over there, perhaps six feet and two layers of canvas fabric distant.

"I'm sorry," the man's voice seemed to be saying. The voice was contrite. Then he said more. Of course the words were unclear, since I didn't know the language, but the man's voice ended distinctly with the slowly-spoken, clearly-enunciated word, "Disneyrand."

Perhaps they weren't clearly aware that Disneyrand was more than a day's drive away. Whatever had been said, there was now silence in the other tent. Then the woman's voice came again, much quieter, with a loving tone, short words, then more silence. There were tiny kissing sounds.

Listening to an argument in an unknown language was challenge enough. The potential of listening to tourists copulate was direr. Listening to that would lead me to contemplate my aloneness, and then I would think of Angelica and Jerome at Lake Tahoe.

That thought ruined any potential sleep. I reached for my water bottle. Half full. Frozen solid. I put it down, felt for my headlamp and my pants, and rushed, stumbling over pine tree roots in the darkness, to the warming refuge of the coin-operated showers.

I spent a full day in the outdoors hiking up to Vernal and Nevada Falls. This was a drought year. The trail was open. I hiked up to the falls, propelled by cashew nuts and curiosity. After dark, as the freezing cold layered over the valley, I took the bus over to the Ahwahnee Hotel.

The Yosemite Valley floor is actually rather urban, and the

jewel in the park's architectural crown is the ultra-luxurious Ahwahnee Hotel, where movies stars go for their honeymoons and the rooms cost a week's pay. Exorbitant.

But then again, complete luxury experienced rarely may be one of life's blessings. Too much luxury and we don't see the good in it any more: it becomes jaded, banal, normal, boring. Perhaps a dollop of luxury in a rigorous life is a stimulant.

At any rate, that was my interpretation, and thus I had made a point of staying at the Ahwahnee one or two nights each year. Last year I had postponed my visit, waiting for that special night with Angelica. That had never happened. At the moment Angelica and the children were at Lake Tahoe with Jerome. Hard as it was to contemplate, all was probably as it should be.

I *had* stayed joyfully with Margaret and the children here in the past. So many memories of those happy, innocent times, before the world burned.

Given my situation, the bar was a definite step up: it was heated, unlike my tent. Unlike the Curry Village common area, there were actually chairs to sit in. I was alone in the Ahwahnee bar, still wearing my hiking clothing. "Hiking clothing" included a well-used set of United States Marine Corps brown suede boots, a set of worn coffee-stain military BDU ("Battle Dress Utility") pants, long underwear (thankfully unseen), and my antique, bright red oversized ski sweater.

Lack of a collar meant the dining room was off limits. I was enjoying my traditional smoked salmon plate with a large Bombay Blue Sapphire gin martini. Life was good.

Actually, I thought, if I had not already consumed half the martini, I would prefer to simply leave: just get in the car, abandon the overnight reservation, go home. Flee the memories and the dreams. Watch some *Game of Thrones* on TV. Stay warm.

I was lost in that reverie, looking through the floor to ceiling glass partition that divided the bar from the hotel's lobby. The giant Christmas tree out there was shining brilliantly. I hadn't celebrated Christmas yet, I realized. The martini was seeping into my soul, ginesthesia, perfect timing. Beautiful holiday lights. Slender women, carefully dressed in flowing dinner gowns. Timeless affluence.

I turned and looked out of the glass windows, which divided us in the bar from the wintery lawn and swimming pool area outside. The lawn was frozen, half-brown, half-green, with white, fist-sized clots of snow scattered across. Those snow clumps gleamed in the darkness, reflecting the lights of the hotel. Beautiful.

Outside, there was steam rising to the side from the pool, the outlines of people in the mist. Perhaps, I wondered, they were settling into the embracing warmth of the Jacuzzi. That would be something, I thought, to be here with Margaret again, or Angelica, to enjoy that Jacuzzi, then to retreat to that warm room upstairs. At this point, it would be mighty fine to do it alone, as an alternative to freezing tonight at Camp Curry. I felt a pang of regret that I had cashed in my reservations here, for Angelica's abortive plan.

And then I saw Cesar and Rose outside in their snow gear, running, laughing. I looked again. Definitely the two children laughing and running, chasing each other, on the frozen hotel lawn, in the snow clothes I had purchased for them months ago. So . . . they weren't at Lake Tahoe. They were here.

I was not hallucinating. I was not drunk. They were here.

I turned in my chair and looked out at the hotel lobby again. There, by the Christmas tree, smiling, dressed in a stylish, sequined, short black skirt, surrounded by Marta, Mike, Rachaela, and a host of other Filipinos whom I recognized from Facebook as her family, was Angelica. High heels, faux-fur black coat, brown and tan Louis Vuitton clutch bag. The men were wearing sport coats, collared shirts, and slacks. Clearly all were dressed for dinner here at the Ahwahnee.

I didn't see Jerome at all. I watched. Sitting in my red wool snowflake sweater, I was utterly conspicuous, should they look through the glass. They didn't look. I ordered a second Bombay gin martini from a smiling waitress, disregarding the expense as I gratefully felt my toes begin to go numb. After smiles and photographs, Angelica and her family walked together away across the classic hotel lobby, towards the dining room for a sumptuous meal.

The second martini, smooth as drinking an ice cloud. Stifling the urge to go peer into the dining room. Afraid, in fact, to move. Finally I visited the men's room, looked up from a urinal, and there was Mike, Marta's husband, looking at me steadily, face passive, resplendent in a gray striped suit and a red tie. There was a hint of curiosity in his gaze. Completely at a loss for words, I said, "Hey, Mike," as though nothing was unusual at all, washed my hands, and left.

Thence to nighttime public transportation in Yosemite Valley, YARTS for "Yosemite Area Rapid Transit System," and a silent, dark retreat in the gently rocking anonymous bus, watching visitors climb off and on at the various stops along the way, finally stepping down cautiously onto the icy pavement myself when I saw the office lights of Camp Curry in the distance.

The desk clerk was heavy-lidded and tired: the normal glut of chilled visitors was jamming the warm room. It was by now ten at night. I waited in line, seeking in vain to access Facebook, and finally I looked up and I was standing at the reception desk. I informed her that I was leaving tomorrow, and she opined that it was sad that I was abandoning my reservation for tomorrow night.

I said, "Well, there's nothing I can do about that, is there?"

"Ahhh, yes, we have an opening at the Glacier Point ski hut."

I considered that. Clearly, Jerome wasn't resting at all. Clearly, my only refuge was to live my life as fully as possible, to follow the path God had laid out. I had no idea where that path was directing me. I only knew that now I was alone, with a deep aching wound deep inside me half-numbed by gin, and with a palpably hollow sense of surrender. I said yes. Cold and questioning kept me awake most of the night.

The ski resort at Badger Pass, high up in the mountains, and thus in the snow zone even in a drought year. Light attendance.

Parking lot only half-full. Bright sunlight.

I stepped into my battered Epoke backcountry skis, and slipped on my worn backpack, for the 12-mile ski to the overnight-catered hut at Glacier Point. This was my first time on Nordic skis this winter. I stretched my inelastic legs, feeling the rhythm from past years returning, remembering Badger Pass ski school from my own childhood with my ski instructor, a smiling French alpine guide named Nic Fiore. Back then, it was all about cables and snowplow turns. Now we had three pin bindings. Down the hill, then up the other side.

After a mile or so in, I skied past Summit Meadows, and left 90-percent of the gawking, snowshoeing overdressed tourists behind. Ahead of me, the green crowded tall pines and firs. An occasional, rust-colored tree signaled death from beetle and drought. Quiet. Quiet. Quiet. I felt the repetitive glide of Nordic skiing come back into my body as the striding became natural again. I heard the hiss of the skis sliding on the groomed snow. Surprise from so much joy. So many good memories. Above me was a brilliant blue sky with only a few white clouds, and the forest white and green around me.

Ahead of me was the Glacier Point hut, with a waiting hot meal made more perfect by the 12 miles of skiing to obtain it. Tonight: wine, a wondrous blazing fireplace, with all the stars of heaven outside the door, and the moon as well. Surely, I was blessed.

As I skied, rejoicing in the natural rhythm of movement, I realized that only disappointment had forced me to this joy. Had I stayed at the Ahwahnee I'd still be down there, in the valley, the mushroom among roses. Unlike the Ahwahnee, this place was true, and it was mine.

— Honor —

Chapter Thirty-seven

January 2014

January 2, 2014, was one of the shortest days of the year. This was an unnatural winter, a brutal drought year, and so it was unnaturally warm here by the sea at crowded Carmel Beach. According to the calendar, it should be cold and rainy, and instead it was warm and dry, about like a normal April. I had suggested that Angelica bring her family for a traditional beach fire. I had suggested that she bring Jerome, that we begin our new platonic friendship with cordiality. It was part of my "move on" plan. Insane.

The sun was setting brilliantly into the ocean, deep yellows and reds painting the western sky, shadows deepening across the now-black sea, the first swathes of darkness and street lights in the curving Carmel streets up the hill, and a warm wind off the water, when Angelica and her visiting family arrived. The sunset would happen quickly now, and we would be in total darkness within the half hour. I counted ten of them, a moving, dense column of people bunched together, groping in the increasing darkness. They walked down the stone stairs from the street with two smaller children orbiting. Those would be Cesar and Rose. Francesca leapt to her feet from where she was sitting near our unlit fire and ran to greet them.

I watched them descend tentatively, clutching the iron pipe railing, from my position at the unlit campfire piled with pine-wood 100 yards down the beach. There was Angelica, there was an older married couple, her parents, her younger sister Sheila and trailing husband Bo Bo, then Mike, and the rest of the family. No Jerome, although perhaps he would arrive later.

I rose and smiled as they strode across the sand in a group. "Hi, I'm Garth. First check out the sunset. It's almost done," I said to the group, pointing to the west. *Ooooh*s and *Aaaahh*s rose as they turned their faces towards the setting sun, and ten hands with phones rose for a photographic salute. They began to turn their backs to the fading scarlet sunset, raising their phones for selfies. A few of the phones sparkled with flashes.

Francesca, Cesar, and Rose ran in circles in the sand, beyond the group. Inviting them over, I placed the flint and steel into Cesar's hands. He struck a glowing spark into the black char-cloth with the first stroke of his steel, and instantly transferred it into a tinder nest held by Francesca. She raised the smoking nest in her two hands above her head, we all blew on it together, and as the first flames sprang to life she dropped it neatly into the pinewood kindling at the center of the waiting woodpile.

The flames caught and grew. I stood back with pride: these three children were learning, and mastering, the ways of our ancestors. I looked up at the Aguinaldo family in the growing darkness. They were all absorbed in their phones, taking selfies, digitally broadcasting images of themselves and the last bit of golden sunset to the waiting world. All except one person, apparently Angelica's father. He was slender, athletic, with crew cut hair and a military bearing, looking straight at me with approval in his eyes, and a slight smile. Then he turned and watched the last rays of light. Wonderful.

Dinner was burritos and wine. The chili verde and carne asada burritos were from a restaurant in Salinas, Tico's Tacos, and they were apparently a source of wonder, much-discussed in Kapampangan. I heard the question, "Where is the rice?" several times.

The wine, a thick purple Zinfandel by Rombauer, was utterly undrinkable to them, the cause of many wrinkled faces, as though they had taken mouthfuls of vinegar. I uncorked a bottle of cheap sweet pink zinfandel, with a smiling nude woman riding a bicycle on the label, and that brought smiles. Marta produced several liter bottles of 7-Up and that was even better. When they weren't looking, I drank Angelica's untouched Rombauer and saved the rest to take home, where it could be savored.

After all that, in growing darkness, we sat laughing around the fire, with the sound of the surf on the beach soft behind us. Stars were appearing. Soon they would be brilliant, since it was a clear night. I looked at the Aguinaldos all in turn, all together, all smiling, Angelica next to me with her flashing smile illuminated in the wavering light of the flames. Her large Louis Vuitton handbag hung on her shoulder. I could see she was wearing high polished leather boots and skintight pants. The sand was going to scour the polish on those boots ferociously.

I pointed out the planets Venus and Mars to Cesar, Rose, and Francesca. Then I pulled a headlamp over my head and I rummaged through my frayed, well-worn picnic basket. Metal skewers, a bag of large fresh marshmallows, a bar of 70-percent dark Lindt chocolate, and a box of Graham crackers.

"What are you doing?" asked Sheila, her white smile shining in the firelight. She seemed so young and intelligent. Bo Bo, her husband, stood next to her, a look of puzzlement on his face.

"We're going to make s'mores," I replied.

"What are s'mores, Sir Garth?" asked Bo Bo.

I smiled. "It's a special dessert."

The three children around me laughed excitedly.

Sheila smiled at Francesca. "Ohhhh, can you tell me what are s'mores?"

Francesca looked up at her. "Well, Mommy says they're like a redneck communion."

At that everyone laughed and chattered in Kapampangan. All but Angelica. Angelica was on her phone, absorbed, looking down blankly at the sand, walking to and fro. As she spun her back to the fire and to me, I looked closer at her phone's screen. "Schatzi." It read.

I turned back to the fire and handed the three metal skewers to the waiting children. The fire was hot on my face, and the wind from the ocean, out of the starlit night, was cold on my back. Beyond me, I could see Angelica's father's arm silhouetted darkly against the sky, as he pointed out the constellation Orion to the rest of the family.

A few days later. I was at work. The stock market had continued to rise that winter. That seemed insane, actually. At some point the federal reserve would have to raise interest rates, and then perhaps the overvaluation would stop. But now . . . it seemed that the speculation would continue forever.

Perhaps my natural sourness had been exacerbated by the discovery this morning of a large steaming turd on our front porch. Another deposit by a homeless person. I scraped it up, I disinfected with rubber gloves, Lysol, and a long-handled brush. I threw out those brushes after each use. Lanie took refuge in the back office, focusing studiously upon spreadsheets. No matter how badly investments were performing, at least they didn't smell like our front porch.

While I worked I kept hoping that an expected mutual fund representative would be late. There I was, an investment advisor managing $100,000,000 in client assets, scraping shit like a sailor scraping paint. Surely, I thought, a successful investment advisor could hire a person to clean up sewage. But that wasn't it: I didn't want to ask another person to do something that I wouldn't do myself.

One last hose-down, and then I was done. I disinfected my hands afterwards, and changed my shoes. I resisted the urge to change my clothes and to take a shower. Then I called the city of Salinas offices to complain. "Perhaps you should install a public toilet in your front yard," the city clerk responded on the phone when I expressed my unhappiness. I was silent.

"The homeless have rights too," she continued.

"I'll consider that," I responded.

"Remember that you don't have the right to verbally assault them," said the voice on the phone.

"So I find a man squatting on my front porch, pants around his ankles, launching a reeking log, and I can't even shout? Not even, "Wow that's huge?" I responded.

— Honor —
248

"I'm concerned about the hostility and your mocking tone," the voice responded. "They have needs and rights. Perhaps your porch is better for them because it is more private. Consider that when you yell at them. They've been the victims of so much discrimination!"

Yes, I thought, life is hard all over. Shitting on someone's front porch is not a blessing, unless you're a blowfly.

I sat glowering at my computer screen, trying to get my brain back into the stock market. The European Central Bank was intent on devaluing its Euro currency via negative interest rates. That seemed as sensible as prostituting for the money to pay for your wedding. How should I deal with that? Bond duration was certain to be an issue.

Alongside my computer, my phone buzzed. A text from Angelica. "I miss you. We need to talk." I had been wondering about the possible child, every day. That child would be two months along now. Growing inside her. Sacred, even if not mine.

Nevertheless, I should just leave her alone. Surely, she and Jerome had reached an agreement on the baby by now.

I answered, "Tonight after work? After my run? How about 4 p.m.?"

I didn't ask who would watch the kids.

Angelica at Rollick's coffee shop. Sitting across from me, slender, in a draped, neon blue silken sari. Actually, it looked a bit like a bright spangled blue plastic bag. Her chest appeared to be growing slightly. More cleavage. Nice legs. LV sunglasses. Bare, sculpted arms. She seemed subdued.

"Soooo . . . how you been?" she asked.

"Life is good." I smiled widely. "How's the baby? What's your plan with Jerome?"

No sense mucking about. Not a lot of upside here. Nevertheless, I had promised Tommy, and I *would* support that unborn child as well. Somehow, that seemed vitally important to me.

"Oh . . ." She stared at her large iced avocado mocha macchiato coffee. Silence.

— Chapter 37 —
249

"I told Jerome," she finally added.

"Is he happy?" I asked. Now I was gentle. Something was wrong.

She looked at me evenly.

"What happened?" I asked.

"He . . . he . . . oh, my heart broken." She looked at her coffee. A tear ran from under her sunglasses. "I go to his work in Oakland and he not see me except in office. He says he works. I am desperate. I tell him I may have baby. He won't see me. He has an employee walk me out."

I sat. Minutes passed. Damn.

"You and me. We should stop see each other" she said.

"You asked me here to tell me that?" I laughed.

Silence. The situation had changed between her and me somehow. Now there was power in me . . . at least the power to push a bit. No more bullshit.

She blurted out, "Jerome tell me he has vasectomy. Jerome tell me about his two college-aged daughters. He doesn't want me to meet them. He says that he is not ready for that. Still he flies into Monterey on his Lear Jet and we make love the next weekend. He won't see me anywhere else. Only La Playa. I don't know what is happening and the baby will grow. Oh, my family."

Her head was down now.

Game-changing information. "Sometimes vasectomies work, and sometimes they don't," I responded evenly. Clearly, Jerome wasn't an idiot and he wasn't bound to this community in any way. He could walk from all this. I couldn't. At least I didn't feel I could walk.

"I don't know what say to him," she said. Tears were flooding down her face now.

"Say goodbye. That's a start," I said. I wrinkled up my napkin, folding and unfolding.

"That might make him want you. Instead of you being on call," I continued.

The irony wasn't lost on me at all.

— Honor —
250

"I don't love you, Garth. I wish I did. God knows I've tried. I wish I did. You would be so good for this baby. I am sorry, but you don't excite me. Jerome is full of energy. Jerome is so handsome. And you are so small in mind, you worry about—"

"All true," I said.

I was thinking about the child, and I did not want to hear any more. I wanted her to be able to tell her children that I had been a help, a good man to her and to them. So ignore the irrelevant words, accept it, battle through the pain, and make a good future for everyone.

I continued, now that she was momentarily silent. "So tell me how I might help this child? How might I help Cesar and Rose? That's what I'm here for."

"Well, I had just miss my period. What if I just late? I feel my breasts are sore. I remember from Cesar and Rose."

"Have you had a test?" I asked. "They're ten dollars at CVS. We could get one now."

"Do not insult my intelligence," she whispered. "I know my body."

"Could there be any other possible father other than Jerome? Anyone else?"

She looked down at her drink and ran a finger along a line of condensation.

Silence. Here she was asking for my help. Oh my. I felt hollow.

"Don't get an abortion, please," I said. I had to say that.

"Why not?" she asked.

"You live in faith, right?"

Again. The only time people talked about God seriously was when we wanted something from Him, or to excuse our own behavior.

Her face contorted as she continued looking down. Tears flowed. She blew her nose loudly.

I continued. "How do you know what God's plan is?"

She sat silently, shaking her head, no, eyes closed, face down.

"Angelica, your child will be beautiful. Whoever is the father, this child will be a blessing, I'm sure."

"Praise God," she finally whispered. "I will be dishonored. I dishonor Tommy. I dishonor my family."

"How can I help?" I asked.

She sat crying silently, and I reached out and covered her hand in mine. I looked around: others were watching. We sat.

After a few minutes, she spoke. "Of course I not get an abortion, but Jerome asking. She presses. I mean, he presses. I don't know what to tell. He says he want only healthy children, he says he too old, he says he happy with his two college girls. He presses. Still I say no to abortion, of course. How can you think I say yes?"

"Perhaps it's my own fear talking, I guess," I answered.

"Perhaps he does not marry me ever," she added. "I am concubine."

We sat in silence for several minutes. *You said it, girl.*

"If there is no other way, you help me with my family? Please let us go to the Philippines and talk with them. You will meet my family again. They like you. They will not disrespect me while I am there with you."

Wow. It *was* a solution. It would allow me to help the child, help Angelica, and see those wonderful people again. Was I mad? Or just crazy?

"When would we go?" I asked.

"Soon, please," she said.

"Yes," I replied. "I'll do that for you."

Damn.

"You know I want to go there. I would love to see them again," I responded.

"Yes, this is important. This is necessary to honor my family and to honor Tommy."

"Have you ever traveled inside the PI before?" I asked.

"No," she responded. "I never seen my own country. Getting away from it was always more interesting."

Afterwards we walked down Main Street in Old Town, and

we passed Andrus Jewelers. "70% Off" said the sign. Another sign said, "Going out of business! Retirement special!" Unexpectedly, Angelica took me by the hand and pulled me tripping, stumbling, surprised, off the sidewalk and into the store.

"Let's pretend. Just for now, just for the memory," she said, looking down into the illuminated cases. Each ring had a sale price listed: substantial discounts, sometimes more than 50-percent. She tried on several rings, white gold, a decently intimidating rock, a blue diamond, slender rings, classics. I watched.

There was one ring, smaller than the rest, small enough to fit on her tiny finger. A blue sapphire, the stone of royalty, but the ring was 50-percent off. Affordable.

"If Jerome was truly to marry me . . .," said Angelica quietly. "We pretend. Let us pretend that we know surely that he is the father of the baby within me."

"Perhaps this is all God's path. Love is a decision. Love is action," I whispered, and instantly regretted it.

Angelica was still watching the ring, fixated, apparently irked at my comment. "You mistake," she said. "You think you know but you doan. You just doan get it."

"What don't I get?" I asked.

Angelica was serious now, looking at the ring. She spoke now as if she was speaking to the sapphire. "You think love about commitment and about decisions, but it isn't. You need follow your heart."

"Perhaps following my heart hasn't worked for me," I responded quietly.

She wasn't listening. She was staring at the sapphire on the ring as though it was a small blue flame, burning now, alight, and there was a small spirit, a tiny godlet, dancing in the flame. For a time she was silent.

Then she whispered, "It all goes away. People get old. They get disease. Or something happen, bad."

"All the more reason to commit," I said. "We think short term but we must live long-term."

— Chapter 37 —

"Oh, commitment. It does not matter. Commit, and there come cancer. Commit, and here a lost job, there a lost dream. It always goes away. It always goes away," she whispered to the ring.

She turned the ring over and over, and slid it off and onto her finger and extended her arm up, examining the blue gem quietly. She was wearing her blue plastic mini dress, hair pulled back tightly, large white pearls in her tiny ears. Her LV sunglasses were now perched on her head. I admired her as she studied. So serious. What was she seeing in it?

Roland the jeweler, a friend of mine for decades, was watching us both silently. I turned to him and I asked him very quietly, "She's captivated. Does this happen often?"

He looked at me, smiled, and said, "Oh, all the time," in a hushed tone. Then he looked back at the tiny, slender, brown woman who continued to extend her arm, moving her hand, watching the light play upon the facets in the translucent blue gem.

"You don't understand," she said, so quietly that I was almost unable to hear above my tinnitus.

I was quiet.

She continued to watch the gem.

"Only beauty matters. The rest doesn't even exist," she said.

Chapter Thirty-eight

January 2014

That very night, I bought two non-stop tickets for Manila. Two round-trip tickets, early in March, PAL, Philippine Airlines. Non-refundable. I contacted Angelica's sister Sheila and Bo Bo via Skype and planned to meet them, and the rest of the family heard us and clustered around the computer camera, distorted in the fisheye lens, full of joy and smiles as always.

I didn't say why we were planning a trip so quickly. I didn't intimate that Angelica was possibly pregnant. Instead I ascribed our trip to my own hunger to see their wonderful land. That was at least partially true. Based on their festive response to our plans, I perceived that they could already guess what was happening.

Once finished with me, the family immediately contacted Angelica, and she sent me a text filled with gratitude and emojis bejeweled with smiles and hearts. Indeed.

Of course I went back to the jewelry store the following afternoon. Unexpectedly, during the night it had changed names: it was now McWherter's Jewelry. Roland was there. The ring was gone. Apparently, Angelica had come back yesterday afternoon and purchased it, leaving Roland richer and mystified.

Roland asked when the wedding was scheduled. I told him, as soon as possible. I felt a bit guilty not adding that it would not be my wedding.

My guess was that once with her family, Angelica would want to be with them. I researched a week of possible solo adventures, which I could pursue while Angelica bonded. Beaches.

Dive resorts. Cebu for the snorkeling, to start. Then Bohol for the beaches, the rain forest, and the tarsiers. Manila for the culture: the Intramuros, the museums, beautiful Rizal Park.

That Saturday morning, en route to a Civilian Marksmanship Program National Match pistol competition with my 1911 Springfield Armory pistol, I dropped by her home with two almond croissants from Peninsula Bakery in a white paper bag.

Oh, she was beautiful, sleepy eyed at 7 a.m. in her polka dot bathrobe, bare legs, bare feet. I climbed back into my XTerra and drove to the Swiss Rifle Club, and shot a 257. I won the match. Barely.

Chapter Thirty-nine

February 2014

"I'm not sure that this is the 'fail fast, fail cheap, move on' we had in mind," said my daughter, Sarah.

Another meeting at my great grandfather's home. Sarah, Ernst, Lanie, and Robert, Tommy's lawyer.

"It all seems rather well thought out to me," I said.

"Are you sure you aren't the father?" asked Ernst.

"Unless sperm fly via telekinesis, I'm sure," I responded.

"Spermakinesis?" Ernst said, and smiled. "Wouldn't be the first time."

Lanie laughed. "I've heard of that too. It's a man thing."

"In this case, absolutely impossible. I've been good," I said, looking down at the hexagonal table. Nice wood.

"That backup joint mortgage is a dangerous thing," said Robert. "We need to watch the potential conflict of interest to make sure you can't be accused of predatory looting. If you buy that house, it's got to be for the benefit of Angelica, Cesar, and Rose. We need total veto power on that decision."

"Absolutely," I replied. Serious now.

"Why the obsession with keeping them in the home? Why the fascination with making Angelica's life better? Why does this unborn child matter to you so much?" asked Sarah.

"I have promised a lot in my life," I said. "For a variety of reasons sometimes I didn't keep those promises. I promised I'd stay married to your mother, and that didn't happen."

"Not your fault," said Sarah.

"True, but it still didn't happen," I said. "I had a covenant with your ancestors to stay on the ranch. That didn't happen. And I made a promise to defend this nation. That didn't happen either."

"None of that was your fault," said Ernst.

"Yes, but it *feels* like my fault, and while I was busy making promises and having them thwarted, it feels like something essential in our lives crept away in the night," I said.

"I understand. You promised Tommy," said Lanie.

"Believe me, I didn't want to do that. But he clearly needed *someone,*" I said.

"Perhaps keeping this promise simply isn't possible. Worse things have happened than losing a home," said Robert.

"How do *you* feel when you see what that bank is doing to Angelica?" I asked.

"Like it's slimy. Like it's immoral. The whole world is nuts," replied Robert.

"We have a chance to do something different," I said.

"By going to the Philippines and lounging on the beach?" asked Ernst. "Sign me up."

"It's not going to be like that. Angelica is going with me to meet her family to tell them about the baby. She's not married. I need to keep that baby alive, unaborted. So this is what I will do," I replied.

"Why doesn't Jerome step up?" asked Sarah.

"Why doesn't anyone step up?" I replied. "Is anyone keeping promises anymore?"

"It's not your child, right?" asked Lanie. "Really, why does it matter?"

I replied, "Of all the people in this situation, that baby is the most innocent, the most helpless, and the most important to me."

"Why?" asked Sarah.

"I don't know. It's a feeling. I'm allowing myself to follow this. I know it's irrational," I said.

Robert shook his head. "What will you do if Angelica wants to be with you the entire time? That's not going to clarify the situation, especially if she's pregnant."

— Honor —

"My guess is that she won't even go," I replied. "Jerome has to step up before then. Surely he wouldn't let her go to the Philippines with another man."

"Watch him. He's like most men. If the milk is free, don't buy the cow," said Lanie.

"What will you do if Angelica flakes?" asked Sarah.

"I called the Royal Globe Travel Agency: 'Angelica flaking' isn't covered under the travel insurance. So all of the expense will be lost if I stay home," I replied. "I need to see if I can deploy anyway."

"What does that mean?" asked Ernst.

"I've finished the PTSD program up at Stanford, I need to live courageously again. I need to go see what happens. I need to follow the path, see where it leads."

"I vote that you just write the entire expense off as a failed business venture," said Lanie.

"I could support that," said Robert.

"What if this trip kills you?" said Sarah.

"That's unlikely," I responded. "Angelica's family are good people. But whatever else happens, I need to see myself keep the promise, if I can."

"Promise-keeping, yes. Groveling, no. Remember to let go if the deal goes sideways," said Ernst.

After all that thought, I decided to make the trip with or without Angelica. Call it a pilgrimage. Before I left there was unfinished business.

The Billionaire stood in his office at his small, round, pedestal desk, staring into a tiny laptop computer, as his assistant ushered me in. Apparently, the Billionaire stood like this frequently, since there wasn't a chair or any other furniture near him in the large white room. The assistant was a very well-groomed young man, about the age of my oldest son, wearing one of the new "skinny" suits, light gray in his case, which made his arms and legs stick out. His must be an interesting life, I thought.

— Chapter 39 —

The assistant asked me if I wanted a chair. I demurred. I would surely be too nervous to sit.

The Billionaire appeared not to have noticed the assistant or me at all. He remained focused on the laptop, standing there, tapping the occasional key. With nothing else to do, I stood and looked around the room.

The room was as large as an indoor basketball court, swooping high ceilings, elliptical, and floor-to-ceiling windows, Spartan furniture, almost bare.

Outside, immediately beyond the windows were statues perhaps fifteen feet tall, bronze, nude, smooth impressionist, of sleek, idealized man and woman, holding hands lightly and reaching together to the sky. Where their bronze metal fingers touched, above their heads, was a starburst of gold colored metal. They seemed to be giving life to the sky, or perhaps igniting it.

I studied the statues. They were facing away from us, so that they were looking down upon the city. I couldn't see their metal faces. I *could* see their green brass buttocks. Nicely done. Who were the models? I wondered.

Beyond them I noticed the 880 Freeway, and beyond that, Silicon Valley and San Jose. Far beyond that, the mountains, the white dots of Hamilton Observatory, and Pacheco Pass. It would be beautiful in those mountains of the Diablo Range. I visualized that, and my mind wandered.

Viewed differently, the bronze giants were granting the gift of fire to the lowly city denizens in the valley below. Or perhaps the gift of the Internet. I wondered if they had genitals. Perhaps in the future the statue envisioned, there would be no sex.

"My assistant said you wanted to sell me a ranch," came a flat, small voice. I turned and saw that the Billionaire was gazing at me with a somewhat bored expression. He seemed muscle-less. Long, bowl haircut. Tight turtleneck, long-sleeved black shirt, black pants. Very slender. About thirty, perhaps. Amazing.

I explained the situation.

The Billionaire listened. I went on. Take a non-development easement with Nature Conservancy. Tax deductions. Add to the

Dos Cabesas Ranch, which he already owned.

The Billionaire turned his attention back to his laptop. He tapped a few keys, and paused, apparently studying something. He seemed a bit bored.

"Oh, I suppose that's good. Actually I'm interested in the land simply to reduce my carbon footprint," he said.

"Reduce your carbon footprint?" I asked, smiling. "It's so much more than that. I could show you my family's special places on Dos Cabesas and Tortuga. It's beautiful at this time of year."

"Oh, thank you but no," responded the Billionaire, apparently mildly offended. "You are one of the prior owners, correct?"

"My parents were the last of about seven generations," I responded. "I grew up there."

The Billionaire studied me sternly, his frown becoming deeper as he looked at me. "So it was *your* family who enslaved the Native Americans and ravaged the land. Your ancestors lived there in an Age of Blood. In one hundred years your own descendants will look back upon them with loathing, and be deeply embarrassed."

Scolding. Listening to his words felt like being beaten. I choked off an angry retort, a sarcastic reply. I looked out the window, at the statues. Mostly we had a very solid view of their perfect eye-level green bronze buttocks. Beyond them stretched the city . . . that had once been wilderness as much as Dos Cabesas or Tortuga. Even this palace on the mountain, where I now stood, was built on what was formerly wilderness.

But that wasn't the point. The point was that to preserve the mountains of the Tortuga from development—from becoming this—I needed the Billionaire to buy the land and preserve it. So I needed to keep my anger in check and my mouth shut.

"Perhaps you are right," I said, forcing the words.

There, I thought. That didn't hurt a bit.

"Dos Cabesas is very beautiful this time of year," I added.

"I've never visited," responded the Billionaire.

I stood there, stunned. Dos Cabesas had been the center of my universe. In my soul today, it was still my unattainable Mecca. Now this boy owned it outright and didn't care.

"Why?" I had to ask.

"Oh, my wife and I bought your family's ranch from its prior owner, the Italian who owned the car dealerships . . . Oh what was his name? Something ethnic. Anyway we bought it to reduce our carbon footprint."

Silence.

"Please tell me more," I said automatically.

I was feeling that the billionaire was as separate from me as a Martian. He was apparently clueless and bigoted. Oh, brave new world. And I had joined the Marines to defend this.

"My wife and I have been very fortunate, thanks to our genius and our foresight, and it seems wise that we should give thanks to Gaia by setting aside wilderness. Our wealth is growing, so we now need more land," he continued.

I nodded my affirmation. Gaia?

He went on, looking now at his computer again. "Your proposal is appropriate for our consideration. We prefer ourselves to see places more beautiful, more genuine, such as the Louvre in Paris or the volcanoes of Iceland, or the Great Wall of China. Everest. We were there last month."

"I'm sure you were," I responded.

"I don't need to actually visit my land, you know. I'm sure it's nice, in a bucolic sort of way. The locals *do* love their cows. It *is* fun to watch the cow-people prance in their hats and made-up costumes, when there's nothing better happening, or we can't get away. But we don't have cows there now. Cows are a major cause of global warming."

"What about the local wild animals?" I asked.

The Billionaire pondered then spoke.

"Of course the animals there are natural, if insignificant. They belong where Gaia made them. But we *can* help Mother Gaia. Right now we are considering a proposal to give birth control to the wild pigs, and to create a goat and a dog sanctuary," said the Billionaire.

I looked at him. I didn't trust my mouth.

"At least that's what the property manager tells me," the Billionaire added.

I didn't have the heart to tell him that wild pigs were introduced in the early twentieth century by rich landowners who wanted to mimic the boar hunting on the estates of Europe. Or that goats and dogs were as unnatural as asphalt. I just stood there.

"You probably can't understand the direction this world is going," added the Billionaire.

Right on that count, I thought.

"Great plans," I said.

Actually deep in my mind I was envisioning billboards for mountain lions reading "Goats-in-a-pen, easy eats at Dos Cabesas." I wondered what Mother Gaia, or Zumu the Sacred Snake, or Widgie the Cosmic Wombat, or whomever California Nature people worshiped, thought of Silicon Valley, or this house for that matter, all built on what had formerly been wilderness. All taken from Native Americans by conquest, duplicitous sale, or disease. All habitat, where now, nothing lived except what man himself, in the form of the Billionaire, decided was natural.

We all have our illusions.

Chapter Forty

February 2014

On the last Friday of February, five days before the trip to the Philippines, Angelica texted me. I had not heard from her in a week. "Take me to lunch," the message read.

"I'm at work," I responded. At that point, I was furious. I reminded myself that the baby was more important than my frustration. I needed to keep that child healthy. I knew that anger on my part would make our contact even less. So I choked down my urge to rage.

In the past month, she had been utterly unwilling to discuss the Philippines trip. Of course, in that vacuum of planning, I was planning to cancel her ticket at the last possible moment. I had extremely low expectations.

But then there was that unborn child. I didn't know what had happened.

"☺ Take me to lunch," she texted again.

I thought about that. I responded. "Tarpy's. See you at 11."

Lanie and Tammy Fay kept their faces expressionless as I stood up from my desk at 10:45, and told them I was going to lunch with Angelica. As I organized my desk, Lanie walked into my office.

"I hope you've thought this through," she said.

I turned off my laptop and slipped it into its case.

"You don't usually miss work like this," she added.

I smiled at her. My smile turned into a grin.

"You *are* going to lunch, right?" she added. "Only lunch?" Now she was smiling too. All sorts of possibilities, some not entirely discussable, came to mind.

"Yes, ma'am," I responded as I walked down the stairs.

She stood on the porch and called after me, "Are you sure this is what will make you happy?"

I stepped out of my yellow XTerra in the Tarpy's parking lot and looked up at the beautiful, old stone building. Drops of mist fell on my glasses. Tarpy's was directly under the landing pattern of the Monterey airport, and as I stood there, a jet roared low and unseen through the clouds overhead. Amazing that they can do that blind.

Then I watched Angelica as she stepped out of her gold Honda CRV parked on the other side of the lot. She was clad in a gold felt exercise suit, and large, dark oval LV sunglasses, which dwarfed her brown circular face. She stepped daintily towards me, dancing to me over the shallow rain puddles on the asphalt. She had tiny, graceful feet in bright turquoise athletic shoes. As she walked closer to me, I could see that her long fingernails had newly painted tiny red flowers on them. There were tiny red Poinsettias painted on each shining, unblemished nail.

When we were seated at a window-side table for two, I watched the rain falling outside, rain in a drought year, washing the cars in the parking lot. It was good that our romantic relationship was finished, I thought. Liberation.

The tablecloth was covered with a sheet of butcher paper. There was a glass of crayons. I drew a flower, a yellow California poppy. Too early for this flower, I thought. The waiter came: slender, young, white skin, black thick hair combed straight back, Spanish-looking, black little soul patch on his chin looking vaguely vaginal. I must be the only man who notices the similarity, I thought. Otherwise, nobody would wear them.

The waiter eyed Angelica in her form-hugging velour workout clothing. She smiled brilliantly back at him, answering his stare as his eyes wandered.

"I'll take a chilled glass of Stella D'Oro," she said quietly.

The young man looked down at her. Then he turned to me and

gazed at me inquiringly.

I looked at Angelica. She looked at me, large eyes glistening, serene. I didn't feel serene at all. That glass of Stella D'Oro said a lot.

"I'll take a ah . . . vodka shooter, with four twenty-five milligram Xanax tablets. And a small chilled Red Bull," I said flatly.

He looked confused.

"A 2009 vintage Red Bull," I added.

The waiter was clearly flustered.

"Relax," I added. "It's a joke. I'm fine with water."

When the waiter had glided away with our order, I waited for Angelica to say something. She sat there, a beautiful sleek cat about to stretch. Finally, I said, "I've been calling and texting. No answer. Are you still planning on going?"

I just said that for transparency's sake. Clearly, I knew the answer.

She shook her small head, looking down. Negative. Even though I had expected that answer, still, surprisingly, I felt a blow of adrenaline surge through my body. I felt anger. I looked at the shining, empty white plate in front of me. Rather than demand her participation in the trip, or screech to her that I could not stand her opacity, her covertness, her willingness to allow me to prepare for a journey she knew I would take alone, if at all, I resolved to cultivate empathy and hide my own dismay. After all, I realized that the reasons for this trip had changed. It was now about me, not her.

My first thought was to make sure my feet were still on the floor. I was still sitting in the chair. Around me, well-groomed people chatted with each other, ate, drank, oblivious to this drama happening only feet away.

"I guessed as much. You've been quiet," I asked. Ultra-cool, I thought.

"What's changed?" I continued.

She gazed at me serenely, opaquely, sadly. Beautiful eyes, beautiful lips. I noticed her highlighted black hair, pulled back into a ponytail, tight against her head. I had a memory, of our lovemaking, her above me in the dark living room with her hair loose and surging around her face. There's nothing quite as honest as deceit.

Perhaps a few minutes passed.

"You can tell me," I said quietly.

"I am unsure," she said. "I have not enough pasalubong."

"I have always regretted my own lack of pasalubong," I responded quietly. "One seldom notices one's pasalubong until it is removed."

Angelica's crestfallen appearance informed me that my joke had fallen flat.

"Sorry," I responded to her silent expression. "Please tell me what pasalubong is, and why it is keeping you from this trip."

"Pasalubong is gift; it is what we give to family and neighbors when we come home. It is . . . it is a social obligation. At least it is good manners. Gifts as well as money."

"To whom do you give this?" I asked.

She gazed back at me and considered that. "It is for the honor of the family that Tommy and I give a lot," she said. "I don't have a lot to give now. You know that. And so if I go, I am . . ."

Silence. I looked at her. Beautiful. Manipulative.

"Dishonored?" I finished. "You mean you dishonor your family if you visit them without your pasalubong?"

"Yes, but it is more . . . it is more. I cannot see them without more," she replied. "Not just pasalubong, but more."

I didn't understand that. I sat there. The waiter arrived flourishing our lunches, flamboyant. He set the food before us, gazed inquiringly at us, and raised an immense cylindrical wooden pepper grinder over my salad. I shook my head.

I wondered: where did that pepper grinder come from? It would take four Marines to operate that thing. Flustered by his lack of opportunity to grind, the waiter turned and fled to the kitchen.

"You really love me, don't you?" she asked.

"How is the baby?" I asked.

I looked at her and smiled as reassuringly as possible.

— Honor —

268

She looked at me, forking her steaming pasta, rearranging a mussel shell. She placed a clam on the side of my plate.

"Love is sacrifice," she said quietly. "You remember that, okay?"

"Speaking of that, are you pregnant?" I asked, looking at the sparkling glass of Stella D'Oro. No sense being coy.

"A child was lost," She picked at her meal. She took a long drink of Stella D'Oro.

"Lost?" I asked.

The idea chilled me. Desolation.

"Lost," said Angelica. She looked at me, pale, deadpan, a new hostility, a new daring in her eyes. Don't touch this, her eyes said.

"Angelica, I'm very, very sorry," I said.

The overweening reason for my trip and even for this relationship seemed to wither in my mind. Why am I here? I thought. Then I steadied emotionally. God has a plan. Follow the path. Keep the promise.

"All babies go to heaven," said Angelica. "This is what Jesus say."

I tried to remember that in scripture. I couldn't. I didn't know what to think. It seemed a great loss to me.

The sensation of a perfectly warm room on a rainy day, with food smells, and the contented hum of moneyed people at leisure. I asked a few questions about the children. She smiled and she answered.

"I will still visit your family." I said. "I've paid for the trip, and I want to see them. I need to get away anyway."

It was time I took charge of my own goddamned life, I thought.

"That is your choice," she responded quietly. "If that's what you wish to do, then you must do it. You are a free man. It is your choice."

"Your family is expecting you," I added. "They won't understand why you aren't with me when we've planned this for months. What do I tell them?"

She looked slightly annoyed at that. She looked at me, her

anger apparently rising.

"What do I tell them?" I repeated.

"Arrrrgggg," she grunted quietly. "I TOLD YOU! You tell them NOTHING! They know what they know. The rest it is PRIVACY!" She stood up. "I need to pee."

She walked gracefully away in the direction of the woman's bathroom. I watched her go all the way in. Then I reached across the table, I moved her plate, and I wrote on the tablecloth.

"Love is sacrifice," I wrote. I moved her steaming pasta to cover the writing.

Then I stood up, paid the bill, and left.

As I drove back to the office in my XTerra, my cell phone buzzed. I pushed the button on my steering wheel.

"Hey! Hey! Can you hear me?" Bull's voice filled the cabin. I lowered the volume.

Damn.

"This is Garth," I responded.

"Great job, cousin!" said the voice. "Your contacts at the Nature Conservancy snapped up that wilderness easement, and the sale has gone through! AND I got that life estate if I ever want to ride my horse there."

That wilderness easement. I felt great about that. I knew the Billionaire wouldn't be able to resist the tax deductions.

"So the Billionaire bought all the acreage?" I asked, elated. No houses. No reservation. Wilderness eternal.

"All of it."

Then a wave of sadness swept over me as I realized that our family was probably gone from that land forever. All those generations.

"You kept the house, right?" I asked.

"Damned straight. Plus the 500 acres around it that you suggested. The hay pasture. And the oak grove."

"How did the real estate broker do?" I asked.

"She damned near wet herself," replied Bull.

"It's a big ticket," I replied. "So what do we do now?"

— Honor —
270

"Well I'm outta debt, but I want to get some cash for the rest of my life, and I'm thinking we should sell the rest of Tortuga. Any thoughts?"

"Let's talk," I replied.

Chapter Forty-one

March 2014

A few days later, I was in my office. Just a last few details of work. One client getting divorced. Another client setting aside money for a grandchild. I hadn't heard from Angelica since our lunch. I hadn't sought her out.

The phone rang. Lanie answered it in the other room. "Globalbank!" she sang out.

I picked up the line at once. Headset in place. Poised. I supposed that Jerome had somehow coped with everything. This must be a follow-up call.

"Hello, Mr. Ericson? This is Jose Jimenez from Globalbank calling. I am instructed to tell you that we have not received payment from Thomas Phillip Narcisco, and thus we will foreclose on the home at 6501 Arroyo de Oro Way."

Big sigh. "It's a relief you haven't heard from Thomas Phillip Narcisco because he's been deceased for over two years. Had you indeed heard from him, I'd recommend a new career path," I responded.

"But he's the only person I'm authorized to contact", said Jose.

"When will you foreclose?" I asked.

"Thomas Phillip Narcisco was notified a few weeks ago via registered mail, but he was unable or unwilling to sign so the letter was returned to us."

"Am I the trustee?" I asked. I was feeling very tired. I was picturing my trip to the Philippines vanishing because I would have to stay here, and fight this, and all the investment in my trip would be lost. Hell no. I would be on that jet.

"No, sir, we have no record of you ever being trustee. My instructions are to talk with Thomas Phillip Narcisco," replied Jose.

"So why are you calling me?" I asked. "If I can't do anything?"

"This is the phone number we have," said Jose.

"Been in banking long?" I asked.

"A few months," Jose responded. "Before that I was a truck dispatcher for tomato trucks. You know, the big rigs. But they gave a computer my position so I moved to Texas. This is a good job."

Hmmm. Talkative. That was new.

After a short pause, I spoke to him. "So if I'm not the trustee, I can legally buy that property, right? Here's the deal. You and I both are looking at the same appraisals. You know that all the debt comes to $550,000 and you know that the home is now worth only $350,000. I'll pay you that now. I can get you a check in two days. Short sale, no foreclosure," I said.

"I can't deal with anything like that," said Jose.

"Please connect me with your supervisor, Jose. It's been a blast talking with you."

"I don't understand, sir," said Jose Jimenez.

"I know," I said.

Five handoffs to supervisors later and we reached a weary compromise. They would reconsider a refinance with my funding. If they wouldn't accept that, I would buy the home for $350,000. Nobody was sure if I was trustee or not. They said I wasn't. Yet they were talking to me.

I called Vivian at Seaforth Bank. The 3.50-percent rate for a prospective mortgage to buy Angelica's home still stood. If I was trustee, then, appropriately, I could not legally buy Angelica's home. If I was not trustee, then I could buy it. Whichever way Globalbank wanted to interpret my role, we had the money for a valid response. The plan was solid: buy the home at the reduced price, and later have Angelica assume the smaller mortgage.

I signed all the Seaforth Bank documents the next day, with

a team of two notaries and Robert, the Narcisco trust's lawyer, watching the process pro-bono. Anything to see those two kids stay in their home. I thought of Tommy speaking to me as he lay dying. Yes, Tommy, I am doing it. As you wished.

Tuesday, March 4, 2014. The cool, cloudy, drizzling day of my departure, with a flight scheduled from San Francisco to Manila for 9 p.m. that night. I was packed. I had checked in at work. My brain wasn't in the game. Tammy Fay and Lanie shepherded me through a few closely watched trades on the lap-top computer, transactions the clients needed right then, right now. I asked Tammy Fay to visit Mom in my absence, and keep an eye on the office. I asked Lanie to tell Angelica that the loan was waiting. The rest we could work out when I returned. Then I left to take my mother to lunch. When someone is ninety-three, you should eat lunch with them as much as possible.

We went to lunch at Bahama Grill. Across from the bowling alley on South Main Street. My mother ordered the fish tacos, without the sauce. I ordered the salmon tacos, without cheese, and we ate. We looked through our chewing at each other. It was a game of verbal chicken: first person to speak loses.

I spoke first.

"You know I'm going because of you, right?" I said.

She studied the contents of a fish taco intently, not looking up. Saying nothing. I thought of a desert tortoise about to devour a cactus flower.

I continued, "You were a geologist. You were a marine bi-ologist, you traveled all over that part of the world. You had adventures all the time. I think I've become a coward since the Marines. I want to be courageous again. Like you. Like the Greatest Generation."

I realized I was rambling, filling the emptiness of her silence with words.

"When you were a child you were afraid of everything," she said, still looking at her food.

"Possibly so. I don't remember," I replied.

"Your father and I, we tried to make you stronger, you know. It's a strong man's world," she added. "But you were afraid. Afraid of dogs, after one nipped you. After a horse bucked you off, you were afraid of those too. Not like your family. I didn't know what we were going to do with you."

I let that sit for a time. There was no use rebutting that comment. Then I added, "Anyway, I'm going to the Philippines today."

"I was in the Philippines three times," she said quietly.

"Three times?" I responded.

"Three times, for a total of, oh, about nine months," she responded. She studied her taco intently.

She spoke quietly again. "You see, here's the thing, your grandmother couldn't really believe that Uncle Sid was dead. She couldn't accept it. You know he just vanished on a work detail out of the prison camp. Until she died in 1965, she thought he was alive somewhere, waiting to be rescued. Somewhere far away, perhaps with a Filipina wife, perhaps without people, maybe on some little island. Later when her mind wandered she thought he was in Red China."

She kept looking at her taco, peering at it, as though she might find a weevil.

"I went the first time in 1946," she said. "Your father was a medical officer in the navy by then, on a fast oil tanker, and he met me there."

She smiled at her taco and spoke again quietly. "1946, in Manila, when you are twenty-six years old and your husband's ship has just come in, after nine months apart, that's really something."

I sat there. I knew nothing of this. I took a bite of salmon taco to avoid looking too amazed. I thought of two young Americans a few months after the end of World War II, when everything seemed destroyed and everything seemed possible.

"The war was just over then," I stated.

"Oh, the place was wrecked. Manila was one big ruin. Hard to describe, really. Death, all over. I mean, dead people, skeletons, in the grass, in the fields, in the ruins, in the forests. In the center of Manila, the old Spanish fort, the Intramuros, was simply one big rubble pile. I was there officially with the USGS, to help restore the infrastructure, find good quarries, identify what could be saved, what couldn't." She paused, studying that taco. Outside it was drizzling slightly. A middle-aged woman in a blue windbreaker walked by the window on the sidewalk outside with a small, sleek, chocolate-colored Chihuahua dog on a leash. The tiny dog was wearing a pink knitted doggie sweater, pop-eyed and strutting.

"We looked everywhere for Uncle Sid," said my mother. "You know there were Japanese soldiers and US guerillas so deep in that jungle that some of them didn't know the war was over. Lubang. Mindanao. Morotai, over in Indonesia. That's what your grandmother was obsessed about. That Sid would be out on one of those little islands, hiding or fighting, not knowing it was over, not willing to take the risk of making contact. Wasn't there some Japanese soldier who stayed in the jungle for decades?"

"I don't know," I answered.

"Read your history," said my mother. "Google it. Hiroo Onoda. They're still out there, creeping around on their bamboo walkers."

She smiled at this. Nice.

"Anyway, I was there that time for about four months. I couldn't tell anyone it was really about Sid. To the rest of the world, I was there as a geologist, looking at harbor repair, things like that. The government. Mostly changing maps to reflect the war damage. They gave me a jeep to go look around, and a couple of Filipinos, former Alamo Scouts, with M-1 carbines, to translate, and that was that. Those fellows were tough customers. I never felt afraid for a moment."

"So that's how you learned to field-strip a carbine?" I asked. "I always wondered about that. I was the only kid in middle school whose mom could qualify with a service rifle."

She looked up from her taco, at me. She smiled and spoke again.

"Actually, when you were very young, almost all the men in your neighborhood were combat veterans and former military. Many of the moms were former military, or, you know, they were 'Rosie the Riveter,' working in the defense industry. I'm just the only mom who showed you. Louise Rukeyser across the street, she built 50 caliber Browning machine guns for the big bombers. She could have told you how to field-strip those."

"Why didn't you ever tell me about the Philippines before?" I asked.

She looked at me steadily across the table, holding her fish taco up to her mouth.

I finished my salmon taco. My thinking was that I wanted to eat it before the big news hit.

"I don't know. I wasn't proud of it, I guess. We never found Sid. After 1946, I went back in 1950 . . . 1952. The year before your sister was born. That was ALL about Uncle Sid. I was a tourist, technically. By then the bodies had been dug up from Cabanatuan. That was the POW camp where the Japanese starved them all to death. After the war, someone dug up all the graves the POWs had made, during the war. The government moved all the bones to U.S. military cemeteries or they brought the remains back for families. They mixed the bones up, you know. It was a mess. Many remains couldn't be identified." She shrugged.

I looked at her. Revelation.

"The final time was in 1970," she said quietly. "Take me home. I'll get a doggie box. I can eat the rest of this for dinner."

I drove her home, unlocked her front door, turned off the security system, and positioned the walker by the front door so she could grab it when I walked her in. We were at her home, on Loyola Avenue, in the most southwestern corner of Salinas. I walked back to the XTerra in the driveway and opened her passenger side door, and she swung herself into position and clutched her cane.

"This trip to the Philippines, this is about Angelica isn't it?"

she asked as her feet slid tentatively down to the driveway pavement.

I smiled. "It's about me now. I'm trying to get myself back."

She looked at me steadily, not walking as I had expected. "You've been lost for decades. Hell, you're all lost, all you boomers."

"Yes," I said.

"Your generation had too much success too soon, and nobody to tell you no. Spoiled children," she added.

"Can't argue with that," I said.

"And as for Angelica, it's not her fault. She's just broken. But you knew this at the beginning. You can't be that stupid."

I just looked at her.

She spoke again. "Well, maybe you *can* be that stupid, so I'll tell you. There's more to it, you know. She was broken before she got here."

"Why do you think that happened?" I responded.

"Oh, you'll figure it out," she replied, slipping her arm through mine and leaning on me as she began to edge forward towards the open front door.

"Come with me to the guest bedroom," she said. We walked, her unsteady, leaning on me, ninety-three years old. I tried to imagine the energetic twenty-six-year-old woman who had searched the Philippines jungles in a jeep with an M-1 Carbine slung over her shoulder.

In the bedroom, she paused over her walker and directed me towards the closet. "There, in the back. All the way in the back," she said. "Reach way back in there."

I pulled out a long, flat, white cardboard box, a box for fine clothing.

"Open it," she directed.

There was a cream-colored satin dress on the top, puff sleeves, elegant, timeless.

"That's for Angelica, if she wants it," Mom said to me. "It's formal Filipina, coconut fiber sleeves, very elegant. I'm guessing I was a bit bigger than her, though. She's welcome to tailor it to fit." She laughed. "Now lift that dress out, I want you to see what's under it."

I lifted up the dress. There was an ivory shirt hidden there, richly embroidered. Long sleeves.

"That's a barong, that's what the men wear when they attend something formal or important. It was your father's. We wore these clothes when we attended embassy parties at the Hotel Manila, after they restored the place. Try it on."

It fit tightly. I could scarcely button it.

"I got him that shirt in 1952. Take it to a tailor. If you are going to ask her parents, you should be dressed correctly."

"I had no idea that Dad was ever in the Philippines at all," I said.

"Oh, you know, the accident happened in 1972. We've had plenty to think about since then."

I replaced the dress in the box and returned it to the closet, and folded the shirt and carried it to the front door.

"I love you, Mom. I hope I'm going there to do the right thing. Thanks for setting such a wonderful example." I hugged her and kissed her hair, stiff from hairspray. Her hair was white now. I stepped outside the front door and looked back at her, hunched over her cane. She looked at me and spoke.

"I hope you find what you are seeking. I deeply hope so. But I have to tell you, your family has been searching those beautiful bloodstained islands for over half a century, and we've never found a thing. Except death."

I arrived at SFO early. At the Philippines Airlines ticket counter, I showed the young Filipina woman my passport and my credit card. "Oh, sir, that flight is late four hours. Manila is congested."

I responded that I was very sorry to hear that Manila was congested. Perhaps Nyquil was in order? Or a sinus rinse? The woman behind the desk was not amused. She looked at me blankly.

"I'll wait," I responded. My phone buzzed.

Angelica. "You don't understand," the text read. I didn't respond.

Another buzz. Another text from Angelica. "You don't understand."

"You can check your bags now, sir," said the woman. "We will plan to board then in six hours, not four."

Apparently, Manila was becoming more congested by the minute.

Philippines Airline's late departure gave me the opportunity to do something I had been dreading. I had been stalling. I knew I needed to visit Lance Corporal Gus. Apparently, or so I had seen on Facebook, they were now living in Burlingame near the airport. Since meeting them at the Salinas California Rodeo, I had friended them on Facebook and afterwards kept my distance. There but for the grace of God. Perhaps being near Gus made me realize how close I had come to being terribly injured myself. Perhaps I merely found it distasteful. Perhaps I was a coward.

My resistance to visiting Gus had eaten at me. I felt quite guilty about it. But as Dr. Pekk at the Stanford VA clinic said, go to the pain. I felt that I had a responsibility for Lance Corporal Gus. Try as I might, I could not evade it.

So when I realized the flight was delayed I texted Gus's wife Honey at once. Perhaps, I hoped, they were out for the day. Perhaps they were busy. Having fun. Sure thing. I would escape meeting them yet have the emotional satisfaction of reaching out.

Honey texted me back at once. They were in San Francisco fitting new leg braces to delay Gus's leg muscle atrophy. I explained my situation more fully. Honey quickly responded with extremely clear instructions: take the BART rapid transit train to the Embarcadero Station, and then walk down one block to the waterfront. They were excited about meeting me at Pier 14, the pedestrian pier, for a brief visit. Emphasis brief. Apparently, Gus was a bit tired.

The BART train left from inside the San Francisco Airport. I ate a freshly-made sourdough grilled vegetable sandwich as the very futuristic monorail pulled away from the airport station and arched into a turn high over the freeways and streets below, heading for downtown San Francisco. It was a clear day. Great sandwich. Far in the distance, I could see the Bay Bridge, covered in scaffolding for a retrofit, then we were in a dark tunnel, moving fast, and the roaring of our train filled my ears.

Honey and Lance Corporal Gus were waiting for me at the pedestrian pier. Gus, in a wheelchair, waved erratically, tried to smile, twisting his head, eyes wandering. He was wearing his light blue plastic hockey helmet. Gold foil Marine insignia roundels on the sides. I reached out and caught his hand as it waved about and shook it gently, and kneeled down and looked in one of his eyes, and I watched as small tears appeared. "D-damn, S-Sir! D-Damn!" he said. I realized that the muscles in his hands were stronger than last time, and his fingers were no longer twisted. Improvement. He was wearing glasses now, and he could sometimes track with both eyes.

"Looking good, Marine!" I said. I didn't know what else to say.

Everybody was wearing coats. It was a beautiful, clear day but cold, with a chilling wind coming off the open Pacific, beyond the rust-colored Golden Gate Bridge that arose to the west, bright in the sunlight. The looming Bay Bridge rose above us to the southeast, grand and triangular. Apparently, when it was finished being rebuilt, it would light up at night. Around the pier, the turquoise dappled water of the San Francisco Bay looked clean. I leaned lightly against the railing of the walkway with the brisk cold wind in my face and pondered what to say.

"How's your daughter, Jody?" I asked. I did not want to ask about Gus.

"Oh, she's 'leven now! Sweet wondaful girl! Did you see her on my Facebook page?" said Honey. Her Southern accent reduced.

Indeed, I had noticed the photos on Facebook. Jody seemed

to be thriving. Honey seemed to be thriving as well. I noticed she was dressed conservatively and stylishly, coat pulled tight, blond hair combed and pulled back. Black polished knee-high boots.

Honey went on. "She is doin' great at school and she loves livin' in California. Did y'all see we took her to Disneyland?"

I had.

"Gus you look much improved," I said. Might as well go straight at it.

Gus grinned crookedly, denture line showing. His head twisted. "Greeeaaat!" he slurred. He held up his hands and flexed them, his fingers opening and closing together.

"Watch this!" said Honey happily. She stood close in front of Gus as he sat in his wheelchair and reached down and gripped him under the armpits. Then she pulled him up.

Shakily, Gus rose and stood, his hands to the side, waving. He was grinning. Honey stood back so that Gus was standing free and whooped in delight.

"Look at mah strong Marine!" she rejoiced.

Gus stood up there in the wind swaying for at least a minute. Then his swaying and shaking increased. Honey stepped back close to him and hugged him supportively again. She helped Gus sit back down. Gus's head rocked back, and he choked and coughed a little. He squeezed his eyes tightly. Clearly just standing up had been terribly difficult.

"Are you tired, Gus?" asked Honey, concern in her voice.

Gus shook his head with effort. No. Then Yes.

"Ya know," said Honey quietly to me "It's not like ya get wounded then ya come home and ya heal. This is moah lahk an ongoin' illness. Nobody really knows what's goin' to happen next, 'cept that it will go on for the rest of our lives."

Terrible, I thought. I pondered how fortunate I had actually been.

"Is there anything I can get for anyone?" I asked. Damn, I thought. That was incautious. Here it comes.

"Newww b-b-bodddeee," said Gus emphatically. Then his

head lolled and he grinned.

Honey was considering my question deeply.

"Ya know what we WOULD lahk is a chance to visit your Monterey sometime soon," said Honey. I want ta show Jody that aquarium of yours. Gus lahks to see ya, don't ya, husband?"

That's all? I thought. No requests for financial aid? No requests for Congressional intervention?

"I'll look forward to that. I'm a charter member at the Monterey Bay Aquarium so I've got passes. Any time. Just let me get back from the Philippines," I responded.

"Oh, an' if ya encounter any recorded readins' of novels, Gus lahks to listen to those when he does his therapy. Used is fine," added Honey.

"Certainly," I answered.

"He's listnin' to Winston Churchill now, aint' yah, hun? *The Hinge of Fate* ahm recallin,'" said Honey.

I considered that.

"We should get home," she added. "Gus is quiverin' from cold."

As she wheeled Gus up the pier to the cab station, she added, "Oh, Warrant Officer Ericson, thank yee for your visit. Thanks for all ya do for us. Y'all the only person from the old unit still in touch with us."

I considered that. Actually, Gus hadn't really been in my unit. Actually, I hadn't done anything for Gus at all.

Nothing at all.

Chapter Forty-two

March 2014

When the 767-jetliner landed in Manila, I was soaked in sweat from the journey. It had been an eighteen-hour ride, the last few hours in darkness and turbulence, grappling with my fears with the aid of a Kevin Costner movie and a Xanax. I quickly texted Angelica's sister Sheila on Facebook Messenger, using the airport's free Wi-Fi, since my cell phone didn't work otherwise. No response. I texted again. Nothing.

As I reclaimed my two bags, one rolling suitcase and one monstrous green military duffle stuffed mostly with dive gear, I texted again. Nothing. Now I was genuinely chilling from my coating of sweat and the airport's air conditioning. I began to consider the possibility of staying at the Manila Hotel if nobody was at the airport to meet me.

Then, at the exit of the baggage claim, in a cavernous waiting area, I saw Sheila and her husband, Bo Bo, watching the flight display board for Philippines Airlines. The board was big, hung on the wall high overhead, and the brightly lit letters were blinking: landings had been cancelled due to thunderstorms. I had literally made the last flight in.

I watched Sheila and Bo Bo as they studied the screen. The frustration showed on their faces. Both attractive, young, intelligent-looking Filipino people. Shorter than me. Very well and lightly dressed. Clothing with logos. Sandals, very appropriate for this hot, humid place.

Sheila looked a lot like her sisters: slender, small, long, thick black hair, graceful. Bo Bo—where the heck had they thought that name up? He was also small, slender, but with a shaved head. For a few moments, I simply watched them, too tired and too relieved at my successful arrival to feel a need for motion.

Then Sheila turned, and she saw me and her face lit up with joy. We had not seen each other since their visit to California in the winter. Blessings. Much discussion of our almost-missed connection. On to the car.

As we left the air-conditioned airport and walked into the parking structure, the hot air blasted us, and I began to sweat again. The car was large, a Toyota Sequoia. It was tan, sleek, and newer than my own vehicle. We shoved my baggage into the back, I climbed into the second row of seats, and Bo Bo began to drive. The freeways were huge megalopolis corridors, eight lanes wide; heading north to Pampanga and Bataan.

There were giant traffic jams, due to many, many haulers and large trucks filling the roads. The air was acrid, polluted. Inside the car, air conditioning, this time mild. Let us count our blessings.

Great discussion: world events, history, the goings-on as they both finished their Master's degrees in education, and the she-nanigans of their two-year-old son. Un-accented English, two denizens of Global America sharing their lives.

The traffic became lighter as we left Manila behind. The speeds became faster.

Sheila was ebullient. Talkative. "Oh my goodness, Sir Garth, this is so exciting! We will enjoy your visit so much!"

Bo Bo was silent. He was driving intently, avoiding the chaos on the highway around us: trucks, buses, motorcycles, every imaginable rolling vehicle with an engine.

As we drove across a flat plain dotted with factories and rice paddies, Sheila began to innumerate her clan. Apparently, about fifteen people lived in one home. It was a new home, built with money from Angelica and Tommy and Marta and Mike, God bless them all. The women were all working as teachers. The husbands were unemployed, for the most part, although they worked part-time as wood carvers and tricycle drivers.

Angelica's father. I remembered him from the beach fire. Such a commanding presence. I genuinely hoped he would like me, that we could create a friendship.

Now we were driving in the city. There was garbage in piles, many raw industrial establishments. Dust and dirt everywhere. I remarked on that. Why were the streets muddy?

"Oh," said Sheila, "After the volcano Mount Pinatubo erupted in 1990, the rivers filled with mud-flows. Now the lowest place is in the city, so it floods always."

"Why do you not build dykes and levees?" I asked.

"It is the government. So corrupt. And that would take more money than the Philippines possesses," she replied. "It is God's will."

"Then why not move?" I asked.

Sheila looked at me as though I had just proposed that we all eat gravel.

"It is our home," she replied.

After an hour of wending through congested irregular streets, surrounded by motor bikes carrying as many as four people, motorized tricycles, pedicabs, all manner of damaged cars, festively decorated jeepneys, buildings peeling paint, drying mud coating the pavement, I noticed a blue-tiled palace, rising from what seemed to be slums. That was their home, I realized. Shockingly different. Literally surrounded by stagnant ponds filled with garbage, especially plastic shopping bags. I stepped out of the car, and there was Angelica's father, Ramon, smiling, trim, imposing. Truly a retired military officer.

In the immaculate, modern Aguinaldo home that night, on the third floor, I took a Filipino bath with the plastic dipper in the bathroom. It was wonderful: no air conditioning, no shower-head, simply the sensation of water evaporating off my body. It occurred to me that Filipinos are some of the cleanest people I know, without showers or hot water. Hot water isn't necessary, since in the Philippines, the world is always warm. All I needed was a bright green bucket full of water, a bright green plastic dipper, and a drain. There I was, clean, feeling the water evaporate from my skin, exultant.

I sat down to a welcome dinner, exhausted and relaxed, sampled a wide variety of Filipino delicacies, which appeared to be variations of meat and fish stir fried with vegetables, and a glass of Tanduay rhum. Smiling, welcoming faces surrounded me.

A slender boy about ten years old appeared at my shoulder, in a blue t-shirt and blue shorts, barefoot, holding in his two hands a white pigeon. He watched me patiently for minutes, until finally I could turn from the general conversation of the table and address him.

Immediately he spoke, in English. He held up the pigeon.

"How beautiful is the dove," said the boy.

"Pigeon," I responded gently. "It's a pigeon in English."

He looked at me smiling, and then held the bird out again.

"How white and pure is the dove," he said.

I did not respond. I smiled. Bo Bo announced that we all needed to sleep tonight, because tomorrow he, Sheila, and I were to climb the local volcano, Mount Pinatubo.

Indeed. I slept like a log that night, in an air-conditioned bedroom in the home that Tommy and Angelica and Marta and Mike had built with their cash from California.

I found myself that dawn with a face full of pumice dust, bucketing along in the open back of a ravaged, red Toyota Land Cruiser, with Bo Bo in the front seat and Sheila with me and a Moslem Filipina in the back.

I had proposed the Mount Pinatubo trip via Facebook back when I was planning the trip for Angelica. I had paid for the trip before leaving California. Sheila and Bo Bo were already showing me that they were superb guides, willing to provide advice and to comment on everything Filipino.

Now, however, there wasn't a lot of conversation. Mostly we were focused on clinging to the roll bar as the driver double-clutched his way across bare gravel lahar flows, and erosional streams that cut through the wide swath of destruction resulting from Mount Pinatubo's 1991 eruption.

— Honor —

As we bucked along in that battered jeep, in the bright tropical sunlight, with the women squealing and laughing across streams, ravines, and pumice flats, I found myself reflecting on how much I had been part of this world in the past, literally and emotionally.

In 1991, while I had been guarding the coastline of California at Camp Pendleton, an entire US Marine Corp regiment had become involved in the rescue and evacuation of civilians from this area. In the middle of the intense Gulf War buildup, they had deployed here, to this very place, to rescue anyone in need.

Now I looked up onto the steep eroded slopes of volcanic ash, and I saw wild bananas growing, in entire glades, the broad wide bright green leaves waving in the wind as the sun rose. All was alive up there, on those hillsides lit by the dawn behind us.

In front of me, Bo Bo was sitting alongside the driver, hanging on and grinning as the vehicle jumped and swayed. Beside me stood Sheila, standing up looking over the driver's canopy, grinning as well. Alongside her stood a young woman I had never met before today, with a broad smile, in a tight-fitting Islamic sheath of a dress. She was wearing an American flag as a Muslim headscarf, in silk or nylon, wrapped completely around her head, exposing only her bright white smile and the bill of a baseball cap.

I looked at that sheath, that dress, and I realized that every curve, the slightest fold, even her thong underwear, was totally revealed as the wind pushed the dress tight against her body. I considered that. I had been all over the Middle East. I had seen women wearing chadors and burkas and a variety of shapeless tents. Only in the Philippines could women turn Muslim clothing into a highly erotic fashion statement.

Eventually the Land Cruiser came to a stop and we got out, and began to trudge.

At the Aguinaldo home that night, I took another bucket bath, and the pumice dust rinsed off me in gray sheets.I stepped back into the third-floor living room, which now was crowded with family members. My bottle of Fog's End rye whiskey from Gonzales was on the table. Also there were eggs. Of course I knew already what they were: baluts, half-germinated duck eggs, with a half-made baby duck inside each one, carefully incubated, killed by boiling when the duckling inside was fully formed. It was like eating a puppy. But then, I had already done that too, in Korea, long ago.

And of course I was expected to eat one of these eggs.

"You've been talking with Angelica?" I asked a widely grinning Sheila.

"Of course." She laughed. "And she told me that this is your favorite food."

I gave her my best, "You must be joking" face, and she laughed again. "You know the story, right?" I asked.

She nodded her understanding.

I had promised Angelica that I would eat one of these eggs when we visited her family.

On the other side of the table sat Bo Bo and Angelica's older brother Ernesto with an empty chair between them. I walked over and sat down. Ernesto was slender, perhaps in his fifties, taller than me, dark-skinned, smiling slightly, wearing the ubiquitous short sleeve t-shirt and shorts. He poured me a glass of rye. I drank it, and felt the fire burn its way into my arms, my core. Delightful vanilla aftertaste. Oh, I need some of that, I thought.

I emptied the glass quickly. Too quickly. That rye whiskey was made to be savored. I was still clear-headed, a condition which wasn't helpful for balut consumption. I drank the second glass.

My vision shifted. Clearly the alcohol was working its way into my system now. I picked up an egg. It was hot, almost too hot to handle. I cracked it on the table and looked questioningly at Ernesto. Is this how I do it? He nodded. I cracked again. Bits of shell fell off, and clear fluid drooled out.

I stopped peeling the egg. I looked around. All the smiling faces. I turned behind me, and there was the boy, Bam Bam. He held up a pigeon.

"See the white dove. Oh how beautiful!" he exclaimed, his young face alight.

I smiled, and then laughed. "Pigeon!" I said.

He smiled even more widely, and spoke again, laughing and insistent and louder, "See the white dove!" he said again. "Oh, how beautiful!"

My heart swelled with love for this boy, this bringer of birds, this ever-present spirit of joy.

Unbidden, my mind leapt through the numbers, the money that must have flowed here to make this home possible. Before Tommy's death, even. Somehow, there at that table, I finally realized what had happened, what Tommy had been trying to say. In the midst of all my searching, I had not seen.

The why of Jerome, the reason for Jerome, loomed up in front of me, through the mist of intoxication, through the laughter and the smiles. I forced myself to keep smiling, stay in the conversation, and peel the hot balut egg in my hand. Even my newly-drunken mind could see what would happen next. An unrolling carpet.

"Look . . . the duck!" said Ernesto. My fingers had absently picked away the shell, and there, revealed, was a duck embryo, a tiny bill, tiny closed dead eye, tiny wet pin feathers. I kept peeling down the egg.

There were laughing people around me. Across the table sat Angelica's father Ramon, smiling.

I took another large swallow of rye.

"Are you, perhaps, an alcoholic?" asked Angelica's mother, Christina, concerned.

"No, no, no, I am not," I responded, trying hard not to slur my words. "It's just that this situation requires a bit of extra medication."

She looked doubtful.

I waved the half-peeled balut at everyone watching, as though performing an incantation, and then . . . and then I bit into it.

It tasted like an egg. There was a little crunch. I imagined

— Chapter 42 —

that would be the bill, and the skull, and the tiny half-formed bones. I closed my eyes, chewed quickly, and swallowed. Not bad. Slightly salty. I was surprised. For some reason I had expected a cheesy taste. It helped to be drunk. The whole situation was better while drunk.

Ernesto, tall, dark, with a flat-top haircut, poked me lightly in the side. "You good?" he asked.

"Never better," I responded. I smiled. I was trying very hard not to sway, not to appear in any way intoxicated, and not to vomit. There were smiles all around me. I saw Bo Bo, behind Ramon, holding up his phone.

"Are you videotaping this?" I asked.

"Oh, yes, we want to play this over and over." He laughed.

I faced him and his phone. I took another bite. Yoke this time. Not bad. No crunch.

Alongside me, Ernesto nodded his approval. "You and I, we eat this together. We face life together," he said.

I made a face. This balut was disgusting.

He looked at me. "You crazy, white man." Everyone laughed.

Ramon pulled a stool over to me and sat down.

"Tomorrow, we will go to Bohol, you and I, alone," said Ramon. You planned to go anyway, right? Angelica told me."

"What's in Bohol?" I asked.

"What you've been seeking," he responded.

I looked up from the table. Everyone was quiet. Serious now.

Chapter Forty-three

March 2014

Ramon and I were on the southern island of Bohol. We had climbed up what seemed like hundreds of cement steps to reach a viewing area overlooking the Chocolate Hills. Bohol is largely forests and rice paddies, all green. Why they call these perfectly shaped green domes the Chocolate Hills is beyond me. Their exquisite parabolic perfection is very like a Hershey's kiss candy, but these hills are gigantic, full-sized mountains all perfectly domed like old-fashioned sugar cakes. To our right these hills stretched in uniform green crenellations into the distant blue horizon. High in the blue sky there were a few white powder-puff clouds.

To the side was a pile of twisted rebar and cement, an utterly destroyed mess, the result of a recent earthquake. The stairs themselves were broken and crudely repaired. Far below, I could see a series of flat, wet rice paddies, water reflecting silver and blue, separated by dikes with rows and sometimes clusters of coconut palms.

I could see the colorful red dot of a motorcycle, carrying at least three people and probably a live chicken or two, as it bumped along the paddy dike to one of the bamboo, stilt-raised dwellings. In the yard of that home, I could see the distant motion of red, blue, and yellow clothing on a clothesline, flapping mildly in the breeze.

I had been in a place like this before, during my time in the Marines. Zamboanga, in Mindanao, in the southern Philippines, high in the mountains, where it looked like this, perhaps with the paddies a bit more kidney shaped, a bit more stepped up the lush green jungled hillsides.

I remembered flying from the LHA landing ship in a CH-53, a giant single-rotor heavy lift helicopter. We preferred those; more range, more robustness, more lift. We flew low under the gray, crenulated cloud cover, bumping in the turbulent air. Then the helicopter hovered, first at one dummy insertion point, and then another, and then I was rappelling down between the palms. The hovering helicopter above me filled the air with roaring, grinding engine noise, loomed heavy overhead, and skidded slightly on the scudding winds while I tried not to land on the crown of a palm tree. Then down, off the rope, I scouted the area with my M-16A1 while others rappelled down to join me.

This was a live, albeit covert mission. I was there with a radio recon team, searching for Lebanese instructors sent by Iran to coach Abu Sayef, the "New People's Army" into ever-more-creative atrocities. We heard them, we listened to them chattering on walkie-talkie radios in Arabic, and we found them in our scopes. Bugs, Mr. Rico. About six of them.

After that, we in the patrol waited hidden in the forest onsite to provide terminal guidance to the coming raid force. They would exterminate the terrorists. We would ride back to the ship with them. At the last minute, the White House called it off: too much chance of an international incident, negative publicity, we were told. Frustration.

I think of that often, whenever the Muslim terrorists post another decapitation video. What would have happened if we had stopped it then? Or at least killed a few of the early team?

One June night long ago, days before the frustration, I found myself, as the rainy season emerged, standing under a sky with intermittent black clouds, ever-gleaming stars, a brilliant full moon, looking down from the forested edge of a rice paddy terrace into a small bamboo hut, not Abu Sayef, just peaceable farmers, just like that building below me now. Back then, my face had been painted green, in greasy, diagonal multihued stripes, and contact had been forbidden. I had stood in the darkness, rain-soaked and warm on that hillside, looking down at the lit windows of the hut, small flickers of colored motion within. Once, the distant hint of laughter drifted up to me as I stood there hidden in the nighttime forest, and I had wondered, who lives there? Are they happy? Sad? What do they think about life? Is there love in that home?

Mostly I remembered an infinite longing to be down there in that hut, in that love, out of the darkness, embraced in the light of a family's life.

That was then. Now, standing there looking down from the remains of the earthquake-mangled observation platform, it was déjà vu all over again. Strong, powerful memories.

Ramon reached up and put his hand on my shoulder. I loved that touch. He held it there as I looked down at the shacks, the palm trees, the rice paddies. Then he held up a small, wrinkled color photo, slightly out of focus. A small child standing unsteadily in the sun, held upright by the hands of an adult, a boy, about one year old at most. He had a big smile, an almost perfect copy of Angelica's perfect smile, and he had those tiny round ears of Angelica's, and her darkness, and her eyes.

"Who is this?" I asked Ramon. "I haven't met him yet? Maybe grown up now?"

Ramon shook his head. "You never will meet him, except in heaven and perhaps in your dreams, if you are lucky. This is Ramon, Angelica's first child, her son. My first grandson. He is departed now."

I needed to sit down. I lowered myself down on the guardrail at the stairway's edge, until as I sat down on the edge of the concrete slab that overlooked the desolated, chopped remains of the rest of the viewing platform. My legs dangled a little bit overlooking the slope of the hill, where the rest of the observation platform had detached and slid down the incline, exposing the bare dirt and rock. I looked at my running shoes, hanging there in the air. I hooked my arms over the aluminum tubing of the bottom rung of the guardrail, and looked down the slope at the closest bamboo hut. Down there, the tall green coconut palms were swaying slightly in the warm breeze. It all seemed so peaceful.

I looked up at Ramon. He sat down next to me with his legs hanging off the edge of the slab.

"Nobody told me," I said to Ramon.

"Nobody knows, not in the United States," said Ramon. "Angelica is like that. She has so many secrets."

I was watching the palm trees rustling in the wind. Such a clear sky, and off in the distance, thunderclouds forming. Far away. I swung my feet in the air.

"Please tell me," I said as quietly as the breeze allowed.

"She was married, before Tommy," said Ramon. "Rick was his name. He was older, Filipino, rich. He owned a petroleum distribution company. He was very nice to us, very proper. We had a wedding at the Catholic Church, a big wedding, and they moved into a new house out by Catamaran, out by Subic. By the water. You could see Bataan from the patio."

"She was married before?" I responded. That was news.

"Oh, yes, and it was a good marriage, at first. You know Angelica. She likes living high. And they became pregnant, I mean she became pregnant, and she was sick, you know, all that, and he was so attentive," Ramon was looking at the palm trees too.

"Rick traveled a lot for business," continued Ramon. "All over the world, mostly in the Philippines. Perhaps he traveled a little too much. When little Ramon was born, he wasn't there, he was at his offices in Davao, on Mindanao, to the south. I think . . . I think he had a special someone there. A special woman. Secret, you know. God damn, I don't know why people keep secrets like that. Secrets are like sharks, biting you when you don't see them."

I watched as far below a tiny dot of a motorbike drove along a mud paddy dike towards the bamboo hut. Covered with people. Perhaps three, perhaps even more.

"It was a hard delivery, but Angelica did it by herself, with a little medication, of course." Ramon was studying that distant red motorbike. The sidecar was polished aluminum. Far below,

— Honor —
296

it reflected silver in the sun. There was a little square windscreen in the front.

"My wife, Angelica's mother, was there at the birth, and her sister, Marta. You know Marta, she is always strong. We used to laugh that Marta pushed that baby right out of Angelica, with her shouting, 'Stop being weak! Push harder'." Ramon laughed softly to himself.

I was silent. So Marta knew all this, of course.

"So there we had him, little Ramon. He was perfect, the perfect baby. He was happy, he fed well, and Rick . . . Rick was gone on business to Davao even more and more. Never at home. Perhaps he just couldn't see himself in his son's eyes. I've always wondered."

I sat there looking straight ahead. I could feel the adrenaline rising in me, for no reason. I did the math: little Ramon would be twelve years old now. What had happened? Where was he now?

I began a ten-count breathing series, to stay calm, wait for it, say nothing. That paddy dike far below, chocolate brown, was a straight line across the green rice paddies, and that motorbike with the aluminum sidecar was going slowly, so slowly. If it slipped into a paddy, it would probably stick in the mud. The silver glint of water reflected off the flat paddy between the green rice stems. All the paddies were flooded now. The sprigs of green rice plants were in rows, like comb teeth, covering the valley floor from where we sat to the Chocolate Hills on the other side of the valley. Far, far away. We sat in silence. It was warm, perfect, with a breeze in our faces and our legs dangling in the air.

Then Ramon began again. "You know, I wish I could still smoke. But I gave that up. The doctor said it would kill me. I can't really drink either. I miss booze. Anyway, Angelica saw some messages on Rick's phone one day, in 2002. He had a girlfriend. A woman he kept in a condominium, there in Davao. Oh, Angelica was crushed. She decided to let him go back to Davao, then to confront him, to surprise him in Davao, with little Ramon."

"So little Ramon was less than a year old?" I asked.

"Little Ramon was a bit older than one year," Ramon said, looking at the distant clouds. "At first her mother and I advised her not to do this thing. Men will be men. It is very sad. I never did such a thing, but so many men do it, and it is part of the world. Rick's secretary, she was the one who lured him away. She was very slender, athletic, always posing for 'selfies.' You call them 'selfies,' right?"

I began to answer, but Rick spoke more quickly, more emphatically now. "Rick bought that mistress of his the Louis Vuitton purses, the high heels, and the fancy fingernails. And Rick's mistress, you know, Rick's secretary, she always wore that perfume, that Chanel Chance, Angelica told me."

I considered that, silently.

Ramon smiled ruefully. I watched him closely. "So Angelica got those things too," he continued. "She thought that Rick would come back if she had these things."

I watched him. Genuinely, he looked commanding, and relaxed. He kept his eyes on the rice fields below, and the hills beyond.

He took a slow, deep breath, as though sighing, and then continued. "When we accepted that she would confront Rick, we asked her to please leave little Ramon with us. Her mother begged her. You know her mother. Quite dramatic. Marta was angry, of course. She's always been very religious. Marta kept saying to Angelica, 'Go confront him with his sin!' For a time Ernesto and Dan Dan wanted to go with Angelica to face Rick, but Angelica said no, she would face Rick with his woman, with little Ramon, alone. I wish now I had done anything to keep her from going."

Ramon was sitting companionably next to me, on the edge of the overhanging concrete slab, feet dangling a few yards above the exposed dirt and rock slope. Swinging his feet, arms laced through the bottom rung of the steel pipe guardrail. It occurred to me that Ramon rarely wore shorts, but he was wearing them today. Green nylon water shoes, no socks. He was slender and fit and he was looking down at the creeping motorcycle on that rice paddy dike, as it made its way far below. Then he was looking at the horizon, beyond the hills, at the distant white mounded clouds so far away. Perhaps thunderstorms, out there.

He spoke again, quietly. "At the airport, in Davao, it was 2003. The terrorists . . . some Islamic radicals, Abu Sayef, they blew up a bomb. Angelica was there. Little Ramon was there. Hundreds of other air travelers were there. Of course, nobody expected a bomb at all. Who blows up children?"

I wondered if they were the same people I had chased long ago. If so, I had failed . . . and the diffidence of U.S. politicians had killed our innocent allies yet again. Guilt.

He shook his head, looking out at the peaceful green paddies and the domed hills. Never looking at me. Then he continued. "Angelica had flown there to confront Rick. She was waiting in the airport for a taxi to come pick up her and little Ramon. IED, you know them, right?"

I knew what an IED was. I didn't say anything. After all, I'd never met one, really. I wasn't qualified.

Ramon was speaking in a whisper now, and I saw his eyes moisten. "A splinter from a chair, or a fruit stand, or something, a big piece of metal about this big . . ." Here, he lifted up his hand and spread his thumb and forefinger as wide as possible. "It went through little Ramon's head, killed him right there, went all the way through him. Angelica was holding him, and it came through little Ramon and cut Angelica right here." He moved his hand along his right jawbone.

"It cut her deeply, into her neck. She bled very much. She almost died. And when we found her in the hospital, we thought she would die. I thought she would die. Little Ramon . . ." I watched his eyes. Wet, but no tears. He looked serenely out at the tropical vista below. His close-cropped gray hair was so thick. Still a little black in it.

"It was such a little coffin," he said.

Then he stopped speaking. We watched the distant chocolate hills. We watched the motorcycle struggling along the dike far below. It seemed to slip sometimes, as though it would fall from the raised path into the water, but still it came on. We sat. We swung our legs.

"So then Tommy came?" I asked quietly.

"Two years later," Ramon replied. "Those two years, like death for Angelica. She almost wasted away. She changed. She became obsessed with the babies of others, but she could not be in the room with them for long. She prayed to the Virgin, she did not eat, she did not sleep. She made a small altar in our home, where you see Tommy's pictures today. She became emaciated, skeletal. Oh, it was hard to see.

"Rick never came home, really. He gave her money, he gave her jewelry. You know she loves her jewelry. But Angelica gave money away, the pearls and the gems, to orphanages, to hospitals, to any child in need. Marta told her, we all told her, to keep some of that money for herself, for her future life. We told her that she would have other children, but that did not move her. She gave it all away. I think she was dying, really, when Tommy came."

"Did Tommy know all this?" I asked.

"Oh yes, he knew it all," Ramon responded. "He knew it all before he came here. It's why he came. He saw her first as a doctor. You know, he was here on a church mission, right? You know he's related distantly to my sister's husband's family. They told him there was this woman, a young, beautiful woman, dying of a broken heart. That's why he came, the first time. To heal her. Before that, he didn't know her. I think he fell in love with her right there, the first time. But he didn't say anything until he returned to the United States. Nobody expected Tommy to fall in love."

He made a dismissive motion with his hands.

"When did she decide to divorce her husband?" I asked. "When did she give up?"

"Oh," Ramon said quietly. "You know there is no divorce here in the Philippines. It's illegal. Actually, there isn't really any divorce anywhere. You know that."

— Honor —

He continued to look down across the landscape.

Far below the motorcycle reached the bamboo hut. Three tiny figures stepped off the machine, and other smaller dots of color rushed from the hut to meet them.

Chapter Forty-four

March 2014

The next morning, after a sleepless night on my part, we flew back from Bohol to Manila on Philippine Airlines. It was an easy flight, amongst the looming thunderhead clouds in the bright blue sky. I spent the time looking out the window at the sky where Japanese and American aircraft had battled seventy years before. Right here, seventy years ago. By now, even the oldest surviving Japanese and American aircrew must be almost dead. Then there would be nobody who remembered what it was to fly a Zero or a Hellcat to battle. So much happens, and yet everything passes.

At that point the aircraft bumped and I had to smile to myself: a few bumps, and I was tense. Imagine me in a Val dive bomber or a Wildcat fighter. I'd be terrified. Next to me, Ramon slept most of the flight.

The jet landed smoothly in Manila and taxied to the jet way, and stopped. Bo Bo and Sheila were waiting for us with the family's Toyota Sequoia SUV. Ramon sat in front while Bo Bo drove expertly on the crowded freeway, full of battered, rusted shipping container trucks and a full spectrum of worn, old, and brand-new autos. Most astonishingly, I saw brilliantly multi-colored jeepneys, traveling at full highway speed, with people hanging out the unglassed portals and windows. The air was acrid with smog.

"You say you want to learn all about our family, right?" asked Sheila. She smiled. She always smiled.

"Of course. Except I will never ever eat another balot egg. It isn't going to happen. I'm still recovering," I responded. "I'm going to need therapy."

"Hmmmm, Tatay tells me that you've learned about little Ramon," she said. Now she wasn't smiling. Her beautiful brown face was serious. She was looking straight at me.

I looked back at her and nodded. "Yes."

"Angelica won't talk about him, will she? She hasn't mentioned his name since he died. So now you will see what little Ramon gave us in return." A hint of smile returned. "God makes everything beautiful," Sheila said under her breath.

How can she think like that? I thought to myself. Are we going to a cemetery? The SUV—bright polished copper color, new—had left the freeway after more than an hour and was now driving through a less affluent world, gradually deteriorating into a crowded, ramshackle slum. I looked out the window. I saw crowds of people looking back. As the streets passed, the buildings became more worn, more congested, and dirtier. Power lines webbed haphazardly across the sky overhead, from building to building. Paint faded. Now, here and there, I could now see an abandoned cement ruin, formerly a home or a business, once even a three-story brick-made factory, slowly succumbing to the vegetal growth of the relentless jungle. Bo Bo pushed a button and my window hummed down, and a blast of hot, fetid stench shoved its way into the cool stillness of the Toyota. Bo Bo parked the SUV near a bridge across a canal, and we stepped out.

The steaming air reeked of carrion, defecation, stagnation, despair, and wood smoke. And there was another smell, something else, worse.

A small, serious man stepped forward with a thick head of gray hair. Slender. Wearing a polo shirt, Dockers, sandals, and bifocal glasses. He extended his hand. I shook it. He smiled slightly. He smelt of soap.

Bo Bo motioned with his hand. "Garth Ericson, meet Jon Jon Marcelas, pastor of Turn to Jesus Ministries."

I smiled politely. "Good to meet you," I said. "Where is your church?"

JonJon motioned with his arm in a circular motion. "Everywhere," he answered. He grinned.

He began to walk, up the teeming road, towards the canal. The street was crowded with motorized tricycles, motorcycles, cars, and a few carts pulled by carabao water buffalo. The hot air was burning my nose and throat. Stench. We stepped up onto the canal bridge and looked down at the bright green water, small slashes and puckers indicating surfacing fish, surprisingly many. Brilliant hot sun on the green water. Slender canoes as long as vans slid across the glasslike green water, directed by men in shorts who steered with their small, chipped outboard motors. Oh, so hot. We began to walk on a well-worn dirt trail by the canal's edge, away from the traffic and the street, and the road noise began to soften. The large canal was to our right, bending gently away from us, perhaps 100 yards across. To our left, in the middle distance, I saw rusting, giant shipping containers, their vestiges of paint blue, orange, brown, stacked three high, doors open, ladders slanted up to the openings. A child looked down on me from one of the open container doorways.

Jon Jon turned to me, walking backwards, and began to speak and point, as though he was a tour guide and this was a national park. "As you know, when Mount Pinatubo erupted in 1991, it dumped lahar ash over everything here. It raised the river bottom by at least three meters, and there are vast quantities of ash still to wash down."

I was wet with sweat. Jon Jon appeared to be unaffected.

I could see abandoned cement buildings, foundations sodden in the few inches of rancid water that apparently never ever drained away. "Does it flood here often?" I asked.

"Every year, for perhaps a month. Perhaps two weeks really high," replied JonJon.

That was stunning. "Why don't they leave?" I asked.

"It's their home. They know it. They work here in Macabebe in factories making toys and whatnots for the Americans. Some work in the aquaculture ponds." He gestured out beyond the abandoned buildings and the stacked shipping containers. I could look between the container stacks and cement walls to brilliant, flat expanses of shining water. Out there, in measured green and silver oblongs of rice paddy and fish pond, it seemed bucolic, rural, the epitome of wet tropical living.

"Sewage?" I asked.

"Of course the established sewer lines are still in place in the old town, the good part. Here, they just use a bucket and dump it in the canal or a pond," responded Jon Jon, "The original lines are all full of lahar."

"Power?" I asked again.

"Look." Jon Jon pointed. "Bootlegged."

We continued to walk down the path in the steaming sunlight.

In front of each doorway, on the ground, there were small cement open circles, a few still smoking, one with the rice pot still boiling, a few sticks burning underneath it. Most of the small stoves were cold. All were outside. That explained the biting acrid smoke in the air. I did the math. Hundreds of thousands of shanties, all burning wood or coal for cooking.

"Drinking water?" I asked.

"Dispenser at the end of the street, for cash," replied Jon Jon.

"Some can't afford it so they just drink canal or pond water. After boiling I hope," he continued. "Sometimes they just drink the water, sewage and all. Then they get sick, and they often die."

We walked down the path for a time. Ahead was a chain-link fence about nine feet high, topped by barbed wire. Inside the fence were trees, and beyond them, a rising building, which seemed to be in use, and recently painted tan and rust red. I saw a sheet metal roof several stories up, rising above the trees.

"The disease must be terrible," I responded. "Awful."

"Dengue, typhus, cholera, tuberculosis, malaria, dysentery, sepsis, to start. Infant mortality was off the charts," Jon Jon said in clear English.

"Was?" I asked.

As we walked, we encountered a small dock in the canal,

well-maintained. From the dock, there was a small paved path, up the side of the low, flattened hill. At the top, a gate in the chain-link fence that stretched away into the distance, with a forest of young trees pressing against the fence from the inside. Standing by the gate was a guard, middle aged and trim, in clean pressed camouflage utility uniform with a boonie hat. He carried a large metal and wood American M-14 rifle slung over his shoulder. The twenty-round magazine was in place in the rifle. Safety on. Muzzle up. The guard looked at us evenly, calmly, unsmiling. Then he saluted Jon Jon.

"Pastor Jon Jon, *Magandang umaga po Kumusta po kayo?"* he said.

I could reason out that "Kumusta po kayo?" was "How are you?"

As we walked through the gate, through the manicured sapling forest by the fence onto a mowed hillside lawn, I noticed that the guard's boots were polished. Jon Jon smiled, shook the guard's hand and spoke with him briefly, affirmatively, apparently in Kapampangan. The guard smiled warmly and waved.

We walked uphill across the lawn. All was clean here. There was a generator building. Looking down, I could see that the trees around the fence were trimmed.

"The guard's wife has a new baby now. She does well. Praise God," said Jon Jon.

"Do they live out there, down beyond the fence?" I asked.

"Oh, no, they live inside, praise God," replied Jon Jon.

"Where are we?" I asked.

"This is Angelica's place," Jon Jon responded.

I was silent. This was way too big for Angelica to afford.

"Angelica paid for all this," said Bo Bo.

I just looked at him. "What do you mean, Angelica paid for all this?" I asked. I looked. Under the sheet metal roof of the porch, there were perhaps thirty children, all in clean little black and white uniforms. All of them seemed healthy, smiling. Even happy. In the back, two little boys had caught a prawn, and the smaller child was waving it to tease the others. That prawn was gigantic, greenish-blue, perhaps a foot long, astonishingly large. At this moment, the prawn seemed dedicated to the prospect of escape. It snapped and flexed and waved its tiny claws, clicking, and the children in the back row tried to hide their laughter and their distraction. The little boy—he was quite small—waved the prawn threateningly at the row of children in front of him, grinning whitely, still neat in his white shirt and black pants.

As intelligent children should behave, I thought. That boy was pushing the boundaries a little. Exactly what I would want to see in my own children.

"I mean she paid for all of this. This school, the food, these children. She had it all built. She doesn't send money any more, but until last year, she was all they had."

I thought back to the giant debt that Tommy had left after his death. I had assumed that all the debt was due to medical expenses, to Tommy's love of flat screen TVs and golf. I hadn't bothered to do any forensic accounting at all, I hadn't gone backwards in time, I had simply embraced the challenge, gone to war over what was owed, and battled until we obtained a restructuring. I had never looked back beyond Tommy's final years, and I had missed it. I had missed the most important part of all.

"Why do you think she did it?" I asked, almost whispering.

"I don't know, really," replied Jon Jon, barely audible over the laughing children.

It's in the book of Genesis, I thought. Timshel. "Thou mayest."

"I think it's in the Bible," added Jon Jon.

Tommy had not had the money to give. It had come from debt. I had battled for two years for a mortgage restructuring, thinking that the debt was from Tommy's medical battle, a lost cause, a valiant yet futile fight against death.

Instead, the debt was a fight for life. Angelica had known this all along. Now, here was the mortgage, the debt for which I had gone to war with banks and lawyers, and it was alive and forgiven, smiling, laughing, running, playing with shrimp.

"Mortality? Disease?" I spoke, half to myself.

"Not here, none in these kids," replied Jon Jon. "We feed

them too, of course."

"Then why the guard?" I asked.

"Oh, local government officials and criminals. Mostly the criminal families of local government officials. They will steal even the lightbulbs if we leave this place unguarded," responded Jon Jon. He walked forward into the building.

A tour followed. A classroom, neat and full of light, where the six youngest students proudly counted from one to fifteen in English. Another classroom where a young girl of high school age was struggling with the computer coding for one of her classes. The dormitories, for temporary use only, apparently also occupied by the students' families during flood times. There was a small room for medical care, occupied on this particular day by a small, wide-smiling nurse wearing the traditional white dress and cap of nursing, no longer seen in California. Finally we walked around the front of the building, across the black asphalt parking lot under solar panels, where there was road access, looking down on another wider gate and another younger guard with another M-14. And there was Angelica's brother, Rafe, on his motorcycle.

Chapter Forty-five

March 2014

That evening at the Aguinaldo home, I looked out of the living room's back balcony at the flooded, deserted portion of Macabebe that was now permanently underwater from Mount Pinatubo's lahar flows. Here and there were snags of old cement and brick walls rising above the water. Aquatic plants covered most of the lake's surface, and garbage, mostly plastic shopping bags and apparently diapers, floated densely in rafts. Brown, sodden water. The dengue, the disease, must be horrific. Down in the coffee-colored water amongst the thick, submerged green vegetation I could see tilapia fish and large prawns patrolling. The back of this stately edifice faced a big lake: the mansion had been built overlooking this sewage lagoon. But if the lake was transformed into a clean environment, the entire place would be beautiful. Why didn't they do that? I wondered. Or why not just move away?

To the side, along the wall, I noticed pigeon coops. They were designed overhanging the water, so the seeds and the droppings would fall down into the lake, into the aquatic vegetation, a distance of about fifteen feet. There was an open wire walkway along the coops, and there, sitting in an accidental hammock of sagging, rusted chicken wire, was Bam Bam, suspended fifteen feet in the air, holding a big gray pigeon contemplatively, petting it, looking down at it, then looking away into the vista of the lake. He looked up and he saw me, and he shouted happily, "Sir Garth! Look! Look at the beautiful dove!"

He held the bird out to me, then tossed his arms up and threw the bird away, straight into the air. It flew away instantly, and Bam Bam bounced up on the wire and ran squirrel-like across the flimsy netting until he leapt onto the balcony with me. Then he ran laughing into the luxurious living room.

I turned, and there was the entire family gathering for dinner. I had given money for lechon, and barbecue, so tonight we would eat well. Bam Bam ran directly to the large slab of roast pig, tore off a piece of crispy skin with his bare, unwashed hands, and, grinning, began to eat it as he held a plate out and women spooned various foods onto it. He must have the immune system of a tank, I thought.

I sat next to Ramon, and someone brought me a plate heaped with too much food. Too much grease, too many calories. It tasted great. Someone brought me a glass of Tanduay rhum. I took a sip. It was smooth, and it cut the grease in my mouth.

"Learn anything?" asked Ramon.

"Life changing," I replied. True.

"What do you want now?" asked Ramon.

"I think it's best to talk with Angelica," I said quietly. "I want to do the right thing."

"So what is right?" asked Sheila, sitting on the other side of Ramon.

"I'm not entirely sure," I said.

"Does not God tell you? Does not God show you?" she asked. I didn't know what to say.

For some minutes, they let the silence hang in the air.

"Let's talk to Angelica," said Sheila, setting a laptop onto the table. Everyone crowded around.

Everyone watched as the FaceTime connection emerged. Behind me, the retinue of curious children chattered.

Angelica answered the call. There she was, beautiful as always. Hair pulled back, smiling. Bright ,even teeth. I could not recognize the room behind her. It seemed bright in the early morning, luxurious curtains. Like an expensive hotel. Greetings to her from the family in Kapampangan. Discussion, growing heated and fast. I couldn't understand.

— Honor —

Instantly her expression on the computer screen turned to rage. "Say nothing or you damn to hell, you evil man. You evil, small man. First Ramon, now this. You intrude my life. It PERSONAL! Never, never mention this again. I never see you again! Hear me! You never see me AGAIN!"

Then there were a few minutes of angry discussion in Kapampangan with the family around me, who seemed subdued, even embarrassed.

"You must leave them tomorrow. Enough of this spying. It is unacceptable. You endanger everything," said Angelica to me. "Go away from them."

Then she ended the connection.

A sleepless night, full of thoughts and wonder. Ramon came for me around 3 a.m. I was half-nauseous from lack of sleep. Dark. A quick bucket rinse. A hastily written inadequate check to the school, taped to the mirror. A hot breakfast of last night's dinner leftovers, reheated, surrounded by apparently the entire family, which had arisen en masse to see my departure. Jon Jon at the door. Tears in the eyes of the women. Angelica's mother, Christina, was overtly crying. Oh my. Hugs, shaking hands, then down the walkway to the street, teeming with people in the darkness despite the hour.

Onto Jon Jon's motorbike. Yes, we strapped my suitcase and my giant green duffle bag loaded with SCUBA gear onto that bike, hanging out the back, and I rode behind Jon Jon, pressed back against the roped tower made of my belongings. I was astonished and a bit terrified as we rode in the darkness, to contemplate the inhuman load that bike must be carrying. I was waiting for it to topple, for my underwear and snorkel and fins and antidepressant medication to spew itself across the filthy road as the bags shattered, but it never happened. Everything held.

There was a brilliantly lit doorway ahead of us on the dark road, a beacon in the darkness. Few or no streetlights. We stopped there, I stepped off full of curiosity, and Jon Jon leaned the motorbike and its giant load of strapped luggage against the wall. He poked his head into the doorway and spoke in Kapampangan with some women working there, with what looked like plastic ice trowels, shoveling newly-cooked rice into what seemed to be ice chests.

A small, worn old man, thin hair, bloodshot eyes, apparently a little inebriated, pushed a wheelbarrow up to the door, smelling vaguely of alcohol and urine. I recoiled a little as he crowded the door. The old man was dressed in a dirty t shirt and dirty, olive drab shorts, and cheap plastic flip flop sandals.

Jon Jon reached out and patted his shoulders, smiling, speaking in Kapampangan. The women loaded one of the ice chests into his wheelbarrow. Then Jon Jon introduced me to him in incomprehensible Kapampangan language. Rick, meet Garth. Angelica's name was mentioned. The small, wizened man seemed embarrassed by the attention. He grinned, he winced painfully, as though he was thinking desperately of escape. I noticed he was missing teeth.

Finally, the man nodded and bowed and accepted some foil-wrapped food for himself from one of the women. Then he stepped out of the doorway, pulled back his wheelbarrow, and pushed it creaking into the darkness.

"Rick?" I asked.

"Yes," replied Jon Jon. "Angelica's Rick. Her husband."

"Isn't he a millionaire? Very, very rich?" I asked.

"Not anymore," answered Jon Jon.

"Did he give it all to you?" I asked.

"Oh, no, we didn't see a dime. God punishes sin in His own way," replied Jon Jon.

"What's he doing? Penance?" I asked. It was a bit alarming to see such a vital, wealthy man brought so low. Rick looked so much older than his pictures. His smell . . .

"Oh, he feeds the street people the rice we cook here at the mission," replied Jon Jon.

"Penance?" I repeated.

— Honor —

"Oh," said Jon Jon. "Rick will be doing penance until the day he dies."

Chapter Forty-six

March 2014

E arly morning at Kon Tiki Dive Resort on the coast at Lapu Lapu City, near Cebu. I was sitting on a hard, unpainted wooden bench under a gigantic, open-sided roof of corrugated sheet steel. The sun was just rising. The air was soft and warm.

I had carefully researched this place when I had planned the trip with Angelica. Now I was here after my hasty departure from the Aguinaldos. No way was I going to run back to California like a chastised puppy, tail between my legs. So here I was, my military duffle full of snorkel and SCUBA gear leaning against my legs, barely coherent.

"Here" was a tiny, rundown resort with peeling pastel blue and red paint, surrounded by urban shacks, on the shore of a small harbor. Apparently, there were coral reefs below. The clear water was still a bit dark, with the sun not fully risen. A scattering of outrigger boats, spidery blue and white, drifted on flat, utterly smooth water. Perhaps ten people gathered around the small, floating pier. The growing beauty of a pink, cloudless sunrise filled my vision.

This large-roofed, open area was clearly a restaurant of some sort, mostly empty, with a few European people eating at square tables. A Filipina woman, aged, red, worn, short-sleeved t-shirt, blue shorts, flip-flop sandals, smiled at me from the counter against the opposite wall about thirty feet away. Missing top front teeth. Bare lightbulbs in the open rafters above us.

I was so tired. Above me something squeaked. I looked up and saw a mouse-sized, cat-eyed, green lizard looking down.

It launched a small turd the size of a bean that plopped dryly against the cement slab floor. Indeed. Greetings.

"Why are you here, sir?" the woman asked. She looked so content, so old. Probably younger than me. I was aware that a toddler was rustling around on the floor near her feet. The child was drooling immensely, unsteady with its newfound walking skills.

"I have a reservation for tonight at this hotel," I said.

"I can feed you breakfast, sir," replied the woman. "Your room will be ready around noon."

She smiled widely and her brown face crinkled up. Missing teeth. Very happy. Very calm.

I looked at my watch. It was almost 6 a.m. I had no idea what I was going to do with the rest of my day. At least I was here.

A sun-worn Filipino man stepped off the walkway near the harbor. T shirt, shorts, flip-flops. He smiled at me. "You on the dive boat?" he asked. "You with the army?"

Damn.

"No, I'm a former Marine, but I'm a diver. What's up?" I answered.

"Oh. This is for the Australian Army," said the man. Mystery of mysteries.

"Oy, mate!" said one of the young men eating breakfast across the room.

Looking at me. I hadn't noticed him before. Clearly military, European, mid- twenties, a new, large, red scar down the length of his face, so much more dramatic and admirable than my own. He was fit, muscular, wearing shorts and a t shirt, flip flops. He stood up and put a military boonie hat on his close-cropped, blond head. Some sort of spidery camo. Australian? "You a U.S. Marine?"

"Used to be," I answered. "Until a couple of years back."

"Good on! Well, if you want to dive, you better come with us. Grab yer tongs and yer bongos. Boat's leaving in fifteen minutes."

I was exhausted. I didn't know these people. I stood up.

— Honor —

"Where can I change?" I asked the lady behind the counter.

The boat—the "banka" or "pump" boat—was a traditional outrigger about thirty-six feet long, painted long ago pastel blue and white. It had an antique stern motor steered with a tiller, a furled sail, and long, slender, tree-trunk outriggers on both sides.

Ten of us sat companionably on benches facing each other under a faded, tan canvas awning on that wooden spindly canoe. We motored across a silk-flat, blue sea under a turquoise sky as the world filled with brilliant sunlight. I had changed into shorts, a t-shirt, and thongs, like everyone else, albeit with my very white complexion and slathered in perhaps half a bottle of sunblock. I was wearing my own bush hat. American camouflage pattern from the preceding decade, green and black woodland, whereas their boonie hats were delightfully splattered in tan and buff.

There was a catwalk in the prow of the canoe. There, far in front, sat a very slender local Filipino man, hatless, skinny, wife-beater sleeveless shirt with holes, faded pastel blue shorts, giant aviator sunglasses, skin black and wrinkled beyond words, with a burning cigarette between his fingers. He signaled slightly with his hands to guide the Filipino man back at the tiller to steer the frail boat away from submerged coral heads. The ocean was flat as glass and mottled in patterns of turquoise to deep blue, depending upon the depth of the ocean.

The young man whom I had met in the restaurant was named Marcus. Still in the Australian Army, late of Helmand Province in Afghanistan, which was, he and his seven military friends affirmed repeatedly, the rotten crotch, the arm-pit, the gaping anal fissure of the entire world.

The young men joked about women, about Afghanistan, about the Australian Army, often in their own language. Except for a gentleman named "Jackers" and our local Filipino boat crew, they were all infantry, and they had recently endured a combat tour in Afghanistan together as a squad or platoon. Marcus, a young unit commander of some sort, had gotten that "binty bait" on his face from an IED, an improvised explosive device set by the Taliban. All this had taken place about four months previously.

Seven of them had been sent on this diving adventure by the Australian Army, for R & R ("rest and recreation") before returning home. Eminently civilized, I thought. I discovered that in fact "Jackers" (rhymes with "Crackers") was an American helicopter pilot who had provided the Australians close air support by flying above them in his Apache gunship. Jackers was regarded as mildly insane by the Australian infantry, I was told, because of his low-level, aggressive flying. Despite the genuine name of Chief Warrant Officer Cromwell Jackson, he was "Crackers Jackers" to the Australian grunts.

Jackers lived in Cebu with his young Filipina wife and child when he wasn't in Afghanistan, had spent a lot of time "layin' down the thirty mike" for the Australians, and had somehow come back to his home with them. Apparently, he was planning to rotate straight back to Afghanistan in a few months to resume flying.

Our Filipino instructor, Jov, was a tall, wiry, brown muscular man in his fifties who was obviously a military veteran, with countless dives to his credit.

The Australians were much younger and much more gripped by spontaneous energy. As a result our conversation was enjoyably mostly about them. There were seven of them onboard but apparently there were more at the Kon Tiki. Apparently, there was a "blue suit" at the Kon Tiki as well. They preferred "the elephant gun," also called the "slam" or "self-loading Enfield", a rifle like our own 7.62 caliber M-14. Vastly more powerful than the M-4 or the "Awg." They were not, I learned, "mangos" or "Muppets."

Through it all, Jov sat with us, and passed out roasted bananas and succulent steamed coconut rice in woven palm bags. "Hanging rice," it was called.

We spent several hours lost in conversation and our contemplation of the overwhelming vista of the flat tropical sea. Green, jungle-clad mountains and hills of islands rose from the ocean in the still far distances, and some of these were crowned with white clouds.

We slowly approached a tiny, low dot of land, which appeared to grow larger, a palm-fringed atoll surrounded by submerged coral reefs. It seemed to be floating on the blue, glasslike ocean surface. I could see roofs, and separate bungalows on piers over the water. Nalusuan. Although I'd read about it in dive journals, I wasn't even aware that Nalusuan was near Cebu. Now, accidentally, here I was, in one of the world's most beautiful dive sites, with people who appeared to be wonderful as well.

There were no anchors allowed at Nalusuan. Instead, dive boats were required to tie off to round, orange floating buoys. The crew handled that, as we suited up for our first dive. I had my SCUBA-pro fins from long ago in the military, which had also served me during my summers as a research diver at University of Hawaii. I had hundreds of fairly utilitarian dives in my past. Today, I was afraid.

I didn't show it, of course. I knew that part of my apprehension was from PTSD. In PTSD, anything unknown is a threat. Part of it was due to my sinus injuries. After Iraq I'd tried to dive again and been able to go only to thirty-five feet. A doctor had cleared me to dive, with the awareness that my spongy repaired sinuses contained scar tissue air sacs which would compress with depth and become painful. No more one hundred and eighty-foot dives. Now I looked over the side with hidden misgivings. But, it occurred to me, I was at last in a place where Jerome was not better. I could do this. Jerome wasn't here at all.

I turned and looked at my Australian comrades, sunlit, standing on the stern deck of the slender banka boat, opposite the outriggers. They were geared up in SCUBA equipment and thin black wetsuits, as was I, and silent as well, for the first time since our adventure began. I looked at Marcus. He seemed subdued. I was guessing that he had his own issues. Certainly, I had

— Chapter 46 —
321

much more experience with SCUBA. It dawned upon me that as little as I could offer them, here was an opportunity to comfort and to lead. Meanwhile we were quickly overheating in our wetsuits. When Jov went over the side into the sea in full gear, I was right behind him.

As soon as I stepped into the ocean, and that cooler water swept over my facemask, I was seized by a terror of falling. The water was so clear. We were anchored at the edge of the reef, so that we were hovering over an underwater cliff face at least three hundred feet high. It was shocking. Twenty feet from us, towards the island, there was coral and a sandy bottom about six feet in depth. There, I could probably stand up with my head above water and breath. Out here, only twenty feet away, there was only the abyss below.

I struggled to contain my breathing, and focus, and my fear-induced tunnel vision expanded. Jackers and the Australians were in the water alongside me, and just below me on the reef face was the entire swirling menagerie of a healthy tropical reef, resplendent and colorful. Trigger fish, giant Tridacna clams in the shallows, and even a squatting yellow frogfish, about a foot long. You don't meet a frogfish that large every day.

The sight was enough to divert me into an unthinking, instant descent to about ten feet, so that I was hovering on the reef face drop-off. I stared at the frogfish. The frogfish, discomfited by the attention, globular and jaundiced, shuffled its feet-like fins and stared back. I realized that there were Australians on either side of me, looking at the frogfish. Joy. The joy of sharing. The joy of being.

Then Jov led us on a tour up onto the adjoining shallow reef, onto the sandy part. I reveled in our togetherness, in the panoply of the sunlit shallow reef, and the many Tridacna clams, some up to three feet wide, mantles open, brilliantly colored, photosynthesizing in the bright shallow sunlight. A mantis shrimp. A sting ray half-covered in sand, which I avoided carefully. A small, boxy calappa crab digging itself hull-down into concealment. I even tracked a slender Terebra snail about six inches long by following its sand trail across an underwater dune. My fear was forgotten. Wonderful.

On the boat afterwards, we rejoiced together while sharing Filipino food. More "hanging rice," some with pork and marinade encased within. Delicious, savored all the more because of my recent triumph over my own fear. Then we were back in the water.

This time Jov led us deeper down the darkening underwater coral cliff face, into a strong current. I hadn't fully expected that. As we descended down the coral face we were met with hundreds of reef dwellers: a large school of colorful, frilled poisonous lion fish. Morays hanging from small crevices. A cowry snail. And my favorite, a deadly cone snail shell now occupied by a fearless hermit crab.

Jov knew about my sinuses, so, as planned, I stopped descending with the group when my face began to ache, and proceeded up current. Marcus and another Australian stayed with me, and we swam parallel to the larger deeper group, looking down on them as they explored the multicolored reef face below us. Diadema sea urchins. Delicate fan corals, giant brain corals, and always in water so clear that the fear of falling was ever present. We seemed to be flying. Below everything, the dark of the abyss.

I looked back and saw irregular bubbles rising from below. That wasn't right. I looked down. I checked my depth gauge. My face was hurting and the gauge read forty feet. About thirty feet lower than us, at about seventy feet deep, there was Jackers, alone, ignored, behind the group, chasing a mid-sized octopus. The octopus seemed to be playing rather than fleeing. It darted back into a crevice on the cliff face, and then reached out an arm and touched Jackers. Jackers petted it back.

Below them was the dark blue of much, much deeper water.

Suddenly, Jackers reached up and grabbed his regulator, and the bubbles stopped abruptly. Nothing. Jackers began to writhe. He groped at his regulator, reaching over his back for the tank. Time for a free ascent, I thought. Just blow out gently and rise.

You've got enough air. Just do it.

But Jackers didn't attempt a free ascent. Instead, he began twisting and rolling, irrationally attempting to take off his gear, perhaps to determine the malfunction.

I looked rapidly at Marcus and the other Australian. They were watching Jackers and they were watching me, the veteran. I motioned for them to follow and descended rapidly to Jackers, clearing my ears as I went, venting my buoyancy compensator. I felt the front of my face and my teeth explode in pain as my sinuses compressed. It took only a few seconds to reach Jackers. I jerked him around and shoved my spare regulator, my octopus rig, into his mouth. I focused on him, looking into his eyes. His eyes widened as he looked at me. I realized my mask was half full of red blood from my cracked sinuses. This had happened before. But Jackers was breathing easily on my rig now.

As the four of us hovered next to the reef face, with the deep blue below us, Jackers reached over and took Marcus's octopus rig, and placed the mouthpiece between his lips, dropping my octopus apparatus as he did so. Apparently sharing a rig with a man with a blood-filled mask was less appealing. As he reached for Marcus he dropped his small Fuji underwater camera, and it fluttered, silver and orange, down about ten feet where it fortunately landed on a large brain coral. I vented some air out of my buoyancy compensator and dropped down to fetch it, with my whole face burning from the pressure. My mind was embracing the question of how long I could stand the pain. As I picked up the camera I turned, rotating with my back to the coral cliff, looking at the camera in my hand. Undamaged. Unflooded. Nice camera. I looked up. No people. They had obviously surfaced without me.

I looked for them intensely, then realized that I was caught in a strong current, which was pulling me alone, away from the reef, rapidly, over the abyss. My face was aching, burning, crushing. I looked at my depth gauge. Eighty feet. I had vented too much air from my BC, and now I was heavy. Sinking. When I looked down, I saw red. My mask was continuing to fill with blood.

— Honor —

324

Quickly I punched the button on the side of my apparatus and air hissed into my BC. I kicked gently, although I wanted to rush upwards to the dim rippling silver of the surface. I checked the depth. Seventy feet. Then sixty. Slow. Go slow.

Too fast an ascent with no exhaling meant my lungs would explode. I'd seen that happen after a military dive, by a boy with too much courage and not enough brains. Pink frothing blood erupting from the mouth. The wheezing, the frantic attempts to breath, the rush to put the rapidly dying young man into the steel tube-like compression chamber to offset the inevitable bubbles. That lance corporal had survived, but it was an ugly near thing. I didn't want that.

I wanted, instead, to vent the blood out of my mask but I also didn't want to attract sharks. They can smell a thimble of blood five miles away, and the snot and blood in my mask could fill at least a dozen of those. I turned 360 degrees as I rose, looking out far into the clear, underwater blue vastness. No people. No nothing. I had drifted far away from the reef now. The current had me.

Off in the distance I saw an aluminum glimmer. Then again. Near it, another. Something was alive, something was big, perhaps a swarm of some sort, and it seemed to be moving fast, straight for me. Too late about the sharks, perhaps.

I thought, courtesy of this current, I'm on my way to Vietnam.

Fear. Fear. They will never find my body. After the sharks have me, the hagfish will rip into what is left of my corpse in the deep depths below, wriggling and ripping into my gray rotting intestines. This is it. I'm going to die.

And yet. And yet, damn it, I am here. I have traveled half the world to come here and perhaps to die, but I AM here, and I EMBRACE IT. Fuck you all who call me craven. Fuck you all who hold me old, or worthless, or at least worth less than Jerome. Thank you, God, for putting me here. Thank you for the joy of living again. Here I am.

Let me see you face this, Jerome. You sure as fuck ain't resting and neither am I.

— Chapter 46 —

Big as Volkswagens, the large fish were almost on me now, moving with incredible speed. Not sharks: they were too bulbous for that. Silver and blue and giant, with eyes as big as tea saucers. Tuna. A school of Bluefin tuna, racing all around me fast as jets, both sides, moving to an unknown destination as though I wasn't there at all. Terror at first that they would collide with me, then rising exhilaration despite the pain in my face, the feeling of being inside a living steel wind, feeling the water pressure as they slipped past in a silent rush, and then they were gone.

I was alone again. I looked up. There was the surface, close above, and there was a silhouette of a banka boat hull, splitting the brightness. I vented the blood from my mask in one great satisfying blow, felt my head expand, and surfaced. To my delight, I discovered that I was still holding Jacker's dive camera in my stressed, aching fingers.

Apparently, when the other group had realized we were gone, they had surfaced, summoned the pump boat, and followed our bubbles. Immediately they had pulled Jackers, Marcus, and the other man from the water and instantaneously realized that my bubbles were outboard of the reef. So while I had lived my drama with the tuna, they had been watching from above.

Jackers was impressed and grateful to receive his camera undamaged. He was also impressed and grateful to still be breathing. He admitted that he lacked experience, and he had panicked. I thought that was a gigantic admission from an Apache gunship pilot.

As the boat steamed steadily back to Kon Tiki, across the smooth ocean in the reddening twilight, Jov discovered that metal sediment, essentially aluminum rust, from a badly-maintained tank—Jacker's own, stored in Jacker's mildewed shed in Cebu through a wet Filipino year while he was deployed—had clogged the filter of the first stage of his regulator.

Marcus recounted the story of my rapid descent towards the struggling man while my mask half-filled with blood, and I basked silently in the retelling. "I look there and oy, he's bleedin'

— Honor —

like 'ees shot and 'ees smooth as pie." Cheers all around.

I smiled. I didn't tell anyone that later I had pretty much panicked myself. God is good, I thought. At least today. That should be enough.

Chapter Forty-seven

March 2014

As we off-loaded the outrigger boat in the brilliant heat of the late afternoon, the Aussies were in full party mode. We quickly agreed to continue into the night. I was silently basking in the adulation of the young divers: I secretly needed to hear the praises of those combat veterans.

As we loaded our empty tanks onto a wheeled cart, a smiling, animated Jov informed us that next door to Kon Tiki, over that twelve-foot high cinder block wall, there were *women*. Young women. Implicitly, fertile women. The energy in the air spiked immediately.

The young men were mesmerized. The obsessions of young men are to move, kill, and breed. God help us all.

Over there, Jov continued to his rapt audience, was a giant plush tourist resort, the Imperial Palace, resplendent, Korean, boasting a large elegant roofed bar, a live band, and, yes, a plethora of young women. I looked. Yes, there the resort loomed beyond the wall, beyond the trees and bamboo groves, multi-storied, white and gleaming, towering like a medieval Japanese castle. I looked at the young Australians. They were watching the wall and beyond, and grinning thoughtfully. I looked at Jov. He was watching the Australians and smiling happily. I looked at Jackers. He was checking his watch. He was married.

I looked back at the high cinder block wall. Broken bottles *and* concertina wire. Either someone didn't want people from there going here, or someone didn't want anyone from this casual, inexpensive, threadbare little dive hostel going there. I wondered what the average Korean tourist would do here at Kon Tiki. Perhaps the Koreans were crazy to escape from the Imperial Palace. Perhaps the boredom was intolerable. That might explain the wire.

A few hours later, newly shaved and scrubbed, I walked alone down the walled entry road of the Kon Tiki and turned into the much newer Imperial Palace driveway. An out of body hallucination was a sincere possibility. I had been awake for about forty-eight hours before our dive day had even begun. I was insensible from fatigue, wearing a bright red Hawaiian shirt, and white beltless cotton slacks, with battered, river-running Teva nylon sandals. It was much too hot for shoes.

I could hear the Aussies before I saw them. When they finally looked up and recognized me, they shouted and welcomed.

"Ayyy, Marine! You look like bloomin' white Christmas!"

Why indeed I did.

I stood there, a bit dazed in the very well-lit, wall-less room, looking over them seated around a large, ovoid table. I could see the place was cavernous, all white, red, and gold, brilliantly lit, one side open to the gentle ocean in the sunset-lit distant beyond. On the opposite inland side was a rock ensemble playing loud, live American music. A beautiful svelte Filipina singer sang the Celine Dion hit "My Heart Will Go On" as well as or better than the singer who had made it famous. Crowds of affluent Asian people.

Waiting for me were the nine Australian men sitting at the large table, interspersed with attractive young Filipina women, all black hair and flower-patterned dresses. The men were wearing golf shirts, except for Jov and Jackers who were wearing Hawaiian shirts more pastel than my own. All smiling. All talking. All welcoming me.Marcus pulled out a chair, and beckoned me to sit. I sat. Jov reached over the table to tap me, and introduced me to his wife, whose name I could not hear in the noise. Something like "Regina." She smiled wordlessly. Middle-aged, almost regal in her demeanor.

At the opposite end of the table, Jackers waved, his blond crew cut reflecting the bright lights of the room, and shouted, "I'm telling everyone how you saved my life!"

He looked large, coarsely vital, wrinkled, and sunburned from the day. His Filipina wife seemed incredibly tiny and incredibly young, perhaps even in her teens. She smiled whitely, showing perfect, even teeth, and said nothing.

Marcus put a glass of some sort of beer in front of me and I lifted it, saluted Jackers and his wife across the table, and drank. Dark beer. Very cold. Absolutely, rivetingly delicious. For a few seconds there was only that beer, and me. Memories of other dark beer: the ranch on hot days, the town of Bath in England on rainy days, Carmel Beach fires in the sunset. Then back to reality.

Next to me sat a delicately beautiful young woman, slender, graceful. I introduced myself.

"What is your name?" I asked.

"Dove," she responded, smiling whitely. Brilliant perfect teeth.

"I love it here too," I answered. I smiled. "But what is your name?"

She laughed. I was aware that my tinnitus, my deafness, had intervened.

"My name is Dove," she said.

Oh my.

"What brings you here, Dove?" I asked. Noisy room. Hard to hear. I spoke loudly.

The young Australian on the other side of her leaned across her. He was smiling. I remembered his name was Stan. He was a lance corporal. Three tours in combat. Clearly Lance Corporal Stan had been drinking a bit. That was fine by me. He reached out to grasp my arm. A star-shaped keloid scar about three inches long wrapped over the top of his tanned hand.

"FANtastic fuckin' divin' today, mate! Damn fine," he said.

"Glad you liked it." I smiled back. I was eager to have him stop swearing in front of this young woman. I looked at her and smiled.

"To answer your question, this bint's a nurse. They're all nurses," said the Australian. "All going to the same place, what?"

"And what place is that?" I asked.

Dove answered. "Qatar."

That stopped me for a moment.

"Tell me more," I said.

She spoke quietly. I had to lean towards her to hear. "All of us here are nurses. We work at a hospital together. Today we interviewed for work in Qatar, all of us," she said.

"Why? What's in Qatar?" I asked. I had bad memories of the Middle East. Al Shark-al-ausat. Sand. Explosions. Shrapnel. For any woman, stares, whispers, brutal indecent comments among the local men, and perhaps abuse.

"Big bucks, Nagib!" said Stan. He pushed his reddened, moist face close to us. Eyes half shut. Perhaps he had consumed more alcohol than I had realized.

"She's going there for the big dinaaries!" he reiterated.

"Faloose kabir?" I asked her. I might as well speak what little Arabic I could remember. Dove simply looked at me blankly.

"Going there for the money?" I asked her.

"Yes, here we are paid about five hundred dollars a month, and there we can make perhaps two thousand a month. Also, they pay our food and our dormitory."

Such small salaries for trained nurses. But I didn't want to comment on that.

"So you can save. What does your family think?" I asked.

"My little daughter doesn't know," said Dove quietly. "But if I want a good life for her, I will leave her with my parents and go there to make money for her school."

"Where is the father?" I asked.

"Oh, he is an American. He lives in Virginia. We met online. He came here and lived here for three months. We became engaged, and when I became pregnant he left," she whispered.

"Did he genuinely offer to marry you? Did he propose?" I asked.

His behavior, if it was real, was offensive to me. Who wouldn't want to be with his own child?

"Oh, yes. On his knees. Everything." There were tears in her eyes now. "We planned to have a baby and make a family. When I told him I was pregnant he said he didn't like my body growing fat. And I went to work that day at the hospital, and when I came home, he was gone." She was whispering. I was leaning close to her to hear.

"Child support? Isn't that required?" I asked.

"He says he has not enough money. He says his job is small," she answered. "He blocks me on Facebook and he doesn't communicate now."

Her head was down. She was quiet, subdued. I realized that my own worn, aged, shar-pei face was almost touching hers. She was very beautiful. She seemed too slender to have had a child.

Stan's face appeared again, close and sweating. I had forgotten that the whole table was there. I looked up. They were all watching. The conversation had faded. "Well, cheer up, Banats, the night is young!" said Stan loudly. "Who wanted to get rogered?"

The women all looked quizzical. The men looked a bit shocked. As quickly as possible, Marcus stood and toasted us all: "Here's to the American frogman!" Cheers.

"Here's to the Kuringai! Long may they battle the Nips in heaven!" More cheers.

"Here's death to the towel-heads! May they fuh-fuh-fuh . . . marry goats and eat grass!" Cheers. Laughter.

Good save, Marcus, I thought.

Confused looks from the Asians around us. They were so smooth-faced. So quiet. So cultured. So effete. Not at all like the ROK Marines. I had served with them for nine months on the Korean DMZ, in 1978. Those men had been snake-eaters, loud, big, muscular, brutal. Surrounding me now were the bespectacled, slack-muscled, pansexual urban elites of the new Asian century. They seemed mildly amused by our coarseness. Silent disapproval of the child-like westerners.

"Who wants more beer?" shouted one of the Australians, usually the quietest. Possibly the youngest. He appeared to be high school-aged.

Smiles, and more talk. I didn't want more beer.

Sitting next to me, Dove was demure, quiet, a bit timid, feigning that she hadn't understood all the talk. Her life with her young, half-American child seemed challenging at best. Her plans to leave her home to work in the boiling misogyny of the Middle East appeared at best a second choice: that erstwhile fiancé had truly defrauded her. She had no idea what the Middle East was going to be like.

I thought of Angelica and Jerome, back in California, undoubtedly engaged in gymnastic sex at the La Playa Hotel at this moment. Then I realized that I *always* assumed that Angelica and Jerome were *always* engaged in something amazing, usually sex. I found myself smiling. At some point, after all, they must sleep. They must blow their noses. They must chew, snore, fart, sweat, and defecate.

"What makes you so happy?" asked Dove.

I laughed, and looked at her, pondering my answer. Suddenly I was very, very tired. I wasn't ready for a late night of alcohol, attempted sex, cerebrodicktosis, and despair. The day had been superb. Let it end well.

"Who wants to SCUBA dive tomorrow?" I asked the table. People smiled. People kept talking to each other, ignoring the question.

Dove looked at me. "I've always wanted to do that," she said quietly. "I've snorkeled but I've never had the chance to SCUBA."

"Another moment to find beauty," I responded. "Shall we meet at 9 a.m. tomorrow at Kon Tiki? Snorkel first, dive after."

"Wonderful," she answered. "An excuse to sleep early. That's good too. I have been interviewing all day long."

We rose.

As we stood together, all eyes turned to us. I realized that they were assuming that Dove and I would leave now to spend the night together. That would help my reputation even more, I realized, and the thought was warming. The reality was that at this point I had been awake for three days and couldn't see straight. I spoke to Jov across the table and arranged our SCUBA dive for tomorrow afternoon. Then I left with Dove and two of her friends. I looked back across the brightly lit room when someone shouted another toast. Those Australians knew how to party.

The next morning was clear, brilliantly sunlit. I awoke feeling reborn. My second-floor bedroom had a balcony overhanging the coral reef, so that I could look down and watch the fish. The sunrise across an azure sea flat as glass silhouetted the outrigger boats riding at anchor. The crews were scurrying in their preparations.

I was hungry. Delightfully, surprisingly hungry. I decided to go down to the open-air roofed area where breakfast was being served. It was 7 a.m. There was a feeling of all things being ordered and right in the world somehow.

As I walked into the open-air café I saw Jackers—Cromwell Jackson—and his wife sitting at a small, round, green plastic table with Jov, our diving instructor. The table looked cheap, like the matching press-formed plastic chairs. The wife seemed tiny, very young, and very tired, and she was holding a restless, small child, wearing boy's baby clothes, about one year old. Jackers stood. "Sir, you remember my wife? Gina, this is Garth."

She rose. She took my hand and put it to her forehead. She grinned silently. "Join us, sir!"

So I sat. It was comfortably warm. The plastic chair bent slightly beneath my weight. I was wearing a Hawaiian shirt and board shorts. So was Jackers. The baby seemed listless, distracted. Gina seemed stressed. Jov ordered for me: sausage, fish, and rice. Delicious. More fat than I was used to. As I reached for my fork I saw Jackers look behind me and become animated, grinning, rising, and extending a hand. I looked. There was Dove. I rose at once, happy to see her.

"I . . . I came early. I wanted to see the ocean," she said as she shook my hand. She was wearing shorts, flip flop sandals, and a white sleeveless t-shirt. She was very, very beautiful. She had well-shaped shoulders, toned arms, smooth legs. It occurred to me that this would be a perfect situation for reality television: "Americano geezer chases nubile Filipina beauty while locals watch and laugh."

I needed to be careful here.

I invited Dove to join us. I invited her to eat. She demurred, at first, and then she picked up a fork and took a little from my plate.

Gina was silent, watching Jackers talk. She seemed bored by the recitation. Tired.

The breakfast was excellent. The fish, apparently pronounced "Bangoose," was delicious.

Dove was watching the baby. Finally she spoke to Gina in Cebuano. Gina answered. Something negative. Gina shook her head.

I asked Dove what she had asked Gina.

"Does he grow?" said Dove.

"The baby?" I asked.

"Yes," said Dove, apparently lost in thought. "He does not grow. I suspect this. See he is tired. And it is morning. He does not play, and he does not watch us."

More Cebuano. More discussion. Gina agreed with something Dove said.

"What does she say?" I asked.

"She says that the baby has a fever at night but she thinks it is teeth. That is what her mother tells her," said Dove.

Jackers was sitting silently, now distracted from his life story. Concerned.

Smiles from Dove. Baby talk. Then Dove reached across the table and Gina placed the child in her arms. Dove glowed, rocking and playing with the baby, and the baby responded with a smile. Dove lifted the child up to her ear and listened to it breathe, making a game of it, so that the child laughed lightly, then coughed once, weakly. Dove listened again. Then she passed the baby back to Gina. More Cebuano.

"And?" I asked.

"I'm guessing the child has tuberculosis," said Dove. "I'm not sure, but I see many babies like this."

Nobody seemed alarmed. I was horrified. I was wondering if I could get back into the U.S. Imagine. Active TB at breakfast, with the sausage and eggs.

"Well, that changes our plans for the day. Skin test, you say?" Jackers asked Dove.

"Yes, now. They will read the results in two days," said Dove.

"Thanks for advising that," said Jackers, seriously. "My mother-in-law is in charge in our home and sometimes she runs our lives with tradition, not medicine. Getting Gina to do something different is sometimes a challenge. You just gave me the ammo I need."

"Ah, yes, tuberculosis is very common here. It kills us." She then spoke gently with Gina in Cebuano or Tagalog.

Something Dove mentioned seemed to excite Gina. They sat and argued across the table in Cebuano. Harsh syllables. Gina looked at me and at Dove, and then at me again, and scowled and she said, *"Hudas!"*

I said to Gina, "Excuse me?"

She said, emphatically, *"Ulol! Burat! Pesteng yawa!"*

Gina did not seem happy. I looked at Jov and he appeared to be choking on his coffee, face red, eyes bulging, still attempting to smile. I turned back to Gina. So tiny, so slender, so quiet. Jackers was slapping Jov on the back. He also appeared to be choking on his coffee. Trying not to laugh.

"What are she saying?" I asked the table.

"She's . . . surprised that her baby is ill, and she says thank you for saving its life," replied Dove.

"Paksheyet! Pakyu!" said Gina, looking at me, frowning.

"You are most welcome!" I said to Gina, smiling gently. She didn't smile back. Dove spoke to Gina soothingly, at length in what was apparently Cebuano or Tagalog. At first, Gina's eyes filled with tears, and her head shook, negative, no, I won't do that. Then, she nodded and seemed to calm down.

"What are you saying?" I asked Dove.

"I am saying don't go to the traditional healer. Don't give the baby herbs. She says the skin test will give the baby poisons. I say it is necessary," said Dove.

"Well, that decision just got made," said Jackers. He was smiling slightly. Next to him, Jov was grinning, red faced, his choking behind him. I wondered if the locally grown coffee was especially harsh.

Jackers stood up and smiled. Gina was reluctant to leave. Jackers looked down at her, patiently, until she rose. Jov rose with them. As they walked away, Jackers said to Dove, "Good on you, ma'am. Courage. My kind of person."

That left me sitting alone looking at Dove.

"What?" she asked, laughing lightly.

I was thinking that Angelica would have hated this place. To me, Kon Tiki was simple and delightful. To Angelica it would be dirty, shabby, and beneath her.

I told Dove all about Angelica, and my relationship with her. It took perhaps ten minutes. She was quiet. She listened. She smiled gently as I finished.

"I know that feeling completely. I am lost without the father of my child. But I go on, as you do. Be patient and wonderful things will happen. Trust in God.

Chapter Forty-eight

March 2014

The water was warm. Dove was an excellent swimmer, and she snorkeled well with worn blue rental gear. Astonishingly, the reef off the balcony was almost as delightful as Nalusuan: clear water, lush with fragile corals, replete with brilliantly colored fish. There were even mollusks, sea shells that would normally be pillaged from reefs so near an urban area. Clearly, the people living here were investing in protecting this.

I found myself at one point about thirty feet underwater holding a cone snail shell, a Conus geographus, a fish eater, one of the great marvels of the world. Imagine, a fish-eating snail. The urge to share this amazing little creature was strong, and I rolled upright underwater and looked up to find Dove. She was swimming on the surface, easily, gliding over me looking down, her slender form silhouetted against the surface. I looked down at the shell to confirm that it wasn't occupied with a potentially stinging snail, and began to rise to the surface, and I realized that I had planned this entire trip, this entire adventure, for a woman, Angelica, who did not swim.

Then there was lunch, again in the restaurant ten feet from the water, and then there was more snorkeling in the afternoon, more sharing, more amazement. More lazy hours with a cold dark beer, "cerveza negra," watching the flat blue ocean, and the bustling pump boats.

After that, dinner with the Australians, so natural and joyful. They had spent the day diving with whale sharks at Oslob up the coast. The brightness of rediscovered life was in their eyes, youth restored. I sat there with Dove, smiling, laughing, carefree, as though I was thirty again. Dove was wrapped in a tie-died sarong over her bikini, and I was in a t shirt, still in my board shorts. Both covered in a layer of crusted sea salt. Magic dust.

The world had turned in just a few days. Perhaps it had turned too rapidly.

"SCUBA tomorrow?" I asked Dove after dinner.

"Yes," said Dove. She was looking directly at me. Eyes no longer looking away. Smiling gently. She was as she had been all day: serene. Quite beautiful.

Jov sat next to us. He quickly volunteered to be our guide, and to provide all the equipment, tomorrow morning. We agreed upon a price.

Jackers, Gina, and their baby arrived, sweating slightly in the heat of the night. Gina appeared mildly angry. Jackers was grateful, and thanked Dove profusely for insisting on the tuberculosis test. Apparently when they had arrived at the clinic the doctors had demanded that the entire family have skin tests. Gina was now concerned that she was poisoned. That was better than an incomplete diagnosis. Dove merely smiled quietly, and nodded her head in acknowledgment. They joined us and sat, sharing in the joy of the Australian's whale shark adventure. It seemed wonderful to me.

I turned to Dove. "Shall we meet here again tomorrow?" As the words left my mouth, I was surprised at them.

"Yes, please," said Dove. "I should wash at the outdoor beach shower first. "There are six girls in my room, to be kuripot, that is, frugal, and I don't wish to wake them."

"Did they interview today? Did you miss that?" I asked.

"I interviewed the day I met you," she answered. "We are gallivanting here for three more days simply to see the sights and enjoy, then we go back to work."

"What did you think about today?" I asked.

"I thought it was a dream. I think all this is a dream. Such wonderful people here," she answered. "I was a military nurse for the Filipino Army. I saw many casualties in Mindanao. The Moslems are here, too, you know. They kill us."

I explained to her that many years before, I had been in Zamboanga with the United States Marines, seeking the New People's Army. I had never seen any combat of any sort, although I *had* gone home with a delightful, much-worn Russian SKS rifle, vintage 1945, which I had discovered immersed in a muddy rice paddy. I had stepped on it while on patrol. Good thing it had not been an improvised bomb.

"Yes, the SKS," she replied lightly. "My father has it too."

"How does he have it too?" I asked, fascinated.

"Oh, now he is farmer in Mindanao, but he is also former Philippines Army. He fought the NPA and the Abu Sayef for many years."

And so we talked. The gecko lizards scampered and chattered in the rafters. We discussed the whale sharks: great, gentle, lumbering behemoths, giant as submarines, utterly silent, breathtaking. And gradually the discussion of the others drifted out of my mind, and I was focusing only upon what Dove was saying.

She was still in love with the father of her daughter. He was African-American, he was very fit, with big muscles, and he lived in Virginia. He had dreadlocks. He worked for the State Department. Very concerned about freedom and women's rights. Apparently, that's why he had been in Mindanao: to study the rights of women of color. It had been part of his job.

He had left within a week of learning that she was pregnant because he didn't like the shape of a pregnant woman's body. He had simply gone to the airport and flown away while she was working. She had never received any financial assistance from him, aside from the three hundred dollars in cash he had left behind when he'd departed.

Because their marriage had been imminent, she had left her family home to live with her fiancé, and, at his request, had not used birth control. Now, since the pregnancy, many in Cagayan de Oro regarded her as an immoral woman. No marriage, no husband, no virtue. She was fated by her community to remain single and care for her parents until they died.

But that was not the life of which she dreamed. She was seeking to move forward, somehow, to reclaim her life, and now she was interviewing to work abroad. She did not want to leave her daughter but the daughter's best schooling required much money, and money required work abroad. She was quite willing to work hard. Although she loved the Philippines deeply, even more since today's coral reefs.

Finally, I looked at my watch. It was 11 p.m.

She caught me. "I should go."

"Shower first," I said.

I asked Jov, "Is it okay if she showers there?" I pointed to the outdoor shower by the stairs that led down to the ocean. It was simply a metal pipe with a u-joint, an industrial on-off valve, and a nozzle.

Jov looked at me puzzled. "Yes, of course, but it will be more modest if she showers in your room. Here there are all the young men watching. Your room will be air-conditioned. There will be lights there. She can dry her hair. Be civilized, man."

He laughed.

I hadn't thought of that.

Dove agreed with that idea. Nervously, we excused ourselves and walked up the open-air stairs in what now, in the night, were balmy breezes rather than the searing heat of the day. Across the lawn, we could see that the party was continuing under the tin roof of the restaurant. We removed our sandals, and I showed her my suite: bathroom, balcony overlooking the coral, bedroom. She had a small "Hello Kitty" bag with her clothes. Both of us were distant, cordial but concerned. The mouse squeak of sexuality so evident in daytime was now a tiger's roar. We both were seeking to ignore that we heard it in the slightest. Both pretending.

Dove shut the door behind her as she entered the bathroom, and I walked to the balcony and attempted to put my mind to other things. I wondered how Angelica was doing: it must be morning there. With Jerome? How were Cesar and Rose, and Francesca, and my other children? How were Margaret? Jack? My mother?

Over there it was daylight. Life was fast.

Here there were warm breezes. Here was a wonderful glass-like sea turned to silver by a half-moon, silhouetting the masts and the spars of the slender sharp-prowed outrigger boats. Far, far in the distance the looming darkness of a small island. Out on the sea, lights. I wondered who they were, those lights. Whom did they love? What were their cares?

The thought of Dove showering in the brilliant light, in that bathroom, utterly naked, soap suds sliding down her flawless slender body, long black hair wet and clean, surged back to my mind unbidden.

Life was good, wasn't it? I had followed the path, and it had unexpectedly led me here. I had expected to die yesterday in that open ocean, and instead God had released me. For what reason I didn't know.

In fact, all my fears had been fantasies. I had followed the path, and here I was, and there was a wonderful, intelligent, courageous thirty-five-year-old Filipina woman in my shower. I had thought that my life was destroyed in so many ways, a few months ago. Most men would change places with me now.

Somewhere in the dark ocean, out on a boat, there was a small, distant unintelligible patter of conversation, and a laugh. I had to laugh as well.

What was waiting for me at home? Angelica was not thinking of me. Cesar and Rose were having a good life with Jerome. Margaret was with Jack. With the exception of Francesca, my other children were adults. Here I was . . . in paradise, liberated, and very much alive.

It occurred to me that Dove had probably finished that shower. I opened the sliding glass door and walked back into the room from the balcony. The air-conditioned air instantly chilled me. I could feel the salt on my skin. The residue of an active day.

— Chapter 48 —
343

I walked to the bathroom door and opened it a tiny crack, and looked in. Steam. Steamed mirrors. Bright light. On the towel rack of the sliding glass door was hanging Dove's orange bikini. It looked very small. Through the distorted glass of the shower door I could see Dove, naked, standing straight, small, and lithe and rinsing her hair in the flowing water.

"All good?" I asked. I had to make myself speak. My voice cracked.

Dove laughed. "Almost done! It's just so GOOD! It's so GOOD!" she replied. Her voice echoed in the steamy bathroom. "I never want it to end."

I stepped into the bathroom and shut the door.

I needed a shower myself.

The next morning, the pinkish dawn light poured in through the windows. I woke and the first thing I considered was that I hadn't taken my normal Ambien. Then I realized that Dove was sleeping soundly alongside me. I felt beneath the covers. Yes, she was all there, and none of her was clothed. She hadn't dressed while I slept.

I remembered everything. So smooth. So wonderful. I rolled onto my side, and looked at Dove. Astonishing. Astonishing.

At any moment, I pondered, a documentary film crew could knock on the door and interrogate me about the sexual exploitation of Filipinas. And what would I tell them? "Yes, she's here, and I feel damned good about it, actually."

Guilt. Pondering exploitation. By whom? I could end this now in frowns and sorrow, or I could go forward with the momentum of our experience. Well, why the hell not? I was all-in now anyway, thanks to my lack of self-control. It was like parachuting: once you leave the airplane, the odds of making yourself go up diminish radically. So . . . onward. Make a decision, Lieutenant. This morning was an entirely new sunrise.

Wandering, drowsing thought: I was curious to see how Dove dealt with SCUBA diving later today. I had planned too many camping trips for women who didn't camp, too many beach adventures for women who did not swim.

The realization startled me fully awake: I was now thinking of Dove not as a chance passing encounter but as a potential genuine relationship. How unexpected.

Well, why not? What could prevent that? What could I find in Dove to keep us from simply going forward from here? Fear. Wondering what to do now. No . . . put all those thoughts away. Let's see how she copes with SCUBA diving.

Dove was sleeping on her back now, snoring very lightly, in a surprisingly endearing way. There was an urge to reach over and kiss her face, lightly. I gently placed my hand on her flat tummy and let it rest there, feeling her breathe.

I realized that without an emphatic step in a new direction I was doomed. Perhaps this was it.

Jov and Jackers were at the stairs to the reef at 8 a.m., smiling widely, with our gear waiting, as though last night was utterly, totally normal. I stepped down the stairs from our room alone, while Dove showered again.

It was a brilliant morning.

Dove came out of our room upstairs, shut the door behind her, and walked down the stairs, and all eyes were on her. Even the elderly Filipino groundskeeper stopped to watch. She was wearing her orange bikini, with a gossamer sheer cover, slender, long black hair and brown skin, and she was beautiful. Magnificent.

Jackers walked up close to me and said, quietly. "Damn, dude, she's a keeper. She's like a princess."

Oh, how the world can change so fast.

Sitting at a shore-side table beneath the restaurant roof, about ten feet away from the stairs to the reef, Jov gave Dove a quick yet thorough basic class on SCUBA. "Don't hold your breath or your lungs will explode out your mouth," and simpler, life-enhancing information. Dove seemed entirely focused on his words. Wise woman.

Since Jov and Jackers were caring so intensely for Dove's preparation, Jackers helped me into my thin, black, short-sleeved wetsuit, hoisted the heavy tank and regulator onto my back, and assembled my gear.

I carefully crept down the worn, wet, mossy—and slippery—concrete steps into the water, with that heavy air tank on my back and my regulator swinging about and smacking into the concrete. Carefully. I realized I was a coward. A coward with undamaged knees. A coward in a tropical paradise. A coward who was SCUBA diving with an intelligent, model-beautiful young woman. I could live with all that.

Beneath the water's surface, the stairs ended and there was a drop into about two meters of water. The wetsuit was already stiflingly hot, and getting in the ocean now, ahead of everyone else, seemed attractive. I pressed the button to partially inflate my buoyancy compensator and felt it swell around my neck as the air hissed in. Then I let myself slip into the water and float with the meager current. Cooling seawater coursed over my skin, under the wetsuit. I looked down, masked face in the water, and did a quick 360-degree scan below me as I breathed through my snorkel. No stonefish. No sharks. No poisonous sea urchins. A riot of color and life as brilliantly colored fish swirled around the coral below me. Joy.

I looked up the stairs to the landing above. Dove was in her wetsuit. Jov and Jackers were helping her into her BC and tank, and her legs were shaking. Fear. We would see now if she would actually dive. I noticed Marcus and two other Australians behind them, smiling and watching, and taking phone photos. They waved at me, mugging and gesticulating. I grinned up from the sea and waved back. Marcus pointed at Dove behind her back, gave me the okay sign, and winked. I smiled from behind my snorkel and gave him an okay sign back.

I put my masked face in the water and did another three-sixty. All wonderful. I looked up, and Dove was being helped down the steps, shaking but smiling. Jackers and Jov didn't have their gear on yet. Apparently, the plan was that she would wait floating on the surface with me until they joined us. Another three-sixty. Underwater, I saw that a few meters away was a banded sea krait, a deadly poisonous sea snake, quite common here and inoffensive unless we messed with it. It seemed more intent on probing into a coral head for small fish to eat. I looked up again. Dove was poised on the final step, legs submerged, shaking and smiling, and looking into my eyes, then she gently let herself topple into the water and into my arms.

Jov was a superb instructor. We spent about forty-five minutes underwater. Jov had a hand on Dove's arm most of that time. After some early challenges clearing ears, we swam down with Jackers taking photos with his underwater camera. We found ourselves luxuriously swimming between coral heads that were the size of cars, about thirty feet underwater. My sinuses hurt. I didn't care. We met anemone fish who emerged from their anemones to challenge us. We swam alongside a green sea turtle. We all watched a banded krait undulate by, ignoring us in its quest for fish.

Lunch, followed by two more similar dives, then showers, then Dove and I and our room and our balcony. We all met for dinner in the sheet-metal-roofed dining area as the sun fell pinkly into the glassy sea. It was very dark tonight, clouds gathering, small waves washing over the stairs down into the ocean. I savored a cervesa negra and contemplated the cold drops of water collecting on the sides of the bottle. Far off there was a bolt of lightning.

We were sitting with Jov and the Australians. All of us in shorts and old t-shirts and flip flop sandals, lit under the open beam roof by the meager light of a few bare light bulbs. The weathered woman in charge of the establishment was all smiles. Jov was energetically telling Dove that she was a natural with a tank, that she should get her certification, and that he should provide that course. The price was mentioned. Dove looked at me. I smiled. I told them that I could imagine nothing finer.

Jackers and Gina and their baby arrived. Abruptly, it began to rain, then pour. The noise of all that rain hitting the tin roof was deafeningly loud, and we all smiled at each other and waited. The rain continued to roar on the metal roof. We ate. We smiled.

I had two more nights left. It occurred to me that I was living very fast. Overhead, the gecko lizards were scrambling across the wooden truss beams under the roaring tin roof. Their lizard mouths opened and they orbited each other, shaking their small scaly heads. Apparently they were barking at each other, but we couldn't hear them. The noise of the rain overwhelmed any other sound.

Chapter Forty-nine

March 2014

We faced a deluge the next morning. Overhead was a solid ceiling of gray clouds, and I could not see where the clouds ended and the rain began. Our balcony provided us with a wonderful vista of pouring rain foaming the flat ocean, as off in the far gray distance the lightning jolted from the sky. I went down to the restaurant and came back with a sweetened coffee for Dove and a rich Filipino hot chocolate for me. So much rain fell on me that our drinks were lukewarm and diluted by the time I ran the sodden few rain-doused paces back to our room.

It didn't matter. We lingered on the roofed balcony holding each other on the couch, and the morning was warm enough that the lukewarm drinks were perfect. We sat, watched the rain, and savored.

After several hours, hunger drove us down to the café. We joined our new friends at several plastic tables pushed together. The rain hammered on the roof. The lizards looked down. We talked louder and we talked more slowly than we had talked last night. I realized that none of the Australians had women with them. There were Jackers and Gina. No baby.

Gina and Dove fell into a quiet calm discussion, and they stood up and walked away from the table to talk by themselves.

One of the young Australians asked the table: "If you could have anything today, what would it be?"

"Real or fantasy?" asked Jov.

"Oh, real, right now!" responded the very young soldier, Australian accent very pronounced.

"I wish I didn't have gonorrhea," said one young man, ruefully.

"Oh, oh, you have to hear this, sir!" added Marcus, looking at me. "He caught it in fuckin' Afghanistan! They should give this little bludger a gong for such a feat!"

"Afghanistan?" I laughed back. "How?"

"Ayyyy! You cane toad fuck! Stick your doodle in a goat, see what happens?" added one young Australian. Everyone laughed.

The young man in question continued to grin sheepishly and stare at his feet. I considered that he might be twenty years old.

"I'm guessing the Italians or the Danes in the next huts over. There were some women there." Smiled Jackers. "Some of them were real jamilahs."

"Ay, genuine spunks," added the young suspect.

"I finished the antibiotics several weeks ago," he added. "So I guess I'll be clean by the time I'm home."

"Seriously, what does everyone really want, today?" said the original speaker.

"I want my wife back," said another young man, quietly.

"I want to be back on the family station," said Marcus. "Been eight years now. Time's up, I think. Time to stop wagging and get back to the bush."

Everyone was quiet. Too quiet.

"I'd like my hair back," I joked.

"No, sir, I mean if you could *do* anything today to change your life, what would you do?" asked the original young speaker.

"More beer?" said another young Australian. Quiet laughter.

"I'd be right here, right now," said Jackers. "I mean, look at us. Life is good."

"Life *is* good," added Jov. "God is good."

"Well it's good when I'm blasting Talibs to bits too. But this is fine," said Jackers.

"In its own very quiet and soon-to-be-boring way," said a young Australian.

Silence.

"If I could do anything today I would fly back to Mindanao to my family with you," said Dove, looking at me.

— Honor —

350

She had rejoined us during our discussion.

"Why?" I asked. "Won't they be angry at me?"

"I have two college degrees, a great job, and a baby without a husband, and I'm old," said Dove.

I pondered that. She was thirty-five. Old?

Dove waved her hand in negation. "They think I am only to care for my parents and no man will have me. I want them to see that I have my own life."

Silence. I considered that. Dove and I had experienced something wonderful and life changing. I wasn't sure what we had experienced, but it was certainly better than the raw despair which owned my life before we met. She was saying what she really wanted. I had it within my power to give her something wonderful even if I never saw her again. Besides, I was flying back to the United States in a few days anyway.

What an insane and profligate idea. I was amazed I was considering it.

"It's going to rain all day," said Jov.

"Not much diving?" I asked him.

"No, not so much. We don't want to be out on the water with lightning," said Jov. "Imagine swimming around in a lightning storm with a steel tank on your back."

"Mostly it's just a day for this sort of thing," Jackers added.

He motioned around the table.

I looked at him. He smiled. I felt he was silently giving me advice.

"No diving?" I said again.

"That wouldn't be the best use of your day," Jov replied, smiling.

"You only live twice," said Marcus.

Overhead the rain was beating down and the sheet metal roof was banging as though someone was dumping gravel on it. Deafening. In the eaves, the geckos were darting in the rafters. Chasing. Chasing after what?

I looked at Dove. She was looking at the geckos too. I touched her gently on the shoulder.

"Let's pack and go to the airport," I said to her.

Her eyes widened.

I stood up. "Gentlemen, please friend me on Facebook because each and every one of you is marvelous. Thank you for your service."

Monstrous turbulence. Our Boeing 737 skidded, yawed, and plummeted, careening between blackness and brilliant daylight. I felt sure we would die. I kept my terror hidden to set a good example for Dove, who seemed utterly unruffled by the bucking, the bouncing, the gut-wrenching drops, and the sodden sideways yaws. Entirely fearless, she seemed. Meanwhile I was considering popping an emergency Xanax, surreptitiously counting the minutes, repeating over and over to myself, "You don't know what is really happening." The seatbelt sign was on, so lurching and stumbling down the aisle to the bathroom to take a pill secretly was out of the question. The flight attendants remained strapped in their seats during the short flight, so booze was not available.

As we taxied to the Cagayan de Oro terminal in the drenching rain, I wiped the sweat off my bald head with a bandana from my carry-on backpack, breathed slowly to calm my racing pulse, and asked Dove, "Flown much?"

She looked at me calmly, deeply unperturbed, and replied, "Oh, no, I always take the overnight ferry. Much cheaper. That was my first flight. Is it always such fun?"

"Seldom," I replied. "This was special."

The airport featured a roofed, open-air terminal. It was raining, sometimes drenching. We selected our baggage from the rotating aluminum carousel and exited into the open breezeway to meet Dove's family: apparently mother, father, sister, nephew, niece, and Dove's daughter, Akemi, and approximately ten people whom I couldn't place. Loud, Cebuano language. Chattering, smiling Filipinos swarming, surrounding, suitcases carried off somewhere, fleeting introductions for me, hugs for

Dove, tears apparently of joy, then quickly into a battered old indigo 4X4 SUV to get out of the rain, driven by a scowling, elderly driver wearing an Oakland Raiders baseball cap.

The SUV seated eight. There were approximately fifteen persons in the car: the adults sitting in seats, sometimes with the smaller women on another's lap, Akemi sitting or sometimes even standing on the storage housing between the driver and the front passenger. The other small children were all standing behind us in the cargo compartment on our suitcases, lined up like small, brightly colored, smiling fence posts. Nobody wore seatbelts.

The man who was apparently Dove's father was in the front passenger seat. He seemed welcoming, in charge, dressed in shorts, flip-flops, and a golf shirt, hair crew-cut, square without being fat at all.

It was stiflingly hot and moist. The hammering rain on the roof and myriad chattering voices produced an ongoing roar of sound that all seemed to blend and match my permanent tinnitus. Unable to hear anything, I simply settled back and let the whole situation engulf me. In a few days, I would be flying back to California. Around us, beyond the SUV's window marked with raindrops and rivulets, surged floods of people on motorcycles and tricycles, all soaked, all weaving through the crowded, slightly flooded streets.

Dove was grinning brilliantly ear-to-ear, conversing animatedly in Cebuano, mostly with her mother. I leaned over to her and said, "Why are all these people here with us?"

She answered, "Oh, to see you and me. None of them can believe it. They are shocked."

She smiled.

Suddenly, the car braked to a halt, and everyone inside surged forward from the inertia, shouting and laughing. I looked outside. Another car? A pedestrian? A goat? Nothing. We were parked curbside in a swirling ramshackle street market. I opened the door, stepped out into bright sunlight and no rain. Instantly, everyone behind me in the car disgorged onto the wet ramshackle sidewalk. The children slid over the seats from the cargo space and began laughing and darting into the shabby roofed stalls, which displayed a vast spectrum of colorful, inexpensive goods for sale.

There was the smell of sewage, the acrid smell of burning charcoal, and the smell of roasting chicken. The bright street swarmed with happy, boisterous, busy people. Most were dressed like the Filipinos I had seen before, but here were also men in ankle-length robes and woven cloth skullcaps, and women veiled in gaudy brightly covered headscarves. Moslems.

Dove's father was talking in Cebuano with a man at a chicken booth, crammed amongst other similar stalls. The booth was made of roughly trimmed sticks with a dilapidated military surplus olive drab canvas roof. Perhaps twenty chickens were roasting over a gasoline-drum barbecue, on long stainless steel skewers about five feet long. The heat from the fire compounded the intense heat of the day, and I felt sweat trickle from under my arms and down my back, beneath my already-soaked shirt. As the two men talked, apparently beginning to argue amiably, the man put his cigarette in his mouth, reached over and rotated the cooking birds, squinting into the smoke. I walked over and stood next to Dove's father.

"Smells delicious," I said, mostly to myself. I hadn't heard English since landing.

"Thanks," the man replied, speaking through his cigarette. No accent. "It's my mom's recipe."

That was unexpected. I studied him. He appeared to be Moslem. Skullcap. Ragged sparse beard. Big, coarsely woven shirt untucked reaching almost to his knees. Half Filipino, half something else. As I watched, Akemi reached out, smiling, and the man put a small piece of cooked chicken in her hand. She shoved the treat into her mouth and began to eat.

"Where you from?" he asked, looking at his roasting chickens, busying himself turning them.

"California," I responded. "Where are *you* from? You speak English superbly."

"Gringo, huh? Oh, I'm from Fremont. Up by Oakland," he answered.

"What the heck are you doing here?" I had to ask.

"My mom is Filipino. Original Moro, man. Dad was US Navy. So I came here. Much less living expense. I'm retired from the Alameda County Sheriff's Department. Born and raised in Oakland."

He didn't look old enough to be retired.

"What do you think?" he asked, still focused on his chicken, nodding his head to indicate the market. The movement dislodged an ash from his cigarette and it drifted into the cooking fire, floating onto the cooking birds. He squinted into the smoke, watching the ash drop. Apparently seasoning chicken with tobacco ashes was acceptable.

"It's different," I responded. "Fascinating. I have a lot to learn."

I looked around me at the crowds passing by. Men in robes. Veiled women. Bright fabrics. Heat. Smells. Most of all, that delicious roast chicken aroma. People seemed happy. Nobody seemed to be interested in me, which I thought was a good thing. Dove was picking through giant coconut-shaped spiny fruits, which were as big as fifty-pound bags of rice.

Dove's father and the chicken monger exchanged friendly words. The man behind the counter removed three chickens from a skewer, placed them on a large wooden well-used cutting block, and dismembered them with a giant square-bladed smashing cleaver. *Whack, whack, whack.* Then he wrapped them in foil and newspaper and handed the package to Dove's mother. I reached out to him with a wad of peso notes before Dove's father could pay.

"Thanks," the chicken man said, and he smiled and passed change back to me. His beard and mustache were short, patchy, and scraggly. He looked sweaty, hot. Who wasn't? It must be very challenging to work here all day. His eyes were amber, not brown like most Filipinos. Honestly, he looked as though he was in his thirties. I wondered why he wasn't wearing sunglasses.

Even from under the makeshift awning, the glare from the street was intense.

He removed his cigarette, smiled and spoke. "You know this is Moslem country, right? You need to get out of here before Abu Sayef kidnaps your ass." He laughed. Very conversational. Have a nice day. Smile.

"That's the plan." I smiled back at him. "Stay safe yourself."

We all retreated across the heated, bright sidewalk to the waiting SUV and its scowling driver, who was glaring straight ahead. The inside of the car smelled like vomit and a dead horse. I looked down. There was one of those spiny giant swollen fruits on the floor, about the size of two military sandbags, between the driver and Dove's father. The fruit was covered in a tarp. Tiny Akemi stood on it happily, clutching the seats on either side and peering out through the front windshield. I contemplated what would happen if we had a collision: the child would fly through the glass. I also pondered what a modern California Highway Patrolman would make of it: probably call child protective services and arrest the parents at the scene. Welcome to Mindanao.

"It is durian fruit," said Dove, pointing at the fruit.

"It has a strong smell," I said.

"Bad smell, good taste," replied Dove.

Gradually, as we drove, the city became less densely packed, and rice paddies more frequent. Suburbs. Small, chaotic strip malls. Less traffic.

The car suddenly swerved over into a bus stop cutout in the road, next to a makeshift roadside stall selling cheap goods. About 300 yards in the distance, surrounded by rice paddies, there was something like an island, with broadleaf trees and coconut palms rising from the water, and amongst them the outlines of a rusted metal roof on a two-story cinderblock building. Behind me, the family swarmed out of the car. One woman carried the giant swollen durian fruit on her head, on the cloth padding, and the children fought to pull my suitcase along on its wheels. I carried the duffle bag. The little girl, Akemi, ran ahead of us down the walkway. I followed.

Large rice paddies on both sides. Smooth clear water, which seemed about six inches deep. Ranks and rows of young rice plants. Small silver minnows darting. A small frog between the young rice plants, looking up at us passing, and then submerging its head as though it could become invisible. A small, smooth-shelled turtle about the size of a pack of cigarettes stroking away underwater as we walked. I had an impulsive desire to stop and watch it, but I kept walking.

In the far distance, beyond the island, a carabao water buffalo, plodding through the shimmering mirage, pulled something slowly, with a man behind. The man was wearing a classic Asian triangular domed straw hat. Beyond both man and carabao rose green sugar-loaf hills covered in mottled foliage.

Beautiful.

Chapter Fifty

March 2014

"How do you like our country?" asked Dove's father. His name was Oscar.

"What I have seen, I love," I replied. That was the truth.

The family had built their multistoried cinderblock home in stages over the years, so that now it was ramshackle and much bigger than the home I occupied back in California. Arguably, it had a much nicer vista: slanted green trees with a view of the mountains. Feng shue, they said. There was a table-top shrine to Jesus and Mary at the far corner of the cluttered living room, in a canopy of gold and red pillars, almost like a very large bird-house. On the back wall of the shrine there was a crucifix, a bloody Jesus, dead or dying, his side pierced, hanging from the cross with nails through his feet and hands. There were many burned candles around that crucifix, with the detritus of worship. Matches. Ashtray. On one side of the shrine, there was another statue, a larger, standing, smiling Jesus, looking very metrosexual and very European, hand raised beatifically, blessing. In addition, there was a smaller statue of Mary, head cocked, sitting, observing the baby in her lap with a gentle smile.

"Watch *Game Of Thrones?*" asked one of the older women. I answered that yes, I did.

There was discussion of a daughter working as a pharmacist in Switzerland, and a son-in-law working as an engineer building skyscrapers in Saudi Arabia. There was a married cousin with news in Virginia; she was pregnant. Another cousin was apparently a petroleum engineer in Vietnam. Reports from all over the world.

"What do you think of Clinton?" asked Dove's father.

"Bill or Hillary?" I responded.

"Either," he answered.

"Corrupt, I think."

"Oh, yes, they are like the old days here. You know, they fornicate with everyone who gets near them for sex and money both. Trump is insane. Therefore, you are like the Philippines now. Or, at least, you are the way we were," he said.

"Why do you think that happened?" I asked.

"Oh, same as here. The government employees want to get rich. The rich want to get richer. People think of their richness first. It is very Asian," he answered.

"You are Asian now. Not Americans." He laughed. "While we have become what Americans once were."

"What do you think of America?" I asked.

"Well, I live there for five years, in San Antonio. I was a cab driver, and I went to college. You know, Texas A&M. The Jaguars."

"What made you leave San Antonio?" I asked.

"I finished my college degree in farming economics, and we had enough money. My family are farmers. We bought more land here. Then your country wanted to draft me, to send me to Vietnam. So I came back here."

"It's beautiful. So you became a farmer?' I asked.

"No, first my country draft me and send me to Vietnam." Dove's father laughed.

"What happened next?" I asked.

"Then I became a farmer. That is what we do now."

"My family were ranchers," I responded.

"Really? Like cowboys?" said one of the women. "You go *bang, bang?*"

She mimicked holding a pistol.

I laughed. "Yes, we go *bang, bang*. And yes, we were cowboys."

Big memories of my childhood on the Dos Cabesas Ranch.

I thought of the 1858 Remington cap and ball replica revolver that had been my first pistol, at age fourteen. I had learned to shoot it from my Uncle Otto, the Bataan survivor. Yes, we went *bang, bang.*

"You still cowboys?" asked one of the boys.

"No, not anymore, that's finished. No more ranch," I answered.

I didn't mention our discoveries after my father died: the girlfriend, the wealth-destroying speculations in the futures markets. Bad investments. Bad secrets. Suddenly it hit me: had it been suicide by car? Here I was sitting at a dinner table in Cagayan de Oro, and that thought had danced into my head un-bidden for the very first time.

Dove's father was contemplating my words. He could see the open question in my face.

"What brings you here?" he asked, changing the subject. Nice of him.

I explained about our family's connection to the Philippines. I could have simply said, "Your daughter."

He translated my response to everyone. They all spoke in Cebuano.

"My father was with Fertig," said Oscar, suddenly switching back to English. "He was guerilla." Abruptly he stood up and left the table. "Wait," he said.

I sat with the rest of the family and looked around the room. There were five women, including Dove, just outside in what they called the "dirty kitchen," cooking with fire under a sheet metal roof. I could hear them chattering companionably in Ce-buano. The children, Akemi among them, were swirling around in play in the yard beyond.

I thought about the last time I had been in Mindanao, with the Marines. The CH-46 had dipped between the rain-swollen clouds, bucking and rolling. I had stood up, hooked my snap link into the rappelling rope, the ramp had dropped, and the rappel master had motioned me forward. Loud, roaring engine. Trying not to slip on the muddy, bouncing helicopter floor. I was the officer so I was first. M-16A1 slung low. Heavy ALICE pack.

A tap, and then I had jumped lightly out and backwards, falling, then I was swaying on the rope beneath the helicopter, sliding fast to minimize the time the CH-46 would be exposed to RPGs.

So green, so wet, so muddy. So beautiful.

I realized that Oscar was back with a blanket-wrapped bundle, about six feet long. I stood up. He placed the bundle on the table, and began to unroll it as children clustered around.

"Dove tells me you are interested so I wish to share our family heirlooms."

I nodded eagerly. I was quite interested.

Oscar gradually unrolled the bundle.

First, a Spanish Mauser rifle, a bolt action, from about 1890, with heavy patina. Amazing. 7 millimeter. I opened the bolt to make sure the weapon was unloaded, and then examined the bore. Clean.

Then an American .30-40 Krag carbine from the Insurrection days, when the Americans had become occupiers. Very used. Rifling almost worn out. Scarred stock, including what looked like a chop from a blade. I wondered at what it had witnessed. I wondered who had carried it.

"My grandfather, constabulary, you know?" said Oscar.

Yes, I did know. The Americans had fought a dirty little war, scarcely remembered now, against the Filipino people after deposing the Spanish. The United States had been occupiers, not liberators as they had depicted themselves. That was decades before the Japanese invaded in turn.

"Also my father used this as a guerilla with Fertig, 1942 to 1945. It has had a hard life, but much excitement. If only it could talk."

I could only agree.

Next was a Japanese Arisaka rifle, a Type 38, an early 6.5 millimeter. Carefully constructed, not like the later poorly made chunks rushed together when they were losing the fight. This had to be pre-war, perhaps the 1930s. It had a long, dark bayonet with it. There was kanji writing carved on the stock. It had probably witnessed atrocities beyond description.

Finally, there was the SKS carbine with the stock soaked black and pits scattered across the rusted brown metal.

"NPA, you know?" said Oscar, smiling broadly. "New People's Army. Now Abu Saif. Still here. However, I have their gun. I found it underwater in a rice paddy. And it shoots!"

I checked to see that the weapon was clear and looked down the bore. Unlike the pitted exterior, the bore was pristine. It must be chrome plated.

I prepared to tell him that I had found its twin in a rice paddy, submerged as this had been.

Then a swarm of women unexpectedly swept into the room with steaming plates of food. Dove smiled brilliantly at me as she placed a pungent bowl of rice on the table. She reached out and rested her hand on my arm. Everyone was watching.

"It is bagoong," she said. "Shrimp paste rice."

I smiled. Everyone was watching.

"I see that my father has shown you the family history," she added. She turned to her father. "Please put them away, Tatay, so that we might eat."

Oscar laughed and looked at me.

"All this history," he said, "and she thinks only of the rice."

I had to admit I was hungry. The food smelled wonderful.

The next morning I slept until after daylight. I didn't expect that. An American could be kidnapped, could be tortured, could be decapitated by Abu Sayyaf here. I should be alarmed, I should be prepared. I should miss my M-16 A-1.

No. Instead, I lay contentedly alone in a hotel bed in a seaside resort I could not name, while the light grew over the flat, gray ocean outside my seaside window. I dozed a little. I remembered the last time I had spent a night in Mindanao, camouflaged, and wrapped in my loosely folded poncho liner, soaking wet, muddy, and half-cold.

That long-ago morning: I had lain in my lightweight camouflage blanket in the early dawn, contemplated the absolute necessity of cleaning my M-16 again, of having my team clean their M-16s again, the complete and suspicious absence of the NPA, the aching question of whether the scheduled CH-53 helicopter could fly in the rain, and the resemblance of my C-ration, still unopened in my ALICE pack, to commercial SPAM. Delicious.

This morning, years later, I was alone in an air-conditioned room with a spotless shower in my immediate future and a breakfast buffet featuring fresh fruit and Filipino delicacies with Dove and her family in one hour. The greatest threat was to my waistline.

I stepped out onto the porch and the sun was only half risen from the sea. I felt a pang of revulsion as my deceit washed over me: I had known Dove perhaps four days. This was all way too early, and I was acting a role based on Dove's needs, not mine. Yet here we were. This being the case, why not walk this path?

Out on the flat sea a banka boat was chugging by. Timeless. Perhaps my Uncle Sid had been here as a slave, a POW of the Japanese. Perhaps, in fact, he had died here. Nobody knew. The Japanese had even executed a captured American general here in Mindanao, General Guy Fort. They had tortured him, and then decapitated him.

I shook off the thought. The world had changed. Yet the past endured. Somewhere out there were the remains, perhaps simply a tiny speck of bone, or dental fillings. They were out there.

Shake it off. Time for a shower.

Breakfast under a roofed veranda at the small resort. The morning air moist, tropical, still slightly cool. The sound of surf in the distance. Fruit, langonisa sausage, baked meat buns, pastries, egg, rice, ham. Delicious. Incongruous, given my thoughts. A small gathering given Filipino standards: perhaps ten people, plus small children running, laughing, and playing loudly around us instead of eating.

"Today we will have thunderstorms," said Oscar. "So first we want to take you to see Giant Jesus, then to the airport. Is that good?"

"Giant Jesus?" I responded.

Dove's mother Helena, eating alongside Oscar, spoke up. "Yes! We have most biggest, giant Jesus in the world. If you go Him and you pray Him, you have your wish. It is important to pray Giant Jesus, to get your wish."

I was feeling a bit trapped. I pondered the concept of praying to Most Biggest Giant Jesus to get my wish.

The waiter approached shyly. "Sir Garth? Do you fly today? Because they close the airport because of thunderstorms in one hour."

Deus ex Machina. God works in mysterious ways.

"Then we should go to the airport directly, and see Giant Jesus another time," I decided.

I looked at Dove. She looked crestfallen. Almost about to cry.

"Is Giant Jesus on the way to the airport?" I asked.

"Yes, yes!" Dove's mother said brightly, spectacles shining.

"Then let's go quickly on the way. I'll get my bags now," I said. I stood up.

Giant Jesus was indeed quite large. He seemed to be perhaps as tall as a ten-story building, with lightning bolts or rays of light—I wasn't sure which—emanating from his sides and buttressing Him from the sides. He looked European. Serene, somewhat meditating. There was a church built into his feet.

"We will pray. We will attend a service. Then in a few hours we will have lunch, and then we will go to the airport," said a woman in our group. Apparently, Dove's aunt.

I looked at the looming stairway up to Giant Jesus' toes. Thunderstorms became worse as the day heated up. Any chance of getting out of here was slipping away as the heat increased. The woman's plan felt claustrophobic.

"No," I said. Emphatically.

They looked at me aghast.

"I need to go to the airport now, please. Another time, we will visit this beautiful place. Now please take me to the airport and help me catch my plane," I said.

— Chapter 50 —

Silence. They were looking at each other, seemingly mildly offended.

Dove spoke. "Please help him and we can return after he flies. After he flies we can even attend mass."

Oscar nodded his head. "That's good!" he said.

At the airport, the woman at the ticket counter confirmed my thoughts.

"Oh, sir, they have one more flight to Manila in thirty minutes and you must rush to catch it. Perhaps even it may not fly, if the storm comes sooner. Rush, sir, rush!"

I turned to Dove. She drew me away from the others.

"Friend me on Facebook," she said.

"Yes, of course."

"Thank you," she said.

"Thank you," I responded.

"Please, please," she said.

"What?" I said quietly.

"We've had a wonderful time, and you've blessed me in the eyes of my family. Our time was so good. You don't need to come back here and it's okay if we are simply friends after this," she said quietly.

"But—" I said.

"But you will miss your flight. Hurry, Beloved, and go to your next adventure. Go! Go! You have blessed me." She kissed me lightly on the lips and stepped back.

I waved at her family, kissed her lightly in front of everyone, and ran to catch my flight. Outside the walkway, the dark clouds full of thunder were towering in the deep blue sky.

The battered cab containing my worn luggage and me arrived at the imposing portico of the luxurious Manila Hotel. I waved to the gate guard and we entered the driveway. I could see the raised eyebrows of the wealthy patrons, most of them Asian, the stares of the two smiling uniform-clad doormen, and the smiles of the women attendants who were there to greet arriving visitors with their 1890s' gowns swirling.

Quickly, the waiting bellman hoisted my heavy bags onto a gurney and rolled them into the security station at the door, where all the contents were x-rayed and examined. A very beautiful girl in the historic costume of a formally dressed Filipina in the late nineteenth century gently escorted me to the vast mahogany check-in counter where another smiling young lady awaited.

I showed her my reservation. My mode of arrival might make her wonder. Then I showed her the Philippines Airlines itinerary for my flight the following day.

"Oh, sir, this is a mistake," she said.

What?

"Oh sir, the times are accidentally in American time. This flight leaves tonight."

What?

"Here, sir, let me check for you."

She walked away from the counter and returned in a few minutes.

"You see, sir, you will fly tonight."

She showed me my flight itinerary in Philippines time. I would leave tonight at 10 p.m. Astonishing. Quickly she cancelled my room reservation. Yes, I would like the hotel car to take me to the airport. Now what?

It was still mid-morning. I was welcome to wait in the bar or the opulent lobby until that evening. I looked around. Someone was playing "Somewhere in Time" live on the piano. Beautiful. Tempting. Across the lobby was a chocolate stand, sure to have cold, dark chocolate for sale. I realized I was hot and tired. If I bought chocolate and sat down, I would probably waste the day.

"Is anything else happening?" I asked.

"Well, we have a tour of Corregidor leaving in ten minutes," she responded.

"Corregidor the island?" I couldn't believe it.

"Yes, the island, the battleground. Would you like to go? You won't return until 6 p.m. tonight, and your flight leaves at 10 p.m. So you won't get much rest," answered the woman.

"Please include me," I said. "I'll sleep on the plane."

Of all the battlegrounds of World War II, there were few so famous as Corregidor. I had been hearing about it literally all my life.

Chapter Fifty-one

March 2014

The ferry was filled with many Asian tourists and perhaps four Americans, only one or two so antiquated that they might actually have been present at the battle. The young Asian women, slim, smooth, smiling in shorts, sandals, sunglasses, and tank tops posed for selfies as the boat cast off from the dock and steered out into the bay. The standard safety brief. I became aware that many people around me were speaking Japanese. Somehow, that was irritating. I went to the prow in the front and attempted to see the island, in vain, until a drenching rainstorm drove me back into the cabin.

Thoughts. After Bataan fell to the Japanese and the atrocity of the Death March began, the last surviving American outpost in Luzon had been fortress Corregidor, lying just offshore of Bataan. It is a small island of about 2,000 acres, shaped like a tadpole, or a sperm, depending upon your mood. The head of the tadpole rose like a flat-topped mountain. Before World War II it was packed with defenses, including a vast system of tunnels named Malinta. There were also strong points on the sides of the mountain, hardened defenses containing batteries of cannon, which could shoot ships or airplanes or even reach all the way to the Bataan peninsula.

The one hundred forty thousand American and Filipino troops on Bataan, starving and ill, my two uncles among them, surrendered on April 9, 1942. The suffering and abuse of the Bataan Death March and the remaining horrors of their years of imprisonment began at once. But the little island of Corregidor held out for weeks longer, the only American refuge surrounded by hostile Japanese forces.

The commander of all American and Filipino forces, General Douglas MacArthur, and his family quickly lit out for Australia on a PT boat, thus earning the Congressional Medal of Honor as a political sop, and my family's undying contempt.

That left General Jonathan Wainwright holding the bag. What went through his mind must have been amazing: he had to know the island was doomed.

My reverie was interrupted by my buzzing cell phone, feeding off the ferry's Wi-Fi.

"Where are you?" a message from Dove.

"On my way to Corregidor," I texted back.

"Amazing!" was the response.

"TTYL," I texted back.

Then, impulsively, I texted Angelica: "On my way to Corregidor!"

Nothing for a few minutes. Then:

"What is that?"

"We should talk," I replied.

Angelica responded with a text: "You are right. We should talk. Things change with me."

I sat back in the air-conditioned ferry cabin. Things had changed with both of us, I thought. Surprising happiness. Freedom. I diverted my attention to the ferry. There was a flat screen TV on the wall. Apparently, a passenger aircraft from Malaysian Airlines was missing somewhere over the Philippines. I couldn't hear a word.

After a thirty-minute ride, the guide came on the loudspeaker to announce that we would arrive at Corregidor in ten minutes. I went out into the rain, staggering a little as the small sea swells rocked the ship, and there was the island, rising like Gibraltar from the water.

As we neared the island, I realized that the ocean foam that had collected against the shore was in fact garbage, mostly diapers and plastic shopping bags. A voice on a loudspeaker pointed out the pier where MacArthur had fled in a PT boat. Engulfed in seaborne trash. We docked. We exited the boat. The guide immediately loaded us on small open trolleys, in small groups, with four trolleys for all the passengers on the boat.

Immediately we went topside to the museum. It was monumental, and somber, without much to see except remembrances erected after the war.

It was peaceful inside that museum. The Japanese tourists took many photos, with the young, slender Japanese women flashing peace signs in front of the heroic statuary as they posed for selfie stick photos. Douglas MacArthur in bronze. A statue of three battered American soldiers in their World War I helmets, metal clothing torn, metal eyes vacant. A Philippine scout and his horse.

Then there was a gift store. I bought a red ball cap emblazoned with "Corregidor." Made in China.

The trolley next pulled up the hill to a small, overgrown ravine. There was some discussion in Japanese. All the other trolley occupants stepped out. A few old men and women with canes, nicely dressed, a few middle-aged Japanese who might have been their children, and the gaggle of young Japanese girls, now quiet, now walking slowly down the path to a small Buddhist monument.

The Filipino guide, a young man, remained with the driver in the open trolley, shaded by the canvas roof. He lit a cigarette and sat back on the cushioned plastic seat, and looked out at the forest around us.

"Where are we?" I asked.

"Oh this is where they buried the dead Japanese soldiers," said the young man in completely unaccented English. Moments before he had been speaking to the others in Japanese.

"Dead Japanese soldiers?" I asked.

"Yep, sir. When the Americans came back in '45 they slaughtered 'em all. About sixty-five hundred of 'em. If the Americans found Japanese bodies, they put 'em all in a mass grave here."

He motioned across the plaza to where the quiet Asians were

— Chapter 51 —
371

clustered around what appeared to be a small Shinto shrine. Clapping and bowing.

"We just found this mass grave a few years ago. Now the Japanese come here. Lots of them visit. I think they believe that their dead relatives can see 'em," the driver added.

The older guide nodded his approval.

I sat on the trolley seat behind them and let the cooling ocean breeze wash over me.

"You know you don't have to just sit here," said the guide.

He pointed downhill. "That's the trail to the batteries," he added.

"The batteries?" I asked.

"If you take it, we'll drive down after these folks are done and pick you up. Battery Geary is right down there."

I had read about Battery Geary. Here there had been two giant cannons in a huge, circular open-air revetment. Those guns could shell nearby ships or even Bataan, lobbing artillery at high angle up and over, plunging down onto the target. Of course after the siege of Corregidor began, the Japanese blasted Battery Geary with thousands of rounds of their own artillery.

In the process, the Japanese ignited an American armored ammunition magazine, which exploded, killing about thirty young Americans. The blast blew the concrete roof apart so severely that a jeep-sized block of cement falling unexpectedly from the sky crushed an American soldier a mile away.

That's what I'd read, anyway.

Now I walked down a small, asphalted trail with regrown forest on either side, downhill alone. After I stepped off the main road, nobody else was in sight. I wandered past the looming concrete revetments, now so worn and mossy that they seemed ancient. I wondered if my uncles had ever been here. In my childhood, I hadn't known enough to ask my Uncle Otto. To think I was here, really here, in this place of heroes.

The trail led past the bunker walls onto a grassy circular depression, broken cement, grass growing tall, clearly the battery floor with one giant heavy cannon barrel embedded into one of the walls. That had happened long ago: the metal had been repainted olive green, the shattered wall was growing grass in the cracks, and moss.

I heard a small cough. I was not alone after all. Walking a few paces, I looked into an open metal doorway in the cement wall of the gun platform. The old doorway: olive -painted metal twisted, clearly blown open long ago. There was a small old, old man, too old to ever have been young, sitting curled and enfolded on his walker. At his side stood a young Filipina, straight and beaming, apparently his aide. The old man was looking down at the dirt through thick glasses, apparently lost in thought, wearing a red ball cap which read "Corregidor Veteran 1942" with the sewn insignia of a white seahorse on a blue oval.

Damn. Here was someone who had served with my uncles. He must be in his late nineties now. He looked it. I noticed there was a small black gas canister attached to his walker. Oxygen? Hearing aids in both ears.

I couldn't help myself. I walked up to him. The tiny Filipina watched me intently, smiling, saying nothing. I could see the uncertainty in her eyes though.

"Thank you for your service," I said.

The man looked up. For a moment we were both silent.

"Hi thar, young man. I was jus' thinkin,'" the old man said in a quavering voice.

He stared at me, smiling slightly, like a tortoise. From his accent, I guessed he was from the southeastern United States.

"Well, thank you for *your* service," he added.

I realized I was wearing a ball cap with the USMC eagle, globe, and anchor.

I nodded.

"Were you here?" I asked.

"Young man, I was right har, in this doorway, durin' the battle. The world has changed soo much, but I was rat har, today, seventy-two yars ago. I was twenty yars ol," he said softly, blinking around the revetment.

I considered that. For a short time, I watched a butterfly,

chocolate brown with iridescent blue stripes, fluttering lightly over some small red blossoms that were growing out of a crack in the cement wall. Imagining this place back then, full of activity, new and polished, young men moving fast, then the explosions.

"I bet this is a lot different than you remember," I said.

I wondered what remained at the roadside in Iraq where my truck had been blown up. Probably nothing.

"You wouldna' thank there had even been a battle har," said the old man.

I watched the colorful butterfly making its way from blossom to blossom along the far wall. Moss, grass, and flowers growing out of the cracks.

"How did you come to be here, back then?" I asked.

"I'm from Oklahoma. Sulfur, Oklahome. Beautiful lil' town. Now they have the Chickasaw National Monument there. It's a good life. Anyways I was sev'teen and wanted to see the world. Or see Kansas anyways. So I enlisted rat out a hah school, sev'teen years old. 1939. Artill'ry."

"Springfields. 03's," I added.

"Good rifle," he said, smiling. "I got expert on that ol' V target. Course anyone from Sulfur could ha done that. Chickashaw country. We grew up shootin'. And ridin'.'"

"Horses?" I asked. I had grown up on horses myself.

"You bet!" he replied. "In fact that's how I got into artill'ry. Most a' the guns were pulled by horse back'en. So they needed young fools who could ride."

He chuckled at the memory, as his gaze wandered across the structure. He was watching the butterflies too.

"Did you get to ride much?" I asked.

"Oh, nah, the war in Europe changed all that. Calvary don't work so well 'gainst panzers. Tanks, ya know. Anyways they put me in coastal defense artill'ry, and then *woop-smack* I was in San Fra'cisco. Great town. Purty gals. Then here."

"How was it here? Before the Japanese" I asked.

He laughed. "Mah unit was wonnerful people. The best of

'Merica. This place was paradise. Weemen. Graht chow. Lawt duty. That changed. The Japanese bomb us. We stayed pretty much intac' till Bataan fell, then they started shellin' us with artill'ry too. That's when this place got blowed up."

"Were you here?"

His face grew much sadder and he looked at the ground, sitting on his walker, hunching over. "Young man, I was takin' a shit. 'Magin that. I'm not kiddin'. I was squattin' over thar shittin' in'a ammo can," and with that he waved across the flat gun revetment.

"I had a little dysentery, I guess. I was stationed in the magazine with about forty of my best friends, and I was supposed to stay thar, but t'was a let-up in the shellin' and I didn't want to shit in no ammo can it front of 'em. No more, fartin' in front of my friends, makin' all that smell. So I went ova' yonda with the can. And then the bomb hit."

We were both silent for a time. There were two butterflies out there now. The Filipina was sitting on a concrete bench deeper in the bunker. It was cooler there.

"I mean, *woop-smack,* it blew me off'n the shitter can and knocked me out. I woke up, I pulled up my pants and run back out and the blast had tossed those big cannons aroun' like straws and blown one rat into the wall. Look, it still thar." He motioned out the door.

"It's a damn big piece of steel," I replied. It was: long as a telephone pole and twice as thick.

"What happened next?" I asked.

"They kept bombin' us, so we couldn't do much movin'," he continued. "But the guns were all out of action and most of us were dayd or wounded. I couldn't har and I couldn't thank, so really all I did was hahd. I helped with a few of the guys who were horribly burn or tore up. One guy . . ."

I sat and waited.

"One guy, my good frien, Fred Peterson, had both legs blowed off, hah up. He'd come out from San Fracisco with me. I mayn, he had a Studebaker cahr in San Fracisco, and it was his prawd and joy, and now he was layin' there with his legs gown and big shrapnel wounds to his guts. Bleedin' out, dyin', even with tourniquet, and he keep sayin', 'How ma gonna shif that Studebaker?' and then he asked for his momma, and then he died."

"I'm sorry," I said quietly.

"Right thar," he pointed back into the bunker.

"Wow," I said quietly.

"I thank of that evera day of mah life. Maybe evera hour," he added. "Fred is always with me. An' ta others."

Silence.

"We were kids," he said.

"What happened next?" I asked.

"I spent a few days hidin'. I was deef, mah head hurt, I couldn't see too good neeter. So I hid in that Malinta tunnel with all the staff and the nurse and such. Nurse was nahs to me 'cause I was so damn deef. Then the Japs landed and thay brass, they given me a Springfield rahful, deef or no deef, and I come out of that tunnel and this 'Merican fellow is layin' there raht at the entrance, heed blowed off, with a big ass Thompson gun. So I picked that up too, and I shoot at the damn Japs an I kill some too, until the Japs they drive a tank raht up to the mout' a that tunnel, and then we surrender. Those Japs they thrash me good boy. Beat me blahk 'n blue. But at least they didn' kill me."

"I've read about that but I've never met someone who actually fought here before," I said.

"I didn know what else to do," said the man. "Mos the tahm I don' know what the fuck was goin' on. Parently, the brass didn' know either."

"And yet you lived," I said.

"No thanks to the Jap for that one, boy. They starve us good. I weigh one hundred sixty when I git here, and eighty pounds when ta war end. They kills us, they starves us, most of us die in the camps, but I live 'cause I can eat Chickashaw."

"Eat Chickashaw?" I asked.

"Yep," the man replied, chuckling. "I growed up eatin' singed squirrel an' stew possum an' pashofa, so I ready to eat singed

— Honor —

rat, stew cat, and whatevah."

I had to smile too. "It's a skill."

"Are you veteran? Koree? Vitnahm?" the man asked me.

"No," I responded. "I never got that far. I went through lots of training. I didn't do anything. My uncle died here though, and we never found him. And another uncle survived, like you."

"Well you were luckier than my son. He die in Vitnahm. Volunteer. Beautiful boy." His voice cracked as he spoke. He put a hand to his face as though he was waving away a fly.

"I'm sorry. I guess we should thank him for his service most of all," I said.

We sat and looked at the giant, dismounted cannon, scarred deeply by the Japanese bombardment, surrounded by the green forest vegetation, trees looming up beyond the walls of the circular pit. The old man continued to wave his hands up by his face. To break the mood I pulled out my camera and I took a few photos.

Then the old man spoke again, looking down. "It all a braht shinin' lah, ya know? All bullshit. All ah it. None ah us should have been har. What happen in the Philippines didn' matter to us'ns moh than a bucket ah cow piss. But here we war. And they just abandon us, all of 'em. MacArthur, the rest ah the country. And so we starve. And aftah the war I wen' home and mah girlfriend was married to an asthmatic farmah. Hayll, he died young anyways. Brucellosis. Ya get dat from da cow."

"What did you do then?" I asked.

He lifted his head and looked at me.

"Welluns, I used mah GI Bill and went to college," he said. "I got a degree in food sarvice and a PhD in nutritin and I become a college perfesser, then we open a dog food company."

"Really?" I asked. What an odd turn.

"Yep, Fancy Chow Dog Food. Ya know it?" he replied.

"One of the big sellers," I said.

"And than I married a beaut'ful woman who thought Aw was a hero. I get the Distinguish Sarvice Cross an' the Silfer Star, ya know," he said.

— Chapter 51 —
377

"Wow," I said. "Impressive."

Clearly there was a bit more to his story than he was telling. He had done something unique for that DSC and that Silver Star.

"It still all a braht shinin' lah, ya know? The rich stayed home and git richer. The pol'ticians stayed away from the fawt. And I live wit' tha nahtmare and the malaria every dang day. An' one a my son think it's all hero shit, and so he go to Vitnahm, and now he dayd." He shook his head, regretfully, looking down again.

"You still stopped the Japanese long enough to keep them out of Australia," I said.

"That don' brang back mah hearin' sonny. We did all this for what? For some dick-smokin' pol'tician to look strong an' macho, get elected, get hisself rich with the bribes and the speakin'fees. My frien's and my son, dey dye for some asshoe back in da rear to make a better lahf for hisself only. Da rest 'a us, we just bleed." The old man spoke heatedly, gasping.

"You really think that?" I said. The old man was going to need oxygen soon, I thought.

"Afterward, we had to set it aside and moof onwards. When my Mary and I built ah dog food cumpnay, we built it despaht the gov'mint. Hell, they let Sulphur and the small folks lahk us rot. They fool us inta fawtin' thar wars. They make the big city folks rich and they dress like womens or mens or whatnot, and they laht us ROT! We done live well despayt the govment, despayts they lies, and whatevah we create, they take, and they give it all away."

"Then why are you here?" I asked quietly.

"Ahm har, mah friends from those past long-go days ain't. Yah know when I thank back, I didn't do it for the gov'mint or tha flayg, or all that. I did it for mah friends. Mah friends, the bes' 'a owa country. Lot 'a mah friends are har, now. Raht har." He pointed at the dirt.

I looked around. Perhaps the spirits were here.

"I'm part Chickshaw on mah momma's side, yah know we believe that the dayd lif on. We really *do* belief dat God is reel."

"Is God here?" I asked him. He looked like a desiccated

vestige, all curled up on his walker like that. Staring out at the cannon and the pit. Too old to ever have been young.

"Oh, course. Course He here. Look 'roun' ya, boy!"

I looked around. He watched me silently. There were birds in the tree branches, and there were red and yellow hibiscus flowers blooming from plants on the walls of the battery.

He continued quietly. "Look roun' ya at mah friends, my brothers. My brothers were the bes' people ah mah life. Aftah that Jap artillry blast through the roof thar wasn't 'nuff left ah most ah them to flush out wit' a hose. So I figga lease partways they all still har. So God is har too."

Chapter Fifty-two

April 2014

The following Monday I was in the office when the lawyer Robert Masters' email came in. Complete with an attached restructuring agreement. Tammy Fay brought in the newly printed, still wet pages, about forty of them. Apparently, my buy-out of the property was not necessary after all. Somehow, we had cajoled, battered, or simply outlasted Globalbank into offering a genuine restructuring. While I had been in the Philippines, the mortgage gnomes had been contemplating.

"Robert says that there's something wrong with it. Check out the title."

I read Robert's letter. It said everything in the first paragraph. "This restructuring agreement is offered to the ESTATE of Thomas P. Narcisco. Legally, there IS no estate. His will was a pour-through. There is only a trust. They are playing word games. This is an invalid offer by Globalbank."

My phone buzzed. Angelica texting. "You see the restructuring?"

I texted back. Yes.

A buzz. A text from Angelica. "Miguel says to sign it. Jerome agrees."

Who was Miguel? Ah, well, it did not matter.

I phoned Robert. "Why is Globalbank doing this?" I asked.

"They are doing this because it's invalid, once she signs it, it's invalid. It's a non-starter," Robert responded.

"What do we do?" I asked.

"Well, you are trustee. Do not let her sign it. I'll call

Globalbank and rewrite all this."

"Will do. I'll get back in touch when I talk with her," I replied.

There were no responses to my ten texts. I was frantic.

"I'm going over there," I told Lanie and Tammy Fay.

Tammy Fay shrugged. "You won't like what you find," she said. Something was different about Tammy Fay recently. She was sullen. Distant.

Lanie just looked at me evenly. "There comes a time when it's not worth it anymore. I think we are just about there."

There was a black, two-seat Mercedes convertible in the driveway of Tommy's home when I drove up in my beat-up 2004 yellow XTerra. Its top was up. There was also a new red Camaro parked on the street. I parked, I texted, "Outside," then I walked up to the home and rang the doorbell.

Angelica answered the door, wearing an olive velour jumpsuit. Her hair was pulled back tightly. She scowled at me. "Why you here?" she asked.

"They think I'm the trustee. I have to be here," I said, and stepped past her into the living room. I looked at the mantle. All the pictures of Tommy. Tommy in his wedding clothing. Tommy and the children. The children by themselves. A photo I had taken last year of Angelica and the children when they learned to make fire at San Juan Bautista. All those photos.

On the far side of the mantle, new photos: Jerome and Angelica and the children, all wearing personal flotation vests, with Jerome smiling broadly and holding a single waterski, with Cesar holding the waterski grinning broadly from the other side. Another of Jerome and Cesar holding a massive lake trout together, standing ankle deep in Lake Tahoe, holding a fishing pole, with Angelica and Rose smiling behind them.

I felt a small pang of jealousy, followed quickly by the realization that this was actually very good for the children. Their father was not being displaced suddenly. The small, square, polished walnut box of ashes, which I had always considered morbid, was still in the center of the mantle. Jerome was creeping his way gently into the family, as he should, respectfully, with love and smiles. Look at all those smiles . . . there were many good memories there.

I was interrupted in my diversion when Angelica said sharply, "What you here for? You stalk me."

She scowled. I walked into the kitchen. There, seated, was a Latin man, as handsome as a Greek god. This was apparently Miguel, the mortgage broker. He was wearing a tank top and very high shorts, exposing his swollen biceps and his chiseled thighs. There, in the nook opposite, about a yard from Miguel, there was Jerome. He looked up and smiled coolly. Greetings all around.

"You already know it won't work, don't you Jerome?" I said.

Jerome looked down at the papers on the table. "I think she should just end this. When they get the restructuring agreement and they approve it, then Angelica can alter the terms. Miguel agrees."

"This is Miquel?" I asked, gesturing towards our weightlifting comrade at the table.

Miguel shook his full head of hair, and the black soul patch on his chin bobbled. He smiled widely. Youth. Perfect white teeth. Superb, unblemished brown skin with his black beard unshaven for a day. "I go with Mr. Jerome," he said. "Then Angelica will invest her inheritance in my special business opportunities. We will make her rich."

"So let me get this straight," I asked. "Angelica signs this and what happens?"

Miguel explained. "Angelica signs this document. Then she sells the investments she received from Tommy's retirement. She pays out $200,000 to pay down the mortgage. I refinance the remaining $250,000 mortgage for only 6.5-percent. Then I invest the rest of Tommy's retirement plan in aggressive investments and we make that $200,000 she paid out grow back in no time."

I considered that. Mortgages were going now for 4-percent at most. The interest rate was clearly excessive.

— Chapter 52 —

"Taxes?" I asked. They were going to be substantial since the money would come from an IRA rollover. Ordinary income. Something like $80,000 in taxes or more.

"She'll grow them back too."

"And your fee will be?" I asked Miguel.

He smiled back at me steadily.

"I make her rich, she makes me rich," Miguel responded.

Jerome was watching all this, smiling slightly, saying nothing.

I looked at Jerome. "Why are you letting this happen?" I asked him.

"Mr. Jerome knows I will make Angelica rich," said Miguel.

If Miguel's scheme actually happened, Angelica's investments would be reduced by about $280,000 in payouts and taxes. It would be *very* hard to grow that back. And we hadn't really put Globalbank to the test yet. Miguel was shady. Too few details. Too much suave.

I turned to Angelica. "This isn't a good idea, at least not right now. Please trust me on this," I said.

"This *viejo* is boring," said Miguel dismissively to Angelica. "Why is he wasting our time?"

She looked at me and scowled. "You have no place here," she said. "Jerome much more wiser than you. He know what to do. And Miguel always does what I ask, while you ALWAYS GIVE ME HARD TIME!!! WHY CAN'T YOU DO WHAT I NEED?"

A struggle for self-control. Finally, I spoke. "Miguel is just a con artist. He's trying to squeeze you like a sponge for $280,000 and he won't even tell you how he's going to be paid."

Then I turned to Jerome. "Why won't you buy this home as you promised?"

Jerome looked up at me and smiled coldly. "Listen to the puppies fight over a bone. You will get the restructuring, because you can't help yourself, because you promised Tommy. You'll do the work, we'll rent it out at a profit, and I can save my cash for other adventures."

Of course. I had promised Tommy. I thought of the Philippines. The thought of Jerome funding the school. That was the plan then. Payback's a bitch.

"Well," Jerome said, looking down and shuffling the pages. "I'm rich for a reason. A lot richer than you can ever even dream. I have Angelica, I have Cesar and Rose, and you do not. I've always wanted a family. Now I have it. You don't."

Both Jerome and Miguel stood up. Miguel approached me now, arms up, palms out, as though he would push me. "I think you had better leave this woman alone, viejo," he said. "The sight of you is threatening this woman."

He loomed towards me. I thought about my Marine combatives training. I would love to break his nose with the heel of my hand. I thought about the strike upwards, the crunch. The reality was that I'd never experienced that. All I had was the training.

I stepped out into the darkness of the night, onto the porch of her home. I apologized quietly while Angelica stood looking out through the closed screen door. She wiped a few tears from her eyes, said nothing, and shut the front door in my face.

But Angelica never liquidated her account. The money stayed where it was. Somehow, at some time, my words must have penetrated her mind.

A few weeks later, Globalbank called again. The Globalbank voice said that the mortgage that Angelica had recently signed was invalid, since it was to the estate of Thomas P. Narcisco, and not to a living individual. A dead person can't be in debt, he said. Perhaps foreclosure would be best after all.

I mentally wrestled my verbal response into silence as a slug of adrenaline pulsed through me.

"Why are you calling me?" I asked.

"You are the trustee. I have instructions to call you first," the voice said. "Besides, you are the person who's been working with us . . ." There was a pause. "For over a year. You have been persistent, Mr. Ericson. It's time to end this."

"Yes," I responded emphatically. "It *is* time to end this. Please take a moment to look through the record. Take your time. Do you really think that I will ever stop? Do you think that I will ever, ever leave you alone about this? Widow and orphans, racial minority, five applications, five denials, fake names, lost applications. It is all there. It's a lawsuit made to be publicized."

"Sir, you know we will counter-sue. I'm not supposed to talk like this but you know we'll wear you down. Big bank, itty-bitty trustee."

My response: "Look, I can Google just as well as the next guy. I can see you've lost in several similar cases already. What do I have to lose? Itty bitty trustee like me."

He could not see that I was entirely worn down. There wasn't any rational need for a restructuring now: no more threat of widow and orphans turned out. Jerome had apparently saved them from that. But I *needed* to finish this. Globalbank was a predator. I didn't want Angelica and the children to simply abandon that home. It was Tommy's home. And I had promised, so long ago. Jerome was right about that.

I spoke into the phone, one last bluff: "You know that before this is over, it will probably cost you millions. Let's not do that. Please reissue the mortgage worded correctly. Then send it here and I'll have our lawyer look at it."

There was a pause on the other end of the phone. "I'll see what I can do. What if we decide we'd rather pay the millions?"

"Do you think I'm going to stop? We've been at this for most of two years," I replied.

"I'll give my people a call right now," the voice replied.

"I haven't seen Texas yet," I responded as the line went dead.

On the following Wednesday, Globalbank emailed the corrected mortgage package to the law offices of Robert Masters. He organized the papers, and called both Angelica and me into his office immediately after lunch for the signature. I walked over to the dark, traditional lawyer's office on Alisal Street that afternoon, and sat alone in the waiting room, decorated in tasteful 1960's style. So many memories. I had done so much of my father's business here, so much ranch work, and now here I was, decades later, waiting yet again to meet a lawyer. I sat there, and

I realized how alone I truly was. Then I reconsidered that. No, I wasn't entirely alone. I would be able to tell Lanie, Ernst, Sarah, and my mother about this in the afternoon, and Dove via Skype at night. No, I wasn't completely alone. Thank you, God.

Robert came out of his offices. He sat next to me. He smiled slightly. "This is the end of a long trail," he said. I smiled back.

The front door to the office waiting room opened and Angelica entered in a blaze of brilliant sunlight, a blinding halo all around her, a blast of traffic noise and disconnected voices from Alisal Street, quickly cut short as she closed the door behind her.

Robert and I looked her over. She was wearing a broad, white Spanish Bay Golf Resort cloth visor with carefully layered hair with highlights. Large, oval Louis Vuitton sunglasses with cream frames hid her eyes. She was wearing a low-cut pink and white silk shorts jumpsuit, with the short gauzy sleeves revealing her gym-sculpted brown arms. Gold and rattan designer flip-flops were on her bare pedicured feet, and her toenails and fingernails were freshly painted in layered designer shades and swirls of pale purple and cream. She was carrying a new small white and pink Louis Vuitton clutch purse with a bronze plaque. The scent of her signature Chance perfume filled the office. She smiled whitely with gleaming perfect teeth. "I'm here!" she announced.

Robert and I both looked at her. Both of us took several seconds to respond.

In this mortgage, done correctly, only Angelica's signature was needed. She practiced her full signature several times on scratch paper as we sat together in the windowless conference room. Then she quickly signed two copies affirming that she accepted a mortgage restructuring, which would allow her to continue to live in her family home with her current diminished income.

We all stood up, we all exchanged cordial greetings, and Robert showed us to the door, hugging Angelica as always, and shaking my hand as I exited last. As I stepped into the sunlight outside, Robert whispered to me from behind, "I suppose I should bill for this after all."

I smiled and I leaned back and whispered in his ear, "She better pay you fast."

And I laughed.

Chapter Fifty-three

May 2014

A Sunday in May: I shocked myself awake at 4 a.m., in the predawn darkness, with a dream that all my friends, my ex-wife, all my children, my clients, Angelica, even Francesca, Cesar, and Rose were in my home, like ants on a cupcake, with the sunlit front door wide open, removing everything I owned and treasured. Everything I owned. The oak chairs from my father's parents. The worn, small, hardwood table from my maternal grandmother's years living in Costa Rica. Even my clothing. I confronted them all in my dream, questioned them as I stood there in pajama bottoms and bare feet, and they told me that I was unworthy, that I had not done enough in life, that all my possessions, my passions, and my relationships were now to go to other men worthier, more accomplished, more brave.

Then I woke up, shaking.

I sat up and I prayed to the usual panoply: God, Tommy, my father, and all my ancestors. Why do you show me this dream? Is it a warning or is it just my mind contemplating the unthinkable?

Quickly, I changed into my wilderness gear, the tan BDU pants and the well-worn USMC boots, and shaved, sunblocked, shouldered my go-pack and .45-70 Marlin rifle, walked out the front door into the darkness to the waiting XTerra. I drove to Arroyo Seco, and I began to run up the Indians Road. There was nobody walking or running there at 6 a.m. The dirt roadbed was littered with rock-fall from the inclines above. The summer-brown mountains ahead of me in the wilderness were shadowed by the mountains behind me. I ran uphill, up the winding road, west, with the sun at my back. The green chemise-covered hills were gradually unveiled into brilliant sunlight as the shadows fell down the faces of the slopes ahead. The sun rose higher behind me.

As I ran I became wet with sweat, and I was lost in my thoughts: loss, Angelica, Dove, and confusion. Then all my awareness was submerged by the vast visual input of the day. A gray fox darted across the road ahead of me. A brown golden eagle soared high in the now-bright blue sky, a small winged speck of feathered brown, effortlessly gliding ahead of me. This was late May in a severe drought year. Even the oak trees seemed to be wilting.

I ran on without saying a word. Wet with sweat. Running step by step. Then there was the trail leading down to my clearing, my secret place. I slid down the scarcely visible path, sliding on the dry sand-colored dead wild oats, down to the flat amidst the oak trees.

I sat on the rock littered with small clam fossils, my seat for so many visits. I struggled to calm my breath, my racing pulse. I could not find serenity at all. I looked uphill. Columns of white blossoms coated the buckeye trees. Beyond the ringing tinnitus in my ears, I could hear the hum of bees, and I could see the bees themselves, tiny specks swirling around the blossoms. Good.

I closed my eyes. My pulse raced, my breathing was ragged. Oh, God, I cannot live like this. Do something. In the distance, I could hear a quail family chuckling to each other, and a scrub jay yapping. There was a quail gathering call, and more blue jay chattering.

I noticed that the glass arrow point I had placed on the rock during last year's visit was gone. I took a new green glass arrowhead out of my backpack. I placed it gently on the rock. The unnamed anxiety was there, all there, and it wouldn't go away.

At the Post Traumatic Stress Disorder clinic at Stanford, Dr. Pekk had told me frequently: Go to the pain. Face it and go towards it.

Okay, God. I embrace it. I am not going to step out the side door by wishing to die. Give me courage and take me straight at it.

Then it came to me suddenly, a campfire taking flame: I was not done.

I was not done.

I was not done.

Angelica and her family quickly accepted my idea. It seemed they had been waiting politely for someone else to suggest it. Putting Tommy's ashes into the ocean meant that we would all accept that Tommy was actually dead.

It was like an oyster growing a pearl. With each death, a grain of sand, always there, always a foreign body, always an intrusion into harmony. Like oysters we just make each loss into a gem. The loss never leaves us. We simply grow a pearl around it.

What would happen now, I wondered. Most of those photos on the mantelpiece would be put away face down in drawers, waiting for the children to have their own homes, to claim their own identities. The mantelpiece would be swept bare, fallow for new memories, new life, life ongoing, life reclaiming its own. New photos, new life, new joys, an upwelling of life. All that in the future, after the cruel necessity of the here, the now, the present.

Lanie came with me to the beach. She did not need to do that, but somehow that was what she chose, perhaps because she wanted to honor Tommy in her own way, with her own participation. Perhaps she wondered if I had the emotional consistency to do what I had to do. Good question.

Lanie was beautiful in black. Classic Northern Italian beauty. I realized that I didn't want to miss noticing her beauty. Beauty is a shout of joy even in hard times, and we should celebrate it, even if only in our own minds.

The locals call this strand "Mortuary Beach" because the steep incline kills at least several people a year, sometimes divers, sometimes swimmers, sometimes merely people who visit the ocean and slide down that steep slope into the maw of the rip tides.

It is a killing place, and today it was exceptionally beautiful. The inshore waves were shining turquoise, and the sky was clear, brilliant blue, with the green cypress-covered headlands of Point Lobos curving into the ocean on our left and the emerald green of the Pebble Beach golf courses to our right. Straight ahead, the Pacific Ocean as far as the eye could see.

I looked down the beach. There, separate from the others, there was Angelica, in a black nylon short dress, her large Louis Vuitton sunglasses hiding her eyes, black flip-flop sandals, her tiny pedicured brown feet half hidden in the coarse sand. Monastery Beach has dreadfully rough sand.

Angelica was holding a wooden box, large enough for softball and a bit more, between both her hands, in front of her, and it seemed heavy. She was looking at that beautiful wooden box. It had an engraving, hands in prayer, there on that lid. It was a nice box. I had seen it so many times. Laser engraved, I thought.

Cesar and Rose stood close to her, hugging her legs. As I approached, they looked at me fearfully. I looked back. Apparently, I was an apparition, an executioner. I looked at their frightened faces. Was I doing the right thing?

I looked at the people. There were about ten. The weather was perfect. There was Marta, and Mike, and Lanie, of course. And there, distant, about thirty yards away, there was Margaret. Surprising. She was wearing a scarf and sunglasses, and she was slender and somber, almost severe, and she looked at me, and she nodded, yes, and I knew that I must do this, see this finished. As an afterthought, I glanced hurriedly around me, at the brilliant sunlit beach. Jerome was not here. Jerome was not here.

I reached down into Angelica's hands and I gently lifted the box. At first, there was slight reluctance, an insect's increase in her grip around that small cube of wood, and I decided that if she wanted to keep those ashes, she was quite welcome to do so. I lifted the box again, gently. She let it go. It was light in my hands. I turned and walked down the slope towards the water.

The ocean was brilliant blue. I looked at the steep slope of the beach. I looked back at the people watching, somber, wide-eyed.

— Honor —

I realized that I could not just empty the ashes onto the sand, make a black stain that the waves would gradually erase. A mark of pollution. No, I needed something more emphatic. Here we go, Tommy, I thought to myself. I stepped down towards the water, and the ocean swept in, and wrapped itself around my ankles, then my legs, soaking my dress pants. I slid the box lid open. There was a plastic bag, and a white plastic tag, a larger version of what you find on loaves of bread. Why had I not expected that? I quickly read the computer-typed adhesive paper label stuck to the top of the plastic bag. Dot matrix, eighties-style type. "Cremated human remains. Handle according to local ordinances." Then below, "Thomas Phillip Narcisco."

I felt my feet sliding down into the water, deeper, as the steep sand beach eroded from beneath them, and another wave rose up and enveloped my knees in chill clear water. Quickly now, Tommy, quickly. Go with God. Go with us all. I reached down and pulled off the plastic tag, and as the ocean swelled up to my knees I carefully poured the ashes out, into the clear water around me, and it was as though the ocean was embracing me, and when the ashes poured into the water they vanished into nothingness and became the clear sea itself. As the ocean fell back, I saw Marta alongside me, up to her knees in the sea, throwing a pink plumeria blossom lei into the water sweeping out into the open bay and I thought "Ohana. Family. Agape, Tommy. Agape."

Chapter Fifty-four

June 2014

The wedding invitation lay on the hexagonal table. It was small, cream-colored, rectangular, elegant. It was thick, with delicate calligraphy and the little translucent papers buffering the pages.

"It arrived in the mail two days ago, and it was addressed to us all, the entire staff, the family," said Lanie.

I looked around the table. Ernst, Sarah, Lanie, Robert the lawyer, and myself.

"Did you get an invitation? I asked Robert.

"Oh, yes, but I won't be going," he replied. He seemed tired.

"If I may ask, why not?" I asked.

"I have leukemia. I'm trying for a bone marrow transplant two days before the event," he replied, matter of factly.

Stunned silence. Concerned looks.

"Is there anything we can do?" said Lanie.

"A new body," Robert smiled. "Seriously, they caught it early. Good prognosis."

Tommy had said that too.

"You've done a superb job at this," I told him.

"So have you," he replied. "The trip went well, I take it?"

"You've seen the photos on Facebook?" I replied. "The Philippines is a beautiful place."

"And there's Dove," smiled Lanie.

"And there's Dove!" everyone chorused, smiling.

"Should we tell Jerome what we know?" I asked the group.

"I'd say he already knows, or he doesn't want to see," said

Sarah. "Besides, it is his job to go to the Philippines and meet the Aguinaldos, if he's going to marry their daughter."

I pondered that. My trip had changed everything. "Then what's my role going forward?" I asked.

"Do what's best for everyone," said Sarah. "Isn't that what love really is? Agape. Do what helps them. Help them marry well. Help them live well."

"That includes Dove," added Ernst. "That includes everyone, especially the children."

"I raised you both right," I said.

I read the invitation. Very beautifully done.

"Lieutenant Colonel Ramon Aguinaldo and Michelle Aguinaldo respectfully request your presence at the wedding of their daughter Angelica to Jerome Princeton Koenigen"

At the bottom of the page there was a childish scrawl. "Please come, Uncle Garth! Please bring Francesca so we can play! We miss you!" And there was a childish crayon picture of the four of them, Angelica, Jerome, Cesar, and Rose. All smiling, with Cesar holding a fishing pole. There was a stick-figure image of Jerome standing next to him, holding a giant green catfish, with long, gray crayon whiskers half as long as the fish itself, and *X*s for eyes. I folded the invitation closed and put it into my REI backpack to take home.

I needed a large chilled glass of red wine. And perhaps some 90-percent Lindt dark chocolate.

Lanie was still working inside. As the darkness of the evening grew around me, I could see the lights in her office. Such a blessing to have her in my life.

My cell phone rang.

"Great job, cousin! Great job!" said Bull's distant voice on the phone.

I was a bit dazed. What great job? Then I remembered.

"The strawberry fields?" I asked. *Damn. Wonderful.*

"Yep! Fuck yep!" responded Bull.

"Did they sign off on the ag land easement too?" I asked. Surely, we couldn't be that fortunate.

"Oh yes!" said Bull's distant happy voice.

"So that leaves you with the middle pastures, the hayfield, the oil wells, and the home?" I asked.

"Plus four million in the bank from the strawberry fields," said Bull. "Can you manage it? Can we invest that? It's time to live right. Kathleen's gonna kick my ass if I don't invest it with you."

"I'd be honored," I said.

We talked a bit more. How was my mom? Wonderful. How was the family? Everyone's great. We discussed a few memories. Horses, cattle, hunting, ranching. The good old days. We set an appointment for later that month to begin the investment process.

After Bull hung up I sat and savored the feeling of doing something right. It was almost dark. To the west, the moon was rising over the rooftops of Salinas. Lanie's office window was bright from the light within.

I delivered Francesca to Victoria and Fred's home later that night. Francesca ran laughing into the bright living room to embrace Victoria, leaving Margaret standing in the brilliantly lit doorway. Since our family blow-up, I had been careful to stay outside. Margaret and I both turned to look into the living room as Francesca's laughter washed over us.

"Everybody at the office has been invited to Angelica and Jerome's wedding," I mentioned.

"So have we," said Margaret.

That was unexpected.

"To take Francesca or not, that is the question," I replied.

Margaret smiled and answered me, "Whether 'tis nobler in the mind to suffer the slings and arrows of outrageous marriage . . ."

I had forgotten that we had studied Shakespeare together at

Hartnell Community College in an evening course, pre-children. In the background, I could hear Francesca talking and laughing happily with her grandparents. Happy sounds.

"I really don't know what to do," I responded, smiling. "Can we talk?"

I saw her eyebrows raise. We stood there in the front door for a frozen moment.

Then she answered, almost a whisper, "Do you know that Angelica specifically invited me to bring Francesca to the wedding?" she asked. "She doesn't want Francesca to miss it. But she hasn't seen Francesca in months. Why do you think that is?"

"Anacondas come to mind." I responded.

Margaret turned in the doorway and I thought she was going to shut it in my face, as she had so many times. Instead, she called out to her mother, who was smiling and reading to Francesca on a couch by the lit fireplace. "Can you watch Francesca for an hour or so please?"

I saw Victoria look up with a surprised expression on her face, smile frozen. She nodded.

Margaret turned me and said, "I'll get my purse."

Patria was full, as always. Every table taken. We took refuge in the wine room, a casual, no-reservations, Swiss antique-style room with tiny, worn, circular wooden tables, and cabaret chairs. Good enough. I held Margaret's chair out for her, and it occurred to me that this had been another restaurant, under previous management, when it was hip, cool, aluminum, glass, and martinis, in the Eighties and Nineties. Margaret's big-hair era. She and I had been here many times. The world had changed around us and here we were, all over again.

I looked at her unchanging eyes. Slight lines around them now. Rob the waiter appeared, shook my hand inscrutably, and we ordered two glasses of Cabernet and an hors d'oeuvres plate, including their marinated fava beans. Some things don't change.

"It's June 6th," commented Margaret as Rob walked away. It was crowded. The place was full of chatter. I was mystified.

"June 6th?" I responded. "Your birthday is tomorrow. Happy birthday."

The wine and the small plates appeared. The food looked wonderful to me. I realized I was hungry. "D-Day. Midway. And Belleau Wood," said Margaret.

Thousands dead, so long ago.

"I forgot," I said.

"That's not like you," said Margaret, smiling. "History nut."

I responded, "I guess I was too busy with Francesca after work today. We made a pinhole camera for today's solar eclipse and it worked *great!* There was the invitation to Angelica and Jerome's wedding this morning. And the stock market went straight up when Caterpillar's earnings came in . . ."

"Life is for the living, after all," replied Margaret. "What do you think all those men who died in those battles would be doing now, if they were alive?"

"Hmmmm, if they were lucky, I guess they'd be living like us," I responded.

"Yep," said Margaret. "We've been blessed."

I looked beyond her, into the bar. I saw a very tall, slender younger man moving, standing up, smiling, reddish blonde hair in the dim light, now sliding into an upholstered booth. White, white teeth. Jerome. Oh, by all that was holy.

Unexpectedly, I felt adrenaline course through me. Angelica was here. The smart thing to do, the correct thing to do, was to stay here, sit here, have the conversation we'd planned. Stay the hell away from that booth.

"I have to use the men's room," I said to Margaret. "It's at the back. It'll only take a minute."

As I walked past, on my way to the men's room, I tried not to swivel my head, to disclose that I was obviously overwhelmed to see Jerome at Patria. Undoubtedly, Angelica was sitting more deeply in the booth. I peeked as I walked past, and I was stunned. There sat Jerome, crisp shirt as always, light pink this time, powder blue blazer, brilliant red tie reflecting the low light of the room. There was an attractive blonde woman sitting with him, long hair, heavy makeup, bright red dress matching his tie, just the right side of heavy, and all curves. He was rubbing shoulders with her, smiling, tilting his head sideways to touch hers, looking down at his martini. She was smiling, leaning into him, touching him with her forehead. Seeing the unknown woman, I skidded to a stop in a sudden reversal of movement that would have done credit to a cartoon character. My heart thudded in my chest. I was staring.

I should let this pass.

The wedding was next weekend.

Shocking awareness that I could end it all, right now. I could talk about the Philippines. I could rat this out to Angelica. I had the mother of all hand grenades, and I could pull the pin.

Jerome looked up, and his face curved into a sarcastic smile. The blonde, I noticed, still kept her eyes on his face. "Oh it's the accountant," he said. "Wassa matter, you gotta count my beans?"

He pushed a half-eaten plate towards me slightly with the back of his hand. Sudden raging anger flared in me on Angelica's behalf.

I forced myself to smile gently. I said softly, "Hello, Jerome. It is good to see you here. You look great. That's a good coat on you."

Impulsively, I turned and looked back at Margaret in the wine room. She was staring at me. I motioned to her to come here, waving broadly. She looked at me questioningly and lifted the two half-consumed glasses of wine. Bring them? She motioned. I nodded back. Then I pointed at the booth seat opposite Jerome and I slid down to face him.

Jerome's face registered surprise, and then perhaps a transitory moment of fear, then Margaret slid down alongside of me, and placed my glass in front of my hands.

"Thanks," I said to her. "Margaret, meet Jerome."

Jerome looked veiled, surprised, calculating. He also looked mildly drunk.

Margaret's eyes widened. She looked at Jerome politely,

offered her hand to shake, and said nothing. I was very grateful to her right now.

Jerome reached across the table and took her hand. He smiled. "A pleasure to meet you," he said. "You are related to this gentleman how?"

"I'm his wife. Ahhh, his ex-wife," she responded. "We have four children together. We're just together tonight to discuss our youngest daughter, Francesca, the schedule."

"Francesca!" said Jerome, looking her in the eyes. "Cesar and Rose talk about her all the time. She sounds wonderful."

"Oh, she's a delight, she really is. I don't know how we were so lucky with all of our four." Margaret laughed. "But then Cesar and Rose are so *active* and intelligent too. They make a great team with Francesca."

I couldn't believe we were having this conversation at all.

"I've never had children before," said Jerome.

The blonde woman looked mildly pained, or bored. She looked pale, sullen, bovine, and fertile. She said nothing. She looked from Jerome to Margaret and me.

"Hi!" I offered my hand to her. "I'm Garth. You've met Margaret." I smiled broadly.

She looked at both of us, vaguely distracted. "Oh, hi, I'm Budgie. Like the bird. Hahaha! Right?"

"Right!" I said.

Budgie reached over and hugged Jerome's arm. He didn't respond at all. He looked at Margaret.

"Are you aware, Madam, that your *ex*-husband is an asshole?" He smiled at her sardonically. Clearly anger there. Frustration.

She smiled back. "Well, we all have it in us." She grinned. "Somehow he still gets the job done."

"Certainly he gets the job done," responded Jerome. "After all you have four children with him."

Margaret looked at me and smiled. "Jerome has no children." She looked at Budgie.

"Think of the freedom," said Margaret, still looking at Budgie.

"The wedding is next weekend," I said. "Big life change."

Let's see what Budgie does with that information.

"The big life change already happened," replied Jerome.

"I need to pee. I need to pee, pee, Garth! Ha Ha! Right?" said Budgie.

"Right!" I smiled back at her brightly.

A box of hammers, that one.

Budgie turned in her seat to look sulkily at Jerome. "When are we going to the movie?" she asked.

Jerome stood up, and helped Budgie out of the low padded booth seat and onto her feet, and she walked towards the back of the restaurant towards the bathrooms. He slid back down to his seat. Rob quickly darted in, took orders for more drinks, and left.

"Martini number four," said Jerome. "Time for you to leave too, please. Movie."

Margaret began to rise, to leave. "Well, anyway, congratulations," she said.

"You know, Jerome, we've had our differences, and we've fought like cats in a bag," I said, still sitting, "but it all worked out."

Margaret sat back down, and looked at me inquiringly. Eye rolls. Let's leave.

Jerome looked at me. Deep in his eyes I could see where the martinis had slackened him, dulled his mind in vodka. Or gin, I thought.

"You're an asshole," said Jerome, almost to himself, quietly.

I began to rise, and I offered my hand. He took it.

"That attempt at a restraining order kind of sucked though," I added, rising. Margaret began to rise as well.

He didn't let go of my hand. Instead, he pulled me back down. Then he released his grip and wrapped his slender manicured fingers around the fresh, frosted martini that Rob had just placed in front of him.

"I don't think you understand," he said quietly yet firmly. Beyond, at the bar, I noticed Budgie laughing loudly, a jarring, metallic sound, talking with another cluster of drinkers.

I sat there. Margaret sat next to me. I became aware that our shoulders were touching.

"All the kids talk about is you," said Jerome. "You did this with them, you did that with them. Angelica doesn't talk about you at all, but I hear all the time of how you damn near lived there. And you helped, and helped, and helped, she'd get a hangnail and there you'd be, like a poodle, a retriever or something."

Silence. I looked in Jerome's eyes. I didn't know what to say.

"I've never been in love like this in my life," he whispered.

Like watching a large trout, in a clear Sierra lake, on a beautiful summer morning, nuzzling my baited fishhook. Patience. Stay still. I just nodded. I looked briefly at Margaret, and she looked at me, silently surprised by this turn of the conversation. Jerome looked at his martini.

"You know I'm rich, right?" he said. His words were almost drowned out by the laughter and excited conversation from Budgie and her friends. Something about a baseball game. Right.

"Yes, I gathered that." I smiled.

"Bigly rich. Richer than you can know," he added.

"Yes," I said quietly.

He looked at the martini and went on. "It doesn't seem to matter. I mean, it *does* matter, it matters a lot, but sometimes I wish you hadn't helped them so much. So I could have helped them instead."

"She said you were too busy," I replied.

"I guess I was," Jerome replied. "And you've met her family, you know them. I don't know them at all. And I see what you've accomplished in life, and I wonder, what's all the money worth?"

"Really?" was all I could say. Jerome felt I had accomplished something? I felt the glow of affirmation, unexpected.

"Really," Jerome said. "Sometimes it feels like she's not really there, not really there at all. Not when we are talking, not when we are traveling, not when we are in bed. It feels like there's someone else. Is this what she did to you? I mean, do you think she still loves you?"

"No," I replied emphatically.

"Does she text you, does she call you, does she message you? Does she ever see you?" said Jerome. There was a hint of pain on his face now.

"Only on business, and then as briefly and as rarely as possible," I replied. "Jerome, I gotta tell you, she's your woman now. You win this one."

"But what have I won?" Jerome's eyes wandered across the room. "She doesn't still think of you? I mean, tell me that in front of Margaret."

"It's not me," I said. "It really isn't me."

"Do you think she's just after the money?" asked Jerome.

I looked him in the eyes, and I saw fear, coagulated in the back there, like cataracts. I thought perhaps he was drunker than I realized.

"I've never been in love like this before. I've never been afraid like this before," Jerome continued. He looked at Margaret. "Tonight was our rehearsal dinner and she started chattering with her Filipino friends in whatever language they speak, and it was like I wasn't there at all. At all. Everything I am, everything I've accomplished, and it's all not enough. It's Filipina World for her. I just got up and left. I mean, I walked out of my own rehearsal dinner."

I sat there. I looked at Margaret. She looked at me. Surprise again.

"What do you do if it's just not there, if it's lost?" he asked, as though to himself.

"You just keep trying," answered Margaret quietly. "You always, always keep trying. Don't leave." She reached out and put her hand over his. I felt a small kick of jealousy.

Jerome looked at her.

"I know that you've been invited to the wedding. I saw you on the list," said Jerome.

I nodded. I looked at Margaret. She looked at me. Yes.

"What do you think?" asked Jerome.

"I think that next Saturday you are going to marry a dream, and you will start your new life, in a new world," I replied.

— Honor —

404

I was thinking silently . . . it wasn't Filipina World at all. It was Little Ramon World, and it always had been.

Chapter Fifty-five

July 2014

Zero hour, 9 a.m. I sat in my XTerra on a sunny day at the Palo Alto Veteran's Affair's clinic. Tuesday. I was there without fanfare. I didn't want my clients to know that I was being treated for PTSD: it was all I could do to convince them that I was not going back to another non-war in a foreign land. I had completed my transcranial magnetic stimulation treatments. I had pushed through ten sessions with Doctor Häyhä Pekk, reliving the trauma moment by moment, deconstructing and reconstructing my life, the events, the emotions. Now I was visiting the VA Center to see if the treatments had worked. How do you possibly judge that?

Two years ago, I had thought I was dead, at least in my soul. Now, I was somehow reconnected. I could feel the sun's warmth on my face. That was really something, I thought. That was beautiful.

I wondered how much of this was due to the VA, and how much of this was due to letting go. How much was due to what I had seen in the Philippines? How much was due to the on-line relationship that I was enjoying with Dove? She was a month away from work in Oman. We were still talking nightly on Facebook.

The VA Center had valet parking, far from the building. It was a Silicon Valley building, somehow looming yet light. Metal. Glass. Shiny. Big parking lot. At the valet's guard box, there was a sign, in big block military letters: "Please do not tip the valet." I smiled, picturing all the mentally thrashed veterans, the patients, feeling grateful, showering fellow veterans now working as valets with all their spare pennies. The valet approached me. A slender young black woman. Unexpected. Athletic. Attractive. "Good morning, Sir! Welcome to the clinic! May I park your car? Do you need assistance entering the building?"

"I'm good," I said. I gave her the keys.

The large, glass front doors opened automatically, and I walked into the lobby. There was a line of people, mostly young, blocking the hall so much that I was able to go into the lobby only a few feet, and then the doors swooshed closed behind me. The air smelled clean. The walls were beige, institutional, new looking, with a few military posters of historical actions hung precisely.

"What's this about?" I asked a young man in front of me. His close-cropped dark hair revealed a cobweb of scars across the back of his head.

"Oh, just check-in," he responded. Friendly. There was a banter of talk down the line, perhaps twenty people in front of me, and a flat screen TV on a mount from the ceiling that was showing us *Good Morning America* or some other morning feel-good news show. Nobody was watching. There was a hum of soft conversations, meetings, comparisons. It was bright. At the end of the line of people, there was a metal institutional desk, someone sitting, head down over papers, smiling. Papers. I didn't have any papers. Vague anxiety.

"Did I forget something?" I asked the young man in front of me.

He turned back and smiled gently. "We all forgot something or we wouldn't be here." That caused the young people in front of him to turn and laugh.

Ahead of me, there was a metal leg, a prosthesis, attached to a young man. And there was another. And a metal arm. A young Hispanic woman—perhaps in her early twenties—with an eyepatch, and what looked like burns across her face. She had grown her hair out and combed it down that side of her head to hide them.

The room went quiet suddenly. Someone softly said, "Damn."

I looked up, around. The TV overhead was showing a picture of a man in an orange jumpsuit kneeling, staring glumly into the camera, in a place with no green plants growing, just sand to the horizon. There was a man in black Arabic dress, his face covered, and the caption said "ISIS BEHEADS AMERICAN JOURNALIST." Now all of us were watching the TV.

"Well, fuck," a voice said quietly.

"You know he was dumb as a bag of cement to be there anyway," said a soft, youthful, feminine voice. The woman.

"I guess we were dumb as bags of cement to be there too," said a young man.

"Do you think 'Mer'ca'll do anything 'bout this?" said another voice.

"Oh, no, we've . . . moved on." Yet another voice. Sarcastic.

"I guess we could fart loudly in their general direction," said the woman gently. Nobody laughed.

"Tell me I didn't give my leg for that shit pile," said a young man, hidden in the queue ahead of me. "Shit, my friends died over there. For what?"

"Ya know . . ." This voice had a southern accent.

"Ya know we didn't choose any of this," the voice continued.

"They attacked us," said another younger voice. "9/11."

Then silence.

"We kicked their asses," the voice cracked.

"Yep." Southern accent "We were there because they invited us with fuckin' jetliners full 'a helpless people. Wherever we went, and whatever we did, we did the right, the best thing. We kicked ass."

"Fuckin' A. Get some."

On the TV there was now a row of prisoners in orange jumpsuits kneeling in front of black-clad ISIS fighters, all leveling AK-47s at the prisoners' backs.

"Ya know we could kill them all, if we go back," said Southern Accent.

"Well fuck, that's not gonna happen. Like we all might win the fuckin' lottery," said a young woman's voice.

— Chapter 55 —
409

The TV screen had now changed to pictures of a movie clip of a very muscular blond Viking with a very large stone hammer, according to the caption, *"THOR."* Apparently, we were now watching a movie review. The people in the newscast were smiling now. The blonde woman filling the screen had a perfect body, perfect smile, and perfect hair.

"Or get struck by lightning," added a voice.

"Or get laid with her," said a younger, boyish voice.

"Easy, gentlemen, it's a harassment-free zone," said an older man's voice.

"Oh yeah, so I can't bust loose on your ass, right?" said a young woman's voice.

"It's a tough job, but someone's got to do it," the older man replied.

Laughter.

The line proceeded. Gradually the line diminished and we all went away to our meetings. As I walked to the elevator behind a young man in a wheelchair—no legs at all—the TV was showing the smiling woman host, with a very attractive woman chef. Million dollar smiles. Apparently, they were cooking pasta.

The following morning I arrived at work before dawn. I was deeply concerned about interest rates in the European bond market. The European Central Bank, bless their bureaucratic tiny little heads, had pushed interest rates even further into negative levels in June, unheard-of in history. Imagine, a negative interest rate, like a ground-tunneling aircraft. Now the economy was not soaring as expected, it was fizzling, and the Greeks were threatening to default on their debt again. So I was looking hard at investing more in Switzerland, with the theory that the Swiss franc should soar as the Euro falls. That, plus investing more in Asia, and gold, and eventually energy, once that got through collapsing.

Somehow, I forgot the time, and when Lanie called from the other office, "Bull on line 1," I realized that it was already 11 a.m.

"Hey, cousin! We should have lunch now," said Bull's voice. He sounded stressed.

"What's up?" I asked. Wary. We hadn't invested his four million dollars yet.

"I saw some friends of yours last night at Giorgio's," said the voice.

"What's up?" I asked again.

"Face to face," said Bull.

"See you in twenty minutes," I answered.

At Giorgio's, Bull was in his customary booth: left side, two down. He was already eating a massive hamburger. I wondered how much fat was in that edifice of meat.

Greetings. I ordered the salmon panini with mixed garden greens. I sat back as my plate was set before me.

"Weeds," grunted Bull, gesturing at the salad. "The cows on Tortuga won't even eat 'em."

I smiled, looked at him steadily, and placed a large forkful of leaves into my mouth. They *did* look like weeds, I thought. I continued to stare at him as I chewed slowly. I reflected on the fact that most of Tortuga wasn't his anymore and he certainly didn't own any cattle. He seemed more massive than ever.

"I spoke with your friends Angelica and Jerome here last night, like I mentioned on the phone. Boy, did you ever fuck up, cousin," said Bull.

My friends?

"What did they say?" I asked. I could guess.

"My Kathleen was shocked. Frankly I'm a bit shocked myself," continued Bull.

There was an element of unconscious irony in that, I thought. I looked at him, wondering how to reply.

"What, specifically, did they say?" I asked quietly.

"Well, your friends said that you lied about your military service and you are obsessive, for one thing," said Bull. He seemed dismayed. He shook his head as he looked at the huge partially eaten hamburger on his plate.

"They laughed about you, and then they talked about your

business," he continued.

"My business?" I asked.

"Jerome says your kind of business is obsolete. He says you are small potatoes."

I wondered what to say. So much misinformation. Alternative facts. Entire generations of anger, secrets, and sorrow. Long-dead uncles living imaginary lives on tiny tropical islands. The constant feeling of never-enough. Never, ever good enough.

"What do you think?" I asked Bull.

"Well, something's not right," said Bull. "I mean you've been crazy before. Running off to the Marines after 9/11 as if it's the fucking French Foreign Legion. Leaving Margaret, the kids, and the business. I mean, shit, that's nuts. I'm guessing you are still at least a little nuts now. That's what they say about PTSD. If you really have it."

"That's what you think?" I asked.

Ironic, I thought. Given that I had just saved his ass.

"It's worse. I mean, after last night, listening to Jerome like that. I mean, he's really rich, so he's got to know something. Kathleen's not going to trust you. So I'm sorry. I'm really sorry," responded Bull.

"Sorry?" I said. I was struggling to completely stifle my need to respond, rebut, reject.

"I'm going to take that four million to a Wall Street firm. Someone I can trust," said Bull. "I'm thinking Globalbank. They've been around for decades, after all."

"You can trust Globalbank?" I responded, silently gritting my teeth.

The Financial Panic of 2008 came to mind. Visions of days of mortgage restructuring. Lies and manipulation.

"They're doing cryptocurrencies now. That's very popular. Bitcoin," he added.

"We're trying to keep you rich for the rest of your life," I responded. "Traditional no load mutual funds and investments, which have been around for decades can do that. Why take the risk?"

"Look, you just don't get it," said Bull, exasperated.

"What don't I get?" I asked. Thoughts of simply getting up and walking back to the office now.

"All your old-fashioned values and your old-fashioned life and your old-fashioned ideas. Long gone, cousin. Long gone. You know your uncles and your father? All those men in C Company? All dead long ago," said Bull.

"The people are gone. But what about the values?" I asked.

"Yep. Think about it. Like when you helped me. You helped me because of my father and our family. All dead. All their ethics, all their culture, all that horse-and-cowboy shit. All dead. That's who your real clients are, Garth. They're all dead."

Behind Dove's smiling face on the computer, I could see her family's grove of trees, on their island in the rice paddies. Here I was sitting in the dark. There, Dove was looking bright, morning-fresh.

I was complaining about the upcoming wedding, and my meeting with Bull.

"He said all my clients are dead," I finished.

"I seem to be alive. You are helping me. Am I your client?" said Dove.

"You are very, very alive. Thanks for being here for me," I replied.

"I am reminded of the spider," said Dove.

Should I be insulted? I wondered.

"Tell me more," I said. Keep it neutral. Nice use of counselling techniques.

"Here. Let me show you," said Dove. She picked up her laptop and the image swirled. Through the door. Into the yard. Images of rice paddies in the distance. Now a tree, a large tree with a giant fluted trunk. Between branches was a large spider's orb web, bejeweled with recent rain, and in its center, there was a very large colorful spider.

"This is a giant wood spider. Isn't she beautiful?" said Dove.

My kind of girl, I thought.

— Chapter 55 —

"Yes, she is," I answered neutrally.

That was one gigantic spider.

"At this time of year, she will have an egg sac nearby, with a congregation of tiny spiderlings ready to emerge," she said precisely.

"A congregation?" I laughed. "Is that what you call it? Perhaps a congress would be a better term? Or a dance party?"

"Ah, now you smile," she said from off-screen. The computer's camera moved closer to the spider as it sat in its web.

Dove continued off-camera. "The babies will go on, many eaten, many killed, but also many surviving, to repeat the cycle of life. As long as she is able, their mother will rebuild that web. Typhoons, invasions, blundering animals, people, deer, pigs, even birds, will rip that web to shreds, and every morning that spider will be back to rebuild it."

"And if the tree is cut down?" I asked.

"If the tree is cut down, then that spider or her descendants will find another tree and build the web anew," said Dove's voice, off-camera. "My family, we are like these beautiful creatures. We must build our home in whatever tree we find."

Ernst and Sarah and I had brought bagels to my mother's home for Saturday breakfast. I felt anxious: I was missing a trail run. Some sort of game was on TV.

"Amazing that we are so fascinated by that. The football isn't even edible," said my mother, chewing slowly on a poppy seed garlic surprise with smoked salmon cream cheese. "We might be paying attention to the world instead. It feels like destruction all over," she added.

Sarah said, "It feels like the world has gone insane. And I'm only in my twenties."

My mother continued, "I wonder what it felt like, to be a Roman in, say, London, about 400 AD. Picture that. You know that what is around you will all pass away. All the splendor. The culture. All swept away by barbarians, because society has chosen to give up."

— Honor —

"And yet eventually good things happened. Brittania became England," said Ernst. "No more slavery. No more Roman tyranny. Being a barbarian wasn't all bad."

"The process must have sucked though," said Sarah. "Many didn't survive. It literally must have felt like hell. Like everything was lost."

"I'm sure my Native American ancestors felt the same way in the past two hundred years, yet here I am, thriving in a different world," said my mother. "It's a pretty good world too."

I told them all about Dove's comments about the spiders.

"She sounds wise," said my mother. "You should get to know her more. She might give this family a good kick in the pants."

"Our pants have been kicked enough." Ernst laughed.

"How about we just have a good life instead?" smiled Sarah.

"No, we need to be like those spiders," said my mother. "Build a good life in the tree we're in. Actually, Dove sounds a lot like me, in 1950. It's the Americans who are strangers to me now."

Chapter Fifty-six

August 2014

The wedding was at First Presbyterian Church, at the big barn on Main Street, the modern church. Looking out from the steps of the church towards the parking lot, at the gathering mix of Lamborghinis, Porsches, F-150 trucks, and minivans, I could see the parking lot was full. There were coveys of press. The media are flies to the smell of vast affluence.

Five hundred people, many of them the same individuals who had been at Tommy's event three years before. There were so many of our shared friends there. Some of them waved or greeted me.

There were fewer from the groom's side, polished, white teethed, carefully coiffed. I noticed a group of what appeared to be the groom's family, escorted by ushers. A tall, slender, gray-haired woman in a light gray gown, with a frothing gray mink stole. She was arm in arm with a white-haired man who looked a great deal like a professor. Then there followed a middle-aged woman and a man who seemed to look somewhat like Jerome, with that auburn hair, so carefully groomed, fabrics in grays and blacks and white, all pressed. These people seemed singularly unhappy.

I entered the church and began to climb the stairs to my habitual place in the balcony. I would see the back of Angelica's head one more time in this church. Lanie had told me that they were all moving away, perhaps to a suburb of New York, somewhere simpler, quieter, fewer memories, more groomed, more affluent.

As I walked up the stairs, Mike, Marta's husband, Angelica's brother in law, ever quiet, ever somber, slender, now wearing a light gray tuxedo and red bow tie, blocked my way on the stairwell. He motioned me to a stop. He had my attention. I wondered if he was going to ask me to leave.

"Angelica wants to see you," he said quietly. That was all he said. I had to follow him, of course. Why would Angelica want to see me? I felt my pulse rise in my throat, the adrenaline surge. After my meeting with Bull, I was here only from duty.

I said nothing, simply nodded, and he led me up the stairs, into the hallway, to a room along the back of the balcony. New white paint. Florescent industrial light, no windows. A crowd of Filipina women, the same as I had seen at Angelica's parties, a few European women. All women. Mostly talking quickly in Tagalog or Kapampangan.

As Mike ushered me in, he reached out and squeezed my hand. I looked at him silently. That was the first time he had ever reached out to me, and this time his face wore a slight smile of approval.

There, in the center, the queen bee in her hive, was Angelica, in a long white traditional wedding gown, slender and tight fitting with a flowing train, translucent veil, small slender perfect body perfectly fit by that custom dress of taffeta and lace. White dress, brown skin, luminous somehow with her own inner glow. On her left hand, there was the new engagement ring, a behemoth of a ring, with a larger Gibraltar of a white diamond, rising up from her finger like a tiny shimmering post, unusually tall for a ring.

Incongruously, the emotion that surged through me was an irrational revulsion, an offended sense of vulgarity. The new diamond was Everest, so overwhelming on her petite hand. I looked at her, and said nothing.

Her black hair was highlighted as always, but straightened, carefully layered and braided so that under the lace veil it formed a delicate tracery down her slender brown back. She spun around briefly, intentionally making the front hemline of the dress flare and the inlaid sequins glitter.

She turned to me, and her eyes, in her perfectly made up face, were welling, wet. A frown, even a scowl. The front of her gown was low cut, modestly yet strategically exposing her lifted breasts. Then I snapped my eyes back to her gaze, and caught the ghost of a smile, as she understood the thoughts my eyes had evoked. Her eyes began to run.

I had come prepared. I pulled a clean Kleenex from my pocket and handed it to her, wordlessly. She pulled it from me abruptly, and carefully dabbed her eyes.

"I am beautiful, aren't I?" she said.

I just looked at her, and nodded. Yes.

"My father is not here," she continued. "I have no father to give me away." She looked evasively away from me, at the far corner of the room. I looked over there and saw Cesar in a small tuxedo, looking up from his electronic tablet. He looked at me sadly. He waved at me, and I waved back. Rose was behind him, hopping on sheets of bubble wrap. The bubble wrap made a crackling noise when it burst.

"Why isn't your father here?" I asked. "What happened? Wasn't he on the invitation with your mother?"

She looked at me angrily, and seemed on the verge of tears again. She shook her fists. "It is PRIVACY! It is not your business!" She stamped her foot under her dress. Then she composed herself and looked at me gravely.

"You will give me away to Jerome."

I looked at her, stunned. I could feel my pulse in my throat. I struggled for air, and forced myself into ten-count breathing. Could she not know how utterly dishonest that would be for everyone? Agape. Ohana. What would Jesus do? I asked myself. Tommy, Tommy, Tommy, what should I do?

"Are your father and mother here?" I asked.

She shook her head, tearfully, negatively.

"Are they in the United States? Or are they still in the Philippines?" I asked.

She answered with a little girl voice. "Still there. They do not come."

— Chapter 56 —

"Why?" I asked.

The tears began to course, and she stared at me angrily through wet eyes. "I invite but they will not come."

She turned away, spun around as though considering running away herself.

"I don't understand, I give them everything," she said to the wall in a puzzled voice. "But they say that the money does not matter. I live to make them all happy. They say that I marry for the wrong reasons. Can you believe that, Garth? I bring them everything. Never enough . . . it is never enough."

Somehow, I felt a clutch of affinity towards her. All she does, I thought.

She dabbed carefully at her eyes with my Kleenex. She turned back to me. The train of her dress twisted. I wanted to bend down and lay it out straight.

"So, Sir Garth, will you walk me in the aisle, or will I be alone woman when I meet Jerome? Will you please walk me to my husband?"

I was silent.

"Remember," she replied, almost whispering. "You of all people know why I am here. Now, I beg you, please walk me."

Eyes staring, she reached up mindlessly and traced the line of the small scar under her jaw.

Tommy, I thought. See it through. Carry them through to the new life. Keep the promise.

"Yes," I said.

"Wait for me downstairs then. Let me finish this. I must give these women what they want," said Angelica.

The wedding march began to play. It reminded me of music for a wind-up toy. The music was live, up on the stage, strings, drums, woodwinds, musicians whom I knew from so many Sundays past.

.Angelica and I stepped together, arm in arm, through the wide industrial doors into the back of the wide cavernous church, and she abruptly transformed into calm radiance, a beaming royal smile turned to the crowded people who looked back at us from their chairs. All the people stood up. Smiling faces. So many friends.

I felt a moment of inferiority, dressed in my suit, not a tuxedo.

There was a ramp halfway down the aisle rising to the elevated stage, and up there, in the center of the stage, was Jerome, with a dozen groomsmen all clad in gray with red bow ties. One of those groomsmen, farthest away from Jerome, was Mike, who only minutes ago had stopped me on the stairs. And there in the center, next to Jerome, was our pastor, Dr. Latham, waiting.

We walked, slowly, down the aisle, matching steps so easily. Angelica was small alongside me. The music changed. "Pachelbel's Canon in D." The musicians were playing beautifully. I focused on breathing slowly. One foot in front of the other. Keep it slow for Angelica, in her tight and beautiful dress. I wanted to run down the aisle and out the other side.

The music changed again, to a modern hymn, "Revelation Song." Played at Tommy's memorial service. The music of all our times, Tommy, alive, and Tommy, dead, and those of us left behind struggling to find a path to this place, many months later.

Angelica was singing along next to me, her small beautiful strong voice, and I heard myself whispering the words, as quietly as I could, and the sound of everyone swelled to fill the room as we walked up the ramp, keeping our small steps together, singing together until the song ended. What is agape? I thought. Agape is letting go. Always, at some point.

Jerome was not singing. As we sang, I saw him recognize me, a hostile angry confusion flash across his face, and then he willed his brilliant beaming smile to return. I locked eyes with him. He stared back, at me, not at Angelica, and a slight smirk twisted his lips, and remained there. I tried to look apologetic, deferential. His glare continued. I have her now, his face said to me. You have lost her. He raised his chin, defiant. He was handsome: the perfect thick red hair, the tallness, the slenderness, the youth, the fitness, the full complexion, the gray tuxedo, the white shirt, the red tie. He was perfect. And rich.

— Chapter 56 —
421

I looked at Angelica to see if she had noticed my stare-down with Jerome. Her eyes were riveted on him, and her face was transfixed with awe and adoration, delicate full lips slightly parted, a look I had never seen on her before, and there were a few tears unwiped running down her face, as she was transformed by an expression of complete and utter devotion. In all our time together, she had never ever looked at me like that. God, Tommy, thank you for showing me this.

A few more steps, and then we were there, at the top of the ramp, on the stage, and Dr. Latham was saying, "Who gives this woman in marriage today?" I looked at Angelica, smiling broadly, whitely, completely, the very epitome of youthful joy, gazing with abject worship at her Jerome, and I said, perhaps too loudly, "I do."

As I walked back down the ramp, my role complete, I looked at the groom's family in the front row, lit by the lights of the stage. They looked as though someone had just run over their pet Chihuahua dog with a semi-truck. Behind them, faces reflecting the light passing through the front row, were my ex-wife Margaret, all four of our children, all our family. One love reflecting another.

I walked straight to the doors at the back, mentally distracted by the events unseen behind me, straight out the door, and into the foyer and thence into the porch, and the stairs, and into the parking lot. Luckily, no late arrivals ran me over. I saw nothing except the need to escape, to flee.

I did not pause to see Margaret and the children. I imagined they wouldn't want to see me, and given my past obsession and my interior meltdown, I regarded myself as unfit company for anyone, not for my ex-wife, not for my children, not for the woodlice in the shrubbery. I drove my Xterra to the reception at Spanish Bay, which was located next to Heritage Bay Eldercare in Pebble Beach by the ocean, while the photographers were filming the wedding party on the steps of the church in Salinas.

It was a forty-minute drive. I needed every minute of solitary travel. When I arrived at the parking lot I could not remember how I got there. The immediate application of a vodka martini completed the effect, and the addition of a second gin martini guaranteed my smiling, speechless amiability when the wedding party began to arrive in Rolls Royce limousines. I had seldom seen a Rolls Royce limousine before, and now I confronted five of them, in the most luxurious venue known to civilized man.

Angelica emerged from the first Rolls Royce, beaming in the sunlight, brown skin, white dress flowing perfectly, arm embracing the tall, strong form of her newly-created husband. Jerome was radiant as well he should be. Then he stepped on the train of her dress, and Angelica turned on him, angry, scowling. He stepped away, and she suddenly smiled her most captivating smile, the world lit up, and they walked into the Spanish Bay resort, door opened wide by gray-clad uniformed attendants, hundreds of guests streaming behind them.

I recognized several celebrities, several of the most public billionaires, and a gaggle of the confused bespectacled techno-rich, emanating nerdness, black-framed glasses, overstuffed blond consorts of multiple genders in full display. Behind them lurked what I had assumed to be Jerome' family, now acting, and looking, as though they were attending a distant relative's funeral. They stalked in late; catlike, looking furtively about as though there might be pit bulldogs hidden in the corners of the room. Perhaps they were considering hiding under the tables in the corner. Duck and cover. That thought made me smile.

I sat at the end of the head table, from whence I could see Angelica, fully attentive to Jerome, radiant smile flashing, and Jerome, resplendent in his control and his attractiveness, focusing his attention away from her, focusing instead on the party and his friends. Angelica was so dazzling, her white smile gleaming, that most of the attention was on her. I saw Jerome follow his friends' and family's gazes to the object of their attention, and his smile faded. I saw his dominant smile reemerge, and then fade as he realized that he was not the center of attention. He brought his alpha-male smile back, looked at Angelica, looked at the people as they focused on Angelica. Beyond his smile, in his eyes, he seemed a bit surprised.

Dinner was a served buffet, featuring chefs and cuisine from Jerome's home in New York. I tried to eat, but I had no appetite, even for the salmon and the ultra-dark chocolate mousse. In the process, I had several glasses of red wine, imbibed as quickly as possible.

The toasts began. I remember I stood and offered some words enthusiastically. I do not remember what I said, but I remember the smiles and the applause, and so I must assume that whatever I said, it was correct, and right and fitting the image which Angelica wished to convey. I remember a grateful expression from Angelica. I remember Jerome looking at me, with an expression of ascendant amusement.

Then it was time to dance. The first dance. I saw Angelica stand and reach out eagerly to Jerome and pull him out of his chair and into the open space, for a slow first dance. I saw her nestle into his arms, white smile beaming across the darkened dance floor as she rested her cheek on his chest. Everyone was watching them. I turned on my heels and walked straight to the glass wall, through the sliding panels, out onto the green lawn outside. *Go, go, go.*

Behind me, the music changed, from a soft slow dance to pounding disco, and I moved faster.

So much out there on the dance floor. Tommy. Tommy's death. My promise. All Angelica's pain and hardship and uncertainty, my efforts and failures, all the lost love, all the wanting, the needing, the never-ending pain, the unrelenting hunger, the images of Angelica's body, soon to be wrapped, joined, with Jerome.

Then more thoughts: with the Marines in Lebanon, my own wedding to Margaret, my children being born, Iraq, the explosion, the hospital, Margaret's anger, Angelica. Angelica. Then Francesca. Cesar. Rose. Jerome. The feeling of that Stanford magnet pulsing through my brain. *Wam! Wam! Wam!* The

Philippines. Love. Angelica's father, smiling. The vision of a Philippine coral reef underwater. Dove.

The noise from the ballroom was louder now. I heard the crowd yell out the lyric in time to the music, "YOU THE HOTTEST BITCH IN THE WORLD!" I turned back and looked through the glass, dimly into the darker ballroom. In the center of the dance floor was Angelica in her white wedding dress, spinning around a smiling Jerome as he held her hands, her head back, hair stretching outwards as she twirled, laughing. All eyes were on her.

Watching her, I had a sudden surge of clutching, gripping, painful awareness, that everything was where it was supposed to be, had happened as it should. I walked farther away from the building, seeking to get away from the noise. Seeking quiet. The noise from the celebration faded.

I realized that I was at the edge of a small cliff, overlooking the ocean, the beautiful blue flat Pacific Ocean. Over there beyond the horizon was the Philippines. Over there was Iraq. Over there. Carmel beach was a white line in the distance, to my left. I looked back, I realized I had unconsciously walked across a putting green, and there were elderly golfers in pastel pants, looking at me as a trespasser, an intruder, a lunatic.

I could not walk any farther without falling off the cliff and into the sea. There was a sense of completion, and exhaustion. Stillness in the midst of chaos. I prayed and my lips moved, and I closed my eyes and turned my face towards the sun hovering over the still flat ocean in the west. Oh God, oh my ancestors, oh Tommy, is there anything left of me at all? Is it all consumed, all gone, all lost? Is it all blown away in the wind?

I heard a golfer give a small curse, an unintelligible soft exclamation, and I opened my eyes and looked back over my shoulder. There was Margaret and my oldest son, Wallace, and his wife, Alexis, and Sarah holding hands with her husband, Osten, and little skipping Francesca hand in hand with Ernst.

They all walked to me, avoided my eyes, smiling guardedly in the face of my implicit distress, paused to look over the ocean.

— Chapter 56 —

425

Margaret came behind them, looked at me evenly, sadly, smiling only a little, knowledge in her eyes.

For a time we all just looked out at the ocean. Silence. Margaret was standing next to me, looking at that great flat blue sea.

"How does it feel?" she asked softly. Behind us, far away in the reception hall, the party was loud. Here, the soft breeze off the ocean was muted.

"Oh, it's good," I responded with equal quietness. My eyes became wet. "It's the right thing."

"I know it hurts," Margaret finally said quietly. She reached up and put her hand on my shoulder. "I know it hurts." She continued to look at the view. "It *should* hurt like hell if you gave everything. Like you have said to me and the kids all these years . . ."

"Nothing worth doing is easy." I finished her words with her.

"We all have our wars, Major Ericson," she responded. "We've all been there."

"How did you get here, anyway?" I asked.

"Angelica invited us, of course," she replied. "Remember?"

My eyes filled with tears and I turned back to the ocean. I felt like a fool, an obsessive idiot. An old, obsessive idiot.

Was I crying about Angelica? No, I realized.

"For a train wreck you look damn good, I'll give you that," said Margaret, louder. I turned and looked at her, wet face and all. Sleek, statuesque, utterly fit. Four kids later and she looked like that.

"You look pretty good yourself," I replied as tears ran down my cheeks. I didn't wipe them.

"It's the grief diet. I see you've tried it too," she said.

"Yes," was all I could choke. The tears were streaming now. I stood there, embarrassed. I didn't know what to do.

"Oh by the waaay . . ." Margaret always strung that word out. "Angelica told me that Jerome bought the home yesterday. Tommy's home. She said to tell you. Angelica and Jerome are putting the home in trust for the kids. So you won."

I had to smile. Winning. What's that?

— Honor —

"It's a wedding. Let's see if we still know how to dance," said Margaret matter of factly, and she reached out for me, the light of the setting sun illuminating the tracery of lines on her slender face. Every line earned, I thought. She reached out and maneuvered me into a dancing position, a few feet back from the small cliff, and pulled me closer, closer, until I was tight up against her, my tears dripping onto her bare sculpted shoulders, and she began to hum softly into my ear, and move gently, rhythmically. I didn't recognize the tune. I moved with her.

"We used to dance a lot. So well together," she whispered into my ear.

She stepped back slightly. She could feel the dog tags through my shirt, the metal tabs. She pulled back slightly, still with her arms around me, and she traced the dog tags briefly with her finger. Then, silently, she pulled me back into her arms, tightly, and began to two-step slowly again to a song without sound.

Beyond, back in the ballroom, beyond the green flat putting green, and the pastel-clad golfers I could see motion, and the image of a small woman in white, dancing some sort of gangnam line dance, twisting moving jerkily, all the distant figures moving, some sort of music thumping in there, and I saw Cesar and Rose leave the building, smiling, running towards us here at the ocean's edge, small figures rushing, and Francesca and her older sister Sarah running to hug them, greet them. Margaret pulled me even closer, and sang quietly into my ear, our song, which had played so often in our lives. "When I Fall In Love." Nat King Cole.

Her arms were around me now, around my neck. She turned me, and I moved, dancing a shuffling uncoordinated two-step slowly with her. I looked around us.

The grown children were smiling, looking intentionally away, looking at the golfers, the kelp, the seagulls. Francesca, Cesar, and Rose were running in circles around the green, attracting the elderly disapproving stares of several golfers. Somehow, the wedding, the party in the ballroom, all seemed so distant, so far away, so separate.

— Chapter 56 —
427

Margaret moved me again, and there was the ocean. God, God, God, I thought as the tears continued to flow onto Margaret's shoulders.

"I'm getting you wet," I said to Margaret.

Her response was to lay her head on my shoulder.

"Yes, you are," she whispered with a slight laugh, looking at her damp bare shoulder, the muscles defined.

I looked beyond her, and the ocean stretched to the horizon, blue, peaceful, and forever. All blue, all clear, and all there was in life.

My face was on Margaret's neck as we danced slowly, eyes shut, and we were turning, just like at our wedding and so many other times, and I rotated my head so that my lips were behind her ear, kissing her where the hair starts, and I was here. Just here. She was letting it happen, pressing her neck against mine.

Then I could hear a cellphone buzzing. That was odd. My face was in her hair and my cellphone was not vibrating. There it was, buzzing. Buzzing. Margaret stepped back. She reached into her small hanging bag, a Louis Vuitton I noticed. Small. Gold chain. Who gave her that? I wondered. Margaret had the phone in her hand and she was looking at me as her face expanded in delighted surprise.

"It's Jack!" she said.

I stood and looked at her, not understanding and not knowing what to think.

"It's Jack! He's here! And he wants to see me now!" she twittered girlishly. She smiled a white grin. Happy. She looked beautiful, animated in her dress.

I didn't know what to say.

"I . . . I've got to go see him! He's at the front desk right now!" she said. She backed away, turning while I attempted to emotionally stifle any reaction. As Dove had said. Let love and peace prevail.

"I'll watch the children," I said quietly to her toned and beautiful back as she rushed up the walk, into the ballroom, where Jack was waiting on the other side.

— Honor —

I didn't belong here.

I caught an early Uber ride home from the reception, got Francesca established in front of the TV watching *Dinosaur Train,* and then bathed and to bed. When she was asleep, Ernst and Wallace came by for a visit, still dressed in their ties, jackets off, looking resplendent in their youth. I had the feeling they were there to keep me company. I didn't know what to say. I was still wearing dress pants, my dress socks, and a white t-shirt. After some awkward silence, they decided to watch *The Matrix* while I retrieved a bottle of iced Kazani vodka. I had placed that bottle in the freezer before the wedding. Good planning, I thought. Great planning.

I just sat and watched people wearing black overcoats and sunglasses spin through the air, contort their bodies and fly. There didn't seem to be much point. Someone was living naked in an egg, and other people were riding inside a giant power drill, or something like it.

I texted Margaret. "What happened? How are you?" No answer. I sent the message again. Nothing. I thought of Margaret and Jack. And Angelica and Jerome. I ached all over. I looked at my two wonderful sons. Both fit, slender, intelligent, both focused on some sort of shootout on the wide screen of the TV. It was interesting, I thought, kids and young people can watch the same show over and over again, and they enjoy it again and again. For me, it was less interesting. I already knew what would happen next. I thought of Angelica and Jerome. And Margaret and Jack. I already knew what would happen next.

I poured my first and final shot of Kazan vodka. I had brought that bottle back from a business trip to Russia in the 1990s. I had rocked that Russian stock market. The good old days, when Russia was Somalia populated by blonde supermodels, all wearing miniskirts and fur. I smiled. I drank.

On the screen, Keanu Reeves was flying in his overcoat and bullets in slow motion were zinging around him. I'd seen it before. Angelica and Jerome. Margaret and Jack. I'd seen it all before.

— Chapter 56 —

It was good, that vodka: like drinking frozen air. I opened my lap top computer as I sat on the couch. It caught on the belt buckle of my black dress pants. I pulled it open, turned it on. The screen lightened. Email.

Email from Philippines Airlines. PAL. Open . . . and there was a delightful bright photo of a tropical beach with a turquoise ocean in the heading, and it read,

"Mabuhay! This is a friendly reminder that the credit for your nonrefundable round trip ticket for a flight from San Francisco to Manila and returning, will expire on November 30, 2014, unless used before that date. Please schedule your economy class ticket now and enjoy a visit to our beautiful paradise!"

Below that,

"Rate changes and trip alteration charges may apply."

I pondered that. On the TV, a woman in a shiny plastic leotard appeared to be dying in Keanu Reeves's arms. I'd seen it all before.

On my computer, Facebook chirped. A new message. I opened it. From Dove. "How are you?" it read. "I know the wedding was hard. I'm sure you did the right thing. I'm worried about you. Can we Skype?"

Time to let God lead me to where I'm wanted. Time to stop watching movies I've seen before. There was so little left of what I thought was mine. Now I could only go forward.

I typed, "Yes, at once."

Credits & Gratitude

Karen Galladora Andresen, my beloved wife, thank you for making this book possible.

Laurie Classen and Jeanne Nakagawa, thanks for helping me focus. Thank you also for the inspiration of your successful marriages and your wonderful lives.

To the Castro and Galladora families, especially Gloria, Talene, Blessie, Shirley, and JoJo Kyle Carencia, and Christian Lee Voth, thank you for showing me your beautiful homeland and helping me see it through your eyes, if only a little.

Richard Botkin, thank you for leading by example, always, in the Marine Corps and afterwards in authorship.

Cinthia Marlene: thank you for the archaic Spanish translations.
Aletia and Robert, thank you for the dance lessons.
Professional editing: Erin Brown, of "Erin Edits"
Cover and exterior design: Gaelyn Mirriam Larrick.
Interior formatting: Bram Larrick Lightbourne
Marketing/publication management: Susanne Andresen/Eric Andresen

Relationship and spiritual advice for this novel: (the "gurus") Thanks to:
David Anderson
Norm and Jean Hoffmann

Scott Stroud
Herb Hoff
Marta Bechhoefer
Ruth Andresen
Lauren Andresen
Lynn & Jeff Miller
Dr. Michael Ladra

To the entire staff of the Etkin Laboratory of Stanford University and especially Dr. Sanno Zack, thanks for all you do to transform the world.

Blessed are we all.